THE
CARTHAGINIAN
HOARD

THE CARTHAGINIAN HOARD

GUY WILSON

First published in 1997 by Malvern Publishing Company Ltd
The Wells House, Holywell Road
Malvern Wells, Worcs.

British Library Cataloguing in Publication Data

A catalogue record for this book is available
from the British Library

ISBN 0 947993 69 X

Designed and produced by Harold Martin & Redman Ltd.
Printed and Bound in Great Britain

1.

A lan would have approved, Claudia thought, from her privileged seat among the high and mighty. In his meticulous and unashamedly vain way he'd fixed every detail of his funeral, but he hadn't known there'd be this memorial service in Westminster Abbey to honour him.

It proved an impressive occasion, with a fanfare of bugles to get them going – that would have especially appealed to Alan. Alternately the mighty organ shuddered the heavy gothic air, the choir stood, white, red and pure-voiced, and at the altar the Dean and a full muster of clergy glided about in their party-best copes like a set of Russian dolls. The front pews were packed with celebrities, it being a three-line whip occasion apparently for selected members of the establishment with a royal and two cabinet ministers included. Someone no doubt – not the state – was paying, but it had almost the feeling of a national wake.

Claudia reflected on her unexpectedly close acquaintance with the great man during the last six months. This had been time enough to realise his shortcomings – his ruthless insistence on what he wanted professionally, his impatience, his egoism, and certainly this overweaning vanity which made him collect and call attention to the smallest compliment paid to him, especially by the renowned. But she had more than liked him. To begin with, in spite of the name dropping, he was in no way a snob. Not himself out of the top drawer, he'd dealt on the same terms with the highest and lowest and, provided they returned to him that basic tribute of respect he craved, he would do anything for anyone. He was capable of acts of extravagant warmth and generosity. Above all she had found him immense fun to be with. Paralysed as most of his body was, he had lost none of his mental energy. Quick, humorous, realistic, he applied his full interest to whatever he lighted on. Though she'd been worked off her feet, there hadn't been a day in which she wasn't entertained and stimulated by his company. She knew there was more than this. She was hardly the first woman to have been physically attracted to him, but she'd known from the first time he ran his hungry, rather seagull-like glance of appraisal over her that if he hadn't been incapacitated she'd probably have had a decision to take. Alan had been a bachelor all his life and had no close family. She dared think she might be regretting Alan's loss as much as anyone present.

Nonetheless after a time longeurs set in in the extended service. Bareheaded herself – along with a few other enlightened women, she'd been thankful to notice – she amused herself by consigning several hats within sight to Oxfam, and then, with nothing else to do began to imagine the conspiratorial tones of a BBC commentator, by turns sycophantic and sentimental, reporting the occasion.

'Now, rising with great dignity from his seat and coming forward to the great bronze eagle of the lectern is Walter Claridge, like Sir Alan an eminent archaeologist – in his case in the field of the Macedonian civilisation – and a fellow member of Sarum University . . .' (And as pleased as a fat cat, Claudia added in an aside, that he was the leading candidate for Alan's chair).

'And now, as the choir embarks on that most beautiful Bach piece, "That sheep may safely graze", let us glance at some of the less famous members of the congregation. Sir Alan rose high, but he never forgot his old friends, whatever their station in life. In the back row of the choir stalls is Mr Archie Fieldhouse who for many years was Sir Alan's batman in the Indian Army – and then on several of his digs, including that first and most famous expedition of all which uncovered the Carthaginian hoard in 1936 in the central Saharan desert. One wonders what he must be feeling at this moment at the loss of his old friend and superior officer.'

What indeed? And what might he and others be able to reveal to her, Claudia thought more selfishly? She reengaged with thoughts she'd had once or twice since the funeral a month back. When Alan had hired her after his stroke to do the biography he couldn't write himself, she'd been initially in two minds. The money was good. She'd be paid a salary during the research period and would halve the royalties with him. She was also sorry for his physical condition, as well as taking an instant liking to him. But with three reasonably successful books under her belt, she could see it was going to be a bit of a come-down to do an official account of Alan's life which, even though Alan had told her she was in charge and that the book would be in her name, was bound to be pretty much a ghost job. She thought Alan would be frank to her on his own terms, but if she tried to go outside the boundaries of research he'd laid down he probably wouldn't be pleased.

But now? Though she'd lost her chief source, didn't this very loss open up others? Wouldn't she be unmuzzled now she was no longer bound by Alan's strong personality and by his determination to keep all the cards firmly in his hand? She could interview people – like Archie Fieldhouse over there, like the other survivor of the Tifgad expedition, Janet Brisbane – who incidentally didn't seem to be here. She'd searched for her while waiting for the service to begin. She didn't expect such investigations would change anything very fundamental, but the viewpoint of others was surely bound to enrich her study.

Guilt at having such calculating thoughts at this time then took over. She stuffed them aside.

Claudia reprimanded herself for her optimism in another way. She hadn't yet had a chance to talk to the trustees of Alan's estate and, though she knew the will had been read, they'd ominously not yet approached her. She was quite sure Alan had never entertained the thought he might die before the work was finished and would have made no provision for its completion if he did. If there was nothing in the will, the quite possible outcome was that the project would either be dropped, or someone else would be taken on more cheaply. As she joined the throng filing up the staircase to the reception in the Banqueting Hall in Whitehall, she was in a more sober frame of mind.

She'd heard that a peer who sat on the board of the British Travel Authority and belonged to Alan's club, the Overseas, had organised and presumably paid for this part of the do. She knew Alan had thought him an ineffective bore and found his attentions irksome, but the man had certainly gone to town to provide a fitting send-off for the man he had so admired, the one attention, she thought sadly, Alan had been unable to deflect. Golden trays full of sparkly champagne, others of bright and tasty-looking canapés awaited the distinguished mourners, presented by an army of waiters and waitresses. Claudia didn't count herself exactly a wallflower, but she felt a moment of dismay as she entered the rapidly filling, growingly animated room. Everyone seemed to know everyone and have items of burning interest to discuss. What was she doing here, a mere biographer, up from the country?

'The leopard stalking its prey, is it?' she heard at her elbow.

It was Vincent Galleon, Vice-Chancellor of Sarum University. She'd met him often, and found him as charming and approachable as Alan but, unlike

11

Alan, Vincent was about the most modest man she knew. A world-renowned atomic physicist, his silver-grey head no doubt bulging with history-making formulas, he had the gift of making you feel that meeting you was the highlight of his day. He was soft-spoken, humorous, almost skittish.

'This is an opportunity for you, isn't it?' he continued, ending the joke and touching her arm, not without an element of flirtation but really in genuine friendship. 'You'll never again get them all under one roof like this. If you weren't thinking along those lines, you should be.'

She relaxed, and laughed. 'I suppose I should. Though it'd be a bit difficult to know where to start, embarras du choix. Anyway, I may be out on my neck now.'

She really wasn't fishing. She'd genuinely forgotten for a moment he was one of Alan's trustees. His kindly features tautened with concern. 'But my dear Claudia, haven't they told you yet?'

'Told me what?'

'The will was read to the trustees three weeks ago. The lawyer said he'd be contacting you at once. In fact I made a point of asking him to put you at the top of the list. The legatees won't be getting their loot for ages of course, until after probate, but I knew you'd be wondering how you stood. Lawyers are the limit. I'm sure a letter will reach you in a day or two.'

He was looking at her anxiously, but still not telling her. 'Well, what's the verdict?' she asked.

'Oh, that you're to go on, naturally. Did you imagine it would be otherwise? I think Alan had rather fallen for you, you know. Yes, there's a very specific instruction that the money's to be set aside immediately – a lump sum plus a generous amount for expenses – and he bequeaths all the royalties to you. I must say Claudia, it's no more than you deserve. No one I know could do it better.'

'Oh, that's marvellous,' she blurted. 'But . . .'

This capacity for instant jack-in-the-box reactions had let her down more often than she cared to remember. She thought she'd stopped in time, but the single syllable was enough for Vincent's rapier intelligence.

'But do you have carte blanche, is that what you mean?' Once again, the skittish grin. 'I see it is what you mean. No instructions on that score. And no instructions are surely good instructions, wouldn't you say? I'd've thought history demands the warts, wouldn't you? Even Alan, in his sublime and

12

reformed state, we must imagine would wish it. Unless I'm much mistaken you liked him, didn't you? If you liked him, you'll be fair – and there's no close family to take offence.'

She thanked him for what was a typical example of his kindness. They fell then to talking about Alan, and how much, in his boyish, enthusiastic, socially-committed way, he would have enjoyed all this pomp and circumstance. In the middle they were distracted. On a raised platform a uniformed flunkey in white gloves began to extend a microphone upwards. He blew down it once or twice, the machine gave a metallic squawk, and the babble slackened.

'My Lords, Ladies and Gentlemen, pray silence for your host, the Lord Froxfield.'

Lord Froxfield assured them he would be brief. But did anyone imagine, Claudia thought, he wouldn't have his money's worth? No such luck. He scraped up every morsel of his 'deep friendship' with Alan, larded on the praise, and recounted a long anecdote whose point was obscure. It was some twenty minutes later they were allowed to lift their glasses, drink to Alan's memory, and be let out of school.

At this, with a humorous lifting of his eyebrows, Galleon was sidling away from her to his next port of call. She felt a very unfunereal surge of confidence and energy. She had her project intact and, yes, indeed – why not? – a free hand.

She saw Archie Fieldhouse standing on the edge of the mob dressed resplendently in a morning suit. She'd only met him once, six months ago at Alan's house, Donnerton Hall where, after making an appointment, he'd come to offer his condolences on hearing of Alan's stroke. She'd had only a brief conversation, but remembered thinking that if she ever got to interview him, she'd need explosives to penetrate the carapace of clichés by which he seemed to live, however omniscient a valet he might have been. 'Sir Alan's as bright as a skylark if you ask me,' he'd said to her as he left. 'Shouldn't be surprised if he hops out of that chair one of these mornings. Can't keep a man like that down. Never say die – that was always our motto when we were together.'

She approached. 'Mr Fieldhouse, do you remember me? We met briefly at Sir Alan's house about six months ago.'

He'd been having a conversation with a waiter out of the corner of his mouth. His mien suggested he'd've been a lot happier helping to hand round drinks and not standing there doing nothing in these fancy-dress clothes. His face showed recognition, though no great surprise at their re-encounter. 'Oh yes, madam, I remember you all right.'

'You'd just stayed the night, I believe, and I was busy helping Sir Alan write his memoirs.'

'Yes, I recall very well. Sir Alan spoke most highly of you.' He paused fractionally, as if selecting an approach. 'So will you now be . . .'

'Continuing with the work? Yes, as a matter of fact I've just heard that I'm able to. It's mentioned in the will apparently. Sir Alan wanted me to continue.'

He looked away – rather foxily, she thought. 'I dare say that's a great responsibility for you,' he said.

'Yes, it is.'

'Posterity wants to know everything, doesn't it?'

'I think it will, yes.'

'It's a great responsibility.'

This wasn't getting them very far. No doubt with bull-like absence of finesse, she plunged. 'You're one of the people I most want to talk to, Mr Fieldhouse,' she said.

He raised his eyebrows in a way she didn't believe in. 'Me? Oh no, madam, I don't think you'll get much from the likes of me. I was only his batman and driver, you know.'

'But you knew him in India – for five years, was it? And then of course in the Sahara, and afterwards.'

'Oh yes, for all those years, and there've been reunions since. But what I'd have to say'd be very commonplace, I'm afraid – shining boots and buttons, bringing him his tea, tuning up the vehicles, that sort of thing, that was my lot.'

'I bet you knew him better than anyone here – his habits, what he thought about other people, and so on.'

'Oh, I wouldn't say that, madam. Very much a workaday relationship, ours. Sir Alan was always very correct, you know. No nonsense with him. He used to say the world would be a better place if there wasn't so much tittle-tattle. Between us, it was the work, start and finish. If you're looking for any personal insights, Mrs er . . .'

'Claudia Drake.'

'. . . Mrs Drake, I'm afraid I'm not the sort of chap you're looking for. Like Sir Alan was, I'm a spade's a spade sort of type. Always tried to be like him, you know. Facts, that's what I try to keep to in my lectures. Sir Alan used to say we could do with more facts and less opinions.'

Claudia had forgotten for a moment that Archie had been giving lectures on Tifgad for some years. Alan had told her when she'd seen a small notice in one of the national papers and brought it to his notice. 'Oh yes, I know about it,' he'd said, 'it gives the old boy an income, and they tell me he's rather good at it.' Surely showing an interest in what he was doing might be a way into his confidence?

'I've heard your lectures are very successful and that you're much in demand,' she said to Archie.

Rather touchingly, he blushed. 'Nice of you to say so, Mrs Drake. I just try to do my best. Can't do more, can we? And of course I only do what I feel Sir Alan would approve of.'

'I'd like to hear one of your talks. Do you think I'd be allowed to muscle in on one?'

'Well – er . . .'

'I mean if it were a public lecture I could just appear, couldn't I?'

'I don't do public lectures. They're all by private request.' He paused, and again the rather foxy look showed. 'I dare say it could be fixed though, Mrs Drake,' he went on, 'if you'd really like to. I'm sure you've heard it all before from Sir Alan, but you never know, there could be the odd spot of detail here and there that'd be new to you. In fact, in one or two instances, I might even be able to guarantee it.'

There was an odd change of note as he said this last sentence. He then rather abruptly took her card and said he'd call her if he'd been able to arrange something.

Archie's cryptic remark left her puzzled for a moment. He stood to attention and rather gauchely said he would be best going home now. But as he turned and marched away Claudia had a curious sensation. Was it possible Archie Fieldhouse wasn't quite the military stereotype she'd been imagining him?

15

She was thinking about this, when a voice assaulted her from behind. 'The simple soldier's view?'

She wheeled round as if she'd been threatened. All the men present wore dark suits if not morning dress. Before her stood an unrepentant figure in an olive green corduroy jacket, and a tie that had parted company from the curling collar to show the undone shirt button beneath it. Rather younger than her own age of thirty-four, he had thick, corn-coloured hair, cut severely, and a fair complexion. His compact, muscular figure gave an impression of barely restrained energy. But she immediately liked his mouth, which was young, agile, and twitchy with potential humour.

'You know Archie Fieldhouse?' she found herself saying, immediately on the defensive.

He didn't appear to hear, and turned his head genially to the crowd in a leisurely fashion. 'Load of old bollocks this, isn't it?'

'What is?'

'Everything. The service, the eulogies, the speech. Total hypocrisy.'

'I wouldn't say so.'

'Silverman was a prime shit.'

'I don't think so at all.'

'You wouldn't, would you?'

'What do you mean?'

'It's rather obvious you liked him.'

She decided not to pursue this and its several implications. 'What do you know about Silverman?' she asked instead.

He turned away reflectively. 'Not much actually, not nearly enough. I only interviewed him twice. But that was enough to know he reeked of hypocrisy. OK, I'll let you out of your misery. I'm press – freelance. Speciality archaeology, and I'm sort of into Silverman, or would like to be some time.' He took a card out of his wallet and held it forward between two fingers. 'I'd like to talk to you some time. Even if you're only ghosting and have practically disappeared up the establishment pardon-me, you must have picked up something between the lines. One of these days I'm going to do your precious celebrity, you know, introduce a few disturbing facts about the bastard. It's just a pity he's dead. I'd like him to have been alive to hear it.'

For some reason, though she wanted to be annoyed Claudia found she wasn't. Actually, something in his manner made her want to laugh. Could

16

this be because she suspected Michael Strode's statements might not be as definitive as they seemed. Could his rudeness be his professional way of asking questions?

'You seem very confident you know what I think of Sir Alan,' she said instead.

'Sir Alan – is that what you called him in your cosy tête-à-têtes? Surely you were a bit more intimate than that?'

'As you appear to know, I'm doing his official life.'

'So what? Silverman made a pass at every pretty woman who crossed his path, even when he was frozen solid below the neck. Right? I can't think he passed you by.'

If this was the man's style of compliment-paying, Claudia was beginning to think she'd already had enough of it. But probably fortunately she didn't have the chance to get stuffy. He was already signing off. 'Well, see you,' he said, turning to go. 'I thought there might be something interesting here, but this farce is a waste of time – except for the drink. So long, might be in touch one of these days.' He put his fingertips to his lips, twiddled them in the air in an ironic simulation of a sentimental suburban farewell, and disappeared.

2.

Claudia was surprised to get a letter from Archie Fieldhouse only a week later. On Basildon Bond blue notepaper with the North Harrow address printed with a do-it-yourself embossing machine, the almost copybook ink handwriting invited her to attend a lecture he was giving in a few days' time in what was described as 'a west-country minor public school called Lavington Hall.' Archie supposed she would be coming by road and suggested they met at Taunton railway station, the nearest to the school, at five-thirty in the afternoon – the time of the arrival of his train from London. Perhaps she would be kind enough to give him a lift to the school? He said that, 'in anticipation' that she'd come, he had told the school she would be accompanying him so it would be convenient if they arrived together. The school had replied, and there was 'no problem.'

For a moment she was mildly irritated. The idea of attending one of Archie's lectures had been more of a means to an end. She didn't think there was much about the expedition she didn't know from the official account and from Alan himself. She'd imagined herself ringing him up when it suited her and fitting it in in the London area, maybe taking him out for a meal afterwards when she could have questioned him more generally about his association with Alan. She immediately reprimanded herself. It had been nice of Archie to act so promptly and efficiently, and she had after all asked to attend one of his lectures.

She arrived with time to spare and was there to meet the nondescript blue-suited figure which appeared at the back of the crowd bunching to get through the barrier, carrying a small suitcase. She waved. He saw her at once and raised his free hand in acknowledgement.

Claudia had already questioned her first view of Fieldhouse as very much the ex-soldier – no doubt practical and effective in anything he undertook but polite and brisk and not overendowed with imagination. In these first moments of their closer relationship he gave her further grounds for a different view. She could have imagined him marching to her car, gallantly opening her door for her perhaps and standing to attention while she got in. But outside the station, he put down the suitcase for a moment and looked about him languidly in the late afternoon sunshine as if they were old friends out for a stroll.

'Well, this is a nicè town, isn't it?' he said discursively. 'Never been here before.' He sat easily beside her in the car, the battered suitcase on his knees. Claudia was itching to use every moment she had in his company, particularly as they might not have much time to talk after the lecture. But he continued to make amiable urbane comments on everything they passed – buildings in the town, then aspects of the countryside. A herd of cattle set him off about the sacred status of cows in India where he'd served ten years in the army, he told her. 'Pity really,' was his comment. 'Economics at war with religion. They could do with the beef.'

There was a reception committee of a besuited boy and a girl in a smart dress waiting for them in front of the main entrance to the central school building, a rather massive tower sporting what must be the school flag. They closed on Archie's side of the car and the boy opened his door.

'Good evening, sir.'

Archie had said he'd been invited to a meal before his talk. Claudia imagined she would drive back to Taunton, book in to the hotel where she had reserved a room for the night and get something to eat, then return in time for the lecture. But it seemed she was also invited. They were to have sherry in the teachers' common room with a Mr Teppit, 'the talks master', which the boy and girl would also attend, then supper at high table in hall where they would meet the headmaster and some of the students.

As they stood with Teppit in a corner of the common room, she wondered how Archie's modest style and appearance would go down in this public school ethos, which was apparent on all sides, and how he'd cope with it. He'd given her some idea in the car of the range of audiences he spoke to – women's institutes and lunch clubs, University societies, city livery companies – there'd even been a request from the Palace. But would a boarding school be different? Boys of this age were not prone to giving quarter if they saw the opportunity for some sport.

A bell began tolling rapidly as if there were no time to be lost, and a vast throng of boys, plus a fair sprinkling of girls of sixth form age, began to sluice heavily across the courtyard visible through the windows. The conversation they were having tailed off as if undermined by this immutable

19

demand of daily routine.

'Perhaps we should go in now, sir?' the boy suggested anxiously to the master as the bell stopped.

They entered the vast hall in which three or four hundred youth stood at long tables, and filed on to the raised top table set at right angles to the others. A boy clanged a brightly-polished ship's bell fixed to the wall and the din of voices was quelled. A gowned headmaster turned to greet them. Watched by hundreds of eyes in a pin-dropping silence, he shook hands, first with her, then with Archie. They were ushered to their places, the Head nodded, the boy who had rung the bell said a Latin grace, and the pandemonium resumed as a long line of women in white overalls and net caps paraded forward from the kitchens and began the distribution of food to the tables. Apparently this school had resisted the cafetaria revolution.

Claudia was seated next to the Head, while Archie was put further down the table among the students. She replaced her initial thought that this might be some ghastly piece of snobbery. Perhaps this was very sensibly to give the kids the opportunity to talk to the speaker. She hoped so. Whatever the case, she felt she had the worst of the deal sandwiched between the Head and Teppit – who, previously garrulous, was rendered virtually silent by this proximity to the fount of power. She didn't care for the Head whose object seemed, not to converse, but to inform in an unnecessarily booming voice. Mostly he boomed about a new science block that was in construction, financed by an appeal. She was happy enough to listen, which was after all her metier, but it occurred to her as he spoke that one definition of a bore is someone who assumes without checking that their pontifications are of interest to their listener. She was cheered to notice that, in contrast, after a stiff start, Archie was soon in his element. Eight eager heads of varied ages and both sexes were turned towards him, out to catch his every word. Maybe the students were not more than superficially overlain with all this tense ritual and conformity. Underneath, they were still ordinary kids with kids' enthusiasms.

The lecture was to be given in a large rectangular hall – some thirty rows of seats stretching back from a wide raised stage and on either side of an aisle. The place was almost full. If attendance was voluntary, Archie must surely be breaking records. Nonetheless, Claudia was glad she wasn't in his shoes as, carrying the battered suitcase with his finger on the clasp, he and the young master climbed on to the stage and the din of youthful voices stilled as if cut off at the mains. If he didn't win their interest, it would surely be very soon apparent. There was a brutal air of the Roman circus – deliver or else. The hubbub stilled to a hungry expectation.

'Privileged . . . Mr Archie Fieldhouse . . . following the recent tragic death of Sir Alan Silverman . . . in a unique position as the great man's personal assistant..' Teppit burbled, turned grinning to Archie, and left him to it.

Archie made an apparently inauspicious start. A table had been set with a chair, glass and water-jug. He'd already put the case on the table. Leaving it, he shambled forward to the edge of the apron and put his toes over the edge as if he were about to take a high dive. 'Well, nice to be here in your school,' he began discursively. He gave a token glance at the very ordinary ceiling. 'Beautiful hall you've got here.'

The tension deepened. Did the man know what he was doing? Would they giggle? The smallest snigger would surely ignite a whole conflagration.

But Archie knew what he was doing all right. Claudia wasn't sure he hadn't deliberately created this apprehension. Did he know instinctively that any speaker probably had these few moments of grace in which to command a total silence? It seemed like it. Just when things seemed in the balance, he plunged into his subject with a quick change of tempo and with total attention at his command. His tone became a lot more business-like.

'Now you may have noticed something as I stepped up here. Did you? What was it? Carrying a case, was I? Of course I was. That case.' He pointed behind him. 'Not exactly your Ritz Hotel luggage, is it?' He got a titter. 'Right. But you're going to be surprised then when I tell you that what that case contains is just about priceless. You don't believe me? OK, let's have a look then, shall we?'

He moved back to the table and sprung the two catches. He drew out a heavy necklace of globular dark stones that looked like malachite and, hanging it over his fingers, held it up like a jeweller displaying his wares. 'Know what this is? Like it, would you, some of you boys, to give to your beautiful girl friends here?' There was another stir of still uncertain amusement. 'Well, if you did, the girls would need to be grateful, because it's nearly three thousand years old, it's Levantine, age about 900 BC. The Carthaginians had bought, stolen or borrowed it and it was part, a very small part, of the great Carthaginian hoard we found in the desert mountains of what is now the Saharan Republic in 1936. I've got some other things in here you might like to see afterwards – which, OK, Sir Alan gave me. I didn't nick them.' The laughter greeting this sally was more confident.

'It's the story of how we came upon this great treasure that I've come down here to tell you about. And I'm glad to announce to you tonight's a bit special. There was something Sir Alan made me swear to all those years ago – for certain very good reasons of his – something I swore to keep quiet about for as long as he lived. Now that Sir Alan has sadly passed away, I'm released from my pledge. You're the first audience I've talked to since he died, so you – and a very special lady who's here in the audience – you'll be the first to hear about it. But we'll come to that a bit later.'

Claudia's ears pricked. So was this what lay behind her prompt invitation? But she immediately downgraded her expectations. She was already beginning to suspect that as a lecturer Archie was full of a busker's clever tricks and surprises. It'd probably be some little detail he'd decided to add – of no great consequence. She fell to thinking about the more pressing concern of how she might hang on to him when this was finished. A drink perhaps in her hotel before the last London train, which he'd said he would be catching? Maybe she could even persuade him to stay the night, at her expense.

A screen had been lowered against dark curtains at the back of the stage. Archie called for darkness and the first of his rather amateur slides appeared. It was a map of the Mediterranean region with a good chunk of northern Africa included. It showed the distribution of Carthaginian influence at its zenith at the start of the fifth century BC. Marked, were the cluster of towns in the western Mediterranean radiating from Carthage, and the wider extension of trading posts in Spain, France, Italy, and islands such as the Maltese group. From Carthage stretched southwards an overland trade route, traced by a dotted line in red ink, which finished in Timbuktou and the vast region through which the Niger river flows. About half-way from Carthage to Timbuktou a shaded area indicated the mountainous area where the find was made.

Archie explained the legend – surely a very ancient one, he said – which had first interested Sir Alan. The Carthaginians, like the Phoenicians from whom they derived, were a commercial rather than a colonial-minded people, who were always looking for new markets. Having penetrated everywhere in the western Mediterranean, and baulked now by the Greek empire in the east and centre of the region, they were even probing through what are now the Straits of Gibraltar down the Atlantic coast of West Africa with the aim maybe of reaching the powerful African kingdom in the Niger basin, fabled to be a producer of gold and of great wealth.

Of course they were a sea-going people, he explained, and it has never been proven that they established or even tried to establish an overland trade route to this region. But being the adventurers they were, and the lure of gold being such as it was, it was not fanciful to suppose that they did. Indeed there is literary evidence that one Carthaginian leader made the extravagant (and unlikely) claim of having 'crossed the Sahara three times without drinking.' Even if he had a drink or two on the way, Archie commented, raising another laugh, it's possible he made the journey. And if the Carthaginians had established such a route, how would they have proceeded? Almost certainly they would have started off in great 'caravans', processions of camels loaded with useful and decorative artefacts gathered from their activities all over the civilised world, which they hoped to exchange for gold. The gold of course would have far greater value in the more sophisticated markets they traded in.

Archie paused dramatically. Somewhere in the region indicated, he went on, legend had it that one particular caravan was waylaid on its way south by a band of thieves. The story was that the Carthaginians were pursued, and managed to conceal their valuable cargo in a cave before they were overtaken. They were massacred to a man but apparently managed to avoid revealing the secret hiding-place of their treasure, which their assailants never found. Archie reminded his audience how all through history attempts had been made to find the buried treasure in those thousands of caves with which the Jurassic rocks of the area is honeycombed. In more modern times, after Sahara – the state in which the area is situated – became part of the French Empire, a number of serious expeditions had been organised. But none of these had met with success.

Though Claudia knew the story, she was surprised to find she was as fascinated by Archie's simple relation of it as if she were hearing it for the first time. Archie was surprisingly literate in his speech, and the unconcealed traces of his cockney origin were part of the charm – this and the amazing fresh energy with which he spoke. He must have given this talk more than a couple of hundred times, she thought, but it was as if he had just come back from the expedition. There was no doubt the students were rapt, as were the two other young masters and their wives who had joined Teppit and sat beside her in the front row.

Having filled in the background to the expedition, Archie moved a step nearer his objective. He began to talk about Alan. He described how they'd met in India in the Indian Army, when he became Alan's batman for five years at the end of the nineteen-twenties. He said what a lively and daring man Alan was, always liking to be in the limelight, whether it was a skirmish on the North-West Frontier where he won the M.C. for outstanding gallantry, or just an officers' mess lark after dinner.

'But though he won promotion to the rank of major at a very young age, British India wasn't enough for a man like Sir Alan,' Archie continued. 'I began to get the sense he was getting itchy feet and was looking for new pastures. He'd already become interested in archaeology and spent all his leisure time reading. One day, out of the blue, he told me he was going to resign his commission, return home, and do a degree course in the subject at a university.

'Well,' said Archie, 'you can imagine how I felt. I knew no other officer in the regiment was going to take Sir Alan's place in my estimation, neither did he. I gave up being a batman and, being a bit of a mechanic, transferred into transport in which I spent three very ordinary years after he'd gone. I almost felt like giving up the army myself, and said so to Sir Alan in the one or two letters we exchanged. I probably would have done if he hadn't advised me against it. Then out of the blue, came the most exciting letter I've ever received – from Sir Alan of course – asking me if I wanted to share an adventure. If I did, he thought he could fix a few months' absence from the army for me. He had raised the money from Afrochem, that large company with interests in Africa, and he was going to look for the Carthaginian hoard in the French colony of Sahara, plumb in the middle of the Sahara Desert.

'Did yours truly want to "share an adventure" with Sir Alan? I never had a moment's doubt. I'd've gone even without the leave of absence. Those five years in India with Sir Alan had been the best of my life.'

Archie now plunged graphically into a description of the six months of hardship and endeavour the four Britishers and six Berbers had to endure, some of it – because the work had lasted so much longer than had been intended – during the early part of the summer in 'what must be one of the most inhospitable places in the world.' Archie explained how though by comparison with other expeditions they had generous financial backing, translated into actual living facilities it didn't seem like that. They had just three tents, one medium-sized for the Berbers, one smaller one for his two assistants – Janet Brisbane and her fiancé, Neil Beazley – and the largest for the equipment, in which Silverman and Archie slept. Apart from the gear they needed for the work – ropes, lighting equipment, a drill (with a small generator) – essential large items were a cumbersome Hudson truck which they used for running in to the nearest town, Tifgad, some sixty miles away, two mules, and a metal water tank. There was an abandoned well on the camp site which they managed to get going, but the water was only suitable for washing and for the animals, and every drop of drinking water had to be humped from Tifgad. There was also an antediluvian stove they had bought in the souk, which had been adapted to run on paraffin.

Archie was reaching the centrepiece of his account, and Claudia could feel the mounting excitement of the audience behind her. He explained Alan's plan. It was almost certain that if the hoard was there it would be buried or walled up in one of the huge number of caves in the limestone rock. Sir Alan suspected that previous expeditions had been forced by impatience or shortage of time to make random plunges on wild hunches. He was not making that mistake. He began with only two assumptions. The first of these was that the ancient trail would have followed the same route as the one that became established in later history. His second thought was that a certain area along this route – where the trail passed through a mountainous area which contained at one point a particularly narrow defile – was the most likely site for an ambush. It was the area which figured in the legend. No matter what bright ideas occurred to any of them along the way, he insisted on a systematic search, mountain by mountain, the areas of search radiating in concentric circles from a central point.

Every day, Archie explained, while he stayed at the camp to guard the belongings and prepare midday food for the European members of the expedition, each of the three archaeologists took two Berbers to search different but adjacent caves. They got up well before first light so as to arrive on site, with one of the mules packed with equipment, at dawn, and worked five or six hours until the heat – which was intense even inside the caves –

and the consequent exhaustion, stopped them. Sometimes they returned in the evenings for a second stint. Silverman would have had them work at night, which would have been much more satisfactory, but the Berbers refused point blank. They were superstitious enough already and would almost certainly have vanished if pressed.

Suddenly, Archie stopped and asked for the lights to be put on. For a moment Claudia wondered if something was wrong. Was Archie not feeling well? But she was soon reassured. He'd got through his very ordinary black and white photographs taken with a box camera and made later into slides. It was, she suspected, no more than another of his dramatic tricks. He'd sensed his audience needed a break. While the students eased themselves in their seats and perhaps realised how absorbed they'd been, he stopped to pour himself a glass of water. He then abruptly recalled them.

'Now I've no doubt many of you will know a bit about the last phase of the story. You'll know, I expect, how desperate we'd all become after these months with nothing found, how the money was on the point of being used up and we'd been ordered to stop, and how on that fateful day Sir Alan, after doing half a day's work with the others, had taken the Hudson to go into Tifgad to make an appeal on the telephone to our benefactors for funds for just a few days more. You'll know perhaps how he obtained these funds, but how when he returned to camp we had to temper this good news by telling him that Neil Beazley hadn't returned with the others for the midday meal and was missing.

'I must tell you at this point a little about Neil Beazley. In the last days Beazley had been behaving oddly – particularly, as I'll explain, on the day before this one when, against Sir Alan's wishes and orders, he'd been working by himself well away from the main party on a different mountain-side. It was probable that on this day of his disappearance he'd been doing this again. Sir Alan didn't think anyway there was much we could do that night. Perhaps he'd turn up during the night. He must already be very thirsty and hungry. But when at dawn he was still missing, it became a real worry.

'Sir Alan realised we'd have to lose some of the precious time that had been given to us to look for him. He declared a day of rest and decided that he'd undertake the task of looking for Beazley with just me accompanying him. There was no point in having everyone there searching. He certainly didn't want the Berbers to witness anything unpleasant, if it had occurred.

And though Janet Brisbane, Beazley's fiancée, wanted to come with us, he made her stay in camp with them. Someone had to.

'I said Beazley'd been acting strangely and had been working alone probably for the previous two days. The difficult conditions had been getting to him more than most – Janet Brisbane confirmed this. It was she who told me that, when they had arrived at the mountain site the morning before, he'd had words with Sir Alan in front of the Berbers. Sir Alan had had to reprimand Beazley, and had actually ordered him to return to camp.

'Now, as I say, Beazley hadn't returned to camp. Sir Alan was pretty certain he'd've gone off again to another cave to continue working by himself, although this was expressly forbidden for obvious safety reasons. What we feared was that on his own Beazley had fallen down one of the countless chasms inside the caves. Maybe the head-light they all wore when working had failed. Some of the caves were half a mile long or more and he could easily have stumbled. Maybe, in his state of mind, he hadn't taken the precaution Sir Alan always insisted upon – of tethering the end of a ball of string to some object at the cave entrance and letting it pay out – and had got lost. In a way we rather hoped this might be the case, for if it was he might simply be sitting firm, maybe injured in some way – sitting firm being the procedure agreed upon in such an eventuality. If this was so, we'd almost certainly find him by shouting. The caves relayed sound like speak-tubes. Though he could be in one of several caves, which were particularly numerous in that area, and not precisely in one of those designated by Silverman to search, he couldn't, surely, be that far off.

'Now our difficulty of course was to know to which cave Beazley had gone, if that was what he'd done. We knew the approximate area, which wouldn't probably be far from where the others had been working. The official account tells that Sir Alan decided we should go first to 'Gold Mountain' – Sir Alan had named all the peaks with the names of minerals – which was the next (and probably the last) area on his planned list.

'Gold Mountain was particularly rich in caves. Its flanks were honeycombed with maybe twenty or thirty entrances. The account tells how we arrived at what Sir Alan had called 'Red Facet', the south-facing slope, and whilst surveying it through our field-glasses from a vintage point saw in front of one of the cave entrances a mysterious cairn of stones which had clearly been built by human hands.

'The story from now on is famous, isn't it? How having gone, apparently by Sir Alan's amazing instinct to the right and as it turned out the fatal cave, we found, not poor Beazley, but on the smooth floor of the main entrance chamber a Berber's knife and beside it a pool of congealed blood. The official report tells how we shouted and searched that cave in vain for a considerable time and how, finding no sign of Beazley, we were forced finally to return to camp.

'When we got back, Sir Alan had me immediately turn the Berbers out on parade – we rather went for military discipline with them in this way, it kept them up to the mark. While I did this, Janet and Sir Alan searched the Berbers' tent. Janet told me that the first bag Sir Alan wanted to search was that of a man called Mustapha Beri. I have to explain that Beri was a cut above the other men. He could not only read and write – in Latin script as well as Arabic – but also spoke a bit of English. Until very recently, Beri had been working with Beazley, and it had been obvious to all of us that Beazley'd had a particularly close relationship with him.

'Why Sir Alan should have chosen Beri's possessions to search first I will not go into now. No explanation is offered in the official report. Sufficient to say at this point, it didn't take Sir Alan long to find that Mustapha Beri's kit-bag was the one which held an empty scabbard. He then found two other bits of evidence among the man's belongings which were to have repercussions a great way beyond Beazley's death. These were two alabaster pots which Sir Alan's expert eye at once dated as sixth or fifth century B.C. Even more telling was a letter written in Beazley's handwriting to Mustapha, telling him he had to slip away and come to "the" cave during siesta that afternoon – when he knew Sir Alan was going to be away – as he would have a "couple of interesting things to show him." He himself wouldn't be returning at midday. The cave would be marked with a cairn of stones heaped in a pyramid at the entrance. This of course was the very cairn that had enabled Sir Alan and myself to spot the cave where Beazley died.

'What were these two "very interesting things"? It was immediately obvious to all three of us what they were, and also what must have happened. The "interesting things" were the pair of alabaster pots, which Beazley must have found the day before. Beazley was a young man with no experience, but he'd had training and would've known the pots were of antiquity. And he'd've known that if they were of antiquity it was quite possible they belonged to

28

the hoard, which might be close at hand. It was possible they'd been dropped by the Carthaginians in their haste to escape their pursuers and in their anxiety to conceal their precious merchandise as quickly as possible.

'What was almost a hundred per cent certain to us was that, unable to speak directly to Beri without arousing suspicion, Beazley had somehow slipped him that note the previous evening and that Beri had not had the sense to destroy it. Almost certainly, Beazley was calling for Beri's help in following up the find of the pots.

'But Beazley hadn't bargained for the kind of man Mustapha Beri was. Mustapha went to the cave all right as asked but, instead of joining with him to look for the hoard, had killed Beazley and taken from him the alabaster pots. Then, in a panic, he left his knife. He was no doubt planning, we thought, to make off during the night with the pots. You might've thought this was small compensation for so gross a crime, but there was beginning to be quite a market for antiquities in those days and as a Berber trader he'd've known this. He'd've known there were Europeans about scouting for the stuff, and he'd probably have pocketed what for him would be a tidy sum for the two pieces.

'Whatever the case, Sir Alan ordered me to place Beri under arrest, which I did. We had a rather primitive radio-transmitter with which we could usually contact Tifgad and on this occasion did so successfully.

'The French colonial police were efficient. They arrived that evening and took Beri away. You may know that some time later the man committed suicide while in custody. I've little doubt that, had he not done so, he'd've been tried for murder, condemned to death and executed, even though Beazley's body, despite extensive searches, was never found.

'Now you may think that the violent death of one of our party would have blighted our whole enterprise and put an end to it. In other circumstances it probably would have done. But, blight it as it did, it was so soon overwhelmed in our minds by one of the most astonishing events of archaeological history, that we felt it less than we would have done otherwise. Sir Alan always maintained indeed that, with the short time left to us, it was Beazley's murder which indirectly caused the finding of the Carthaginian Hoard. It has to be said therefore that, unsatisfactory character that he was, his death was not entirely in vain.'

3.

*I*n the last minutes Claudia had been aware of a change in Archie's manner. He seemed to be hurrying and to have lost some of the immediacy of his narrative. He'd talked almost perfunctorily about Beri's suicide and the failure to find Beazley's body – surely both matters warranting more than cursory mention. Was it because, having dealt with the diversion of Beazley's death, he was now impatient to return to the finding of the hoard? Apparently not. For a moment, as he paused, he looked almost uncertain, certainly nervous. He gripped his wrist and stared at the stage boards in front of him as if he must steel himself for the final phase of his story.

Suddenly he threw his head back. 'I told you earlier, boys and girls, this evening's a bit special to me – a bit special because I'm about to tell you two or three things which've never been told yet, and which force me to relate the last bit of the story in a different way. These details have never been told yet because, apart from Sir Alan, I've been the only man alive who knew them, and as long as Sir Alan was with us I was under oath not to talk about them. They concern the actual finding of the hoard, the crowning moment of the expedition.

'The main part of this story is, as I say, now old knowledge, and it'll remain as it is for the rest of time. But the real story isn't quite as it's always been told. It's never come out, for number one, exactly why Sir Alan had to reprimand Beazley on that morning of the tragedy. Before I tell you about that, I must point out something else.

'You'll be appreciating that among our difficulties was the fact that we weren't working in British territory – as we'd've been in, say India or Egypt – but in a French colony. Sir Alan had had to get permission from the French Colonial Administration. He'd been very careful to tie up an agreement with them in advance, an agreement that stated clearly that if he was successful in his mission he'd be entitled to export his find back to Britain. Sir Alan thought they'd agreed to this because, firstly, French archaeologists might well find themselves in similar circumstances in British territories, and probably second because they didn't believe the treasure existed, several reputable Frenchman having tried in vain to find it. Well, he had his agreement – but there was always still a difficulty for, whatever its wording, it seemed we'd still in certain aspects be subject to the very complex French-Saharan law of what we'd in England call "treasure trove", which no private contract could alter. I wouldn't say I ever mastered this – I'm not sure Sir Alan did – he used to joke about it and say what a bird's nest it was. But what we all understood was that the actual person making the find could have rights. In practical terms what it boiled down to was that if one of the Berbers actually came across the hoard there could be complications about its ownership.

'Sir Alan wasn't taking any chances. It was because of this we only had six Berbers with us and not double that number, which we could certainly have used. And it was also because of this that, as I've said, for work they were at all times divided into three groups of two, each pair being either with Sir Alan, or Janet Brisbane, or Beazley.

'I go back now to that quarrel between Sir Alan and Beazley. Beazley, as I say, had gone rotten on us. There had been other incidents before, in which Beazley had taken the Berbers' side in disciplinary matters – against Sir Alan. He'd more than once come out with the idea that if the hoard was found it ought to belong to the Saharans – and by that he meant the indigenous population of the country, not their French colonial overlords – because it was in the Saharans' land and we were just invited guests working on behalf of what he called "culture," which ought to have no national frontiers. On this particular morning, or actually the one before it, the matter came to a head. I have mentioned Mustapha Beri, and Beazley's relationship with him. Sir Alan didn't like it. He considered Beazley was getting much too friendly with the man, which in the less democratic nature of those days I'm afraid was something most people accepted. It was the day before the tragedy that Sir Alan had re-formed the working parties, so that Beri worked with himself and not with Beazley. Beazley had one of the two men who had been with Sir Alan in place of him. Beazley had appeared to accept the new arrangement and had gone to the cave designated him for the day with his two men. But during the morning he apparently left this cave and went to another – which one he refused to reveal when questioned by Sir Alan that lunch-time – and sent his two helpers back to camp. That was almost certainly, as I've said, the day when he came across the alabaster pots in the fatal cave on Red Facet.

'When Sir Alan discovered this he was of course furious. He was normally an equitable and courteous man but on this occasion he told Beazley he would either carry out his orders or go home. On the morning of the tragedy, on arrival at the working site Beazley again began causing trouble and saying it was ridiculous he couldn't work with Beri. This time Sir Alan really lost his cool, and ordered Beazley back to camp. I relate these few extra details in defence of Sir Alan. I've heard it said from time to time that Sir Alan was at fault in the treatment he gave Beazley, that he was unnecessarily harsh. In my view it was quite the reverse. He'd been remarkably tolerant and only took action when he had to. He'd spent all this energy and know-how and endured all this hardship – so had we all – and here was a young man just out of university disobeying his instructions, telling him what he ought to do with the spoils, and jeopardising the whole expedition.'

Archie paused, as if again to draw breath for an even steeper climb. 'I come now to another matter,' he said, 'the exact details of what happened subsequently on that fatal day of Beazley's disappearance. I've said how Silverman had gone into town that day, and that it was when Janet Brisbane returned at lunch-time with the Berbers that I first heard that Beazley was missing. Sir Alan had said nothing to me when he came through camp to pick up the Hudson vehicle. What's never come out is what happened that afternoon. This is the second thing I'm going to reveal to you now.

'I gave Janet Brisbane her lunch and, as usual, afterwards they all – that is, Janet Brisbane and the six Berbers, who cooked their own food – retired to their tents for siesta.

'Now I've referred to how touchy the Berbers could be. They were especially so in these last days of our so far unsuccessful campaign. Sir Alan was afraid they might all push off. He was always telling me to keep an eye on them. He hadn't said anything particular on this occasion, but I thought at this crucial time it was down to me to be especially vigilant. When I'd washed up, I went to the tent I shared with Sir Alan but, instead of turning in, I thought it was my duty to keep an eye on the Berbers. I kept the flap of our tent open so I could see theirs – it was about fifty yards away. At about three, when the heat was really basting down and when no doubt the rest of them were snoring, I saw Mustapha Beri steal out and make off approximately in the direction in which the parties had been searching. I was immediately suspicious. When I'd satisfied myself he was not just on his way to the

Berbers' latrine – and that he was not running away, because he didn't have his kit with him – I decided to follow at a discreet distance. Was it something to do with Beazley's failure to appear for lunch? It seemed very much like it.

'Following Beri wasn't easy. He was obviously setting out on something of a hike, and the Berbers had had rather more practice than we had of moving across this territory in the hottest part of the day. He kept up a lively pace. And I had another problem. Apart from occasional outcrops of rock, there was no cover – not a tree or a bush in that barren landscape. For an hour or more I followed in the burning heat, always waiting until he was out of sight before making my own moves forward. I was soon pretty sure he was going in the direction of the area where the party had been working that morning. At the end of one of my advances, some mile or more from the present working area, I had gained a long ridge and was in expectation of seeing my quarry ahead of me. I was then alarmed to find the valley below me, and the mountainside rising beyond it – need I say it, this was "Red Facet of "Gold Mountain?" – was deserted. Beri had clean disappeared.

'Beri would not have had time to surmount the further ridge ahead, and it was at once obvious to me that he'd entered one of the numerous caves there were on this particular mountainside. But which one? Then I made out in front of one of these spots that strange cairn of stones I've mentioned which couldn't be natural, built in the shape of a pyramid. Very weird, I thought, unless one of our party had set them up for some reason. But why here? This mountainside hadn't yet been searched. I kept my eyes glued to this area, and sure enough, after quite a short time, Mustapha Beri appeared, right by the cairn. He stood for some moments, looking about him – it seemed to me he was nervous and uncertain what he should do. He had both hands, I remember, thrust into the folds of his djellabah.

'Was he fingering those two objects inside it, which Sir Alan later found in his belongings? In the light of what happened the next day, it is possible to say he almost certainly was. It is also certain that while I had been observing that empty mountainside he'd been in that cave murdering Beazley.

'After this short period of uncertainty, Beri set off back to the camp. Until he was well past me, I hid myself more thoroughly behind the rock from which I'd been observing. Then I made my own way back by another route.

'Of course I knew nothing about a murder, or the pots, at this stage.

Though he would appear to have given up rather easily, I just thought Beri had been looking for Beazley and hadn't found him. Consequently, I didn't say anything to Janet Brisbane, thinking Sir Alan would prefer me to keep such strange behaviour under my hat until his return. I was right in my thought. Sir Alan returned, as I've said, after dark, and heard that Beazley had still not returned to camp. Because of the talk about this he had with Miss Brisbane, in her tent, it was quite a time before she retired and I got Sir Alan on his own in our tent. I told him then. He thought for a while about what I'd said, then he seemed pleased. The first thing he did was congratulate me, first on my vigilance and initiative, and second on my discretion. Almost certainly, he said, Mustapha's movements must have something to do with Beazley's disappearance. Could he have known what Beazley was up to and had come looking for him? But why, if this was so, had he been for such a short time in the cave with the cairn, and why had he apparently abandoned his search so quickly? He decided, however, not to get Beri up now to question him. We'd go together in the morning to the cave, he said, which I'd be able to point out to him by means of the cairn. He was sure there'd been no cairn on that mountainside before. He would've seen it on the way to the site they were working.

'Well, I've told you what happened the next morning. Sir Alan and I found the cave all right, but not on this occasion because of Sir Alan's deduction as has been stated in the official account. I was happily in a position to identify the cairn of stones and lead him to it. My little expedition and its consequences is the second new set of facts I'm revealing today.'

Archie, Claudia noticed, was now almost transfigured. Was it her imagination, or had his face turned paler? Certainly he was tense. He stood, his feet slightly apart, his fists clenched at his sides, every fibre strung like an opera singer about to deliver a taxing aria.

'I come now to a third point, perhaps the most interesting. In my opinion, Sir Alan's greatness and professionalism never showed itself more clearly than it did at this moment when we had arrived together at the fatal cave. We'd found the knife and the blood on the floor of the cave. We'd shouted Beazley's name until we were hoarse, and got back only echoes of our voices.

'My mind of course, as any ordinary mortal's surely would have been, was fastened at this moment entirely on the tragedy which seemed to have occurred. Surely, there was no doubt Beazley had been struck down by one of the Berbers, almost certainly by Beri in view of what I'd seen. If this was so, I couldn't rid my mind of the thought that if I'd followed Beri to this cave and not stayed observing on the further mountainside, I might've been able to intervene. But when we had completed a search of that top chamber of the cave and found no body – indeed, there was nowhere obvious it could have been concealed – Sir Alan's mind switched.

'"Archie," he said, "it's here, very close. I'm sure of it. Perhaps within yards of us."

'At first, in confusion, I thought he meant Beazley's body. But then I realised he was referring to the hoard. He said we had to search the walls of the cave – not wildly, but systematically, section by section, as always. He told me which side of the cave I was to work on, and I set to.

'I'm telling you, I take no credit for this. It was pure luck – and Sir Alan's intuitive feeling the hoard was there. But it was just my good fortune to be the one who came upon it. I was on the opposite side of the cave to Sir Alan. While I was searching the rock face, my feet stumbled on what seemed like loose stones. This was immediately unusual. The floors of most of these caves were smooth, as this one was. Most had had running water in them at some point in geological time. I shone my head-lamp downwards – I'd been looking upwards towards the top of the cave wall, where I'd already noticed a faint, vertical fault line. There was indeed a scattering of stones and crumbled dry earth at my feet. I then looked up again and saw that there was a hole in the wall in the line of the fault not more than a foot to eighteen inches in diameter at about waist height. I'd been so intent on looking upwards I hadn't seen it.

'I must have shouted out. Sir Alan was at my side in a flash. I remember he brushed me aside quite roughly in his haste. He detached his head-lamp, held it forwards through the aperture, then followed it with his head for which there was just enough room.

'It could only have been a matter of seconds, but it seemed more like minutes of silence. Then, "This is it, Archie," he shouted, his voice muffled inside the cavity. "We've done it. We've found the hoard. It's got to be it. It's beautiful – a huge mound of miscellaneous artefacts – gold objects, too, I think. It's beyond belief" – that was the actual phrase he used.'

'It was some minutes before I was allowed a sight of it, he was that excited. He kept looking. His head, and the arm holding the light, were thrust through the hole and blocking it, so I couldn't see a thing. His voice was now only just audible. "Votary objects," I heard him call out. "And – the most incredible small terracotta figures, dozens of them, a silver mask, glassware, bronze objects, some of copper I think, jewellery."

"'It looks like a cross-section inventory of fifth century Mediterranean and Middle Eastern civilisation," I remember he said to me a little later. In that, of course, he was proven a hundred per cent accurate. Some of you may have seen the museum at Salisbury where the collection is housed. If you haven't, you should go at the first opportunity. I suppose the set of small terracotta figures, like those larger warrior figures later found in China, are one of the greatest archaeological finds of all time, giving such a vivid visual account of so many aspects of everyday Carthaginian life.

'When I eventually got a look, it was undoubtedly the most exciting moment of my life. To my untrained eye, the objects did not seem at first so much. They were in a great untidy dusty heap, some clearly broken, piled one on top of the other – there was no doubt they'd just been thrown in there anyhow. It reminded me for a moment of a lot of old useless junk accumulated in an attic. But when I thought about what it meant, and when Sir Alan's excitement began to penetrate to me, my feelings swelled. As Sir Alan said, we were being privileged to witness "a suspension of time and to look upon the encapsulated achievement of another age." I remember those were the actual words he spoke, and I repeat them to you exactly.

'I wasn't allowed to look for more than a few seconds. Again I had to stand aside, and Sir Alan began to hack at the hole with his rock axe to widen it. He wanted to get inside of course. It was clear what the Carthaginians had done. There was this fault line in the rock, which widened at its lower end into a space a man could squeeze through to the sizeable chamber behind. All they had to do after stowing their loot was stuff loose stones and a matrix of wetted clay into the crack of the fault, up to the ceiling. The fault line was visible, but even an expert might not have noticed it had been filled in this way – fault lines down which water has passed at some time are often choked with small rubble. And the concealment had lasted intact all these years. If I hadn't stumbled on those stones and seen the hole, I probably wouldn't have noticed it.

'Sir Alan had only been working a few seconds when he stopped. He stood there reflecting, the axe in his hand.

'"Archie, we're going too fast, a great deal too fast," he said. Then he asked a strange question. "How long did you say Beri was inside this cave yesterday? Think as accurately as you can. Was it seconds, minutes?"

'I thought as carefully as I could. I told him I thought it had been about ten to fifteen minutes.

'"Exactly," he said. "Almost no time at all. That bugger Beazley." You'll pardon the language, ladies and gentlemen, but that was the word Sir Alan used. "Beazley had obviously made the find, probably only yesterday – it must have been Beazley who hacked out this small hole in the fault. But I'd guess that for some reason he realised he was near it the day before. Somehow, that evening he must have tipped Beri off that something was in the offing. Beazley knew I was going to be away the next morning. He must have fixed for Beri to come up here yesterday afternoon to help him. Well Beazley paid a high price for his treachery, the bloody idiot – so much for his love and care for the Berbers. Clearly it was Beri who did him in."

'Silverman broke off at this moment. Something else had occurred to his rapier mind. "What interests me now, though,' he went on, 'is whether Beri knows about the hoard. If he's Beazley's killer, you'd think he must do. The discovery would've been, you'd think, the first thing Beazley said to him when he entered the cave yesterday afternoon. But it puzzles me he was in the cave for such a short time. If he murdered Beazley, he did so almost certainly for gain, and surely he'd've wanted to see the hoard, perhaps widen the hole and begin to help himself to some of the objects. But it looks as if he didn't. If you're right about the period he was in here, he wouldn't have had the time."

'I asked what was in Sir Alan's mind.

'"What's in my mind," he said to me, "is that we shouldn't act too swiftly. If Beri knows about the hoard, he can make up any kind of story. He can say he found it, that Beazley attacked him, and that he killed him in self-defence. In other words, the French being what they are, we'll be in trouble. I'm going to wall up this crack again – until we find out what Beri knows. If Beri does know, as I say, we're in trouble and we'll have to think again. But if by any lucky chance he doesn't, we can know nothing about the hoard until a later date. I can then come across it myself – it had better be tomorrow before any police get here – with no ugly 'treasure trove' questions arising."

'We made a good job of shoring up the crack. We put the stones back in the breach and cemented just the outside edge of the fault line with clay. We had to make use of the water in our two water bottles to do this – the same method the Carthaginians probably used.

'Let me finish the story. After filling in that hole, we both, I think, realised we'd allowed our excitement over the discovery to overcome our anxiety about Beazley's fate. I don't think either of us had any hope he was alive, but we began a further brief search for his body, and called again. When we again drew a blank, Sir Alan said, "Look, the body can't be far away if Beri was only in here a few minutes, but we may not find it for some time. We could be up here all day. First, we've got to get back to the camp to deal with Beri." He'd realised of course how important it was to interview the man – if indeed, he was still there. Having seen us go off looking for Beazley this morning, we thought he might well have taken flight.

'I've told you what happened when we got back to the camp. Beri hadn't fled. The discovery of Beazley's letter in his kitbag, and the absence of his knife – clearly the one we had found in the cave – as good as put the noose round the Berber's neck without my evidence about his movements the afternoon before. The two alabaster pots enabled us to prove that Beri's motive was theft.

'Beri denied he knew anything about the pots, which was of course a downright lie. He had to admit to the letter of course, but he said all he had done was to go up to the cave as ordered, find Beazley was not there, and so return to the camp. But after intense and clever questioning by Sir Alan, there was nothing to make him think he knew Beazley had found the hoard. Sir Alan concluded, almost certainly correctly, moreorless as he had surmised up in the cave, that what had happened was as follows.

'Beazley had probably found the pots, but not the hoard, the day before his death. It was these he referred to as "two very interesting things" in his note to Beri. By the time Beri arrived at the cave the next afternoon, he must have found the hoard – maybe he had only just done so, hence the very small hole he'd hacked in the fault. It's probable anyway he had the pots in his hand and maybe was about to tell Beri about the hoard, but that Beri had decided to kill him. He did so, then probably panicked, dragged the body somewhere out of sight, and ran for it, with the pots concealed in his clothing

– as I surmised from my own observation of him as he came out of the cave. You remember he had his hands inside his djellabah as if he were holding something.

'Anyway, as you may know, the matter of whether or not Beri knew about the hoard and whether it could therefore be construed that he'd had any hand in its discovery – even if the French had thought of raising it, which they didn't – very soon became of no consequence. He stuck to his story of innocence with the police, but a few days later he took his own life when in custody. Clearly he knew he was for it. The day after the murder, Sir Alan made the great "discovery" of the Carthaginian hoard which startled and amazed the world, before the police made their on-site inspection of the cave. The only mystery was that Beazley's body was never found.'

Archie was grinning, and looking a great deal more like his usual relaxed self. 'Well, there you are, that's my little bombshell, ladies and gentlemen. As a matter of strict accuracy it wasn't Sir Alan who made the discovery of the hoard, it was Neil Beazley. As very much a footnote I can claim to have played a very small and secondary part in the event myself. These few extra facts in my view make absolutely no difference to the renown Sir Alan rightly earned himself for this expedition. But, as I say, facts are facts in my book and must be told – even when they are somewhat supplementary and told a long time after the events took place. Better late than never.'

Claudia didn't take in much of the last few minutes of Archie's lecture. He was talking more about the contents of the hoard and how they shipped them home. This continued to fascinate his audience, but she was mulling over what he had just revealed.

What did it amount to? Her first thought was, as she had surmised might turn out to be the case – not so much. As Archie had said himself, his action probably made no essential difference to the story. It's just possible that if he hadn't followed Beri, the dagger and therefore the hoard wouldn't have been found. But Alan knew approximately where Beazley had been working. Gold Mountain would have been the next for exploration – she had seen this herself in Silverman's diary. And the dagger, it seemed, was not far inside the cave. It was difficult to think one of the party wouldn't have immediately come across it. If they had found the site of the murder, they would certainly have found the rock fault and the breach in it. Neither did Archie's description of the other events in the cave on that morning he went there with Alan alter anything fundamental. All right, Archie had played his part in the discovery of the rock fault – and would gain the little bit of kudos which was no doubt the object of his revelation – but more than this? There was only one interesting aspect of the information, as Claudia saw it – Alan's decision to suppress this bit of the story. But Archie had already supplied a good reason for this. Alan wanted to eliminate any suspicion that Beri had played a part in the discovery, which might have hindered his easy export of the spoils. In the modern climate of greater respect for countries in which archaeological finds are made, this might seem grasping and high-handed. In the prevailing, still imperialist, mores of the times, it was no more than common practice, and pragmatic good sense. Any European archaeologist, including a French one, would have been likely to behave in the same way.

Claudia was reengaged with the present by the thunderous applause which broke out as Archie finished, which continued for at least half a minute. She joined in enthusiastically. The excellent lecture had reinforced her belief that Archie could be useful to her on more general points about Silverman's life, especially the Indian bit.

But she certainly wasn't going to get him going down here, she realised, unless she could persuade him to stay the night in Taunton. It was now after nine and the last train was at half past ten. When he had finished, excited students surged on to the stage. Then, just as with Teppit's help he was extricated from their eager questions and they began to move off, a local reporter waylaid them and caused another delay.

'So Silverman deliberately falsified the story?' the journalist asked, when he had scribbled down a few details, as they walked.

'In these small details and for the reasons I gave,' replied Archie.

'So he could take all the glory?'

Archie was horrified. He stopped in his tracks. 'Oh no, not for that reason at all. I have given the reasons.'

'You mean he did it just to fool the French?'

'Exactly so, to protect the find, and to shield me.'

The reporter also wanted to know more about the failure to find Beazley's body. Archie shrugged. 'The police out there weren't exactly Scotland Yard, you know – in the heat of summer. And, after all, with the evidence against Beri, and his suicide, it was a cut and dried case, wasn't it?'

Archie refused to stay the night. 'Oh I never do that. Must get back to Bounder, who'll be expecting me,' he said. 'The school offered to put me up.'

Bounder apparently was a dog. Claudia conceded defeat. She had enjoyed Archie's performance, but from a professional point of view it had proved a rather less than satisfactory jaunt. She'd have to nobble him another time.

4

A s the next senior to Sir Alan Silverman in the department of archaeology at Sarum University, eminent in his field of ancient Macedonia on which subject his books were surely paramount, Walter Claridge considered his candidature for the chair of archaeology by any decent standard unassailable. On the other hand he recognised that in an inequitable world standards are not always decent. Sir Alan, he knew, had not favoured his succession. How could a man of Silverman's sort, flashy, limelight-loving, charming, popular and manipulative, have favoured someone like himself who shunned publicity – especially the type trumpeted on television – who kept to the strict academic disciplines of patient verification, and who as an administrator tried to be fair and even-handed? He had also heard that Vincent Galleon, whose Vice-Chancellorship he so respected, opposed his election and would do his best to block it. Silverman had known how to cultivate Galleon of course, as he had always cultivated anyone he considered useful. The matter couldn't be considered decided.

But in university elections as in any others the ballot does not always favour those holding power. A few days after Sir Alan's memorial service in which Claridge's chalky voice had been heard reading the lesson, Claridge received a formal letter from the Vice-Chancellor informing him that he was the Senate's choice. The appointment would be announced officially in the University Gazette next week.

By the time of Archie Fieldhouse's lecture at a west-country boarding school, Claridge's daily arrival at the Faculty was already beginning to acquire an established punctuality and routine. Whatever he might be doing later in the day, just before eight-thirty he could be seen in his usual dark suit making his way with his rather trudging walk from his car towards the large office Alan designed for himself on the second floor of the building. Normally his route lay through the main entrance and up the main staircase – at this time of morning there were no students to impede his way. On the morning in question, precisely three days after Fieldhouse's revelations, he used the entrance to the Silverman Collection, which was on the side of the building. During the night he'd had thoughts about the museum, and wished to confirm to himself when nobody was about how the changes he envisaged might work out in practice. It was some time since he'd been in the place. He let himself in with the keys he had acquired, relocked the door – for the collection was not opened to the public until ten – circumvented the turnstile by opening the iron gate beside it with another key, reset the burglar alarm, and mounted the stairs to the first floor where for security reasons the exhibits were housed.

Among the flashily arranged showcases – and, worse, within sight of the appalling tableaux rooms which led off from the main hall – Claridge endured moments of intense distaste. Really he'd forgotten the extent to which Silverman's propensity for the plebeian could go. It was like Madame Tussaud's. He fled in horror from the room which depicted the cave in which the murder had taken place, wax figures enacting the event. That would simply go for a start. He concentrated on the material in the cases in the main hall, which needed proper classification and grouping. The lay-out as it was was stagey and meaningless. He decided what he would do. He'd first have an inventory of the artefacts made – it was a disgrace, but he did not think a proper one had ever existed. He would then, when time offered, sit down and work out a new strategy of deployment. Probably he'd call someone in to put into practice principles he laid down. Encouraged by his decision, he continued with a lighter step through another locked door at the far end of the room which led into the Faculty proper and to what was now his office.

The office, too, he had decided, would need instant changes, its walls being lined with a gallery of autographed photographs of Alan snapped with the great and notable – on dig sites, outside the Palace after receiving his knighthood, and so on. This matter, too, had been receiving his overnight mental attention. As he entered the small outer room in which his secretary, Felicity Warboys, sat, he was on the point of inviting her to secure for him some samples of new wallpapers that might be suitable. It was as good a topic as any with which to start the day.

He was not immediately allowed to mention the wallpaper, however. Felicity, a young woman he had employed before to type his work and whom he had immediately brought in to replace the decorative person who had continued to work on in the office after Alan's stroke, rose anxiously as he entered, clutching a pale green cardigan over her not over-prominent bosom.

'Oh, good morning, Mr Claridge. I . . .'

'Good morning, Felicity.'

Claridge sensed there was something the girl had to say but, choosing to ignore it, he preceded her into the inner tabernacle towards the impressive mahogany desk. Here, turning, he stood for a moment. He could not help for an instant savouring again the grandeur of his new position – whatever it was that was troubling Felicity, who had followed him in.

'I fear there is some news that may not please you, Mr Claridge,' said Felicity, her disquiet now plain. She had in her hand a copy of the main news section of yesterday's Sunday Times. She placed it on the tooled leather blotter, neatly folded at an inside page.

Faintly smiling – for what could a newspaper produce which could be more than a moment's difficulty? – Claridge looked downwards. Centred was a photograph of a figure familiar to him, a small man with spectacles whose baggy trousers somehow looked too big for him. He was standing with a black and white dog outside a semi-detached house apparently about to scrub the front door step. Felicity had ringed this photograph in red pencil, also the column-long piece beside it.

'DID SILVERMAN LIE?' Claridge read.

Claridge read a few more lines, sufficient to learn what this lunatic ex-soldier had apparently said in a lecture at a public school – also he registered the slant being given to the statement. The journalist – or was it perhaps Fieldhouse himself? – was more than implying that Silverman lied out of the sordid motive of his own glorification and of cheating Sahara of its birthright.

Claridge permitted an eyebrow to rise. 'So, it's that fellow Fieldhouse again, is it? Sir Alan encouraged him, I'm afraid. The man should never have been let loose on the public.'

Miss Warboys seemed encouraged. 'The paper appears to say,' she went on more eagerly, 'that Fieldhouse – and another man called Neil Beazley, I think he was the one who got murdered, wasn't he? – were entirely responsible for the Tifgad find, not Sir Alan, and that Sir Alan suppressed this fact in order to keep all the glory for himself.'

'So I read,' said Claridge. While he read further, a clock on the solid marble mantelpiece seemed to stop ticking. It was gathering itself to strike nine. It did so. Warboys waited, like a maid who had delivered a note on a silver tray.

'Hm, a one-day wonder, I don't doubt,' Claridge said, and threw the paper onto the desk.

'But do you think there can be any truth in what Fieldhouse says?'

'Of course there isn't.'

'You mean Fieldhouse, or the journalist, invented it all?'

'One or the other, or both in collusion. There's no one to gainsay Fieldhouse now, is there? Strange he never said anything of this sort when Silverman was alive, isn't it?'

'Fieldhouse says Sir Alan swore him to secrecy because of possible difficulties with the French colonial authorities.'

Claridge was preparing, after this brief irrelevance, to begin his day's work. He sat down and rearranged one or two items which had got out of position. 'If you believe that, I shall have to think you capable of swallowing anything, Felicity,' he said. 'The French colonial authorities disappeared thirty years ago. The man clearly makes a living out of this sort of thing. It is a gnat bite on the tough hide of the profession, no more. Now, the mail if you please, Felicity.'

Claridge had introduced the subject of gnats. Not much later, Felicity Warboys had cause to reflect further on the habits of this species, in particular its habit of persistence. The phone rang. It appeared to be a journalist wanting an interview. 'No comment' – the verbal swat handed to her by Claridge to deal with the intrusion – proved quite inadequate. The same man, who announced his name was Strode, rang again a short while later. He understood, he conceded, the Professor's reluctance to comment on a sensitive issue, but didn't he realise – didn't she realise on his behalf – that silence on his part might be construed as a cover-up? The caller was at pains to instruct Miss Warboys that for the Faculty of Archaeology no news was terrible news, that comment was essential if a total breakdown in public confidence in a revered and recently buried national figure was to be avoided. A responsible column in The Sunday Times yesterday might become a headline in a daily newspaper of a much lower standing tomorrow.

When Strode actually appeared in Felicity's office accompanied by a cameraman, Felicity's not robust resistance was crumbling. She said faintly that Mr Claridge didn't see people without appointments. Sitting uninvited in

45

the two chairs, the men didn't appear to understand this. They could wait, Strode said. In a dither, she went in to Claridge and made sure to close the door behind her.

Claridge was reviewing lecture subjects in the department, which Silverman had allowed to get wildly out of hand – there was duplication and no attempt at a rational coordination. He was also well aware that where the press were involved an aloof silence would nearly always be the textbook advice. But why shrink from this very early opportunity in his professorship to make plain his attitude towards publicity? There were one or two colleagues who might be given cause to think by a few succinct remarks on this matter. It was at least The Times, not a tabloid, and a short definitive statement would surely end it. The very persistent gnat was granted an interview.

Claridge commented, with the cameraman in attendance, that in his view the fact that Sir Alan Silverman had never mentioned to him any confidential circumstances relating to the Saharan find of 1936 made him entirely confident the story of the discovery was exactly as Silverman described it. He was asked if he thought Silverman wanted to steal the limelight by appearing to have used almost intuitive powers to find the right cave in which a murder had taken place. Claridge, whatever might have been the temptation to do otherwise, was not found wanting in defence of his calling. What monarch after all favours regicide?

'I think you will find that truly professional men and women do not need to employ such subterfuges,' he pronounced.

Did this imply then, the interviewer pursued, that Claridge thought Archie Fieldhouse's story a fabrication?

There was here an outbreak of humour. 'That might be a conclusion which will be drawn,' was the reply, accompanied by a smile as majestically distant as a January sun.

Michael Strode was in luck. There was a shortage of news that day in the editorial department of The Times. On an inner page, accompanied by two juxtaposed photographs, Claridge's revelation of 'the professional mind' was coupled with the fruits of a further interview Strode had with Archie Fieldhouse.

Archie was asked by Strode to comment on Claridge's statement. 'He wasn't there, was he?' Archie replied. 'He wasn't even alive, now I come to

46

think about it, so how can he know?'

What did Archie think of Claridge's saying, or implying, that he, Fieldhouse, had invented his own part in the find?

Archie's answer – he didn't think. Claridge's sayings were his own business, nothing to do with himself, whose priority was the giving of talks and the telling of the truth.

The second picture alongside the piece was of Archie emerging from a supermarket. It caught the ex-soldier looking down with appreciation at his black and white mongrel dog, which at this moment was giving priority to a female poodle tethered to a pram.

5.

As Archie Fieldhouse woke in his North Harrow semi-detached, for a moment he fancied he heard the call of a bugle and the clink of a mule's harness. The sun's rays, brimming through his window, appeared to be those from a Saharan or an Indian sky. Then he realised what he had heard was the sound of the milkman's bottle on his doorstep.

Fully awake, he realised a lot more things which were not quite as they should be. He remembered that two days ago his lecture revealing new information has been reported with uncalled for slants in a Sunday newspaper brought him by a neighbour. On the same day he had been cornered outside his front door by a journalist and asked questions about a professor at Sir Alan's university, which he was happy to answer in a factual manner. The answers he gave to these questions had also been interpreted quite wrongly by The Times newspaper. Since then he'd had to answer a dozen telephone calls from other newshounds. What he had intended was that a written record of his little contribution to history would be made by Mrs Claudia Drake, the official biographer approved by Sir Alan, not by these jackals who daily hunt the streets for offal. Disquieted anew, he turned out of bed smartly.

By the time he had washed and shaved he had things in a better perspective. No milk spilt, he thought, when all said and done no harm done by anyone except the one or two who wanted to twist the truth. All he'd done was his duty. He put on working clothes, this not being a talking day, then went downstairs to give Bounder his breakfast and get his own. Archie believed in starting the day with a good lining to the stomach – on which a soldier marches after all. By the time he'd fried an egg, bacon and a sausage, Bounder had finished the plate of meat he'd put down and jumped on to the other chair pulled to the kitchen table, licking his chops appreciatively.

'That's it, Bounder,' Archie said, 'you give your whiskers a clean. Nothing to worry about, you know that. The odd bean or two spilt – but just to put the log-book straight.'

Embarked on his plateful, later he glanced up at the large, signed

48

photograph of Sir Alan which occupied pride of place over the tiled fireplace, and raised his laden fork to it on the way to his mouth. 'Know you won't mind, sir, now you're where you are. You'll have a good laugh most likely – like we used to round the camp fire when the day's work was done.' He returned his attention to the dog. 'No, Bounder, his lordship won't mind old Private Fieldhouse having his little moment of glory. Not now, not after sixty years. No confidences broken after all, all our kit pukka clean and mustered for your inspection, sir.' The highly intelligent dog, wrinkling an eyebrow and lowering a lustrous eye, seemed to agree.

On the kitchen wall hung a diary. Consulting it, Archie read that opposite that day's date it said: 'Blitz the garden.' He didn't imagine he'd get through the morning without being disturbed again, but he saw no reason to interrupt his routines. The world had to go on whatever the weather, however many of these people with notepads and pencils were flying about like maniacs.

He began with the privet hedges. They'd been brought back to square one in the autumn, but spring growth had taken them up again. He spread a sheet of hessian on the pavement, gave the blades of the shears a stroke or two on either side with the dry stone, and began. Unknown to him a female neighbour opposite, drawing aside a lace curtain with a forefinger, smiled. You could set your watch by old Archie Fieldhouse. Fancy him being in the news like that.

The hedges trim back and front of the house, Archie mowed the small patch of grass, weeded and loosened the soil of the beds surrounding it – in one of which stood two ranks of African marigolds dressed by the right. He was mixing a bucket of whitewash to freshen the stones which lined the beds, when the phone rang inside. Here they come again, he thought. There was no rhyme or reason in it. Surely he'd said all there was to say? He was getting to feel he wouldn't bother answering the phone.

This call was at least a variation. It wasn't a journalist but a rather hesitant female who said she was a secretary of some sort. Then he caught the words 'Silverman Museum' and 'Salisbury,' and he made connections. It was apparently this Professor Claridge again, who had clairvoyant insights into events in the past at which he was not present, on behalf of whom the woman was speaking. Archie gathered that Professor Claridge wanted to come and see him this morning.

'This morning?' Archie said, thinking he hadn't started on the back patio yet.

'This morning,' the woman repeated as if he were being obstructive. 'Professor Claridge finds himself in London today, and it would be convenient for him to come to North Harrow in the later morning today if that's possible for you.'

As a matter of fact it wasn't all that convenient for Archie, who found himself in the situation of having promised a neighbour he'd fix a drain when he'd finished in the garden. But Archie Fieldhouse had not been conditioned to defiance of this sort.

'Towards midday then.'

Archie had almost finished his work in the front garden and was beginning to think a can of beer wouldn't come amiss, when a large black car the size of a hearse pulled up on the other side of the privet. An individual in a peak cap lowered the driver's window.

'You a Mr Fieldhouse?'

'Right first time.'

The peak cap got out and opened the back door to his nibs on the back seat. A large dark-suited gent in a brown felt hat emerged and, looking up and down the street, seemed not instantly delighted to find himself in such a neighbourhood.

'My secretary telephoned you earlier, I believe?'

'She certainly did, Mr Claridge.'

'Good, and I see you know who I am. Well – er – perhaps we can go inside, can we?'

Archie had an immediate difficulty. He didn't feel his sitting-room was constructed for persons such as Walter Claridge. For starters, rather in the way of an animal caged in a city zoo, he seemed much too big for the armchair. Bounder was more outspoken on the subject. He stood by the door of the room in these tense moments, uttering the low growl he reserved for times when he considered his master menaced.

Mr Claridge had refused a glass of beer. He built his fingers into a pyramid. Tapping them together as if he'd come to a decision, he cleared his throat.

'You may well be somewhat surprised by my visit,' he began. 'I could of course have spoken to you on the telephone. But I fear a situation has arisen

50

of – er – some delicacy, which needs, in my estimation, a more private conversation.' There was no direct question here, but Archie felt a response was being demanded of him. Sitting on one of the upright chairs, he nodded encouragingly. 'I could think, Mr Fieldhouse, that you might imagine my motive in coming to see you like this is hostile. I have to admit that, when I first read of your recent revelations in the newspapers, I did tend to be sceptical about their accuracy. In my profession – as you might have come to appreciate with your considerable contact with it – caution is an instinctive part of one's equipment.' Another nod was being canvassed here, which Archie again supplied. Mr Claridge, he thought, was beginning to look extremely uncomfortable and in need of nods. He was attempting to smile but the grimace seemed to be jamming half-way. 'I do confess to having some continuing doubts about some aspects . . . however, let me make it plain, my object is in no way ill-willed. Indeed, it is constructive. Let me put it to you in this way. It would have been so easy, wouldn't it, for you to have been carried away by the drama of your graphic descriptions at that school? I've no doubt you have a very strong sense of drama, which I'm sure brings colour and excitement to your – er – lectures. But where there's drama, I've no doubt you'll agree, there's always the danger that the facts will slip a little.'

'Oh no, Mr Claridge, not that.'

'Er – not what exactly?'

'I don't twist the facts. Facts is what I'm after. Sir Alan taught me that. I never depart from the truth. What would be the point?'

Archie saw Walter withdraw for a moment. It seemed he might be thinking this wouldn't be the easiest of interviews. 'I've no doubt you never intend to distort reality,' he continued with a renewed output of patience. 'But you must surely concede there are times, talking of events that took place more than half a century ago, when total veracity might elude you. This question of Beazley's prior discovery of the Carthaginian hoard for example, and of your allegations at a public school that Sir Alan decided to conceal it . . .'

'Oh, that's plain fact. Some of the newspapers have messed the story, but as I told it, and will go on telling it, it's the truth and nothing but the truth. Sir Alan, of course, knew it was the truth.'

'You're saying Sir Alan knew about these – er – embellishments of yours, and decided to suppress them? If that's the case, why is it now we hear about them when he is no longer with us? Why did not Sir Alan speak of them himself?'

'I've said that, sir. Sir Alan was aware at the time of the extreme delicacy of the situation. Beazley was hobnobbing with Berbers – or rather, with one in particular. He didn't want difficult questions of treasure-trove arising. And over the years, I suppose, even though there was no real reason not to bring these facts to light, he probably didn't think it was important to do so. He had more important things on his mind, I dare say.'

'And this story of yours about trailing the Berber the previous day? Why is it we hear of that only now?'

'Oh, that's easy, sir. It was entirely in my own interest, as Sir Alan saw it, that that didn't come out. He thought if it became known that I had been up near that cave that afternoon, the French authorities might accuse me of being involved in the murder of Neil Beazley.'

Claridge raised a token hand to his lips and coughed. 'If that was so, then isn't it still the case? Are you not still in danger of that accusation?'

Archie, whom life had taught to take things as they come, had not frontally considered the motive of his interviewer to this moment. He began to do so now. Who did this man think he was exactly, he was forced to ask himself. Was it only from his own authority that he spoke? 'You'll pardon me, sir,' he said in another key, though with impeccable respect still latent. 'You are Mr Claridge – Professor Claridge, Sir Alan's successor at the University. Would I be right in thinking that you speak of course as a friend of Sir Alan's, a person, naturally, concerned to honour his memory?'

Archie saw a flush of annoyance appear on Claridge's rock-like cheeks. Did he perceive this last question as impertinence? Was this private solidier daring to question his motivation – was this what he thought? It seemed very much like it. Archie noticed a distinct abandonment of subtlety. Was it that Claridge had hoped to head off a wayward soldier without the use of heavy artillery but now saw no result would be achieved this way?

'Mr Fieldhouse,' he began, 'I really haven't come here to bandy words with you. I had hoped that we could come to an amicable agreement without telling you what I shall now have to. Very well then, I must make it plain to you what has happened. As a result of your recent remarks there was a small press coverage. This would no doubt have passed off in a day or two in the normal way of such things. Unfortunately, a very undesirable and not unpowerful party has become interested – the Saharan Republic. Their embassy here in London noticed the story and has taken it up with the Foreign Office. As a result an extremely serious international situation has arisen.'

'Serious, sir?'

'Sahara is demanding the return of the Carthaginian Hoard – for whose care I am responsible in Salisbury – to the country of its origin. It is a ploy of course, and not the first time an attempt of this sort has been made. But they're arguing, because of your remarks, that as Sir Alan's evidence, used during previous discussions between the two Governments, appears to be altered, the whole matter of the custody of the artefacts should be reopened. You may perhaps see now why it is cardinally important the story remains unchanged.'

Archie was horrified. 'You mean the Saharans are saying we should give the hoard back?'

'What I am saying is that what is at present a private diplomatic exchange might well become a very open one, and an international dispute which could have political and economic ramifications potentially very damaging to this country. I am assured of this.'

Claridge had gone too far. Trained by Sir Alan to identify, and have a healthy disrespect for, political jargon, Archie was overtaken by a spirited scepticism which quickly dispelled his momentary alarm. 'After sixty years?' he said with a grin, the sort of grin with which he supported some dangerous enterprise of Sir Alan. 'But we're not going to give 'em back, are we, sir? It's like the Elgin Marbles and the Greeks. The Greeks have been over here trying to get their property back and it hasn't done them any good. The museums of the world'd be empty if every country gave back things they'd found elsewhere. And if we aren't giving them back, what's the fuss?'

Claridge began to lose control. 'Now look, Fieldhouse. I can understand your wanting to grab a bit of the limelight. I can understand it may be lucrative for you to do so. I dare say if subsequent events become front page news, as they well may, newspapers will be offering you sums . . .'

Archie also began to understand the drift of things, and blushed. 'Oh, it's not the limelight I want. Certainly not cash.'

'Then what do you want?'

"The truth. That's what I do in my talks. I don't want all these journalists

53

buzzing about – nor politicians either, if you're telling me they're interested. What I do in my talks is tell the story as it happened – all of the story, as I now can. History. For when all's said and done, that's what it is – history.'

'You're saying the national interest means nothing to you?'

'What national interest?'

Claridge was brought to his last resort. He stood up with his back to the trinket-laden mantelpiece, summoning a last residue of tolerance.

'Fieldhouse, I have not told you quite everything. I said that to this moment the matter has been confined to discreet exchanges behind the scenes. This is true, but it will no longer be so. The matter between the Saharan Embassy and the Foreign Office has been leaked, and I am given to understand that there is a back bench Opposition question down for the Foreign Office this very afternoon, which the Minister will have to answer. Hence his approach to me, and my very unusual visit to you here on his behalf. The approach of the Saharans is to be revealed, and the Minister is to be asked what he intends to do about it. It is too late to stop the question, but what I'm asking you to do is to undertake to retract your story – say you were carried away – and not refer to it again in the future. This will give the Minister the basis of a firm answer.'

Archie had often noted with pleasure Sir Alan's lack of reverence towards established authority, but never in his life had he thought this empowered him with a similar right. But – perhaps it was the accumulated effect of the events of the last days – he felt at this moment that he had reached an impasse in which a natural wish to extend courtesy was absent. 'If you'll excuse me, Mr Claridge,' he found himself saying, 'I've promised to fix a neighbour's drain.'

Archie's neighbours, one or two of whom had monitored the arrival of the large black car, observed that the gentleman in the dark suit departed from Archie's house a great deal faster than he entered it. They also noted that he had opened the back door of the car himself, got in and shut it, before the chauffeur could recover from his doze and assist.

Men like Walter Claridge don't take kindly to fruitless visits to North Harrow, least of all when on the encouragement, through an underling, of an Under Secretary of State, and when sitting in a Foreign Office car put at his disposal, mobile telephone and chauffeur included. As the chauffeur negotiated his way out of the suburban labyrinth, he grasped the status-enhancing tassel with his left hand and turned the pages of his diary with the other. He found the number and dialed it. The number put him in contact with the civil servant, Ian Cobbald, who had seen him in Whitehall that morning. Primed to do so, Cobbald passed Claridge swiftly to the politician himself.

'Professor Claridge? Good of you to call so promptly. I do hope all this is not being too inconvenient for you?'

Claridge was in a dither. He could think of no correspondingly relaxed preliminary. 'Minister, I apologise. I fear, as I forecast might be the case to Mr Ian Cobbald, the man is sticking to his story.'

There was a momentary ministerial silence. 'I see.'

'He refused point blank. Though he denies it, no doubt one of the papers has offered him a fortune for the on-going story. We can probably expect worse to come.'

There was another silence and another 'I see.' 'So – your advice, Claridge?'

There was a complex problem here for Claridge. He was used to being asked for advice on Macedonians from lesser eminences than his own. But this did not concern Macedonians, and the question was not from a lesser eminence. Furthermore, barely minutes ago he had been growled at by a mongrel dog and insulted by an ex private soldier. Claridge produced an uncharacteristic rush of unconsidered speech.

'The man's a liar. He thinks as Silverman's dead he can say what he likes.'

'You're sure of that?'

'Sir Alan was sometimes vain and he cared for acclaim, but he'd certainly have told me and others if there'd been anything untrue in the Tifgad story as he revealed it.'

'Very well then. I'm grateful. I'll know how to perform this afternoon. Nothing libellous of course, but a firm disassociation from an old man's memory – on your advice.'

When he'd put the phone down, Claridge wondered, especially in view of that last phrase, if a reconnection would be advisable. But, exhausted by the visit and the interview, he left things as they were.

On his return to his family in Salisbury, he watched on television the very rowdy question time in the House of Commons that afternoon, in which the Foreign Office Minister was accused of the defence of a national theft.

He heard the Minister say, when pressed, that the information upon which he had denied ex-Private Fieldhouse's allegations, came from 'an eminent authority within the profession.' At this moment Claridge switched the set off.

Claridge had talked to Felicity Warboys of a 'one day wonder.' There'd already been seven or eight. Would this now be the end of this irrelevance?

6.

*I*t amused Claudia Drake when, intending kindness no doubt and after a decent interval following Jack's death, two people she knew well asked her if she was thinking of 'marrying again some day' – as if, given a reasonable supply of sexual attractiveness, 'marrying again' or living with someone permanently was a state of mind, something one just decided to do ahead of the event like booking a holiday or acquiring a pet.

It was five years now since Jack died, so suddenly and unexpectedly that for a whole month or more she just hadn't been able to believe it had happened. Jack had originally been a lecturer in Linguistics at Sarum, but for the year or two before his death he'd been in charge of University external relations and promotion and he'd had to be abroad a lot on extended journeys. After he died, she kept waiting for him to ring from Heathrow, which he had done more than once, saying he'd got back earlier than expected and wanted to be collected. Perhaps this was merciful. Through what might have been the very worst of the pain, she had subconsciously anaesthetised herself in this way.

The pain had come on of course. It had lasted well beyond the statutory year. Claudia guessed she and Jack had been about as happy as a couple can be, and his loss was like a mental amputation. But like everyone who is bereaved and who isn't abnormally melancholic, she had come out of grief by a process, not so much of will, as of natural erosion. She began to look at other men, especially when they looked at her. She even slept with one or two on a basis understood to be temporary. But she counted her real interests. She decided she really preferred what is called her 'freedom.' She was able to compromise on most things, but didn't think she ever could about the person she lived with.

By the time Alan Silverman offered the job, she had begun to love her life again. She had her idyllic Test Valley thatched cottage, her village and, if she wanted it, selected aspects of University life. The friends she had shared with Jack were still there. Approaching her mid-thirties, she could be seen to be in what Jean Brodie would say was her prime. Above all she had her work which, on becoming a widow, absorbed a good three-quarters of her energy. She'd like to have been a novelist, but the next best thing was delving as deeply into the meaning of actual people's lives.

Claudia watched with entertainment the small, then the much bigger, fuss over Archie's lecture. She couldn't believe Archie had told anything other than the truth, and it was patently obvious what the Foreign Office Minister was up to in implying he was a liar to the House of Commons. She was only surprised the minister had got old Claridge to stick his neck out as far as he seemed to have done – for she was sure, even before she knew it for certain, that Claridge was the 'eminent authority within the profession' the minister had referred to.

The morning after the Commons question, the story made the front pages of the newspapers. Now it had become political Claudia found herself less interested, though it had not escaped her notice that a certain Michael Strode was the journalist who had released the cat from the bag. Given what she was now sure was his desire to do down an eminent man, the furore caused by his reportage was no doubt giving him great satisfaction. But . . . Sahara would make a fuss, there'd be a diplomatic row, she foresaw – as there was over the Elgin Marbles from time to time – then it would all die. Sarum wasn't going to yield up its treasure any more than the British Museum was, and what could politicians do about that in a democracy?

Claudia turned her back on the matter, and went to work as usual in Alan's house, Donnerton Hall, which was south of Salisbury, not far from Fordingbridge. The house was to be sold, but because of the usual protractions that follow someone's death, this would not be for ages yet and the trustees of his estate, the chairman of whom was Vincent Galleon the Vice-Chancellor, said not only that she should go on working in the library there where all Alan's papers were, but that she should also have full access to the papers, which she hadn't had when Alan was alive.

Upset as Claudia was at Alan's death, she was having a field day in his library. She realised for sure what she had hitherto only suspected, that he'd only fed her a small selection of the stuff. Not surprisingly for a collector of archaeological valuables (though very surprising for someone who so jealously guarded his image) he seemed to have kept most of the personal letters he'd ever received, and a vast quantity of the official, professional and business ones. There was also an intermittent personal diary, which she hadn't known about. The only diary she had seen was the very practical one relating to the Tifgad expedition. She had a slight (not unenjoyable) sense of prurience delving into all this, though it very soon became apparent that, spots as there were here and there, the good image she had of Alan was much more likely to be enhanced than tarnished by what she read. What was beginning to come over to her was a man of very lonely spirit – both Alan's parents had died young and he'd been brought up by aged grandparents in a small Warwickshire village. Was it potted psychology to think that it was not just archaeological bits and pieces he collected, but also people – to fill an emotional vacuum? If this was sustainable it would explain so much about his life.

This certainly seemed to be a relevant idea where his relations with women were concerned, to which Claudia owned she found herself awarding an unprofessional priority. His activity in this sphere was certainly in a Don Juan category. They reminded her of Mozart's famous aria, sung by Leperello, enumerating his master's female victims and documenting them by nationality. A cool twenty here, fifty there . . . 'Ma, en España . . .' They were an immensely varied collection of women of all ages upwards – from a Neapolitan girl clearly no older than her mid-teens to a Mayfair duchess in her sixties. They were of several nationalities, and in terms of class equally diverse. What struck Claudia was the remarkable lack of recrimination from the women when their inningses had been declared closed. Sadness, yes, pleas for his reappearance and for the continuation of their relationship as a 'friendship', but never bitterness. It seemed all of them knew when they took up with him that their days were numbered, and all accepted the precondition. Through the letters she sensed again vividly Alan's vibrant zest for life. The worst one could accuse him of was vanity, which was not surely a deadly sin. He was not in her judgement guilty of pride or arrogance, which was.

On this particular morning, she happened to come across a letter from Janet Brisbane, the fiancée of the murdered Neil Beazley, who had been one of the four British members of the Tifgad expedition, and who had been absent, she remembered, from the memorial service in the Abbey, though, as Claudia well knew, she was very much still alive. The letter was still inside its original envelope, but the post office mark was only partially legible. It had been posted in Tiverton, Devon, but the date was smudged. Then she realised the faded stamp bore the head of Edward VIII. This surely proved it was 1936, the year of Tifgad? Interested, she took the letter out.

It was tantalisingly brief, with not even 'Dear Alan.' 'You left your pyjamas,' it stated baldly. 'I've sent them.' It was signed 'Janet.'

She was intrigued. There couldn't be two Janets – in 1936. Pyjamas – and obviously a visit after the expedition? She began a search for more correspondence, which would stand out from other letters, she thought. The handwriting was distinct, also mature though she must have been very young at that time – Alan, she knew, had snatched her, and Neil Beazley, straight from Oxford with the ink not dry on their degrees. She could find nothing else from or to her in the file of that year or the one after.

Claudia had not in her other reading been fastening especially on the Saharan episode which, important as it was as an event, was only a small part of the whole life. But the fact that this seemed the only letter from Janet, her absence from the memorial service, and the recent press and political fuss over Archie's lecture, made her wonder if she shouldn't make an effort to see her while Tifgad was still hot in her mind. It would be as well to confirm, she thought, that Archie had been telling the truth in his revelations, especially about Alan's motivation in handling the story as he had. It would be extra ammunition, too, it occurred to her as an afterthought, if Michael Strode ever carried out his threat of contacting her again.

She was pretty sure Janet still lived somewhere in South Devon – which married with the Tiverton postmark. As an intrepid traveller, writer and broadcaster on radio and television, Janet was often in the public eye, even these days when she must be something like Archie's age, and Claudia remembered seeing an article on her in a Sunday magazine recently – one of those 'Profiles at Home' features with colour photographs of the décor. She remembered, because it was her and because she was linked to Alan, and also irrelevantly because of the décor, a rather picturesque shambles of crowded bookshelves, worn-but-much-used-and-loved-looking furniture, arty lampshades – a juxtaposition of objects which on a miniature scale she would like to think described her own small abode. Janet had looked in good shape physically, which wasn't surprising considering the hikes she'd done about the world and still did. And there had been a cat, her memory now added superfluously, a beautiful white creature with a flat cross-looking face, curled on a smooth black and red (Saharan?) rug in front of the fire.

Janet's name was not in Alan's address book. She had come over in the article and from her own viewings of her on the box as a rather caustic if not arrogant person, overconscious of her fame. Claudia wouldn't have been surprised to find she was ex-directory. But there was her name in the first volume she tried from the comprehensive collection Alan had in his reference library. 'Tor House, Bovey Tracey.' That was near Newton Abbott, wasn't it?

Janet answered the phone herself. Claudia knew it was her. The upper-crust, blue-stockingy voice had also, she realised, stayed strongly in her memory.

'Interview – about Silverman? What on earth would you imagine I'd have to say about him?' Janet then said she was on the point of going to Scotland – but not for two days, it transpired. The upshot of this was that Claudia managed to get her to say reluctantly that she'd see her the next day. She really felt she'd had to get her foot in her door to persuade her.

Claudia's car was being serviced, so she took, first, a train to Newton Abbott, then a nippy bus which bombed northwards through lush countryside with the southern edge of Dartmoor looming ahead.

Bovey was the last little town apparently before the road started the steep climb to Haytor. When she got off the bus she went into an estate agent's opposite. She began to speak to the girl at the front desk, but a youngish man in striped shirt and cufflinks came forward beaming from an inner office, presumably the boss. She asked him if he knew Janet Brisbane and where Tor House was.

Was it her imagination, or did the smile diminish a notch? If so, was it just disappointment she didn't want to buy a house? Anyway, he knew Janet all right. 'Quite a lady,' he remarked, as he kindly led her out into the street to point out the very substantial, white-painted house nestling comfortably half-way up the wooded slope to Haytor. There was a footpath she could take, he said which branched off the road before you got to the end of the drive and which cut off quite a chunk. He then lowered his eyes fractionally to her bust and up again, and offered to drive her up. She thanked him, but said she'd been sitting in a train and a bus and felt like the walk.

She did relish the walk. There'd been two days of rain. Now that good weather had returned, the countryside was fresh and fragrant. She followed the main road for a way, then found the footpath. It wound through woods which were filled with echoing May bird-song and smelt powerfully of newly-fledged trees and the abundant damp bracken shoots.

After a steep climb, the footpath found the unmade drive only a few yards from the house. Proceeding along it, she was confronted suddenly with the solid two-storey stone building, staring away over a magnificent view of the lush red soil of the county to the distant blue of the Channel.

There was a sizeable well-mown lawn, spongy with moss, in the middle of which was an old-fashioned sun-canopy and under it a lightly-trousered figure sitting reading in a comfortable-looking, much-cushioned wooden chair with a footrest. Her head was helmeted in a tightly-drawn chiffon scarf, making her look like one of those pictures of Edith Sitwell, or perhaps Isadora Duncan dressed for her roadster. It had to be Janet but, playing it safe and feeling very British, she kept her eyes averted and properly approached the front door at the side of the house.

'Hallo?' said the peremptory voice. The bandaged head had ducked under the fringe of the canopy and was looking towards her.

As Claudia approached, she put a marker in the book she'd been reading and laid it carefully on the wide flat arm of the chair. 'I suppose someone like you was inevitable,' were her first words, as she eased herself in the chair. There were clearly not going to be any preliminaries and she certainly wasn't going to get up to greet her. 'After all this hype, there was bound to be a biography.' Claudia didn't think it worth mentioning she'd started the book several months ago, and waited.

'They've commissioned you, I suppose,' Janet went on. 'That's the trouble with publishing these days. Not even the publishers, but their accountants or market researchers decide what the "public" wants – whatever that word means – and writers get their orders as if they were waiters or cooks, or scriptwriters for films. I'm thankful to say I've never had to run about like that. I'm old enough to write what I want and get away with it. I'm off to the Andes again this winter, you know. At least there are plenty of places out there tourism hasn't reached yet, though one can't rule out that it soon will. Tourists are worse than locusts. Look what's happened in the Galapagos. Darwin's having nightmares in his grave no doubt . . .'

She went on in this vein quite a bit more, leap-frogging from one subject to another. Claudia was obliged to stand there, until she realised if she didn't do something about this Janet wouldn't. She suggested she might perhaps find herself a chair. It was as if she had made a faux-pas. Somewhat crossly, it sounded, Janet interrupted her monologue. 'Oh yes,' she said airily, 'do get yourself one. There are some in that thing over there.' She fluttered her hand vaguely in the direction of a shed.

In an old but well-kept potting-shed whose timbers smelt of some treatment, Claudia made a selection from a stack of deck chairs. Before she had set it up, the high imperious voice had resumed its inventory of the shortcomings of the modern world.

She had to decide. Did she let this blow itself out, or did she intrude? She had always liked people, usually academics, who plunge into subjects that interest them regardless of circumstances, which spoke of absorption and passion and didn't always imply any lack of concern for others as it was sometimes supposed to. But as she listened, she found herself making an exception in Janet's case. 'She's selfish and overbearing,' she thought, looking at the pronounced high cheek bones of her face – which had a curious reddish tan, perhaps from exposure to the sun in high places – the sharp nose whose nostrils were flared into a kind of involuntary sneer, and the rather worm-like lips. Even her amazing blue eyes seemed cold. Was her garrulousness – so far, totally about herself – the cause or the result of loneliness? She'd had a husband, Claudia knew from 'Who's Who', from whom she had been divorced long ago. She certainly looked pretty solitary living down here.

It was a gust of dislike, anyway, which made her switch the subject somewhat brutally at the first opportunity offered. This was when Janet sneezed, and then blew her nose rather loudly on a large man-size handkerchief.

'You weren't at Alan Silverman's memorial service,' she said.

'Damned hay-fever,' Janet continued as, uninhibitedly and obnoxiously, she looked to see what the handkerchief had garnered. 'Always get it at this time of year. It's the new bracken.'

'It was a pretty full house otherwise,' Claudia persisted. She waited while the linen was elaborately refolded. Had she even been heard?

'No, of course I wasn't at the service.'

'I think you were invited?'

Janet looked away horizonwards, and for the first time seemed to show some emotion Claudia felt might be personal. She looked cross.

'There were enough people there, I dare say. There always were.'

'It was quite an occasion.'

'I've no doubt.'

'Am I right – you sound less than enthusiastic about Alan?'

'I didn't say that.'

'But you didn't go to his memorial service?'

'I'm too old to flit about unnecessarily.'

The absurdity of this was patent. To anyone else of her age it would certainly not have been, but – she was planning an expedition to South America and she was saying a couple of hundred miles on an Intercity was too much for her? She seemed to realise the incongruity herself.

'No, I can't say I'm overexcited about Alan Silverman,' she went on. 'A man of quite extraordinary egotism.' Two of a kind, Claudia wondered? But she was given no further opportunity to explore – Janet also switched the subject. 'And I'm reluctant to leave this place in the summer,' she continued. 'I've always loved the Moor, one of the few bits of southern England – those tors at least which are not being bombarded by army guns or overrun by trippers – where you feel man has not made a poodle of nature.'

Claudia feared now her quarry was back in again she might get no further. After a tedious monologue, the interview could end abruptly and she'd be given marching orders. This happened often enough. But once again she was surprised.

'Now I'd expect you'd like some tea,' Janet said suddenly. 'Claudia, I think you said your name is, didn't you? My woman made some scones this morning. They should be edible, certainly with the cream they do down here. I'm afraid I guzzle it.'

As soon as Janet got up, Claudia realised how physically agile she was. She must be over eighty, but she strode ahead of her to the house and positively crashed about the kitchen, buttering, creaming and jamming the scones, throwing tea-leaves into the huge black pot with a large kitchen tablespoon, then manipulating the immense kettle with both hands. The said white cat, having got wind of activity from some hide-out in the garden, leapt through the open window and began to nose the plate of scones. Janet swept him to the floor.

'Get off, Potty, you incorrigible beast. You'll have yours at the appointed hour. We'll go into the sitting-room, shall we?'

Claudia began to like the woman a bit after all. They settled into the room she recognised. Even Potty – clearly a realist who knew he wouldn't preempt his mistress's habits concerning his mealtimes – settled on the Saharan mat she had recalled, which had clearly had some wear. It was a good lead.

'You didn't get that in Tifgad, did you – the mat I mean?'

'Yes, I did. Worn pretty well, hasn't it?'

She asked her how she'd decided to go on the expedition. 'Oh, I suppose it was Neil really.' She was eating voraciously. Pausing, she licked several fingers onto which cream had adhered. 'A sad man, Neil. We met in the Faculty – at Oxford. He didn't have a very cheerful background. His father worked in a travelling circus. Not even a lion-tamer or a clown – I think he just helped put the tents up. His mother ran off with someone when he was quite young. He had largely educated himself, probably sitting in a caravan, and got himself the scholarship – an achievement that was of course rare in those days. He sort of fell in love with me, and I thought he was worth a great deal more than the public schoolboys I knew who ponced about thinking they owned the world. I didn't love him. I think it was in fact partly to teach a lesson to another young man – the son of an earl, Balliol and the rest of it – that I took up with him, and under pressure agreed to be engaged. Then we went on that mad expedition together. I was fond of him and I respected him. He was a good archaeologist, who had already been on a couple of important Norfolk digs in summer vacs.'

Claudia asked how they'd met Alan. 'Oh, Alan had come to Oxford to give a lecture to our undergraduate archaeology society. He was not much known then, and had only got his own degree in the subject I think three years before. But with typical panache he'd made a study of the excavations at Troy, had been there, and published a book which, without producing anything original, brazenly summarised all that had been written. The book was selling like hot cakes. Because of this, and the publicity he'd won, he got himself taken on by a lecture agency. Neil and I were interested in Troy and went to the lecture.

'Among several other famous names he dropped was naturally Schliemman's, whose buccaneer methods had so outraged the serious archaeological world. He praised him as a man of great imagination, and as a publicist. The profession needed publicity, he said, as literature needed best-sellers. Most archaeologists were such stick-in-the-muds. Neil, a serious student, was insensed by this. He asked a barbed question and, not getting a satisfactory answer, stormed up to Alan at the end of the lecture, me trailing behind.

'A hardened soldier and adventurer like Alan didn't find it hard to defuse someone like Neil, who'd never even left British shores. Exerting his charm, which one has to say was considerable, he soon had Neil at his feet. He finished up asking us to have a meal. He tended to be drawn to people who opposed him, he said, and I suppose he liked us. He always made up his mind quickly, some would say rashly. Before the evening was out, he told us of his new idea and asked us if we'd like to come. I was game, I knew even in those days that what I wanted to do was travel, and despite his misgivings about Schliemman, Neil didn't really have a doubt, either – it was an opportunity for him. It also, for both of us, filled a post-graduate vacuum.

'Looking back, I shouldn't have gone. Going about with Neil in Oxford as an inoculation against the attentions of other men I didn't want was fine, but landing myself in the desert with him for months on end under pretty trying conditions was another matter altogether. The strains soon began to show. Neil was possessive, easily wounded, moody. And because I was sleeping with him, to justify indignation if I showed the slightest deviation from total admiration, he had all the historic weight of the male monopoly behind him – evident to an even greater degree in those days probably among the working classes from which he'd come. I don't think Neil was gay, or if he was, he was both – though at the more conventional sort of sex he was not a high performer. But after a giant bust-up in our tent one night he went into a hundred per cent sulk. He wouldn't even speak to me. Very soon he struck up this romantic relationship with the Berber. They worked together and perhaps, yes, for all I know they got up to other things, too, in those caves. I'd like to have gone home. I don't mind hardship – I've voluntarily undergone plenty in my time. But living with this situation was no fun . . .'

'But you had to stay?'

'Naturally. We'd given our word.'

'And that went on for – months?'

'Three at least after the row with Neil.'

Claudia knew suddenly what had happened. Janet was cutting the cake now, two large slices of extremely rich-looking fruit cake with a topping of almonds, also home-made. (How did she keep her excellent figure if she ate like this, she thought footnotally? Some people had all the luck). She waited, wondering if Janet would volunteer the information. She noticed the curiously white, dead area under her eyes, and didn't like her again. There was something ruthless about her, she thought, not just the ordinary, healthily selfish variety.

'You had an affair with Alan?'

She didn't bat an eyelid, and must have known in advance her secret was being guessed, if secret it was. 'Oh yes. Who didn't?'

'Out there?'

'We had to go into Tifgad in the Hudson truck to collect drinking water and stores once a week, and Alan always had cables to send. We used to take it in turns when we first arrived out there to go with him as a sort of treat – Archie, Neil, and I. It became established finally that I always went, except once or twice when I had the curse. We took a room in the one-horse hotel.'

'Overnight?'

'Usually not.'

'But the other two knew, or guessed?'

'I imagine so. Neil certainly. It turned him several shades moodier – if that was possible. He became impossible to Alan.'

'As Archie Fieldhouse illustrated recently in his recent revelations. You read about them?'

'How could I avoid it when it was in the papers, and Sahara has started asking questions?'

'And do you confirm what Archie has said – the amendments to the story?'

She looked bored. 'I suppose so.'

'Including Alan's motivation for what he did?'

'Probably.'

'You mean he was worried about the safe export of the find?'

'That sort of thing.'

Claudia had the feeling she wouldn't get any further on this line. While she still had something like attention, she reverted to Janet's relationship with Alan. 'I came across a note you wrote to Alan the other day. It must have been 1936 – it had an Edward VIII stamp. Apparently he had been to Devon to stay with you. You wrote to say he'd left his pyjamas behind.'

Her face was still a mask. 'Oh yes?'

67

'The envelope had a Tiverton postmark.'

'Yes, my parents' home.'

'So he came to stay with you after the expedition, and met your parents?'

'Yes.'

'Did your parents know that you and Alan . . .'

'Yes.'

'They were fairly liberal about that sort of thing then?'

'Far from it. They thought he was going to marry me.'

'I see. And then when you didn't . . .'

'If Alan had been at hand when it was clear he wasn't going to marry me, I'm quite sure Father would have horse-whipped him. He was the type. "Only one good sort of a German and that's a dead one," that's the sort of thing he said, sort of Mitfordesque. He did actually have a riding-crop hanging in his study, if not precisely an entrenching tool with the hairs of a German on it. He used the whip on me on occasions in my childhood.'

Claudia's mouth was dry. She could swallow only with difficulty. 'Did you expect him to marry you?'

'I'm exceedingly glad he didn't.'

'So you do, or did, dislike him?'

'Silverman was a bastard. Totally ambitious, totally conceited. He was single-minded, greedy, and a filthy lecher. Women to him were sexual objects he used with no modicum of affection or regard. When he was finished with them he threw them aside. No, I didn't attend his memorial service. Nothing would have induced me to.'

'You never saw him again after that time?'

Claudia got no answer to this question. Janet rose. 'Look,' she said. 'I haven't minded your coming down here to speak to me. As I've said, I expected someone to sooner or later, and I'd decided before you rang to say for the record what I've said about the man – and you look to me as if you might attempt to get somewhere near the truth. Far too many people, especially women, were deceived by Silverman – like that little ass of a soldier who doted on his very shadow. Make of it what you will. Now, if you don't mind, I do work after tea. I'll have to ask you to excuse me.'

She got up, collected Claudia's cup from the table and hers, and bore the tray to the kitchen. Claudia followed her. She was excited by what Janet had said, and desperate to prolong the interview. They hadn't even touched on Beazley's murder, or the find. But the interview was over. Janet led the way to the front door. 'Perhaps we could meet again at a more convenient time?' Claudia tried as it was opened.

'Oh, I don't think there would be any point in that. I've told you all that's relevant. Goodbye.' The voice was debonair, dismissive, as she stretched forward her hand. The door had closed before Claudia had walked a couple of paces.

The second person who thought Silverman was a bastard, she registered as she walked down the hill. Michael Strode had an ally. She wondered if Strode's motive was as patently obvious, and personal, as Janet's.

7.

The quirks of human mating never cease to amaze, Claudia thought. Maybe this was smug of her, for her own marriage had involved no startling contrasts – she and Jack had come from the same sort of background, they had the same interests, degree of energy, and ration of intellect. But do not the tall couple with the short, the fat with the thin, the beautiful with the ugly, and when it comes to personality . . .

The Claridges were surely among the most quirkish of pairings? Where Walter was dull, plodding and unsociable, Marjorie was jolly and gregarious. For Walter one felt life was always difficult, a dense intellectual labyrinth which could only be unravelled by painstaking effort. Marjorie's very manner suggested that life's problems were easily surmountable with the application of a little common sense. She was not at all academic, but moved as easily among University people as she did with her fellow cathedral-goers. But the Claridges had two attractive, healthy children, a girl aged ten and a boy of six and were, Claudia was sure, a very happy family.

They lived inside the Cathedral Close in a lovely wistaria-covered Queen Anne period house which had beautiful wrought-iron gates and a sizeable garden. Walter's family had through two generations made a lot of money from commerce in India – notably, Claudia had once discovered to her secret amusement, from the invention and manufacture of a male 'hairwash' named Lotus which had cleansed the scalps of the Raj. Walter bought the house when his latter-day-nabob father died and he inherited what's called 'a small fortune.'

If she'd had something better to do Claudia wouldn't have gone to the Claridges' tea-party. Marjorie's note explained she was trying to get together 'all the people connected with the Faculty' as Walter was anxious everyone should know as much as possible about 'what other people were up to.' Walter my foot, Claudia thought, this was Marjorie knitting social quick-stitch as usual and enjoying every moment of it. But it was Saturday afternoon, she didn't have anything planned, and if she got the chance she thought she might try to prod Walter into a confession that it had been him who'd given the Foreign Secretary the means to deal with his Commons question. If it had been him she would also tell him that in her opinion – which seemed to be reluctantly supported by Janet Brisbane who had been on the expedition – Archie had been telling the truth.

It didn't seem there'd be much opportunity to prod Walter, however. There was quite a throng. Claudia arrived late when things were in full swing, and found herself talking – not to Walter, whose large figure loomed at the other end of the lawn, bestowing his wintry smile, accepting no doubt late congratulations on his elevation – but to Felicity Warboys, whom she thought might be second best.

By sympathetic nods she unlocked an unusual flow of confidence from the not very prepossessing-looking secretary. Felicity told at length the story of how, the day after The Times article on Archie Fieldhouse's lecture, she had had to withstand the attentions of 'a most insistent young man from the press who wouldn't take no for an answer.' She thought, in the circumstances, it had been very decent of Mr Claridge to see the man, though perhaps on reflection not very wise in view of the slant which had been given to his words. But on the more recent incident involving the Foreign Office, Felicity would only say darkly she was 'not allowed to comment.' She went on garrulously about how ruthless journalists can be, yet how she supposed, now Professor Claridge had achieved this eminence, she must expect to have to withstand their assaults from time to time.

Though Felicity had confirmed by her 'no comment' attitude that Walter had been the Foreign Office Minister's fall-guy, Claudia still wanted to talk to the man. Did he really think Archie was a liar? But as Felicity talked, she saw with dismay a little rostrum had been prepared near the open french-windows into the sitting-room, which had been covered with a purple cloth. Another speech to be endured, she thought, like the eager and garrulous lord in the Banquetting Hall, this one from Walter. Well, perhaps she'd be able to nail him after that, when he was feeling pleased with himself. Just as she thought this, she saw him detach himself from the group of guests he'd been talking to and move into the house.

More than ten minutes passed. Some half a dozen uniformed waitresses had now appeared and were standing in a knot behind the food tables. Felicity, still in full flow, broke off for a moment to look at her watch. 'Now I wonder where the Professor's got to,' she said. 'He's due to be making a speech about now. I wonder if I should, though I suppose . . .'

Her question was answered. They both watched, and saw Marjorie, who was talking to a clergyman some yards away, also glance at her watch. She turned to speak to her daughter standing by her, who ran into the house. After a further pause she went in herself. She reappeared soon after, with the girl, looking distinctly disturbed. She spoke a word to the woman she'd been talking to, then walked quickly to the waitresses and said something to them. They deployed, two going indoors for the urn, the others to the tables. Marjorie also went inside again, this time with both children.

Why was Walter delayed? Claudia moved with Felicity to the knot of people which had formed around the clergyman. 'He seems to be not too well,' she heard. 'I expect it's the heat.'

They all looked towards the french windows, which remained Walterless. Claudia couldn't believe it was the heat. It was warm, but not oppressively so and Walter, she suspected, had the constitution as well as the appearance of an ox. But he didn't appear, neither did Marjorie or the children. As the news disseminated, conversation began to die, until some fifty or sixty of them were facing the house as if they were an audience at a theatre waiting for the curtain to go up.

Marjorie came out suddenly, looking pale and uncharacteristically distracted. There was immediate total silence as she stood on the raised terrace outside the window.

'I really am dreadfully sorry,' she said, raising her voice. 'Walter was going to say a few words, but he's had some kind of a collapse. I think he's all right. I'm sure it's nothing serious. But I've persuaded him to see the doctor, who is on his way. Walter's asked me to apologise to you. Please don't go, and continue to enjoy this lovely sunshine. But you'll forgive me if I disappear. I feel I should be with Walter until the doctor has been.'

Claudia knew she hardly qualified as a close acquaintance, but an Elephant's Child curiosity of the insatiable variety impelled her to linger with two senior members of the Faculty while the rest of the guests filtered away through the garden gate The two were waiting to see if they could help. Just as the last guests were going, Marjorie bustled out again – the children, looking frightened, behind her.

'Oh good,' she said, 'some of you haven't gone. I can do with some

72

support. The doctor's with Walter now. Come in.'

They stood in an awkward knot in the large comfortable sitting-room which was crowded with evidence of a family in full swing. On the grand piano was a gallery of photographs, Gideon's tricycle was parked with its front wheel sideways by an encyclopaedia cabinet, one of whose volumes was lying open on the top. One thing was surely in all their minds, Claudia thought – that Walter must have had a minor stroke.

'It must be the heat, Marjorie, isn't it?' suggested bespectacled Lillian Gladstone, petrologist.

'But it isn't that hot,' said Marjorie, 'and he's never minded the heat all the time I've known him.'

Andrew Craven wondered if he could have been worried about the speech. Marjorie didn't think it was that. 'It was only to be a few words,' she said, 'and, as you know, he likes speaking. Yet, when I went in he was just sitting in his chair, as white a sheet.'

'Could he – er – speak all right?' enquired Craven.

'Yes.'

'What does he say it was?'

Marjorie was almost abrupt. 'He says it was his eyes – the glare outside. It's true he had taken his spectacles off and was rubbing his eyes.'

'Well, the doctor will pronounce in a moment, Marjorie,' Craven continued. 'I'm sure it's nothing serious.'

They went in for another bout of awkwardness. Marjorie got them to sit down. Lillian began to say, too brightly, what a nice party it had been. They all contributed other bits of conversation which died. Meanwhile, through the open door and the closed study door on the other side of the hall they intermittently heard the doctor's muffled voice and once or twice, more faintly, Walter's.

After what could only have been a quarter of an hour, but which seemed much longer, they heard the study door open. Marjorie leapt up and they followed suit.

The doctor appeared. A small bustling man with a curious quiff of hair standing up like a baby's, he was fastening the clasp of his bag as he walked.

'Fit as a fiddle,' he said to Marjorie. 'Absolutely no cause for concern. Heart's bashing away like a steel band and all systems functioning normally as far as I can tell.' The obvious question loomed. If it wasn't a stroke, what was it? The doctor preempted any such curiosity. 'He seems to think it was his eyes. They're OK, too. It was some purely temporary derangement. Known it happen before in the summer. He has a bit of asthma, doesn't he, Marjorie? Probably an aspect of that. Touch of nausea maybe. Nothing to worry about. I've given him a mild sedative. He should lie down for a couple of hours and he'll be fine.'

Marjorie went with him to the front door. There was some relief in her voice, but Claudia thought there was another note, too – was it of continuing puzzlement?

They all went into the study. Walter was sitting like a doge in the high-backed chair. Claudia thought he looked ghastly, his normally rubicund face grey. His glasses lay still on the table. Without them he looked exposed and vulnerable, like an Easter Island effigy.

'Sorry about this,' he began, 'damn silly.'

Marjorie bustled. 'Doctor says you must rest, darling. I think you should go straight up, don't you?'

A thin smile was bestowed on them. 'Perhaps I will, just for a while.'

At this stage Gideon, the younger child, who had been clutching Marjorie's skirt, emerging probably from shock, burst into tears and buried his head in her thighs. His act broke the spell of awkwardness, and gave them their cue for departure.

'It's nothing, darling,' Marjorie said. 'All over, Daddy's all right now.'

They took their leave briefly as Marjorie comforted the child. She was half-laughing. It occurred to Claudia she was still very confused.

Marjorie *was* confused, she repeated to herself as she made her way to her car. She was confused because she suspected, as she did herself, that the explanation was not as simple as the doctor had said. It dawned on her-Walter's appearance had not been that of a man who'd suffered a momentary bout of faintness or nausea, it was something far worse. Something, which had happened in those few minutes he'd been out of sight of his guests, had terrified him. She was sure of this. Was it some fortuitous and temporary mental breakdown he had suffered? Had it, unknown to Marjorie maybe, happened before?

An alternative thesis was that some exterior event had occurred in that short space of time, out of sight of the rest of the company.

Claudia's imagination continued to supply possible sources of terror. Did Walter's life contain some lurid variation from the straight and narrow path he gave every indication of having followed since birth? Had someone blackmailed him on the telephone? She even invented a clandestine love affair for him. Perhaps he'd chosen this moment when everyone else was in the garden to phone her, and found the woman was dead or that she'd ditched him? The more obvious thing was to think the doctor had been right, but she found she couldn't. She kept remembering Walter's face.

The next morning about ten she was in the kitchen making herself some breakfast. She didn't like to phone Marjorie, knowing she was probably being besieged with calls, but she'd just spoken to Lillian Gladstone who had. Apparently Walter was still a bit shaken, but seemed all right. Marjorie had said she felt easier about it.

Claudia was planning to spend the day in the garden and was thinking in what order she'd tackle the jobs, when the phone rang.

'Claudia Drake? Oh good, I've got you. Michael Strode, remember? The man who nobbled you trying to pump the good soldier Fieldhouse in the Banquetting Hall?' He left a space. She didn't fill it. He gave his funny, ironic laugh. 'OK, fish not rising this morning, are they? Fair enough. Look, what's all this about Walter Claridge?'

'What's all what about him?'

'No, well you wouldn't know obviously. But I just thought you might have an angle on what he's done, as you live down there and because of your connection with Silverman and the Faculty of Archaeology. You know him of course?'

'I know him, yes. "Done?" What are you talking about?'

Claudia thought she must have sounded like someone accused. Michael gave another laugh. 'He hasn't run off with the Dean's wife, I'm afraid – nothing nearly so exciting. No, the old codger phoned The Times this morning and told them he wants to make a statement to a journalist, and for some reason won't do it on the phone. The News Ed's got on to me as I did the other story.'

'A statement? What about?'

'Fieldhouse.'

'What kind of statement?'

'That's what I was hoping you'd be able to answer. What kind of statement do you think he's likely to want to make?'

'I thought he'd made one already.'

'Exactly. I'm wondering if it's even worth coming down.'

'You're coming here?'

'That's what he wants.'

She debated. It seemed pretty clear Strode didn't know of the events of yesterday afternoon. Should she tell him? The question seemed to be asked in a non-central part of her brain. She found, when she came to, she was already into the story. She told him the bare facts, nothing about her suppositions.

'Well, well, well,' said Michael when she'd finished.

"There must be a connection between the two events.'

'You think?'

'Don't you?'

'I doubt it, but we'll see. I suppose I'll have to see the old boy then.'

'When are you coming?'

'He wants today, damn it. I was going fishing.' He paused. Would he ask her to meet him? Was that really why he was phoning? What would she say if he did ask? She was deciding to say no. 'So you can't give me any kind of an idea what he may want to say?' he said.

'None.'

That was practically the end of the conversation. She got another statement about the theft of his day's fishing, and he rang off.

8.

Michael Strode, that Sunday morning, preparing in his small terrace house in Finsbury for a day's fishing in Essex, had been in two minds about Nic Brown's call from The Times.

'I've had a call from this Salisbury archaeology don of yours again,' Nic had said. 'Wants to make a statement and won't do it on the phone. Probably nothing in it, but in view of the Sahara fuss, it could be interesting. Would you follow it up?'

Strode had said he would. Freelancing on archaeology didn't bring in that amount of work – and as there was nothing technical, Nic could have offered it to one of the regular crew. But if Claridge had more to say, it would almost certainly be some further and redundant condemnation of Fieldhouse. Strode was quite convinced Claridge was the 'source' of the Foreign Office minister's denial in the House. Another statement from him now would have the news potential of an old folks' outing. He could not think, either, his relations with the man would be at an all time high after their last meeting and his piece about Fieldhouse. A substitute for a day in the country and a trout for supper? It had to be an open question.

He had then thought of the delectable 'La Drake'. She was in with the University crowd down there and might have a view of what the old boy was on about.

La Drake was as uppety as before, but came on with a story about Claridge collapsing at his own tea-party. It was hardly relevant, but it was a plus point. Probably Claridge had been approached by the Foreign Office again, pressuring him further in some way. The Saharan ambassador was on the box last night, practically calling the minister a liar. If nothing better, there was always the chance that, under stress, Claridge would reveal he was the impeccable source the F.S. had referred to and maybe that could be made into something after all – a new aspect of sleaze perhaps? He saw a headline: 'Government's academic stooge.' Less reluctantly, Strode dialed Claridge's number, anticipating as it rang the airless voice and fusty personality of his quarry.

He was answered by a child. He adopted his usual gambit with juveniles of treating them like adults – which was no special deal. They usually were adults in terms of nous, especially if female. 'Hallo,' he said, 'is your surname Claridge by any chance?'

There was a pause, but a confident, if conditional, answer. 'Yes?'

'Can I speak to your dad then, please?'

He'd met his match. It transpired he had on the line Ursula, who did seem to be to all intents and purposes an adult, though from the voice she couldn't be much more than twelve. He had certainly underestimated her class-consciousness.

'I'm afraid my father may not be available at present,' he heard.

He absorbed the semantic correction. 'I see. But "may not," you say. That sounds hopeful. When do you think "your father" might be available?'

There was another pause. 'Who are you?'

Strode introduced an element of mystery. 'Someone I think you'll find your father wants to talk to.' This was going a little beyond even Ursula's sphere, and apparently Claridge was by this time at hand.

'Sorry about that,' Strode heard. 'I have rather a protective family. You're perhaps from The Times?'

'Michael Strode.'

'Ah yes, I believe we met before.'

This strangely didn't seem, in the short term anyway, a bar to further intercourse, Strode thought. There was a superfluous but encouraging statement about how kind it was of him to ring, about how difficult it would be to say what he had to say on the phone. A remarkably different tone, Strode noted. The man must want something pretty desperately. He interrupted. Three o'clock at Claridge's house then, he suggested?

There was a more clipped response to this. No, not his house. At the Faculty as before. It being a Sunday, Strode had better enter through the museum, which was open to the public today. Claridge would inform the girl on the desk he'd be coming.

The Sunday traffic was thin and Strode arrived in Salisbury with half an hour to kill. He went straight to the Faculty and thought he'd take a look at the Tifgad museum. He hadn't seen it for years and hadn't had time to more than glance at it on his last visit.

He told the girl in the pay booth of his appointment, pointed out he was early, but that he'd cast an eye on the collection if that was all right. There was no problem, and he was at once immersed. On the walls of the two rooms were still the blown-up photographs of Silverman in various poses of self-glorification on the Tifgad site, which he remembered from before. What a creep the man was. He shut these out and concentrated on the show cases – the fascinating display of pottery, the gold, silver, copper and faience objects, ranged in deathly sleep inside them, the wonderful collection of beads and scarab brooches from all over the fifth century civilised world. An old ambition stirred as he gazed and read. If only things had been different, he might have been digging up things like this himself, instead of watching and reporting others doing it. Then he noticed that the side room, in which he recalled the terracotta figures had been and which he was saving up to look at last, was curtained off with a ceiling-high green tarpaulin. Beside it sat the attendant, half-dozing on his stool.

'Modifications?' The man jolted into consciousness and, looking vacantly at the tarpaulin, nodded indifferently. 'What modifications?'

The man shrugged, and looked aside. 'A new curator has his ideas of course,' he murmured with a timeless grimace.

Strode guessed what sort. He'd gathered there'd been no love lost between Claridge and Silverman. Good for Claridge, and one in the eye for Silverman. Wouldn't this also be the perfect lead in?

At five to three, he heard a car below and, through the window, saw Claridge pulling into the car park in a spotless black Rover. He emerged from it in the Sunday best suit in which he'd no doubt attended Matins in the Cathedral with his family that morning. Within seconds he was hurrying from the lift. 'Mr Strode, sorry to keep you waiting.'

Definitely, there was no personal hassle – yet. Principally just the guilt at being late – which he wasn't – and, surely, an advanced state of agitation. They entered the Faculty through a door Claridge unlocked and entered the holy of holies, where there were also (completed) changes. Gone were all the further photographs he'd seen on his last visit of Silverman enjoying social intercourse with the great and renowned. Substituted, a rather drab and unadorned old-gold wallpaper. Strode gave further silent approval. Archaeology wasn't about messing with presidents, monarchs and film stars, it was about mud, levels and artefacts. Pity the old bastard was so tedious.

They sat. There was more fuss. There were apologies and obvious explanations of why there was no coffee. Could an ounce of flattery be risked in the context of their apparently newly-orientated relations? Strode decided it could be.

'A change or two in the collection next door, I see,' he said as soon as he was able to. 'Can I guess the drift?' He was fixed with a stare he could only describe as scared. 'Towards a more cerebral presentation perhaps? Less' – Strode feigned to search for words that were all too available – 'less naively pictorial perhaps.'

Walter blinked, and there was a fleeting response. 'I think one or two modifications will be attempted, yes,' he said parchedly. But at the same time he was reaching for an ivory paper-knife on the blotter as if he needed it for self-defence. 'You'll have gathered from your superior that I have something I wish to say,' he blurted. 'I'm sorry to bring you down here like this, but I didn't want there to be any chance of a misunderstanding.'

'That's all right.'

'The fact is I've – er – changed my opinion somewhat.'

'On Fieldhouse?'

'Precisely.'

'On what he said in his lecture?'

'When I spoke to you before, I fear that – I erred.' Strode's interest kindled. 'I inferred I thought Fieldhouse's remarks concerning the Tifgad business were inaccurate, that he had made them up, that now Sir Alan is dead he knew he could not be argued with. I've been examining my conscience, and find that I allowed prejudice to overcome temporarily my respect for the truth.'

'You mean you agree with Fieldhouse's statement – that Beazley, not Silverman, found the treasure, that Silverman walled up the breach Beazley had made, then pretended to make the find himself?'

'I've no reason to think it wasn't like that. Fieldhouse was after all there.'

'So Silverman did lie?'

'It's possible he did not tell the exact truth, no.'

'For reasons of personal aggrandisement?'

'No. I very much doubt that.'

'If not that – for what reason then?'

'Probably simply the reason Fieldhouse gave.'

'You mean he was afraid the real story might lead to possible confiscation by the French Colonial Government?'

'Yes.'

Strode straightened himself in his chair. 'This seems a dramatic turnabout on your part, isn't it?'

'That's as it may be. It's what I wish to say.'

There was a moment of supreme awkwardness. Strode quickly focused all his energy. His mind was on red alert and was reconnoitrering well ahead of the conversation. Claridge was now displaying the utmost unease. He rose, as if he wished to end the short conversation he had been so at pains to arrange. Strode flicked over a page of his notebook and poised a pencil. 'I see. Let me get this absolutely straight, Professor Claridge. You now wish to say exactly the opposite of what you said to me before.'

'Yes.'

'You'll forgive me for saying this, but I was expecting you to take an even more hostile line towards Fieldhouse – in view of what's happened.'

'Well, I'm not.'

'You were approached by the FO, weren't you – by the Junior Minister himself perhaps – who was faced with an awkward question in the House. He asked you to repeat what you said to me at our previous interview, that Fieldhouse was making things up, and presumably you did so. You are the "highly respectable professional source" who let the Minister off the hook he was on in the Commons?'

Claridge had turned a very chalky shade. He was looking aside as if he'd just been forced to view a corpse in a morgue. 'I could have been, but that's neither here nor there.'

'Isn't it? But you'll understand why I'm surprised by your statement. Presumably the Foreign Office pressure is still there, made worse by the fuss the Saharans are kicking up? Could it be you resent this Government pressure?'

The large figure turned and for a moment managed even to appear menacing. 'I've no wish to go into the matter more than I have. I've made my statement. My conscience has been worrying me, and that's all. I trust you'll report that, and nothing more.'

'Conscience about Fieldhouse, I understand. And conscience perhaps also that you've been over-defending a colleague?'

'I've no idea what you mean by that last statement.'

'I mean, Professor Claridge, that your instinct before, as a professional man, was naturally to defend Silverman. Would it be true to say that you have now realised this is untenable when the result is to defame an ordinary ex-soldier?'

'It has nothing to do with Silverman.'

'But it has – most courageously, if I may say so – to do with Fieldhouse. What you're in fact doing is releasing him from a calumny in the teeth of strong pressure from the Government. You must realise, too, I'm sure, the repercussions this new statement you're making is likely to have. The Foreign Office won't like it at all. Sahara will almost certainly seize on anything my newspaper publishes and renew its pressure for the return of the contents of the museum next door. The eventual result could even be the loss of the Silverman Collection.'

'That's as may be. Events must take their course. Now, Mr Strode, that's really all I wanted . . .'

'It has to be, Professor Claridge, as I see it, an act of courage. I'm quite sure that's how I'll want to write up this story – with your consent.'

'If you wish – with the latter as your own opinion, not mine. But I'm sorry, where facts are concerned I've said all I wish to say. I'd now be obliged if . . .'

Strode saw he was losing his subject. 'So it's just your conscience, then?'

'I'm afraid you must excuse me. I must ask you to leave. I will see you through the door into the museum.'

He did so, closing and locking the door when he'd passed through it, himself remaining in the Faculty. For a moment Strode stood there. Claudia Drake had said the man had been ill yesterday. Perhaps he was. Should he tell someone – the girl on the desk downstairs perhaps? In the end he didn't. He wasn't the social services, and it was hardly his business. Instead, he sat in his car and wrote five hundred words there and then. He used the Government sleaze angle and headlined the piece: 'SILVERMAN COLLECTION CRISIS REVELATION.'

He then went back into the museum and asked the girl for the best hotel in Salisbury. He drove into the town. More disillusioned every moment that passed, he faxed through his story. Brown would almost certainly cut it, including the headline. What did the conscience of a superannuated don matter? Possibly Brown would cut it altogether – which would leave him with expenses if he was lucky, and no trout. He made a decision. He wouldn't mess any more on the fringes with this high-minded tittle-tattle. A hunch was a hunch and needed a full-scale investment if it was to mature into a real story. Tomorrow he'd go and see Nic Brown and put to him a much larger picture.

9.

*E*ven Vice-Chancellors don't expect telephone calls from ministers of state as part of their Tuesday morning's work.

Vincent Galleon, whose unpretentious office in the central University building commanded a fine view of chalkland slopes, was at work at his desk. He had just attended a meeting of the Building Committee which was involved in plans to extend the theatre complex. A single tinkle announced that Elizabeth, his secretary, was on the line.

Elizabeth, mother of four, watchful, warm, open but of impregnable discretion when necessary, spoke in an almost normal voice. 'It's the Under Secretary of State for Foreign Affairs coming on the line for you,' she said, her tone subtly encompassing the Vice-Chancellor's likely reaction – some surprise and puzzlement maybe, but not overdone. It was unlikely to be high policy, probably a favour being asked – a nephew or a niece coming up next year or something of the sort.

Galleon, appreciating anew the laid-back tone of his attractive and mature employee, acted in the same low-key way. 'Right,' he said, 'put him through.'

The male p.a. the other end confirmed it was Galleon's voice on the line, and after a minimal pause connected. 'Galleon?' said the minister. 'Hallo. We met recently, I recall. Strasbourg, wasn't it – the European academic qualification equivalents business? If I remember, you spoke most eloquently in favour of advance in this important matter.'

Galleon remembered the encounter. The man was a great deal less than interested in the subject, he'd thought. He discounted the compliment as a preamble, and made the appropriate noise.

'Er – Galleon,' the man continued, 'I don't know if you've seen The Times this morning? I can't think why they're bothering with this, but they've given quite a lot of space to an extraordinary statement one of your people appears to have made on Sunday – Walter Claridge. I believe he has the chair of archaeology? It's an inner page, but quite enough to make things extremely embarrassing for me on top of the row we're having with Sahara. Have you seen it?'

84

The Vice-Chancellor hadn't – though the offending newspaper lay unopened on the side of his desk. The politician continued.

'You'll be aware, I'm sure, Claridge was in the news a few days ago when he was asked to comment on certain statements made by this ex-soldier Fieldhouse who was on the Silverman expedition to Tifgad and gives lectures on the subject. I think I owe you an apology about this for going ahead without consulting you, but as the Saharans started a fuss over the Tifgad Collection because of the statements, on advice from my staff I contacted Claridge direct, and asked him to go and head Fieldhouse off. He failed, but told me categorically he thought Fieldhouse was making it all up. This gave me the chance to deal with a difficult question in the House. Someone should, I realise, have contacted you about this before, but you'll appreciate that at that time we felt the fewer people involved, the better. And I'm sure, anyway, you knew about it – perhaps from Claridge?'

Galleon said he hadn't been informed by Claridge, but that he had concluded from the minister's phraseology in the House, and from Claridge's previous involvement, that something like this might have happened. He had not raised the matter with Claridge as he had assumed it was confidential.

The minister praised such discretion with a sympathetic 'mm.' He cleared his throat to indicate that the nub of the matter was at hand. 'Claridge has now done a complete somersault. With no prior communication with us, he's apparently said he's changed his mind and thinks Fieldhouse has been telling the truth after all. It couldn't put me into a worse situation. I didn't mention Claridge by name in my Commons statement, but The Times makes it perfectly clear in today's piece that it was he who gave me the advice. At the very best, my judgement will be called into question for having accepted Claridge's opinion. I'll be accused of pressuring him, and so on. And of course internationally the man has opened an extremely unpleasant can of worms indeed. The Saharans are at our doors, threatening to create a king-size affair. They're threatening to take the matter to the International Court, and a lot else. You know what a ruthless lot they are. In the normal way of things we could ride something like this, as we have before. These art treasure dramas tend to spend themselves very quickly – and are usually linked to some domestic motive on the part of the individual concerned. But, without going into detail, at present we're involved in some extremely important negotiations in the Middle East, with enormous economic consequences in the balance. The last thing we want is a Moslem outcry about "a neo-colonialist art robbery," which it's plain the Saharans are only too keen to orchestrate.

'Now what I want to ask you first, is what you think of Claridge, and what you think he's up to. I never met him, but I was told he seemed someone of accuracy and integrity. Would that be anywhere near your judgement?'

'Claridge is certainly accurate in his work, and I'd say he has integrity.'

'So what the hell's he up to?'

Galleon needed only an instant's pause. He had anticipated the question and had his answer ready. 'I cannot say. But I do know he had some kind of a physical collapse at a garden party he and his wife gave last Saturday.'

'Collapse?'

'Some kind of a fainting spell, it seems. I gather his doctor came and pronounced him fit, but he was too upset to make a speech he was planning. I don't know when or how he made this statement to the press, but presumably the two events could be linked. It's most unlike him, but it's possible, if he were ill, he may not have been fully aware of what he was doing.'

'A form of amnesia perhaps?'

'It's possible.'

There was a noticeable change in the voice. 'Look, Galleon, what you say is most encouraging. What I want to ask you is if you'd see the man. After a couple of days in which to recover, and without the duress of a reporter present, maybe you'll get to the bottom of it. I'm sure – even with a little gentle pressure from you, if that were to prove necessary – he'll see reason. The physical collapse is most useful. With his corroboration we can use it to say he was disturbed, which I'm now quite sure he was. I'm much relieved.'

Galleon said he'd try to see Claridge that afternoon and that he'd immediately inform the Minister of the outcome.

Claudia Drake was soaking in a bath that evening in a delicious daze as she reflected on her day's work. Janet Brisbane's view of Silverman had temporarily rocked her a bit, but the more she read of him through other people's eyes, the more sure she was that Janet's view was jaundiced and distorted. She was developing almost a greater respect for Alan from her researches than she'd had for him in the flesh. He was not, she'd known from the start, a profound man, his success could annoy unrequited ambitious people (such as Michael Strode?), but the way – from humble beginnings – he had jinked his way through the complexities of life, succeeded, and left only amusement and affection behind him, had to be admired.

She was jerked from her reflections by the phone ringing. She contemplated not answering it – but why did one always do so in the end? Curiosity, she supposed – the hope of something unexpected and exciting. She was glad she did. She got her dripping hand to the receiver probably just in time. It was Vincent Galleon.

'Claudia? I've got something rather unusual to talk to you about, and somewhat urgently. I suppose you're not by any chance free this evening? If you are, I was wondering if I could offer you some dinner.'

The invitation was surprising enough, even more so when she heard it was not to be at Vincent's home but at a rather chic new French restaurant called 'Le Poisson Futé,' which someone had started in the next village in a converted schoolhouse – another infant school casualty of educational horn-withdrawing. She was doubly pleased. The food would be good, and Vincent's house, a remarkably ordinary modern dwelling in the southern environs of the city, was not renowned for its cuisine. Min, Vincent's wife, warm and considerate and entirely nice as she was, was congenitally uninterested in the home-making arts. It was, secondly, flattering to be asked out by such a person as Vincent, whatever the 'urgent' matter was. Half-past eightish then, he suggested, as he had to go to a duty function first.

Dress was a minor problem to be surmounted. Something more than day clothes was clearly indicated. On the other hand anything too showy might seem presumptuous of more than was intended. She knew she wasn't the first woman in the world to choose black as the way out of the dilemma, a well-cut dress she'd seen in the Salisbury spring sales and snapped up. She dithered over the relative gaudiness of several paste jewels and settled for her pretty malachite necklace – real as it happened. She realised, as she dithered over these details, that she was imagining Vincent monitoring her in absentia. He was the sort of man whose integrity and eagle perception made you think what you meant even in the matter of clothes. Out of respect for this, she thought it a further declaration of modesty to get there first.

As it happened, he was late anyway. She installed herself at the rather chichi little bar which had excluded the still bright daylight and substituted candles. Muted Debussy waved like reeds on a current in the background. But only the chef was French apparently. The bearded manager-owner, his appearance a cross between Marx and Rasputin, was heavily English.

'Can I offer you a complimentary aperitif, Madame?' he said, overstressing the second syllable of 'aperitif' in needless and phoney French.

Vincent arrived, hot-faced and with a flattering degree of fret. 'Claudia, I'm sorry to keep you waiting. At these functions people are so aggressively adhesive One has to weave and dodge like a boxer. You've got started anyway, good,' he said, observing her drink.

Accepting the same free sherry for himself, he climbed onto the bar stool beside her and began to relax. He was looking extremely distinguished in a smart dark suit, a purple tie pulled to a pristinely sharp white collar – for the function he'd been to, she reminded herself severely, not for her.

But he was clearly pleased to be out for a decent dinner and accepted the extra attention immediately awarded him by the restauranteur – who knew him, it seemed, from a previous visit and no doubt thought he was on to a good thing with a hinterland of food-discerning dons in the offing. 'I hope the cooking's as good as it was when I brought a French colleague,' Vincent said to her as they were left at their table. 'He thought it passed muster.' There was an air of boyish conspiracy, Claudia thought. She supposed he was being reprieved from Min's cooking. He made it clear they were going to do the menu justice.

Claudia soon overcame her momentary guilt about poor Min. Whatever it was they were going to discuss, it was on ice for the moment. They enjoyed together the further fuss bestowed first by the beard, then by the head waiter – whom she saw being tipped off in the corner to give them the full treatment. Vincent took the menu very seriously and, though she usually had fairly pronounced views on what she ate, found herself following his lead.

They talked at once about Alan, whom Claudia knew already he'd liked and admired. 'What was unique about him,' Vincent said as they tucked into an incredible hors d'oeuvres which included stuffed artichoke hearts, quails' eggs, and little pieces of Bombay duck, 'was that he was completely uninfluenced by anything anyone had said or done before. He had unique vision, which saw everything freshly. How are you getting on with the work?'

he asked as he lifted the half bottle of Chablis from the ice-bucket and topped up her glass.

She told him about the women in Alan's life, and the vision of the man she was getting through them. He listened intently.

'Someone in England without a puritan conscience has – or certainly had when Alan was young – such an advantage. It isn't fair,' he said.

'You think?'

'Don't you?'

'I suppose so.'

He reflected. 'As someone from a similarly nondescript background, and something of a plodder, I always admired that quality of his. If I've achieved anything it is largely to do with pleasing people – on their terms as well as my own. Alan also pleased people but entirely from his own agenda. He was the perfect case of having one's cake and eating it. I can see from what you say, this was particularly so in his relations with women.'

This more general talk about Alan, she knew, was the lead in to the reason for their meeting, which she'd already decided must concern Alan in some way. She had a sudden fear. Was she for some reason being taken off the book after all, and was this the soften-up ? She wasn't kept in suspense for long. Soon after the arrival of salmon en croûte, cooked with a wispy fragrance of ginger and an unidentifiable herb, Vincent came to the point. 'But over Alan's grave we have, I suspect, a very nasty business brewing,' he said abruptly.

Claudia didn't know of either The Times story of that morning, or of course of Vincent's conversation with the Foreign Office Minister. Succinctly, Vincent told her. 'And this afternoon I saw Claridge,' he went on. 'He tried very hard to avoid seeing me or to postpone it, actually claiming to my secretary – in a second telephone call he made after the meeting was fixed – that he had a headache and felt he ought to go home and rest. Elizabeth had to be a bit brutal and mentioned the minister had called.

'Well, I spoke to him. I said I thought it very strange that he should have before spoken out so strongly about Fieldhouse and now done this U-turn. I asked him for an explanation. I made it clear how embarrassing his new remarks were for the Government and how they could also have repercussions for the University and put the collection at risk. I asked him if his health was all right.

'He assured me on the latter point, then went off into a rambling almost Gladstonian analysis of the workings of his "Christian conscience" – I do dislike the habit some Christians have of trying to make out their consciences are different from anyone else's, don't you? I think we probably both know Walter's an odd cove and given to mental constructions of ponderous dimensions, but this display really takes the gold medal. It was soon clear that whatever I said and however much I pressured him, there wasn't the remotest chance of getting him to take back his retraction. There was a punch line about "the truth being sovereign".' Vincent looked at her intently. 'Claudia, I may be being naive – or worse, acting from hidden pragmatism, as the Foreign Office clearly is – in wanting to find a different motivation for Walter's behaviour than the one he states. But for Walter to go in for a volte face of these proportions is straight out of character. It's as if the Pope had said about one of his ex-cathedra statements, "Sorry about all that – correction, I got it wrong, what I said wasn't quite what I meant." I've honestly got the feeling something sinister has happened. Walter is as transparent as one of the showcases in the museum. I was convinced, as he was speaking to me, that the man is dead scared about something, and I'm sure it's not his health. Am I being unnecessarily dramatic? Look, Claudia, you were at that garden party, weren't you? Marjorie said that you were very kind and offered help. What did you actually see?'

She beamed in at once and told him how she'd had exactly the same impression about Walter's behaviour. Vincent listened intently.

When she finished, he reflected for a moment. 'And you think then, as I do, that Walter is not telling the truth, that there is a connection between his collapse, or whatever it was, and his statement to The Times the next morning? He must actually have called the paper himself. They had no reason to get on to him again.'

'He did call The Times.' She told Vincent how the journalist, Michael Strode, had phoned her on Sunday morning.

'So – he phones The Times because he has to, because he's been scared by something. We have to ask ourselves – if he was scared, what by?'

Claudia felt she had the slight advantage that she'd been mulling over it for three days. Vincent's cue made her eliminate the more lurid and less likely explanations she'd thought up, and she was left with the residue. 'He went indoors just before he was due to speak, probably to get his notes or something. I think, while he was in his study, he had a threatening telephone call.'

'Did you hear the phone ring?'

'No, but there was quite a babble. I don't think anyone on the lawn would have.'

'So if there was a call, who was it from?'

'There's only one real candidate, isn't there – if we're right that he was frightened? There's only one party I can think of who wants Walter to clear Fieldhouse.'

'The Opposition?'

'Hardly – do you think? I wouldn't have thought parliamentary double standards had gone that far, would you?'

'Someone who dislikes Silverman then.'

'You could put it like that. But also someone who'll profit from Silverman's name being blackened. Surely it has to be the Saharan Republic? They're a pretty ruthless bunch, aren't they? Their ambassador certainly didn't mince words after the Commons question the other evening. And the minister has told you what they're after.'

'You mean you think they threatened Walter's life?'

'Or Marjorie's, or the children's – or threatening something.'

'Heavens, poor Walter.' They kept a requiem of silence for a moment. 'We've got to help in that case,' Vincent said then. 'Look, I think it's very possible your theory is right. And if it is, there's only one way I can see out of this. I could suggest to the Foreign Office what we suspect, but I very much doubt if they're going to react to such a suppositional idea. Even if Claridge were to come clean, which I doubt if he would if his family's being threatened, they'll still say he was acting under stress. Such a phone call could never be proved, and to suggest it had been made would make the political situation worse than it is. But I'm not going to stand by and see one of our professors being threatened into saying things he never meant. We've got to take the initiative and try to switch this one off. And I've just thought how you, Claudia, could help. As Alan's biographer, you have a unique excuse for poking your nose in where other noses would be suspect. Would you be prepared to do what Walter did – go and see Fieldhouse, and try to get him to call the hounds off? He probably doesn't need to make a statement, just to stop adding these postscripts to his talks. Your charm will succeed,

I'm sure, where Walter's probably rather inept performance failed. I'll be
honest. I did actually have something like this in mind when I asked you to
meet me tonight. But what you've suggested makes it seem even more like
sense. Would you do it?'

10.

On reflection, and freed from Vincent's persuasive presence, Claudia didn't like her mission at all. It really wasn't her business, she thought, and apart from coming to Walter's assistance it seemed largely to be about saving a politician from an awkward personal situation he'd got himself into. She was also as sure as she could be that Archie had told the truth in his lecture. Why then should anyone try to pressure him to say otherwise? He'd intended no attack on Alan, and none should be inferred. She felt crossest with Michael Strode, who seemed to have been responsible for making all this todo, very probably out of some purely personal dislike. She remembered the nonchalent virulence of his remark about Silverman at the memorial reception.

But she'd given her word, and she supposed she'd have to go through the motions at least of carrying out the mission. It was also true she wanted to see Archie again for her own purposes. She got him to see her the next day, letting him think the interview was entirely on her own initiative and for her own purposes as Alan's biographer. She went up by car, and found his house in the suburban labyrinths of North Harrow. Archie had gone to immense trouble and carried a sumptuous tea into the tiny room on a huge tray covered with a linen tablecloth – two plates of neatly cut sandwiches, biscuits, buns, and what looked like a home-made cake. She also made the acquaintance of the amiable mongrel Bounder who, perched on a third chair pulled to the table, was an alert witness to the proceedings.

Embarked on one of the plateful of neatly-cut sandwiches, she felt she had better get the difficult bit over with first. Discretion suggested she should adopt one of the ruses she'd thought of on the way up to get Archie to take out the new bits from his lecture. Faced with his presence she was swept by a feeling of candour. How could she beat about the bush with this surely honest and straightforward man? No doubt she was being indiscreet, but she launched at once into Walter's apparent predicament, saying what had happened at the tea-party and what had been her own guesses at the cause of his collapse and his subsequent volte-face with Strode – which Archie said he'd read about. She made as much as she could of the possible danger to

Walter and his family. She made no suggestion as to what Archie might do, hoping he'd volunteer the solution. Having done what she felt was her bit, she sat back and renewed her consumption of the delicious egg and cress sandwich.

Archie had listened to her short account with attention, though feeding a sandwich to Bounder at the same time. She watched his amiable though inscrutable face as he considered what she had said. Would he realise what she was driving at?

Suddenly, he grinned. 'Lot of old wogs,' he said. 'If that's what they're up to, they're just trying it on, aren't they? Probably think that with a man like Claridge they'll get away with it – and have, as it looks. In my book, if Claridge wants to say I've been telling lies he should stand by what he's said and not cave in to a bunch of crooks.'

She reminded Archie that there might be a danger to the Silverman Collection if credence was given to the idea that Silverman hadn't told the full story.

Archie's grin did not slacken. 'Do you think so, Mrs Drake?' he said. 'After all this time? I don't think so. I thought of that before I gave the lecture you heard. Sir Alan did nothing wrong, and he was dealing with the French in those days, not this Mafia. What do you suppose Sahara'd do with the collection if they got it – sell it most likely to the highest bidder. No, if their embassy's been doing what you suggest, our Foreign Office should put them in their place. Kick their ambassador out if necessary. We can't have that sort of thing going on in England.'

Claudia was relieved. Though she still wondered if the affair could be reduced to quite such simplicity, Archie had voiced her own sentiments a great deal more clearly than she'd been able to. She laughed, said she rather agreed and, having done her duty, got him to switch to topics which interested her more directly.

She couldn't say she culled any startling new insights into Alan's life from Archie, but he confirmed a number of things she only half knew – especially things in India. The one thing he told her she didn't know was that when on active service in the Khyber region, unrecognised by authority, Alan had twice saved the life of a comrade by personal gallantry. She left refreshed by Archie's directness and loyalty.

As she was in London, she'd fixed to spend a couple of nights with Jack's unmarried elder sister, Beatrice, who lived in Stepney. Seeing her, at her own home or at Beatrice's, was frankly a chore which she made herself undertake from time to time out of loyalty to Jack. He, too, had found Beatrice a strain. Claudia doubted if Beatrice's financial situation was very different from hers – she'd inherited the lion's share from the sale of the father's successful buy-and-sell furniture business, also the house she lived in, but her mien and vocabulary was selected to remind her constantly how lucky she'd been compared to herself. There were snide references to Claudia's 'university friends' and her 'idyllic rural existence'.

It was to reduce the time she'd have to spend with Beatrice that she evilly fixed her interview with Archie in the afternoon. She told her she'd probably have to take Archie out for a meal and that, if she didn't mind her arriving so late, she'd be at her place by about nine. 'Oh well, we'll have the whole of tomorrow,' Beatrice had said, faintly. 'I mustn't be greedy, must I?' Claudia knew exactly what was in her thinks balloon. 'You're just using me as a hotel.' If only she knew how much she'd have preferred a hotel.

Archie declined her invitation to have supper, and she could have gone straight to Beatrice and taken her out instead. On the way into London she had a further fit of selfishness and under cover of her alibi thought she'd enjoy the additional reprieve of a meal by herself. She did want to think about one or two things Archie had said and note them before she got swamped by Beatrice, who tended to act like blotting paper on her energy and imagination, and even her memory.

She remembered an Italian restaurant she and Jack had been to several times in the dockland area. It was one of those very reasonable trats, well-frequented, in which the whole family worked themselves to the bone. They had always been treated like lost friends even after a long absence. It would be nice to be welcomed again and it must be only a mile or two from Beatrice's flat.

She couldn't remember the name of the street, but was pretty sure she'd find the route – which was through the City, down to The Tower, then east. She saw Pennington Street, which rang a bell. Wasn't it off here somewhere? She cruised, stopping to look at the names of side streets. Surely she'd remember the name if she saw it?

Just ahead she saw a man coming out of a building and thought she'd ask him. As she drew level, he'd reached the edge of the pavement and seemed to be staring at her. She imagined he must be looking for a taxi and thought she might be one. Then she realised it was Michael Strode and that he'd recognised her.

'Lost your way? You're staring at it,' he said, with total sang froid. She didn't know what he meant. 'The Times you want, is it? You haven't got another tasty tidbit about Claridge, have you? If you have, you want me, not the paper. I'm the shit collector on this subject – remember? You should've called me.' He was getting in to the passenger seat as she realised she was right in front of the newspaper's premises.

'I'm looking for a restaurant,' she said, aware she sounded huffy.

'Really?' His tone was of humorous disbelief.

'An Italian restaurant, called Dino's.'

'Ain't no wop eating place in these parts, lady.' He paused. 'But you really are, aren't you?'

'Really am what?'

'Looking for a restaurant. A date, is it?'

'No. My husband and I used to eat there sometimes.'

Claudia was sure several ironic thoughts were coursing through his mind at what must sound her haughty tone, but perhaps he decided to censor them. 'Well, I'm sure the place has disappeared,' he said. 'There's certainly no Dino's now. But look, if you don't have a date why don't we have a meal together? I'm feeling peckish myself. I know a place – not far – that does good fish.'

She told him she couldn't be long, because she was due at a relation's for the night.

'You really mean you didn't know The Times is down here now?' he said as they drove.

'No.'

'And you were here simply because of your relation living close?'

'That, and the reason I gave you.'

'It has to be a pretty extraordinary coincidence then, doesn't it?'

'I suppose it does.'

'Perhaps it's fate,' he said. 'Fate ticking me off for not contacting you before. You know, I nearly called you again when I was in Salisbury on Sunday. I told you I wanted to see you. But by the time I'd faxed the story it was getting late for interviews. You saw it?'

'Saw what?'

'My piece on Claridge?'

'I certainly did.'

'They gave it more space than I thought they would.'

Did he know of the later development from the Foreign Office, their call to Galleon, and her afternoon mission to Harrow? How could he? That at least was a mercy. But her resentment against his activities surfaced.

'I really wish you hadn't started all this, you know.'

'Of course you do.'

'If you hadn't written that original piece, it would have stayed a paragraph in a provincial paper. The Saharans wouldn't have got excited, the Foreign Office Minister wouldn't have been embarrassed, and Walter Claridge wouldn't have been involved in this frightful way.'

Michael chuckled. 'Frightful you call it?'

'I told you when you called what I think happened to Walter. He's continuing to be in a complete dither, and no wonder. Incidentally, the Vice-chancellor thinks as I do. He also thinks he's been threatened in some way.'

'Nonsense.'

'Is it? If you don't think Walter's been threatened, what's your explanation of his behaviour? Not as you wrote in your report on the interview, certainly – you don't think it's his conscience. The irony was plain.'

Michael went serious. 'You didn't get what I was implying? I thought I'd made it clear. Claridge may be an old stick, but he always despised Silverman. He loathed the man's guts. You know he's pulling the museum apart, getting rid of all traces of Silverman? And now he's seen a way of exposing him once and for all. That's all this is all about. Take on board Archie's revelations, and Silverman becomes the liar he was.'

'If that's so, why did Claridge stand up for Silverman in the previous interview?'

'Reflex action probably. Got so used to doing it when Silverman was alive. Professional solidarity and all that, the nasty probing press – until he had a think about it. Then he realised he was missing several tricks. No, it's Claridge five, Silverman nil, I'm afraid. And this is only the beginning.'

'You're saying his collapse at the garden party has nothing do with it?'

'No. Unless it was a Moses-and-the-burning-bush episode – the searing conversion to the truth. I could imagine him bringing it on himself, a sort of do-it-yourself stigmata episode.'

'Then why didn't he immediately tell his family? Why did he say he'd got eye strain and let his wife think he was ill?'

'God knows.'

She was near to repeating her own feelings on the matter, and Vincent's, but she didn't have to decide. Michael changed the subject.

'Anyway, I'm bored with Claridge,' he said. 'My guess is I've screwed all the juice out of the story there is for the moment. How's the book progressing?'

She still felt resentful at his attitude, and the attitude of the press generally, but she accepted the change of subject. This and other small-talk kept them going until they arrived at the restaurant.

It was a posher place than she'd imagined. White table cloths, gleaming silver and glass, waiters in white shirts, red bow ties and dark trousers over which they wore long white aprons. The menu, written in gothic script on a sort of vellum, was nestled in a heavily-embossed leather cover which looked like a papal bull and weighed a ton. The prices matched.

'Don't worry, it's on me,' Michael said, reading her thoughts.

'Of course not,' she said, 'we're going Dutch.'

Michael smiled, and she had to admit it was an attractive smile. It belied everything about him she was trying to dislike. 'I asked you,' he went on. 'And anyway, how do you know I don't want something from you? Can you imagine me ever doing anything without a motive?'

She was on the point of saying, if he was offering to pay, he almost certainly did want something and that whatever he wanted he was unlikely to get. She kept her mouth shut. 'We'll see,' she said, and concentrated on the menu.

They ordered. When the wine waiter came, Michael seized the list and did the macho act, choosing a Sancerre which she was sure was an astronomic price.

It was second nature to Claudia to question people. When the ordering was disposed of, to fill what might have been a gap she began to ask him about his life. As most people do when given the chance, he talked freely. She learnt that he'd been reading archaeology at Nottingham and had to give up in the middle of the second year because of a bad illness. By the time he recovered, it meant doing a further year. He found he couldn't afford it, and drifted into full-time provincial journalism. When his widowed mother died, he'd moved into the house in Finsbury. He'd decided if he couldn't do archaeology, he wanted to try to write about it. Menial jobs, and later a small legacy from an uncle, enabled him to build up his freelance work. Now he was doing reasonably. He'd found a corner which, apart from celebrities asked to do specific pieces, no one was occupying on a regular basis. He'd been able to give up other bread and butter jobs.

She was beginning to think there might be a few mitigating factors in his favour after all, when her nascent goodwill was rudely dispelled. 'You know why I was in The Times building just now?' he said suddenly. 'I saw Bellerby, the "News Review" editor of The Sunday. He turned my new idea down, as I knew he would. It's much too general and historical a topic to interest them unless it's linked to current news of some dimension – and anyway the mean sods aren't going to pay expenses up front. But it is a news item at present, and I know I tickled him. If I turn in the goods, as I think I can, and the Sahara row rumbles on, I think there's a good chance he'll run it in spite of what he's said – possibly more than one instalment. If he does, it'll be for the kind of money I haven't commanded yet. It's the biggest chance I've had, and I'm going to do it.'

She stared at him. She'd listened carefully to what he'd said, but had no idea what he was driving at. Did he think she had clairvoyant powers? 'You're going to do what?' she said, with some irony.

He took no offence. 'I'm talking about Beazley's murder of course,' his tone suggesting a weak intellect on her part. 'I've always suspected there's more in it than meets the eye. Archie's new footnotes have made me certain. I'm damned sure Archie knows more than he's letting on, too. I'm going to Sahara.'

'Sahara? What on earth for?'

'To find out what happened – particularly the murder. I've never believed the Mustapha Beri part of the story makes sense. Why should a Berber kill Beazley for a couple of alabaster pots? What use were the pots to him? Whatever Archie said, he'd've had enormous difficulty selling them in the circumstances. Beri denied all the charges against him. He then allegedly commits suicide in prison and, strangest of all, Beazley's body is never found – when it couldn't have been far away from that cave.'

'But the evidence? It was virtually watertight.'

'For a start I'm going to try to find Beazley's remains. I've got a feeling the reason they weren't found is because no one looked very hard.'

'What would they show, even if you found them?'

'Beazley is supposed to have been stabbed with a knife, isn't he – Mustapha's knife. If I know those Berber knives, they have sizeable blades, curved and bloody sharp.'

'So?'

'So there's a strong probability that if Beazley was stabbed to death, a bone would have been struck somewhere and traces of the blow will remain.'

'And if you found traces, what then? The story is merely confirmed.'

'If there were traces it might be. My guess is there won't be any, and there'll be something else.'

'Are you trying to suggest the Berber may not have killed Beazley?'

'I want to find out. For, if Mustapha didn't do it, who did? There's a prime suspect, isn't there? We know Silverman had already quarrelled with Beazley. Beazley had found these pots, so he knew the hoard wasn't far away. Not only would Beazley, as the finder of the hoard, raise hell with Silverman over its possession, he'd rob Silverman of all the glory he thirsted for. So Silverman murdered him and somehow set it up to incriminate Mustapha.'

'This is totally fanciful. Silverman didn't know about the pots until after Beazley disappeared, and he was in Tifgad for most of that day. How . . .'

'How did he do it, and how do I prove it? That's what has yet to be shown. That's why I'm going out there at my own expense. I'm not only going to get the scoop of the year, I'm going to bust Silverman out of his coffin and expose him for the crooked charlatan he was.'

She felt a mounting anger. 'This is all total supposition. You haven't a shred of evidence. Why've you got it in for Silverman? You never knew him. You never even met him, did you?'

'Twice. Once on a minor dig near Hadrian's Wall, and once on a Cro Magnon jaunt in the Dordogne. That was enough to tell me how little he knew about archaeology. His degree was only second class, you know, and if it hadn't been for Tifgad he'd never have been known except for some pretty cheap rehashing of other people's work. Claridge is dead right about him. Also, in the second interview, I questioned him about Tifgad. That's what gave me my hunch. I knew he was covering up something. Archie's lecture the other week, which Reuters picked up from the local rag, just gave me the go-whistle. Whichever way you look at it, the story's riddled with holes. I only wish the bastard was alive to hear what I'm going to dig up.'

'But this is going to stir the Saharans even more than they have been already.'

'Like hell it is. And that's a major reason, as I say, why Bellerby will print it.'

'It'd be crazy to go out there at the moment with all this fuss.'

'Why? I'm on their side. I'll probably get a presidential car put at my disposal.'

'And you want the Silverman Collection to go back there?'

'It's where it belongs. Silverman stole it.'

'Alan acted perfectly legally.'

'Did he? That's what's in question, isn't it? Besides, Sahara was French then, and the French hardly had a leg to stand on as far as nicking the art treasures of the world was concerned. Now Sahara's independent, it has a right to its own stuff.'

'But that's absurd. Just imagine the chaos there'd be if the great museums of the world returned their exhibits to the countries of their origin. Many were bought anyway.'

'I make a distinction between art objects – such as pictures – which are bought and sold on the open market, and objects which can be said to be part of a national heritage like the Parthenon Marbles. How incredibly arrogant, incidentally, to call them the Elgin Marbles. In my view the Carthaginian hoard is part of Sahara's cultural heritage whether or not their president is a thug.'

'Sahara doesn't give a hoot about the hoard. For them it's entirely political. If the hoard went there nobody would ever see it. I can't imagine Sahara has any kind of a tourist trade. Even if they did, the Saharans wouldn't know how to display it. Look at the way even the Egyptians house their precious objects in Cairo Museum. Anyway, the hoard artefacts aren't Saharan, they were gathered from the entire civilised world of the time.'

'They were found on Saharan territory where they'd been for two thousand five hundred years – and it's a matter of principle. The Saharans have a right to decide what to do with their own property.'

101

Claudia was getting really steamed up. What was utterly galling was that, beside her rage, Michael was entirely unmoved. 'Ah, principle,' she said sourly. 'An ambiguous word.'

'Ambiguous, or inconvenient?'

'I don't think you're acting from principle at all. You're thinking of your own career.'

'That certainly.'

'And for some reason you've got it in for Silverman. I think for some reason you're grossly prejudiced against him.'

'You can think that. But I could say the same of you, you know. Just because he made a pass at you – the way he's done to countless other women – you think he's a great hero. Great archaeologist, great lover, great entertainer, spreading charisma and animation wherever he went – that's going to be the theme of your book, isn't it?'

'I'll try to see him as the man he was.'

'And you're being paid a nice little sum for your pains, I hear.'

'Who told you that?'

'Want to know – really? I heard it from you, when you were talking to the big ship Galleon in the Banquetting Hall.'

She was furious. 'Do you go round eavesdropping on everyone's conversation?' she said.

'No. Only selected people's.'

'And why should you select me?'

He grinned maddeningly. 'You must admit, there wasn't so very much to fascinate one at that absurd charade. No, seriously, I'm joking. You did interest me, and I'll tell you why. I knew who you were – I've actually read one of your books. Bloody good. And I thought it would be nice to know your view on Silverman. I watched you talking to Galleon, and before I heard any words I knew what you were up to by the look on your face. "She's pretending to be in with the establishment," I thought, "but against herself." Even with Galleon, you were keeping your powder as dry as a bone. I know from your book you're not one of them. Your tone is shrewd, healthily ironic, even gently iconoclastic in bits. You know what – I think we'd make a good partnership.'

She reared like a horse at a ten-barred gate. 'What?'

'I've just thought – come to Sahara with me. I knew there was a reason why I should pay for this meal. It's just come to me, I need you. You know far more about the trappings of Silverman's life than I do, which could be essential. And you need me to put you straight on your viewpoint. Just think what a much better book you'll write if you've had Sahara sand in your sandals.'

For a moment she was too flabbergasted to speak. Was there no limit to the man's self-belief? 'I wouldn't dream of it,' she said then in a calmer tone.

He wasn't listening. 'It'll cost you a bit, but you can probably afford it more than I can with Silverman's little legacy to you. And by the way, there's another thing. I've discovered there's a French Consul out there, still alive, who was apparently Minister of Justice in the French Administration at the time of the find. Talking to him will be interesting. Well, are you coming?'

'I can't see why on earth you imagine I'd even contemplate it.'

'Because you're intrigued.'

'By your social hang-ups, you mean? Of course I'm not going on such a crazy wild-goose chase.'

'I need your scholarly approach.'

'Then go back to university and complete your course.'

They finished going Dutch.

11.

Claudia did her duty with Beatrice for two nights quite convinced she meant what she'd said to Michael in the restaurant, and returned home the following day with no deviation from this. She'd only been home half an hour when Michael phoned.

'Where the hell've you been?' he said as if she were at fault, 'I've been phoning you for thirty-six hours.'

'I told you, I went to visit a relative.'

He swept this aside. 'You're coming, are you?' he said.

'Coming where?' She genuinely couldn't for a moment think what he meant.

'To Sahara of course.'

When she put the phone down five minutes later, she couldn't believe what she'd done. She'd said yes.

OK, there were respectable reasons – which she'd supplied to Michael on the spur of the moment. On reflection, a bit of local colour wasn't such a bad idea for the Tifgad chapter in her book. If she went to the place where Alan had earned his world-wide fame, she was bound to learn something about him – there was this French Consul Michael had mentioned for a start. She had also made it quite clear, when Michael began to say he might be able to 'wriggle' her into his expenses somehow if he ever got any, that she'd be paying her own way, so she wouldn't be beholden to him in any way. But she admitted to herself afterwards that in that secret part of the mind where such inaudible decision-making goes on she'd probably elected to go because of Michael's tone. Until she'd said she'd go, his every inflection had suggested she wouldn't – wouldn't because she was a chicken middle-class housewife. What kind of a motive on her part was that?

She contemplated ringing Michael to tell him she'd changed her mind. She'd tell him she'd forgotten about the summer holiday she'd been promising herself, staying with a family she knew in Wensleydale who'd given her an open invitation. Then she realised that going to Sahara – even in what had to be the blazing heat of summer – was a great deal more exciting. She let it stand.

Perhaps in her relatively untravelled state, she was chicken, Claudia thought when Michael phoned again to say he'd fixed the air-tickets and to ask if she knew she'd need a visa for Sahara and Algeria. They had to go via Algiers and spend a night there. Visas somehow suggested official difficulty and obstruction before you started. All she knew of Sahara – quite apart from what might have happened to Walter Claridge – was horrific, and she'd heard of Algerian xenophobia from friends. A journalist she knew had been arrested in Algiers for no reason and held for two days when he was trying to report an international conference.

They went via Paris. Waiting in the Orly transit lounge for the Air Algerie flight her fears were reborn. You'd have thought at this time of year tourism would be flourishing, but it looked as if the plane would be three-quarters empty, and most of the travellers were po-faced male Arabs in European dress. She concentrated on forming a romantic vision of the one unmistakeably Arab family who, unlike most of the travellers, were dressed in the full rig. Were they from some outlying region, right down in the desert perhaps? The mother and eldest daughter were veiled with only their hennaed hands and their eyes showing. While the enormously fat man strode up and down the lounge, his hands behind his back, the four well-behaved children clustered round the mother, the eldest daughter taking charge of the smallest, the two little boys, wide-eyed and good as gold with their legs dangling from the seats, watching the antics of two other children who were rushing about. A real family, she thought, a real unit, moving about the world like a close-knit flotilla. She almost remarked as much to Michael, who was already busy with maps and diagrams she'd supplied him with from Alan's papers. Fortunately, she didn't. Michael already had enough to lambast her with.

On the plane they were able to spread themselves. Michael, spotting she wanted the window seat which was one of the two allotted to them, offered it to her. She was sure the smirk which accompanied the largesse was meant to show her what a seasoned traveller he was, and that he would find more cerebral things to do than stare at the geography. He sat on the aisle with an empty seat between them, still poring over the information she'd given him. He was soon immersed in some selected photocopied sheets of Alan's diary with a total absorption she had to admire. He didn't even look at their pretty air-hostess.

When they left behind the brown distances of southern France and the blue tray of the Mediterranean slid beneath them, she still hadn't had a squeak out of him. Had she been mad, she thought, to saddle herself with this opinionated, concessionless man? They could be a lot more than a week together. At least, if this route was as little frequented as it seemed, it wouldn't be difficult to choose any date for her return flight.

Algiers airport seemed a normal enough place. They negotiated passport control, but after a half-hour wait for their bags they were halted in customs by a sinister female official in white nylon gloves who took their two modest-sized suitcases apart. The woman seemed convinced that either, with their cameras, they were bent on espionage or that, just because they were British they had to be smuggling porn or some dire drug. She ferreted in her very old suitcase, and Michael's very new one, for secret compartments. She drew from her sponge-bag a tube of Maclean's toothpaste and fingered it with frowning suspicion. Was it paranoid, Claudia thought, to conclude that the British, in their enfeebled state, drew down upon themselves a particular amount of retributive aggression from the third world? It did seem like it. If so – it had to be considered the sins of their fathers, she supposed.

Finding no evidence of their non-gratadom, the woman seemed suddenly to lose interest. Actually, Claudia thought she had trodden on a button under the counter. 'Attendez,' she rapped.

She was right. Two uniformed men with machine-guns slung on their shoulders emerged from a door and bore down on them. Her stomach went to water. She looked at Michael who, she wasn't comforted to see, was not alarmed but cross. Surely anger would make it worse. 'Qu'est ce qu'arrive?' he barked at the woman superfluously. The woman turned away with insolent indifference to deal with the next person.

They were marched in the direction of the same door. Through it there was a passage between two partitions, behind which appeared to be a number of rooms on either side. Each had a door. With a hitch of the head it was indicated they should separate, one of them one way, one the other. Claudia was marched to the end of the corridor by one of the men. He pushed open the door with his gun and again headed her in as if she were a football being nudged between the goal posts. It was small cubicle with a bench seat and a hook on the back of the door. Unbelievably the door shut behind her and the lock was turned.

The heat had hit her like a physical blow as they left the plane – and this was only a mile or less from the temperate Mediterranean coast. Though she had dressed for it, she was already soaked with a girdle of sweat round her middle. This claustrophobically confined space made it worse. She sat miserably on the seat and waited. It seemed they were the only people getting this treatment. She'd heard what she thought was Michael's door being slammed at the other end of what she could now see was one big shed. Since then there had been nothing except a low hum of flies, which were everywhere. There were at least a couple of dozen in this cubicle, crawling on the wall and the partition. She thought of cases of people being condemned to death or given life sentences for carrying drugs someone else had planted in their baggage.

She thought of trying to call out to see if Michael could hear, but quickly abandoned the idea. Her instinct was not to oppose in any unnecessary way. She was already crafting her Ciceronian defence against this appalling injustice.

It was nearly half an hour before someone came. She heard a door slam and voices, then footsteps coming her way. The key turned, and another white-gloved horror appeared.

'Déshabillez-vous.'

Claudia marshalled some French to resist this. 'By what right . . .' But a mixture of wisdom and faulty French syntax made her desist. While the woman stood in the doorway half-turned from her she pulled her cotton dress over her head.

'Tout,' she heard, her gaoler's head still askance.

OK, dignity at all costs, she reminded herself. She gave the woman the benefit of two more garments and stood defiantly in her shoes. Perhaps the biggest insult was that the bored official was completely impervious to her nudity. She almost snatched the bra from her hands, turned it over, and threw it distastefully on the bench. She then proceeded to look with the same total detachment in a place Claudia never expected anyone other than a doctor to inspect.

She departed without a word but left the door open. Trembling now with untetherable rage, Claudia replaced her clothes. Michael emerged from his cubicle almost simultaneously. He got the brunt of her feelings.

'It's an outrage,' she burst out.

Michael was fastening a cuff button. Apparently the temperature wasn't affecting him. He chuckled. 'Down to the basics, was it?'

'By what right can they do this?'

'Worry you?'

'Of course it worried me. Christ, if this is the way they treat people down here.'

'You'll wish you'd stayed in the Test Valley?'

In this moment she felt angrier with Michael than with White Gloves. But the incident had one result. It resolved her that whatever happened she wouldn't be going home ahead of time to make him feel one up. By thinking this she managed to stifle the rest of her outrage. Then when she least expected it, he put his hand on her shoulder and gave it a squeeze. It wasn't fresh, or patronising, just kind. She very nearly burst into tears.

Their first evening didn't pass off so badly, either. As their flight to Tifgad left at six-thirty in the morning, Michael had booked them into the airport hotel, which was air-conditioned she was grateful to find. As they entered its cool clean hall, the tiled floors pleasantly decorated with gaily-coloured Algerian rugs, she already began to feel better. In an alcove a gathering of djellabah-ed male Arabs were sitting drinking coffee. In niches and on the reception desk were examples of what seemed to be the artefacts of North African civilisation – decorated objects that looked like gourds (actually, Michael told her, the dried stomachs of camels), model camels with brightly-coloured harness, and buff-coloured prehistoric-looking ducks with attractive black and red decorations on them, a variety of leather goods. In a glass case were shelves of Tizi-Ouzu jewellery which she'd heard of – lovely deep blues and reds predominant. The discreetly piped Arab music was monotonous, but it was a great deal more soothing, she thought, than the usual smash, crash and nasal wailing of European pop output.

The employees were warm and pleasant. Michael had already lectured her on the theme that there was a contrast in Algeria between official 'disagreeableness' as he called it – sometimes, he confessed, of Kafkaesque proportions such as they had experienced – and the general sweetness, frankness and generosity of the ordinary people. And Michael, it seemed, now they were embarked on their mission, was becoming quite a bit more tolerable. Was it possible, she thought, as they climbed onto bar stools, that he wasn't after all so entirely functional? Could it be that abroad, engaged on a scent, he became a different man? Was it somehow England, the narrow perspectives of the English, on which subject she had also listened to a sermon – and possibly the connotations of these with things in his childhood and adolescence – which drove him to a good half of his iconoclasms?

During the meal she received a further diatribe about food. 'I like the whole concept of couscous, as well as the taste,' he enthused as they tucked in to a good example of the dish. 'It's like paella in Spain, or bouillabaisse or any soupe du jour in France. You take a basic and readily available commodity like rice or fish remains or bones – in this case semolina – and then throw into it anything at hand. If you're rich you throw in rich things, but the poor, throwing in cheaper items, do not necessarily eat worse.'

She agreed, but couldn't resist a leg-pull. 'You mean a people's dish?'

'A people's dish, certainly.' She was allowed a short grin.

Relations improved further in the morning. It was a reminder how much nearer the tropics they were that they had to get up in the dark, which always seemed to Claudia an unnatural act. But by the time they were on their way to the airport in a taxi the day was dawning. The air was cool, the road was lined with stumpy little palm trees which she thought were like the feet of baby elephants. She had a thrill of positivity and excitement. She thought Michael maybe felt the same. Emboldened, she made a first mention of her fears about Tifgad. Did he think the Saharans understood and approved of what he was up to? He had warned them they were coming and about the reasons for his visit, had he, as he'd said he would do?

For once, seeming to understand her anxiety, he didn't play games. 'No, there won't be any fuss, don't worry,' he said, for once without connotations about her cowardice. For once she allowed herself to believe him.

Algiers airport was almost deserted. They had to wait for someone to appear to check their bags, similarly to have their passports branded. In the lounge there were only two other travellers, an Arab in a rather hairy-looking brown habit – in which Claudia thought, like Black Sambo, he would surely melt later in the day – and a ragged character in baggy once-white trousers and a battered straw hat, either a European or an American – he could have walked out of a Somerset Maugham story. Resting his elbows on his knees as if he were ill or hung-over, he was smoking, blowing long billows downwards without moving his head, and staring lugubriously at the floor in front of him.

'Sahara doesn't seem to be exactly a mecca of tourism, either,' she said.

'It's July,' said Michael as if it would have been a lot different had it been December.

The light broadened into full day. There didn't seem to be any sign of an aircraft. Would it arrive from the sky in transit? But just when she was beginning to think they'd be returning to the hotel, something began to throb, and presently the most amazing old crate with two propellers was wheeled into view by a tractor.

'Not that?'

As she said this the other two men, and Michael rose. 'We may have to hold on to the wings,' he said. An official appeared and walked, as they did, to the exit gate.

It was actually the most exciting flight Claudia had ever made. She sat in what would have been the co-pilot's seat had there been one. The other six seats were immediately behind. The pilot had to roar the engines to busting point to get them airborne, then they climbed, swaying and bumping, to what the altimeter claimed was little more than five thousand feet. Algiers, the Mediterranean, tilted briefly in front of them, then they levelled and plunged southwards into Africa. For twenty minutes there was green and plenty, then a wide barrier of mountains, finally – nothing – an endless grey rock waste in which a couple of tiny oasis towns they passed over were events. But it was lovely, Claudia thought. You really felt you were flying.

It was a long way – much further than she'd thought. 'Well over a thousand miles,' the pilot shouted, over the roar of the engines. Even at this altitude it began to get uncomfortably hot. Not before she was beginning to feel she'd had enough, the pilot moved the stick forwards and his hand reached for the power control. The land now was not grey but reddish-brown. Ahead, something glinted. She saw that it was a town, a little bigger than the others they'd seen. It must be Tifgad.

It was only eleven o'clock but as they emerged from the plane the windless heat was terrific. For a moment she felt quite scared. She really wondered if one could survive such a temperature. Some vital thermostat had surely broken down here, as in one of those hot planets. As she clambered down the block of half a dozen steps which had been wheeled up by hand

and whose metal rail was too hot to hold, she thought she might pass out. Fortunately, even though it was a short distance to the tiny airport building there was a bus with open doors waiting to transport them across the tarmac over which hung a curious shimmering pool like a mirage. It was a mirage, she supposed. There were palm trees upside down and she wondered if she was, too. She prayed for air-conditioning in the hotel. The plus side was that the airport was deserted like a branch-line railway station – there wasn't even passport control. Thy sailed through unmolested

They drove to the hotel in the only taxi with what proved to be the American. 'Name's O'Grady,' was all he grudgingly vouchsafed when she asked. It seemed like a ghost town. There wasn't a soul in sight on the pitted unmade roads, whose reddish soil reached right to the houses with no pavements. The small flat-roofed houses of unpainted concrete, most single-storeyed, were more like fortifications than dwellings – like wartime pill-boxes perhaps, some without even slits on the outer walls. There was a small mosque whose inverted saucer roof was painted a crude faded blue. It looked like a child's sandcastle abandoned on a beach. They passed a single shop, already shut – its iron grille was pulled down – and the Hotel Oasis hove into sight.

A look at it was enough to tell Claudia there'd be no modern con-veniences, least of all air-conditioning. With its three storeys, tiled roof, its drawn once-green wooden shutters and a balcony on the first floor, it was a cut above the other buildings, a brave attempt to bring a semblance of style and civilisation to this forsaken place. But it seemed to have given up the struggle. Bricks and mortar showed in several places where the rendering had fallen. The first 'S' of Oasis had slipped like a groggy soldier on a Foreign Legion parade, barely supported by his fellows. The 'O' of Hotel was missing.

The monosyllabic American who had sat in the front seat paid the taxi driver, made no reply to their thanks, and disappeared into the hotel with his small suitcase. Nobody exactly rushed out to greet them and carry in their bags. They struggled in through the cheap bead curtain that defended the front door. Claudia was thankful only to escape the vicious thrust of the direct sunlight. O'Grady had already disappeared. Presumably he had a permanent room here for there was no one at the reception desk.

The hall was dark. All the windows were heavily shuttered, and there was only a single naked electric light bulb illuminating the desk. As they stood there, Claudia wondering if the huge fan which turned above them at a leisurely speed made any difference to the temperature, there was an abrupt snore from the shadows on one side. They made out the shape of a man stretched on a recamier-type sofa. On the counter was one of those old-fashioned bells with an upward protrusion which is meant to be smitten with the palm of your hand. Michael smote it. There was a crescendo of snorting and grunting and, eventually, movement. The man lugged his feet off the sofa and came towards them, muttering.

It didn't seem to matter whether or not he had their booking. A huge leather-bound registry book as large as a lectern bible lay open on the counter. The man dipped an antediluvian pen fastidiously in a tiny silver inkwell, tapped the nib on the edge of the well, and handed it horizontally to Michael. 'Une chambre?' he said.

Michael made it plain he'd booked two. The man shrugged. While Michael signed, he produced two enormous keys that would have unlocked a castle.

'Premier étage.'

Claudia knew it was like Oliver Twist asking for a second helping. 'Vous avez des chambres qui sont climatisés?'

She didn't get an answer. Was it a lesson she hadn't yet learnt that in the desert one doesn't waste energy on unnecessary speech?

The room faced inwards onto a well in the centre of the building. It was minimally furnished, but – the most exciting feature – it had a huge bathroom with an extravagantly tiled floor and walls. In anxiety she turned the taps. The hot one, rather irrelevantly, produced nothing, but from the cold, after a wheeze, a cough and a gurgle, issued a brownish liquid in quite a solid volume. The water was tepid, but tepid, she guessed, in Tifgad was the equivalent of ice-cold. She filled the bath, stripped, and lay in it. It was bliss. She dried on the minuscule towel and lay thankfully on the bed whose sheets smelt faintly of sewage. If she could get into that bath several times a day she might just about survive, she thought. She drank water from one of the battery of plastic bottles she'd bought in the Algiers hotel, and must soon have fallen asleep.

A whining dog woke her. She had the idea it had been whining for some time. It seemed to be tied up below somewhere. She heard a chain rustle. Then she realised a breeze was blowing quite briskly. A shutter slammed. It was noticeably cooler. She looked at her watch. Nearly five. She couldn't believe it. She must have been more exhausted than she realised.

She got up quickly. She and Michael had agreed downstairs that they would wash, then try to find something to eat. That was more than five hours ago. She cursed her weakness. He'd now have something new to crow about.

She knocked on his door, the next room down the dark dank corridor. There was no answer. Any hope that he, too, had fallen asleep was dashed. She went down and there he was at a sort of bar, talking to a young Arab she thought she'd seen before. As she appeared, the man sloped off towards the front door, his sandals scuffing the tiled floor.

'He's still here all right,' Michael said, eagerly. 'Older than Silverman apparently. Must be in his nineties.'

She wasn't yet firing on all cylinders. 'Who's still here?'

'Petit-frères. And I've collared that taxi by the way, indefinitely. It seems to be the only one in Tifgad.'

For a moment, in her torpor, she couldn't think who Petit-frères was. Then she remembered – of course, the French Consul, ex-Minister of Justice in the colonial period.

Michael was sitting on a tall cane stool at a makeshift counter. In the same front hall opposite the reception desk, the area was illuminated by another naked electric light bulb. Behind it, attached to the wall with crude metal brackets, was a series of shelves, but empty except for a few non-matching glasses most of which advertised something like Dubonnet. In front of Michael was a half-empty bottle of Pernod and one of the plastic water-bottles he'd also bought in Algiers. He pushed the Pernod towards her.

'I've commandeered this. All they have apparently. And the fridge has broken down, so forget ice. Get yourself a glass.'

She thought he'd make a rude remark about her involuntary siesta. That he forgot to, she was sure, was only because his mind was on other business. 'That was Ouboussad, the taxi-driver, I was talking to. He's coming at four in the morning,' he went on. 'He seems to think it'll take us two hours to get to the site. Should be just about light then. We'll find the camp, then the cave. With any luck, we can be back to the car by ten.' With two hours' driving in the heat to come, she thought, but kept it to herself. 'Ouboussad's a find,'

Michael went on. 'A bit surly, but his French is pretty good. The only problem may be his vehicle, which is not in its prime.'

'Is he a mechanic, do you know?'

'I'd think it's most unlikely.'

'So, if we break down?'

'It won't be pleasant. I did ask him this. He says his cousin has a car. I suppose if we didn't return he'd come and look for us.' It had to be encouraging, she thought, that Michael could also consider such practicalities, and do so without sneering at her lack of experience 'in the field' – a phrase he'd used more than once.

She took a gulp of the tepid aniseed. Its arrival in her empty stomach coincided with a rush of generosity. She had naturally considered the professional advisability of sharing any more knowledge of Alan than she had to for their expedition. But if they were going to cooperate, she thought, it was surely stupid to withhold any information. Their motives were entirely different and there was no necessary clash of interest. She hadn't told him about her visit to Bovey Tracey.

'You know Alan had an affair with Janet Brisbane?' she began. 'It's just occurring to me this is presumably where the trysts took place. I suppose in those days the place was in better shape.'

His glass stopped on the way to his mouth. 'Janet Brisbane?'

'It's strange to think of them here together, isn't it?'

'But Janet Brisbane was Neil Beazley's fiancée, wasn't she?'

'Didn't Archie tell you? No, now I think about it, he wouldn't have. He doesn't like talking about emotions and personalities. Perhaps he didn't even know. According to Janet she had befriended Beazley at Oxford to defend herself against the attentions of a young man who thought his social background gave him a passport to her affections. She wasn't in love with Beazley and the affair broke up out here. Alan cashed in on the débâcle, I suppose.'

'Janet told you that?' For a moment he couldn't conceal his interest. He quickly masked it. 'You bet Silverman busted the romance,' he continued. 'The bastard probably set about it on purpose – he probably thought he had "droits de seigneur."'

She didn't rise. 'Six of one and half a dozen of the other would be my bet,' she said instead. 'I'd say they were both pretty single-minded people.'

114

He pondered, swilling the liquid in his glass. 'You know this woman?'

'I met her, yes. As you know, she's an intrepid trekker in the Andes and elsewhere, and I knew of her. I noticed she wasn't at the memorial service, which struck me as mildly odd, and anyway I wanted to see her for my Tifgad chapter. I managed to persuade her – rather reluctantly – to give me an interview.'

'And?'

'And, among other things, I discovered why she didn't go to the service. You have an ally. She's the only other person I've come across who hated Alan.'

'Because he ditched her.'

'I suppose so. She implied as much – if there's any dropping to be done, Janet is the kind of woman, I guess, who likes to control the action.'

Michael raised his glass and drained it. 'So, motive number two for Silverman to murder Beazley.'

'Nonsense. If Alan was having an affair with Janet, which he clearly was – probably from about half-way through the expedition – he had no need to remove the opposition. There wasn't any. Anyway you aren't going to convince me Alan was that much in love with Janet, or any other woman in his life for that matter. Alan, with women, was a taster, never an obsessive – as he was where his work was concerned. To him the affair was an interlude. It was possibly Janet who took it seriously for a while. It's an irrelevant detail.'

Michael bridled. 'We'll see if it's irrelevant,' he said rather childishly. 'My guess is you're going to get plenty for your book out here, Claudia – and it won't be what you expect. That is – if you have the courage to face evidence that upsets your social prejudices.'

Not this, again. Wasn't this exactly her charge against him. Was this how they were going to go on, locked in mortal combat? She supposed it would be. A pity – surely what they both wanted was an open mind. But for the moment they left it at that. She felt light-hearted. It seemed to her that after this opening skirmish she might consider herself to be a point up.

12.

*B*ell himself would surely have recognised the single telephone the Oasis Hotel possessed, Claudia thought. It was a box attached to the wall behind the reception desk with a mouthpiece you could adjust up or down. On a hook beside it hung a receiver shaped like one of those weights athletes once used to strengthen their biceps.

Michael had written to Petit-frères announcing their arrival in Sahara, but he'd done so too late to get an answer. He was now all for descending on him without an appointment. She managed to persuade him to phone first. She imagined an ancient and frail French Colonial still enmeshed in protocol and clinging to life by a thread. Why start off at a disadvantage?

She was glad her advice was followed from more than one point of view. First, Michael got his appointment all right, and second, as they unlatched an iron gate set into the mud wall which surrounded Petit-frère's property, an exceedingly agitated Alsatian, snarling and barking frenetically, was straining at the end of its chain attached to the wall of the house. It was quite possible the animal was allowed to roam the garden untethered unless a guest was expected.

They entered a large unkempt area, which had no doubt once been a tidy garden but was now covered with some desiccated whitened weed that stood chest-high like a ghastly company of skeletons. The European-style bungalow, of brick not concrete, whose tiled roof extended over a wide balcony, was surely the most desirable house in the town. It was built on one side of the area of palm trees and cultivation (green even at this time of year) which was the actual oasis on which the town depended for its water, nourishment and existence. As they approached, a barefooted Arab boy aged about twelve came out of the front door.

'Monsieur Petit-frères?' Michael called.

The boy seemed to be activated not by the question but by a shout from within. He disappeared quickly into the house. By the time they reached the house he'd reappeared and stood back for them to enter the door, grinning shyly.

116

In a room cluttered with massive French furniture, curios stood knee-deep in dust on every available surface. On the wall were African shields and bunches of spears like Roman fasces. Several haphazardly-built bookcases were crammed untidily with French paperbacks. Over a grate hung a grinning mask made of black metal. Petit-frères sat in the middle of the room in a wheelchair. He was thin and reptilian, with some remnants of ginger hair draped round his white scalp. He had a huge Gallic nose. Claudia thought his purplish rubbery mouth was mean and voracious, his spectacle-less eyes piercing and active.

'Que voulez-vous?' he said irritably with a strong Mediterranean accent. 'Moi, je suis vieux. Comme je vous ai dit, c'est fini ici, tout fini. Il n'y a maintenant que le soleil, les muézins, et les lézards.'

Michael had told her he'd said in his letter that he was a journalist interested in acquiring information about the 1936 Silverman expedition. Characteristically he sat down uninvited and plunged in with no sociabilities, certainly no apology.

'Vous avez bien connu Alan Silverman?'

Claudia watched the shrewd old face closely. Continuing to look reptilian, it made no movement. His age and perhaps his experience had surely taught him to operate behind it with almost total concealment. But just for an instant she was sure something glinted in his eyes, like the sun on a distant object. Was it a glimmer of excitement, curiosity? The conversation continued, he in his dialect of French, she and Michael in their faulted versions.

'What if I did? I've known a large number of people.'

'I don't know if you've heard,' Michael went on, 'but Sir Alan died a short while ago. Because of his death certain facts have come to light which indicate that the archaeologist didn't tell the entire truth about the last days of the expedition here. What has become clear is that the find was not made by himself, as was stated in the official account, but by a man called Neil Beazley, one of Silverman's two assistants, probably in conjunction with Mustapha Beri, the Berber helper accused of murdering Beazley and who's alleged to have committed suicide after his arrest. Did you by any chance hear about this? The story appeared first in The Times, but was repeated by other papers. I think Le Monde carried it.' The face remained as blank as a death mask. Michael continued. 'Silverman was clearly afraid that if your Government knew that one of the Berbers had had a direct part in making the find, the law pertaining in Sahara at that time might have made it difficult for him to export the hoard to England. Would you confirm that?'

'Silverman had a contract with us for his operation.'

'But which didn't entirely protect him from Saharan treasure-trove laws.'

'Silverman exported what he found quite legally, as I remember.'

'But would he have been allowed to if you had known the exact circumstances of the find?'

Petit-frères gave an almost imperceptible shake of his head. 'The matter did not arise.'

'But it does now, doesn't it? It's already plain the present Saharan Government is extremely interested in the new version of the story. It may enable them to take the matter to the International Court.'

'I've nothing to contribute on this matter.'

'You're not interested in the Saharan Government's suit?'

'I'm too old to be involved.' He paused, and looked away disinterestedly. 'And it won't make any difference anyway.'

'You mean, Britain will refuse to go to the Court?'

'Precisely.'

'And will suffer the hostility of most of the Third World in consequence.' Petit-frère's shrug was his largest so far. Michael switched his line of approach. 'Monsieur Petit-frères, I'm not only interested in the politics of the matter. The story of Silverman's lies has led me to think there could be other interesting deviations from the story as recounted up to now. My newspaper also wants me to conduct an enquiry into the circumstances of the murder which took place in the closing stages of the expedition. You were, I believe, Minister of Justice at the time?'

'What if I was?'

'As Minister you would have been somewhat involved with the case?'

'Not at all. I was Minister. Politicians in democratic states do not interfere with the course of justice.'

'Of course not. But you remember the details of the case?'

'Naturally I remember the case. I have an excellent memory.'

'You – don't recall anything at all unusual about that murder? No body was ever found, was it?'

'Not as I recall, no.'

'Though it cannot have been very far from that cave where the murder happened. The police searched thoroughly?'

'Presumably.'

'Then there was Beri's very convenient "suicide" in gaol. Beri maintained his innocence throughout, I believe?'

'Did he? He would have done, I imagine. But he committed suicide. That was hardly evidence of his innocence.'

'If he committed suicide.' Again, the blank look, which verged on the hostile. 'What puzzles me is why a man like that should kill Beazley apparently for no more than two alabaster pots.'

'As I recall, the evidence against the man was conclusive.'

'Almost too conclusive? Monsieur, what I want to do is to try again to find Beazley's remains. If they do exist they might still tell us something.'

Claudia was expecting another irritable shrug of the fleshless shoulders. But this time it didn't happen. Petit-frères wore an ancient pair of leather gloves. Clutching the wheels of his chair, he swivelled it and impelled himself to the antique low fender which surrounded the area of the grate. Attached to the hideous fender at both corners were two metal boxes, presumably meant for storing fuel, but which were also seats. They had padded leather tops. He opened the lid of one of them and drew out another form of fuel – a whisky bottle, and a glass. He helped himself generously, returned the bottle, snapped the box lid shut, and returned to them. He took a deep slug of the neat alcohol and wiped his mouth with the back of his hand.

'Et ensuite?' he said, with clear ill-humour.

'I was wondering if you could give us any kind of information that could help us find that body?'

Petit-frères stared lidlessly. 'Of course I can't.'

'You don't remember at all where or for how long the police searched for it?'

'I've told you I don't. I was not a policeman.'

'There must be police records somewhere. Would they have been transferred to France at the time of independence?'

'They were almost certainly shredded.'

'Shredded? Why?'

'You have forgotten perhaps there had been a war.'

An impasse stared them in the face. She could see Michael himself knew he was unlikely to get anywhere. Direct assault had failed. While Michael was wondering what his next move would be, she wondered if she could contribute something a little less intense. 'Monsieur Petit-frères, I'm not a journalist. I'm Sir Alan's biographer. My interest is therefore more personal than Mr Strode's. I wonder if I could ask you about another aspect.' She got a look which was equally hostile, but was there not that same tinge of interest again? 'You must have got to know Sir Alan quite well during the expedition?'

'I knew him professionally.'

'Would you say he was a straightforward man – generally speaking?'

She thought Petit-frères was for an instant surprised at her question. She'd used the French word 'direct' for 'straightforward.'

'"Direct", vous dites?'

'Yes. Was he an easy man to deal with – honest, frank?'

Petit-frères looked away at the floor beside his chair. 'I have nothing especially to complain of – from what little I saw of him.'

'Are you surprised at the recent development, which it does seem to me you know about?'

'At my age, madame, there is very little that can surprise me.'

'You can't suggest to us a reason why Silverman didn't tell the exact truth in his official account?'

Petit-frères shook his head.

Michael entered the lists again with a last ditch attempt to gain some advantage from their visit. 'As an ex-Justice Minister, and French Consul, would you give this search your blessing? We're obviously going to need the cooperation of the Saharan authorities. No doubt you have some influence here?'

'I have no influence.'

'You couldn't put in a good word for us? We may need equipment, proper transport.'

'Out of the question. These days I deal with only a few commercial matters. If you want to conduct this search of yours that is your affair. I must tell you, however, I think you're wasting your time. Now – I am sorry – but I must ask you to leave me. I do not normally receive visitors.' He shouted something in Arabic.

The boy appeared. Petit-frères nodded his head towards the door. They rose. Claudia thought it was worth a last shot. 'I'd like to ask you a last question, Monsieur Petit-frères. Did you like Alan Silverman?'

The pale blue eyes confronted her coldly, expressionlessly. 'In my position it was not – is not now, as French Consul – my duty to like or dislike people,' he said.

'But if you hadn't had an official position, would you have liked him?'

'Suppositional questions are a waste of time.'

They didn't get another syllable out of him. As they filed out, he was already wheeling himself and the empty glass back to the fender-box.

She wondered irrelevantly where he got his whisky in this country, whose regime Michael had told her was ostensibly even more puritanical than Algeria.

As they left the place the muezzin started up, broadcast from a loud-speaker in the mosque. To the west spread the most beautiful sunset Claudia had ever seen. The sun had already disappeared behind the rim of sand which shielded the oasis on that side. Behind the palms a powerful pink was glowing. While they looked, and the sad voice wailed, the pink was dissolving into the purest yellows, then greens and mauve. Outside the garden gate, they stood watching it together, transfixed.

The wind which had woken her earlier had dropped again. It was still hot, but now quite bearable. It was an enchanted moment. After the total deadness of the heat, it seemed that briefly, before the rapid darkness fell, everything came alive. While they stood, as if switched on, a great joyful chorus of croaking frogs began all over the oasis. It was almost deafening. A huge bird soared in smoothly from the direction of the mountains which lay to the north. It circled majestically, then with a brief commotion of its wings settled out of sight amid the dense vegetation. Had it come to drink, to feed? The muezzin ceased and left them alone with the frogs. Claudia wasn't religious, certainly not in any denominational sense, but the scene induced an awareness of nature, of the power and beauty of the universe, perhaps what others call worship, which she'd seldom felt so strongly. She was sure Michael was feeling it, too. For these minutes at least, wasn't it true, they could forget completely why they were in this place and were at peace with each other?

They had come in Ouboussad's taxi and had asked him to come back for them in an hour if they didn't phone. They could have waited for him, but decided to walk back. They did so in silence as the sky darkened to indigo around a crescent moon and round the most incredible stars, which seemed twice their normal size and triply brilliant. They seemed to bulge. Claudia thought they would fall from the sky like huge incandescent raindrops, they looked so heavy and vibrant.

Ouboussad met them with the car before they got back to the hotel. He seemed surprised they had walked, almost cross. Apparently Europeans never walked, even when moving into the next street.

Claudia was wet through with sweat again. After another bath, she felt ravenous. Even if they offered sheeps' eyes she'd gulp them like oysters, she thought.

The meal didn't include sheeps' eyes. It maintained, however, despite its simplicity, the relics of French standards and ritual. If the Spanish nobleman sells his cloak last, does the French equivalent hang on to his eating habits, Claudia thought? She had more than once pondered how amazingly resilient European civilisation had proved to be in many parts of the ex-colonial third world, which had every reason to bundle it, bag and baggage, from its territory. They got rid of its politics, but not, it seemed, its everyday trappings of life.

In the small room, which boasted three electric light bulbs, the two plastic tables in use had paper 'couverts' and little glass pots containing, each one, an exotic orchid. They had a thin garlic soup with an egg poached in it, an omelette flavoured with an oniony herb Claudia didn't recognise, some rather small pieces of lamb, a pungently goaty slice of dry cheese, and a plate of moist and sticky dates, the most delicious she'd ever tasted and quite unlike anything purchasable in Britain, plumply full of treacly flavour. She could now believe it was possible to live on dates. The fridge had started working again so the bottled water was cold, and there was flat unleavened bread. They were served by an amiable boy – teenage boys seem to do all the work in Tifgad. To her it was a banquet.

At the other laid table was O'Grady and two other Americans. These two were little more loquacious than O'Grady, but one of them revealed to Michael that they were geologists. They were prospecting at a place a hundred miles away, looking – rather hopelessly, it seemed, from the way they went on talking – for either gas or oil, Claudia couldn't gather which. The gusto of their eating contrasted with the meagreness of their exchanges.

As for Michael and herself, Claudia was relieved that their dispute about Silverman was kept at a discreet distance. They talked in depth about Petit-frères, and agreed that though he'd been pretty inscrutable, they couldn't believe he was totally disinterested. Why would he have agreed to see them otherwise? He hardly seemed a man impelled by a desire to commune with mankind. They also agreed that he'd been thoroughly well-informed about recent events. Michael's letter had alerted him to the subject of Silverman's expedition, but he seemed to know quite a bit about the case. Had he looked it up? It seemed like it. And what had been his motive in seeing them?

They decided finally it must have been little more than defensiveness. However perfunctory his consular duties had become, he'd naturally have wanted to inform himself about their intentions in a matter that might well, from a French point of view, throw unfavourable light on the Colonial Administration in 1936. Claudia was quite prepared to concede the French might have thought they'd been gulled by Silverman (rather adroitly in her opinion). As for Petit-frère's less than friendly attitude to them, perhaps that was easier to understand. As Minister of Justice at the time, he could hardly have welcomed Michael's questions about the murder and the insinuations that an injustice could have taken place.

On the latter point Claudia rather took Petit-frère's side, but she kept this to herself. She'd already decided while having her bath to let Michael chase his hares while she got on with what interested her. Apart from 'local colour,' she thought she might well get some new insights into Alan by being here. Petit-frères had come near to giving her one. She'd received the impression he hadn't liked Silverman. She knew from Alan's notebook that the two men had seen a great deal more of each other than Petit-frères had suggested, so she couldn't believe his professed indifference rang quite true. That, she thought, discounting Michael, doubled her tally of people who disliked Alan. Janet, now him. But had Petit-frères, like Janet, a personal reason for doing so?

As they were eating she then remembered something Michael had said during the interview, which she'd only half-registered. 'Hey,' she said, 'I meant to ask you before. The sunset put it out of my mind. You asked Petit-frères for help with the Saharan authorities. I thought you had their cooperation already?'

'Not yet.'

Her stomach leapt like a fourteen pound salmon. 'But you said you were going to get it?'

'I didn't.'

'You mean they don't even know we're here?'

'We got our visas.'

'But a direct approach to the Ministry concerned – "Culture", didn't you say? I thought that's what you meant when you said you were letting them know of our appearance here.'

'I'll do it, when I'm ready.'

'Well they'll know we're here now. Petit-frères will tell them.'

'All to the good then.'

'But why didn't you write in advance? No wonder there was no fuss at the airport. Why do you always want to do things out of the blue?'

'Because, in this case, I want to suss out the ground a bit, and perhaps get some evidence, before I see anyone. Don't worry, there won't be any fuss. Why should there be? I'm on their side.'

On the side of a bunch of thugs? It ruined her temporary and hard-won peace of mind.

13.

Despite their contretemps, Claudia and Michael went to bed in an amicable frame of mind. Over dinner, Michael had been as cocky as ever, but the way he'd talked to her at least suggested she was his rational assistant, if nothing more. That had to be seen as an advance.

But perhaps because she'd slept so long in the day she lay awake. When she did get to sleep at last, she had a repetitive nightmare in which she was bound, naked, about to be tortured by a woman in white nylon gloves. Beside her, looking on emotionlessly was Petit-frères. She woke after the last of these dreams, sweating and shredded, just before her alarm clock was due to shrill at four o'clock. For good measure, as she put the light on, she saw at least half a dozen cockroaches scuttling for the cracked wainscotting over the filthy moquette with which the concrete floors were thinly covered.

Perhaps because of this she started the day in a bad frame of mind. It seemed likely to continue in this vein. They had ordered breakfast at this ungodly hour, but apparently someone had overslept. Downstairs there wasn't a sound, and they witnessed a lot more cockroaches running for cover. Furthermore the front door was locked with the key removed, and all the windows were heavily barred. It didn't seem they'd be able to get going, even without breakfast.

For once Claudia was glad of Michael's forthrightness. Her conditioning to courtesy and deference would never have been capable of the anger he mustered. He hammered the bell on the reception counter until at last there were movements and their somnolent patron appeared in his pyjamas, grunting and muttering.

'Qu'est ce qu'arrive? Nous avons commandé le petit-déjeuner á quatre heures et demi,' Michael raged.

The Arab's ill-humour was upstaged. He attempted lamely to blame the boy, who must have overslept, he said. Michael forced him to put the coffee on himself. If he didn't, he said, he would. On such driving energy and certainty, no doubt, Claudia thought, were empires built.

The next problem was their driver, Ouboussad. He was also late. When he did arrive, Michael denounced him roundly, and he went into a sulk. This, unlike the hotel manager, was a mistake, she thought. It was conceivable their lives could depend on this man.

She kept quiet, but after a decent interval, during which they had driven free of the town and had settled down at a comfortable seventy kilometres an hour on the dusty road northwards, she broached from the back seat what she hoped would be an amicable conversation with their disaffected driver. She asked him about his family, about the town. He answered in sullen monosyllables. Eventually she had to give up. It was her bad dream, she knew – dreams attack one behind one's back and leave a residue which only time eliminates – but Ouboussad's continuing ill-humour worried her. Was it just because Michael had been cross with him? If so, it was surely an excessive reaction.

There was another thing. Ouboussad had said yesterday in an off-hand way that he'd no idea where Alan's camp-site had been. She and Michael had studied one of the photocopied pages of Alan's diary – a diagrammatic sketch of the route from the camp to Tifgad. Sitting in the front seat with a small torch, Michael had the paper on his knees, and was prepared to give instructions to Ouboussad about which turnings to take. Ouboussad now didn't appear to need them. Once, when they had turned off the main metaled road, they were approaching a crossroads where there were three tracks to choose from. Michael was uncertain which was the right one and told Ouboussad to stop while he checked the map more carefully. Ouboussad didn't stop but careered confidently on to one of the tracks. Michael confirmed it was the right one. So he did know the way. Obviously he had consulted with someone overnight, Claudia conjectured. This might have been thought a constructive, cooperative move on his part, but in her jaundiced mood she found it additionally sinister. 'You know the way then, Ouboussad?' Michael said. He didn't get an answer.

Michael had timed the journey well. Since soon after leaving Tifgad they'd been able to see the mountains, which rose dramatically out of the plain of the desert and were silhouetted against the brilliant night sky ahead of them. As they reached them after about an hour and a half, they became aware that the amazing amount of light in the desert night sky was being supplemented from the east. They should arrive, as planned, with enough daylight for the bit of serious map-reading they would need to do before they plunged on foot off the track.

The track entered that amazing valley Archie had talked about in his lecture, which threaded its way through the entire range from north to south and which Alan's find almost confirmed had been used by travellers to penetrate the mountain barrier, certainly since Carthaginian times. The incline was imperceptible. It seemed they progressed along an endless, twisting, flat-floored valley. But they were climbing. In deference to the ancient motor, Ouboussad dropped their speed to fifty kilometres an hour and, as they progressed, the valley sides grew steadily more precipitous and closer together.

Then as daylight was really broadening and beginning to extinguish the stars, the valley unexpectedly widened somewhat. Confident that Ouboussad knew what he was doing, Michael had stopped trying to direct him. Ouboussad began to peer to the right. Suddenly he seemed to spot something. He pulled the old Mercedes off the track, and they began to bump and lurch over the stony terrain as if they were mounted on bucking broncos. They were making for one of the many reentrants that had once, she suppose, in more pluvial times, held tributary streams feeding the main river. Ouboussad gave a small grunt.

At first they could see nothing. Then Claudia made out a small blackish object about half a mile ahead and pointed it out to Michael. This last bit of the journey must have taken ten minutes, the ground was so bad. She was terrified they'd have a puncture and was near to suggesting they should walk – they wouldn't have progressed much more slowly – but Ouboussad seemed set on what he was doing. Then she saw what the black object was.

'Good heavens, it's the old cooking-stove they used,' she said, 'which was adapted to use paraffin. I remember Archie mentioning it.'

Astonishingly, it was almost the only solid relic of the camp. No doubt because of the political involvements and xenophobia, there'd been no effort to commemorate the place, and of course there was no tourism to visit it. Here was the site of one of the most exciting archaeological finds of history and all that marked it was this domestic detritus. There stood the stove, still upright, probably just as it had been, unrusted in the bone-dry climate, defiantly banal. They searched in a radius of a couple of hundred yards. They found evidence of two camp fires – one for the whites, one for the Berbers? – and a metal tent stave. That was all.

Claudia took snaps of what there was with her inexpensive but trusty camera. She wanted to make a longer search. She wanted more evidence of the camp, something that would enable her to imagine the scene more vividly, personal belongings perhaps. But Michael was rightly impatient.

'Come on, we know it's at least an hour's hump.'

She was only too well aware. It was still seductively cool. In another hour it would be hot, later an inferno. If they weren't back here somewhere near ten they'd be cinders.

If Ouboussad knew the way here, did he also know the route to the cave? While they'd been looking round, he'd opened the bonnet of the car and was busy pouring water into the radiator from an old petrol can he'd brought in the boot. Michael probably had the same thought she did, and seemed about to go over to him.

'Let me speak to him,' she said.

Shrugging his shoulders, Michael concurred. She approached, smiling her best. 'Are you coming with us, Ouboussad?' she said. He wouldn't look at her. There was no doubt he was put out. 'Are you angry with us about something? Is it because Michael was cross outside the hotel? If it is, he's sorry.' Ouboussad shook his head strongly as if irritated by the triviality of such an idea. 'Then, will you come? Have you been out here before? Perhaps you can help us find the way.'

She became definitely alarmed at this moment. Ouboussad was not annoyed, she saw, he was hostile. 'I driver, not guide,' he said, in his few words of English, turning away rudely. He'd finished pouring and was screwing on the radiator cap. For him the conversation was finished.

'I suppose we'll be about three hours,' she said, 'you'll wait here?' He made no reply, and picked up the can in order to replace it in the boot.

She returned to Michael, who was sitting on a rock with the contour map trying to work out the route. She told him what had transpired. There was a thought nagging her. Should she mention it? She thought not. But when they'd started, he came out with it for her.

'If that surly bugger does a flit, we'd have to wait until dark. Must be about seventy miles. Probably do about a third of the journey during the night and the early morning then, clear of the mountains, hope for a truck on the main road when we reach it.'

She was relieved. She knew Michael had guts, but the rational variety of courage is a great deal more comforting to a coward like herself than the reckless sort which never considers contingencies.

Both of them had light rucksacks in which they had head-lamps, water, and some dates Michael had wisely bought yesterday evening. They'd added this morning some of the unleaven hotel bread. Michael had brought a long length of light-weight nylon rope which he carried over one shoulder. Now they were started, she began to feel a bit better. After all, they were only doing what Alan, Beazley, Janet Brisbane and the Berbers had done every day for more than six months, and they hadn't had a hotel to return to. Why was she being such a pussyfoot?

Michael's idea was to identify the cave where the find had been made and then assess the problem of searching for Beazley's remains. He wanted to calculate on the spot what equipment he would need and how many people he'd have to hire, within what he could afford, to have a reasonable chance of achieving his purpose. As he'd told her, he did intend going to the Ministry of Culture to ask for their help, but he wanted to know what he was talking about before he did so.

Michael rather fancied himself as a map-reader. She'd had from him already an account – highly complimentary to himself needless to say – of his use of a map in the East African bush on one of his jaunts. This little expedition wasn't going to be a doddle, either, he had pointed out to her last night. In this featureless landscape you'd only have the contours to help you. They had from Alan's diary a six figure reference of the cave from this same ancient French Survey map Alan had used in 1936. The first stage of the journey was obviously to continue on up the tributary valley until they reached a point where they would need to turn west up the steep flank of the mountain on that side. As they trekked up the valley, which already had quite a gradient, Michael kept a good hundred yards ahead of her. Fortunately he had to keep stopping to pore over the map. This enabled her to catch up.

It seemed then they were getting into difficulties. They'd been going about half an hour. The heat was rising by the minute. They'd for some time moved out of sight of Ouboussad and the car – still, mercifully, stationary when it was last in view – and it was a case of picking the right point for their left-angle turn. Claudia realised only too fully that, if they picked the wrong point, they could be in serious trouble with the sun. Michael, clearly in two minds, had stopped for long enough for her to catch up again.

'I'm really not sure if it's here or round the next bend,' he said, his look suggesting some shortcoming in the map. He began another bout of, alternately, staring at it and looking up at the landscape.

The map was not the only thing they had. Alan was a good draughtsman, and his notebook was peppered with graphic diagrams and sketches, which Claudia had been careful to bring. Among these was a series of notes and drawings of the various routes the party had followed in their search of the region. One page contained a diagrammatic sketch map of the actual route they were following now. Michael had pooh-poohed the idea of using it when she'd suggested it last night. 'May have been all right for him,' he said airily. 'He knew the area backwards. I prefer to stick to the contours, not unintelligible shorthand.'

Unintelligible, she thought – Silverman, the arch communicator? That was surely the last thing he ever was, even in his own notes. She'd slipped the page into her rucksack and now drew it out.

A look at the mountains surrounding them confirmed at once how effective Alan's map was. It wasn't to scale and there were no contours. What he had done was make use of his draughtsman's skill. There were three diagram drawings designed to be used at three points where a choice of direction was required. They had plainly reached the first of these, for he, as they were doing, had begun by following the tributary valley for some way. In each diagram Alan had sketched peaks or prominent features which would be in view, identifying each with a quick drawing which was instantly recognisable. These were orientated in relation to each other. By holding the page up and lining it up on one of them, you could know at once if you were in the right position or not. If you weren't, the other two wouldn't line up, or one of the features wouldn't be visible. She saw at once by aligning Alan's map that they were at the right spot. An arrow indicated they had to turn left at forty-five degrees and, to confirm the instruction, Alan had also drawn a remarkably smooth egg-shaped boulder (marked: 'The Easter-Egg') which lay slap in the path of their new direction about five hundred yards above them. She showed it to Michael.

He hummed and ha-ed and pretended to confirm it by further Delphic starings at the map. Claudia kept her little triumph to myself. It amused her, when they came to the second hinge point on the crest of a ridge, that he was more inclined to accept Alan's posthumous guidance. He stopped, and asked for Alan's map.

While she slumped behind a rock which still bountifully sported a shadow – by midday there'd be no shadows – Michael consulted the map, then ranged the mountainside ahead of them with his field-glasses. It was now getting very hot. The sun was right up and they were fully in its rays. She was wearing shorts and a tennis shirt. Round her middle and under the arms she was soaking, and another ring of sweat girdled her head under her wide-brimmed straw hat. She heard Michael catch his breath.

'I don't believe it,' he said. Despite her discomfort and semi-exhaustion, she jumped up. 'Look – there.' He pointed. She could see nothing out of the ordinary. 'That's surely the cairn. It's still there for God's sake.'

He passed her the glasses, but before she raised them she saw it, too, with her naked eye as Archie must have done that afternoon he'd followed the Berber. She trained the glasses. Unmistakeably, beside what seemed a cave entrance, was a stack of sizeable rocks, surely those which Beazley had built getting on for a lifetime ago to mark what proved to be not only the site of the Carthaginian hoard but his death chamber.

'What an incredible stroke of luck,' she said.

Michael was already off again, striding downwards from their hard-won contour on a bee-line for their objective.

It was a cave all right. There was a tiny entrance – you had to stoop to almost half-height to get through it – but once inside you were in a vast chamber which their head-lamps illuminated as they switched them on. Michael shouted. At first the sound seemed to rush frantically around the chamber they were in, then after it had seemed to escape there were the most hideously prolonged series of echoes which seemed to travel hundreds, perhaps thousands, of yards into the bosom of the mountain. What was still eerier was that having almost disappeared, the sound then grew again on a return journey until it snapped off suddenly.

'Crippin,' Michael said – an apt choice of expletive, Claudia thought.

She was glad to see Michael's first idea coincided with her own. 'Operation Theseus, I think?' he said, swinging off his rucksack. She had persuaded him in England to this safety precaution of Alan's. He took out the ball of fine nylon, a mile of it. He tied the end to one of the light metal staves he'd brought and, as it was impossible to hammer it into the solid rock floor, covered it with a stack of heavy stones.

It was plain to both of them from another of Alan's sketch maps that they were in the actual chamber where the hoard was found. Tacitly instructed by it, they moved together towards their left, and there above them at chest height was the breached fault line behind which the Carthaginians had hidden their merchandise. The hole that had been made was still relatively small – just enough to allow someone to get in and out. They both moved forward to peer through it into the empty cavity beyond.

Claudia had only once before had the same sensation she now underwent – in the remains of a villa in Rome buried deep underground below the church of San Clemente near the Colosseum. The villa had been nothing to look at – just a series of damp underground rooms. But when you realised it was possible that St Peter, a known friend of the family who lived in the villa, had once stood in this very spot, one's feelings took off. One hears the cliché about time standing still. For Claudia – for both of them, she thought – the phrase took on vivid meaning as they stood in this amazing, historic place, somehow made so much more poignant by the fact that it had been left like this, undramatised by tourism. If the trip proved useless in all other ways, this one instant justified it. If they – she and Michael – felt like this in face of an empty chamber, what had Alan felt when he saw the amazing objects which filled it – after months of fruitless and stressful labour?

But again, as with the camp site, there was nothing to record what had happened here, just a few rock-axe marks where Silverman, maybe Beazley, had hacked. Having stood staring for some moments and having realised there was nothing more to see, they looked at each other. Claudia was beginning to get used to thinking the same thing as Michael in the same moment, which in view of their antagonism and rivalry had surely to be a paradox. What they were both thinking was – where exactly was the site of Beazley's murder? This had not, rather understandably, figured on Alan's sketch.

'How long does a blood stain last?' Michael said, confirming what he was thinking.

It seemed a rather pointless and certainly macabre thing to do but, a bit guiltily – certainly on her part – they began a more or less systematic search of the floor. They crossed the floor some half a dozen times about six feet apart, swinging their heads, and therefore their lamps, from side to side.

Claudia had a feeling of sickness and disgust as she imagined the appalling scene, the flashing blade, the cry, perhaps the agony of the dying man, the drenching blood. But they found no traces.

As they moved, they were approaching the further wall of the chamber. In their first cursory view of the whole place, it had not seemed there were any interior exits (which, because of the prolonged echo they'd heard seemed odd) but she suddenly noticed on her right that there did seem to be a breach in the wall. Happily abandoning their ghoulish search, they went towards it. It was indeed a considerable breach, which was not visible until you got right up to it, as it was not head on but like the side door of a front porch with a salient of rock bulging over it. When they came right beside it, they saw that a narrow rock path plunged steeply downwards. Could this lead to other chambers?

Making sure the nylon thread was paying out freely, they decided to descend the path. Claudia was pretty sure what was in Michael's mind. Was this the answer to the problem of the disposal of the body? As Michael was paying out the nylon, he made her go on ahead. They must have walked downwards for about ten minutes. As they did so, the stuffy air seemed progressively to close on them to the point almost of suffocation. 'It's not a place,' she thought, 'where humans are supposed to be.' She imagined a Gorgon behind every turn in the path. Then the gradient became less steep. The stuffiness seemed to relent a little, and they were precipitated suddenly into another chamber with a flat floor.

The chamber wasn't nearly as big as the upper one, but it seemed to feed off into a number of paths like the one they had descended, running off in all directions. They began to inspect one of these. Michael supposed the two chambers had once contained lakes. Water had then found these outlets, perhaps along fault lines. How many tunnels were there and how deep did they go? Not knowing quite what to do next, they stopped and had a conference. Michael suggested they should walk round the chamber in opposite directions and inspect the exits for any that were larger, or different in any way.

They were embarked on this when Claudia had a ghastly shock and drew in breath sharply. She'd been idly shining her lamp just ahead of her. What she'd thought was another path wasn't. It was a huge vertical hole about six feet across. Another pace or two and she'd have fallen down it.

She must have cried out. The next thing she knew Michael was beside her. He picked up a sizeable rock and let it drop down the cavity. It grazed twice against the side then thumped to a stop. It didn't seem the hole was very deep.

'This could be it. I'm going down to have a look,' Michael said.

She thought he was crazy. This was a reconnaissance, she said, and they had no proper equipment. The stone could have come to rest on a side ledge, the pit could be bottomless. It probably finished up in hell, she added to herself.

Argue with Michael when he'd made his mind up? He threw two more stones from different angles, with the same result the first had had. He began unravelling the length of nylon rope, laying it out on the cave floor in a long line of large loops. He fished out a stave and began to look for somewhere to knock it in. The rock was as hard as it had been above, but eventually he found a small crack in the cave wall some yards from the hole. It was possible to hammer in the stave firmly. To be doubly sure he took the rope round a large boulder that had broken away and put other large stones on it on the floor on the way to the hole.

'Shine your lamp as I go down to give maximum light,' he instructed her.

He threw the loose end of the rope down the abyss and was rewarded by a kind of slap-noise that suggested it had come to rest, as the rocks had. He then threaded the rope across his back and one shoulder, holding it in both hands held outwards. He gave several hearty tugs on the rope to test it, then stood out almost horizontally across the chasm and began to descend in commando fashion. A few feet down, the hole took a trip sideways, so he disappeared from Claudia's view. The rope seemed held firmly enough but she had a vision of its being severed on the rock it was bearing on, and now he was out of view she couldn't imagine her lamp was doing much to supplement his.

'Can you see all right?' she called.

'Enough.'

He dislodged a couple of stones which made her think he'd fallen, and there were several oaths.

After what seemed an age, and when a terrifying length of rope had paid out, the rope suddenly went slack. He was down on to something.

There was a long pause. She had to stop herself shouting to ask what was happening, which might have distracted his concentration.

It must have been only a couple of minutes. What was he up to? Then the rope stirred, and tautened. 'I'm coming up,' she heard – from much further down than she'd imagined.

There was another frightful period of falling stones, and now panting and straining from Michael. At last he came into view.

The last bit seemed to Claudia to be the most dangerous. Michael's strength must be ebbing, and the hole was just too wide for him to be able to span it with his body and lever himself out with his feet. But by clinging with one hand to the taut rope on the cave floor outside the hole, with a last effort he managed to swing one leg over the rim and, using his free hand for balance, somehow he scrambled out. He lay on his back panting for a few moments. Then, triumphant, he rolled onto his side.

'I can't believe our luck. The first place we look in. It's Beazley. It must be. A human skeleton, including the skull, which will be identifiable. There are three fillings in the teeth, one up and two down. And the skull's got two holes through it, one on each side. There's no doubt – he was shot.'

Claudia was too thankful he was all right to take this in fully or to reply. Then she realised what he was doing. He began to haul in the rope. Long before it came into sight, she knew what would be on the end of it.

He'd threaded the rope through an eye socket and out through the neck. As the skull came into view, the implications to Claudia of what Michael had said were a great deal too disturbing to allow what would otherwise have surely been a feeling of horror and revulsion. Michael hauled it up, unknotted the rope, and lay it between them. Sure enough, the skull had been shattered on both sides. One perforation was neat – where a bullet seemed to have entered – the other more fractured.

Her instinct was to resist the idea with all the force she could muster. 'The skull could have been cracked when the body was thrown down the hole,' she said.

'Hardly – in that way.'

'We have no idea it's Neil Beazley's skull, anyone could have fallen down there – and if it is Beazley someone could have put a bullet through it after his death to make it look as if . . .'

Michael wasn't even listening. 'I'm willing to bet none of those Berbers had guns,' he went on. 'The only member of the party carrying one was Silverman. In fact, we know that, now I think about it. It's mentioned in the diary that it was the only firearm. And the gun appears, in a holster round Silverman's waist, in several of the photos. It's clear in broad terms what happened. Beazley found the hoard. Silverman discovered him at it. They had some kind of a row and Silverman shot him.'

Claudia flared up. 'That is total supposition. You just want to believe it. If these are Neil Beazley's remains, which must be open to huge doubt, it could have been suicide. We know he was in an unstable frame of mind.'

'Suicide – when he'd just found the hoard?'

'What about the dagger – and the blood on it? If Alan shot Beazley, why was it there?'

'That's obvious. It was put there – by Silverman, after the murder, to frame Beri.'

'That's crazy. How could he possibly have done that?'

'I don't know. But I'm willing to bet any money that's what he did. The bastard sent an innocent Berber assistant to his death to save his own skin, and I'm going to find out how he did it.'

It must have been delayed shock, but Claudia was suddenly overcome with emotion. Here they were, sitting in this ghoulish cave in the middle of a desert and here was this self-certain lefty journalist telling her chirpily that the man she'd worked for and respected and with whose biography she was entrusted, a national hero, was a murderer. He was going to make up some plausible story, publish it, be paid handsomely, and several million people would believe what he wrote. She got up in the biggest huff she'd mustered in years.

'I just don't believe it,' she said. 'What you say is entire speculation. There can be any number of explanations for the holes in the skull, and for all the other events. All you're interested in is a cheap sensational story which you largely wrote before you came here. Alan Silverman was many things, but he wasn't a murderer. What you, and the press, do, is in my view filthy. You pose as upholders of the truth, but in fact constantly and deliberately distort evidence for your own purposes. The Times isn't much better than the tabloids. If you've the remotest remnants of decency you'll return those poor bones to the place where you found them.'

Michael had turned away from her. He hadn't taken his small flash camera down the pit with him. He was now taking it out of his rucksack. She watched him place the skull on the edge of the pit, adjusting its angle as if it were any object to be snapped. He was hardly aware of what she was saying. She marched off.

She was thankful for the nylon thread without which she would surely have lost herself. By the time she reached the cave entrance she'd cooled off a bit. She didn't at all regret what she'd said, but she realised a good deal of her anger must have been delayed shock, allied with a refusal to go along with Michael's self-induced conclusion-jumping. She thought about the skull more soberly. If Michael's theory wasn't right, what was? Loath to go out in the sun, which was now blazing down, she sat in the entrance, and ate a piece of bread and a few dates.

Returning to a more normal frame of mind, she realised something she'd already thought subconsciously – their amazing discovery was just too pat. The police must have searched every corner of this cave for the body. They must have come across that abyss, as she and Michael had, at a very early stage. Why had the body never apparently been produced? And if, just supposing for a moment Alan had murdered Beazley – if indeed the remains were Beazley's, which had yet to be proved – would he really have taken so little care to hide the body? Of course not. He must have known how easily it would be found and that when it was – with two bullet holes through the head – he must be the prime suspect. She couldn't believe it. There was something most odd about this instant success of theirs.

As she reflected, she noticed a small object lying beside her on the cave floor in the half light. She leaned to pick it up. It was a cigarette butt. It hadn't been trodden on but thrown carelessly to one side. It was burnt almost to the butt. She smelt it. The smell of the Arab tobacco was pungent. It must, surely, have been smoked very recently. Someone had been here – she guessed in the last days, maybe the last hours.

She thought of Ouboussad's strange behaviour earlier. She thought of their visit to Petit-frères and the almost certainty that he had informed someone about them. She tried to link the three things. What party, she thought, wanted them to find that skeleton at the earliest moment?

She sat just inside the cave, thinking. The cave floor sloped slightly upwards from the narrow aperture, so she could see out of it into the now

137

blinding white light outside, across to the further mountainside where they had made the second hinge point on their journey up. Just then her eye was caught by something on that ridge, a movement was it, or something glinting in the sun? She saw it again. She went outside to look, and the heat hit her like a blow on the neck. She stared.

There was nothing. Was it another mirage? Had she imagined it? Or it could have been someone, Ouboussad perhaps, spying on them.

By the time Michael came up she'd taken refuge inside the cave again. She could see from the shape of his rucksack that he had the skull packed into it. He was looking even more triumphant.

'I think something odd's going on,' she said at once.

'Oh?'

'I just can't believe we'd've come across a skeleton like that. It's too much of a coincidence.'

'What you mean is you don't like the coincidence.'

'It isn't just that.' She showed him the cigarette butt. He took it and looked at it for a moment.

'Probably fourth century BC,' he mocked, returning it. 'In this climate it could've been dropped years ago.'

'Still smelling of Arab tobacco? Also, I'm almost sure there's someone on the ridge over there, watching us.'

He took out the binoculars from the rucksack, went outside the cave, and rather pointlessly ranged the mountainside for a few moments. He put the binoculars away.

'The heat's getting to you. We'd better start back,' he said. She put the cigarette butt into her trouser pocket inside her handkerchief, and shut up. Exhibit B to add to the skull if it ever proved relevant, she thought defiantly.

As they began walking, she tried again to make herself think clearly. Could those bones have been placed there for them to find, after someone had put a bullet hole through the skull? Were their movements being monitored at this moment? It was a perfectly possible hypothesis, as possible as, in fact a great deal more likely, than Michael's.

But she couldn't sustain any concentration. The immediate discomfort and the thought of the physical ordeal ahead took precedence. Thank God the hike back was mostly downhill. For the next hour she thought of nothing but survival. If Ouboussad had left them, she thought, she would expire on the spot.

But, thank heaven, as they rounded the last bend, there was the car, and if they had been followed by Ouboussad, he put on a very convincing act. When they reached the car they found him asleep on the back seat, his legs protruding through one of the open doors. Claudia could have embraced him.

14.

On the journey back to Tifgad Claudia wished she hadn't come on this mad expedition. She was getting her local colour all right, but at what cost?

She had endured worse things, but never such concentrated physical discomfort as during that hour and a half's journey. Because of the dense cloud of reddish dust the car raised, they had to keep all the windows closed or they'd have been choked. The heat, added to by the engine, and the dust which got into the car despite the windows being shut reached the level of torture. She felt her heartbeats thumping at double their normal speed in her chest and wrists and temples. She tried to lie back in the front seat Michael had awarded her, put her head back as far as she could, kept her arms away from her body, and tried to relax her muscles. She tried breathing through her mouth like a dog, but soon abandoned that. In a few seconds saliva dried, and one had the feeling of being strangled by thirst. She felt faintness constantly swaying upon her and had to fight it back by an effort of will. Her only consolation was that in the back seat Michael seemed to be suffering the same discomfort. Even Ouboussad looked distressed. He drove like the wind, but his head was tucked downwards in a gesture of grim endurance. If the car broke down, she kept thinking, what then? 'Please God don't let the car break down,' she recited like a mantra, until she reminded herself that God, given to habits of genocide about the world, was hardly going to care about three crazy people in a desert. They passed the several carcasses of whitened bones which must be the remains of camels. How would God or nature be concerned if three more, human, skeletons were added to the collection?

Safely back, but exhausted, she wondered if she should pull out and go home. What was the point of being a half-despised accomplice to a raving journalist with a chip on his shoulder bent upon proving the most unlikely theory? She'd once thought she understood something of why people like Janet Brisbane were drawn by danger and discomfort, but she wasn't the type, she argued, it wasn't how she got her kicks. This was Michael Strode's scene, not hers.

She staggered upstairs to her room, quenched her immediate thirst by drinking most of a bottle of water, stripped off her sweat-sodden, grimy clothes and filled the bath. Then, lying back in the blessed cool of the water, she began to recover. She made upward undulating movements and felt the water sluice pleasantly over her. A few moments later she was beginning to feel differently. She was rather proud of herself for her part in the morning's work. She'd whinged to herself, but not out loud. She hadn't passed out and become a nuisance and, apart from an outburst of anger, she reckoned she'd contributed a lot more sensibly than Michael's obstinacy allowed him to recognise. Also, here in this hotel, she felt closer to Alan in a way than she ever had in the flesh. He might have sat in this very bath. It was certainly old enough.

Rational again, she took more balanced stock of the enquiry she'd allowed herself to be sucked into. On the one hand she no longer doubted there was some mystery about the 1936 expedition, that things were not exactly as they had been related – even in Archie's recent update of events. But she still believed that, if the skull turned out to be Beazley's, there was some explanation for those holes other than that Alan had shot him. She returned to her fears that their movements out here were being monitored in some sinister way and that they were being set up – an unpleasantness to which her opinionated travelling companion was so obstinately blind.

It didn't take her much longer after this to discard completely her little bout of defeatism. She wasn't going home yet, she thought. Quite apart from her own purposes, Michael didn't know it but he needed her. He needed her most of all because she wasn't encumbered with a mad theory and could look evidence in the face. She'd bide her time watchfully.

When she went downstairs, Michael was telephoning at the top of his voice. She was relieved to hear he was talking French. At least he wasn't on to his paper with a story, which could have goodness knew what consequences for them out here until he'd squared things with the authorities. She went into the dining-room and sat at their table.

Michael came striding in and just for a moment she had a nice feeling of admiration for his vigour and confidence – misplaced as she thought it – and not a little for his appearance. Like her own no doubt, his face – notably his strong Roman nose – was ludicrously red and his lips were chapped, but his blonde head and square strong body dressed in a clean white shirt and a clean pair of light-weight trousers, was unconsciously direct and sexy. She was also, as she had been the first moment she met him, in an underlying way amused by him, however annoying he was. What was it – his lack of guilt? His indifference to manners and propriety? Was it his expectation that life would always be surprising, never the same as before?

'Got it,' he said, swinging a leg boyishly over the chair back before he sat on it. 'Tomorrow at ten. So your anxiety in that direction can be laid to rest.'

He was talking in conundrums again. She grinned. 'Which particular anxiety?'

'A permit, and help. I've got an interview with Mohammed Salek, the Minister of Culture. I spoke to his chef du cabinet.'

'Did you tell him what you're doing?'

'Not exactly. I said I had important information about the 1936 Silverman expedition and wanted their advice.'

'You didn't say you were a Times journalist?'

'No.'

'Why not?'

'I'll let Salek know tomorrow.'

'I think you're crazy.'

'Why? I don't want anyone in on my little bombshell until I've spoken to the Minister. He'll be flattered probably I've kept it for his ears alone. From what I've heard he's an ambitious bastard. He'll probably have some little game of political kudos he wants to play, and I'll trade it for what I want.'

'Which is?'

'Three things. First, permission to export the skull – I don't want trouble at the airport opening a suitcase with that thing inside it. Second, assistance in the cave to recover the bullet, which must be in there somewhere. Alone we'd quite possibly never find it – we'll need ladders to search the walls – and without it we can never prove it was fired from Silverman's gun. Finally I want access to any papers which may still exist on the Beri case. I don't take Petit-frères's word that everything would have been shredded at Independence.'

All her fears returned. She considered shutting up, but couldn't. The

142

difference between Michael and herself was that she believed the Saharans had threatened and blackmailed Walter Claridge, and he didn't, and that she didn't believe they were oblivious to their arrival here. Michael did. She poured it all out in a heap, including her suspicions about Ouboussad. If the Saharans didn't know before what they were doing, they surely must now after their visit to Petit-frères last night. They were bound to misinterpret it.

Michael listened, and to her surprise was reasonable. 'So, supposing you're right,' he said when she'd done. 'Supposing they are the sinister lot of mafiosi you seem to think they are, supposing the police are on to us. So what? As I said to you before, I'm on their side. I advocate the return of the so-called Silverman Collection to Sahara. I've proved it by my pieces in The Times. And tomorrow Salek will have the whole picture. I can't think what's bugging you. What are you suggesting – that we pack it in, ditch Beazley's cranium in the gash bin, and scuttle home?'

She knew this was coming and had her answer. 'No, of course not.'

'So?'

'I just have an uneasy feeling, which isn't, I admit, entirely rational. I think you're closing your eyes to possible danger, that's all.'

Again Michael surprised her. She thought he was going to mock her for still trying to protect Silverman. He didn't.

'It'll be all right,' he said. 'We'll get Ouboussad to take us to Lagoued this evening when it cools off. It's about three hours apparently.'

He wasn't patronising, he was gentle. But maybe because he was, her reaction was illogically and ungratefully harsh. 'We?' she snapped.

'You're coming to Lagoued, aren't you?'

'No, I'm not.'

It seemed to hit him for a moment, as if he were disappointed. Then he seemed to take her refusal on board and his face cleared. 'OK,' he said, 'maybe it's not really necessary. I could be back tomorrow night with the entire Saharan boy scout movement under my command. Stay here then and get some more for your book.'

It was not at all what she'd expected, and it made her feel worse than before.

15.

When Michael Strode phoned Ouboussad, a woman answered in Arabic, as before. She appeared to speak no French or English. When she heard Ouboussad's name, she put down the receiver with a clatter. He heard Arab music piping and skirling in the background, and an exchange of Arabic. A male voice came on the line, not Ouboussad's. The French was minimal but explicit.

'No taxi.'

Michael elaborated – it was a ride to the capital he wanted, overnight. There'd be extra money and accomodation for Ouboussad in a good hotel, a nice meal.

'No taxi.'

Michael increased his outlay of simple words which might be understood. Could he speak to Ouboussad himself please?

The phone was put down and the French dialing tone, inherited with the rest of the telephone system, succeeded. Michael cursed. He re-dialed and the phone was not answered.

The imbecilic hotel proprietor was lurking in the room behind the reception counter. Michael called. Reluctantly the man appeared. Michael asked him if he could explain the breakdown of communication with Tifgad's only taxi. He got a two inch shrug.

'Prenez l'autobus,' was the suggestion. The man disappeared and shut the door behind him.

Michael didn't tell Claudia about the apparent rebuff. There was no point in adding to her fears. He said Ouboussad had wanted too much and he was going by bus. And what did it matter? He wouldn't have to endure Ouboussad's dourness, and he'd get to Lagoued as fast. He couldn't imagine the desert road would be teeming with stops.

At seven, when the sun had set, he walked to the open-air souk which at this hour had stalls selling food and other necessities. It was a wide square area of impacted mud which apparently was also used as a football field –

two goalposts sagging like rhombuses were visible at either end. In one corner, like a prehistoric animal, waited an ancient bus. Michael approached it. Its roof-racks were crowded with luggage. This included livestock – there was a silent trussed sheep panting rapidly, and two hens in a basket cage. He enquired of a ragged individual with a red sheish if the bus was for Lagoued. The man nodded. Michael paid him, and took one of the few remaining seats in the bus among a number of Arab men and several black-veiled women who were sitting patiently.

They started. Michael had a few words of Arabic. He deployed them sociably at the top of his voice – the engine noise was deafening – but to no effect. He was stared at, then the heads turned away. Amused, he abandoned the idea. Sending him to coventry, were they, or were they just dim, or shy? He fell back on his own thoughts.

Claudia. Obstinate as a mule of course, certainly where Silverman was concerned – though he'd hardly expected otherwise from her on that subject. Nobody after all likes the carpet pulled from under their feet – as the day's events surely must have done. (What a scoop, he thought again). But so far, La Claudia was not totally lacking in guts. She clearly believed the Saharan authorities were about to do him in, but he couldn't believe her unwillingness to come to Lagoued with him was funk. Neither, he thought, was it physical exhaustion despite the rigours they'd undergone. What was she up to then? Though it was himself who'd suggested she came out here, he couldn't think she hadn't already got the message about Tifgad. A dump, full stop. What else could she imagine she'd learn there unless up at that cave?

His thoughts soon strayed from Claudia's shadowy intentions into a more brightly lit area. He savoured anew the now almost certainty that his hunch about Silverman was true. The greasy ponce was a low-minded double murderer. Could there now be any reasonable doubt he'd done in Beazley then sent an innocent Berber to his death? So much for the Abbey service and the rest of the hypocritial pomp Silverman had incited in his wake. Not entirely fancifully, there was a distinct chance he was on the brink of the best story of his career. He'd already worked out the hypothesis on which he was going to reconstruct the rest of the complex events – including Archie's recent revelations – in terms of Silverman's guilt.

Lagoued, the capital, was four or five times Tifgad's size. It had ministries, no doubt, a presidential town residence, embassies, a television centre, several mosques, the rest of it. But at night, Michael thought, it wasn't so dissimilar a town to drive into. The principal differences were the few lights strung on wires that hung across the centre streets and – joy – a concrete hotel of five storeys. Surely it might just about creep into a guide-book with half a star?

It seemed it might. There were 'a number' of rooms with air-conditioning. He secured one. He'd rather hoped for a note from the Ministry at the desk confirming his appointment. With a wilder hope hatched by what was now certainly his fatigue, he invented news of a Government car which would be at the hotel at nine-thirty to convey him. For Christ's sake he was a VIP, wasn't he, a key figure in an international incident? But his key was given him wordlessly. He asked the reception counter if there were any messages for him. There were none.

In the morning it seemed even hotter than in Tifgad, but he decided to walk to the Ministry, which turned out to be only a couple of streets away. The Department was a very ordinary building of four storeys, its concrete walls at street level adorned with torn green posters indicating Marxist endeavour – a column of men of spurious fervour, carrying hammers and sickles, was marching towards a sunrise. Certainly no Berlin walls had fallen in this place. He attempted to crash the long queue waiting to speak to the reception clerk. A uniformed man approached, taking the gun off his shoulder.

Michael braced himself. 'J'ai rendez-vous avec Monsieur le Ministre . . .' he began, but the nozzle of the weapon pointed at his stomach strongly suggested conformity with the reception rules.

Twenty minutes later, after another attempt to persuade the gunman that he had an appointment with the Minister who might not like to be kept waiting, a lot sweatier he reached the desk and stated his business, in French. The bespectacled clerk looked bewildered, searched apparently without result among papers out of sight, and eventually lifted a telephone and waited. After a long pause someone seemed to answer it the other end. The man said something. Apparently an instruction was communicated back to him. He put down the instrument and opened the window which protected him from the public but for a small open area at the bottom. He spoke, not to Michael, but to the guard – a monosyllable. The guard looked at Michael, then back at the clerk. An intelligence seemed to pass between them. Michael was escorted to an uncarpeted concrete staircase and was handed over to

146

another guard who led him up four flights. There was a lift, but apparently it was a non-functional variety. He found himself in a room which had two armchairs covered with torn plastic, a small brass table, and a reek of tobacco.

It was suffocatingly hot, flies crawled on the walls and the filthy window-sill, but there was an inner door which offered some hope. Was this really the Minister of Culture's ante-room?

At last the door opened. An unveiled woman in a white haik came out. She said nothing but stood in the doorway inviting Michael to pass. He passed. She closed the door behind him and went unobtrusively to her desk.

It was like passing from hell to heaven. The room was air-conditioned, the floor was tiled. In the centre was a large Berber rug. The armchairs were not torn, but modern-looking, commodious. And behind the huge desk in front of a large photograph of 'The Honourable' Larbi Djebal, President of the Republic of Sahara (the title appeared in French as well as Arabic) a small man was rising. Unsmiling, somewhat unshaven, he said nothing.

'Monsieur le Ministre?' Michael enquired in his Sunday best voice.

He wasn't at once enlightened, but motioned to one of the chairs. The eminence, whoever it turned out to be, sat in another and eyed him. Michael waited.

'Why are you in Sahara?'

'Monsieur, could I please first know who you are? You are Monsieur Mohammed Salek, the Minister?'

The man looked annoyed. 'Chef du Cabinet,' he muttered.

'Ah, it was with you I spoke yesterday?' There was no answer. 'I see. Well, as I explained, I have information which I think may be interesting to you concerning Sir Alan Silverman's expedition here in 1936. I'm a freelance journalist employed by several English newspapers, but on this matter for The Times. From your London embassy, you may be au fait with recent revelations concerning the expedition. I was the journalist responsible for them.' The man was looking hostile. 'We've reason to think that there may be other sensational discoveries to be made, not only about the circumstances of the find, but also about the unfortunate assassination of one of the party. I had hoped the Minister would find himself free to hear . . .'

'You can talk to me.'

'You mean that Monsieur Salek is unable . . .'

'Talk to me.'

147

Michael accepted there were tiresome foothills to be climbed. Should he withhold the whole picture until the summit was reached? He decided there was no point. A man with air-conditioning and this degree of insolence must be someone of substance. There was nothing to be gained by antagonising him.

He began to tell the story, including some of the details about yesterday. The man tapped a pencil on the desk as he listened, like a weary schoolmaster listening to familiar material. Michael began to take a little more seriously the cigarette butt and Claudia's mirage on the mountainside. If Ouboussad wasn't a sleuth, it was possible someone else might have been. He actually said more than he'd intended. He described the descent into the hole in the cave floor and the discovery of the skeleton. Only, at the last moment, he mentioned neither the skull nor its perforations, nor the fact that it was in his possession. Would even a sleuth with binoculars have noticed the bulge in his rucksack? He finished by saying that he wanted to cooperate with the Saharan Government, that he believed historic artefacts of the magnitude of the hoard should be returned to their countries of origin, and that he hoped the Saharan Government would wish to assist him in his mission, which was surely in the interest of Sahara.

After this, Michael expected a thaw. There was none. When he had finished, the politician rose, went to the woman, and with his back to Michael said something to her in a low voice. He then disappeared through the door he'd entered by, closing it behind him. The woman lifted the phone and said something in Arabic. She then exercised her fingers, frowned at the copy beside her machine, and began to type.

There was a hiatus of a quarter of an hour. Any moment Michael expected to be summoned to see the Minister to whom, surely, the matter had been referred. Once he tried a smile at the woman when she momentarily raised her head. She at once turned her expressionless face downwards. At last her phone tinkled. She lifted the receiver, listened, said nothing and put it down. She rose, so did Michael. She went not to the door through which the name-shy official disappeared, but the other one through which Michael had entered. She opened it and two guards were visible. She said something. They entered.

It was at this moment Michael realised he was being arrested.

16.

U neasy as she was about it, it hadn't been fright which made Claudia cry off from Michael's trip to Lagoued. Since their visit to Petit-frères a subconscious memory had been tripped but not fully revealed in her mind. She knew it was there but couldn't get at it.

It was something Alan Silverman had said to her one day when they'd been discussing Tifgad. She knew that at the time she'd thought it a trivial matter, but now, in the capricious way in which the sub-conscious plays cat and mouse games, she was allowed to suspect it could be relevant in some way. The usual thing happened. She'd almost given up when, in the middle of lunch with Michael, there it was suddenly, bright and shining, like a lost object, in the most obvious place.

'Poor old Petit-frères, he never really had a chance,' that's what Alan had said.

She remembered more. The remark had been an irrelevant aside. They'd been discussing the removal of the hoard from Sahara and its shipment to Britain. Petit-frères, whom Alan had come to know quite well, had been helpful in easing things with the French Colonial Government, which had been especially necessary, she'd gathered, because of Beazley's murder and the likely legal complications.

Claudia's visual memory was better than her verbal filing system. When she could bring something down like this, she often had the clearest picture of the scene. Uttering that phrase Alan had looked aside for a moment, as if paying his respects, but what he'd said hadn't been for her ears. He'd hurried on with something else.

She decided to find out more about the taciturn Consul. Why did he 'not have a chance', and surely there must be things he knew which would be useful and which he'd concealed from them? It would be useless to try to pay him another visit at the moment – but an oblique approach, an attempt to find someone in Tifgad who knew him and who could remember the events of 1936 and his connection with them? Shouldn't she try to do a little investigation of her own while Michael was in Lagoued? All right, there was as well an element of rivalry with Mr Big Shoes, she admitted it.

The morning after Michael's departure she was up at dawn. As she entered the dining-room, their three fellow-guests, the only ones they'd seen in the place, had had their coffee and were on their way out. They were off on their prospecting jaunts all day long. She'd made friends with Hocen, the hard-working waiter-cum-hotel-dogsbody who, short of cooking, seemed to do everything about the place that needed actual physical effort, and whose French was excellent. He even had a few words of English. He had a sweet, cooperative and intelligent face, and she supposed he liked her because she was female, took some notice of him, and showed her appreciation of his services.

'Do you know Monsieur Petit-frères, Hocen?' she said as he brought the handleless brown ceramic bowl ready-filled with black steaming liquid. Hocen had remembered from yesterday that they preferred to do without the contribution of a sheep in their coffee.

'Oui, Madame,' he said, pleased to linger.

'Does he ever come to the hotel?' She was told he did every now and then, to have a drink with another old Monsieur when he was staying. 'A drink?' she enquired. The boy smiled, understanding at once what she meant. When this other Monsieur was here there was always a drink, he said humorously. 'An alcoholic drink,' she pressed?

'A whisky,' Hocen revealed with a worldly frown.

'I see,' she said. 'And this Monsieur – who is he? Is he French?'

'Oh no, Madame.' Hocen seemed almost offended at the thought. 'He's an Arab.'

'And he comes from somewhere else – Lagoued perhaps?'

'France,' announced Hocen proudly. 'Monsieur Ben Abbis is a trader, very rich. He gives me . . .'

He stopped in mid-sentence. Hocen really was a charming boy. Claudia was sure he was going to say the wealthy visitor gave him a fat tip, but had realised how she might misinterpret this and think he was fishing for one from her.

Because of this near gaffe as he saw it, he blushed, and began to move back to the bead curtain that concealed the kitchen. She tried to detain him. 'And have they known each other for a long time?'

'Many, many years,' said Hocen over his shoulder. He disappeared.

It wasn't much to go on, but something was better than nothing. When she'd finished her coffee she went into the hall. Standing behind the dimly-lit reception desk was the lethargic manager, whose name, she had discovered, was Tadj, engaged on a seldom-seen bout of work. At least one could presume it was work. He was bending over a ledger. In an access of energy he was probably calculating how much he was earning from his five guests.

She debated whether to be brisk and business-like or conversational, and chose the latter. She sauntered up as if she had nothing to do and put her arms on the counter. They'd heard from Hocen that Tadj was the owner of the hotel as well as the manager and that his father and grandfather had owned and run it before him. How about a good cliché to get things going? In French it didn't seem quite so fatuous.

'You must have seen a few changes here in your time, Monsieur Tadj?' She got a grunt. 'Especially after Sahara's independence. Were you here then?'

From his age she guessed he'd've been in his middle or early twenties at the time. Would he have been helping his father? There was a non-committal rocking of the gross head. She waited a moment or two then tried another tack. 'Your Hocen's a nice boy.'

Tadj was immensely fat and breathed badly through his mouth. He had absurdly delicate, half-lense spectacles perched on the end of his nose. He dipped the old-fashioned nibbed pen into a near-empty inkpot tilted on its screw-top.

'He's all right.'

'He was telling me about one of your regular guests – Monsieur Ben Abbis.' An elephantine approach, she knew, but in this country of elemental values it might achieve a better result than an attempt to be subtle.

The obese hotelier looked up at her, a faint interest showing. 'What did he tell you about Monsieur Ben Abbis?'

'That he's fairly well-off?'

'He's certainly that. What else?'

'He said he's a friend of Gérard Petit-frères, and meets him here.'

Tadj discovered an obstruction on his nib. Holding it up in the gloomy light he attempted to remove it with a podgy finger and thumb. 'Ah, poor Petit-frères,' he said, reflectively.

The exact repetition of Alan's phrase gave her a frisson. '"Poor" Petit-frères, you say?'

There was a lengthy pause while Tadj apparently put his mind to the matter. 'He was Minister of Justice, you know, when the French were here.'

'Yes, I did know that.'

'In those days he was important.'

'I suppose Independence finished his political career?'

'Oh, he was finished long before that.'

'You mean he fell from grace in some way?'

'What I mean is he liked Arabs. He spoke our language and worked for the people.'

'But – was that a disadvantage? Surely many good colonial servants did the same? Do you mean he was politically too friendly with Arabs?'

'Gérard has always been a good Saharan. He was never one of them.'

She was beginning to get interested. 'And you're saying it was because of that they . . .'

'They just ditched him – after twenty years of service.'

'But why? Was there a particular incident, do you know?'

Tadj gave her an odd look, coughed through an obstruction of mucus, but again did not answer. So it was to be a twenty questions game, was it? – with herself doing the guessing until she got it right. She fired in a very long shot.

'When did this happen? I suppose his dismissal didn't have anything to do with the Silverman expedition, did it?'

'You'd better ask him that. I wasn't born then.'

'But doesn't he talk about it ever? He comes here sometimes – Hocen told me. He must have felt very bitter. Has he never mentioned it?'

'Gérard doesn't burble.' ('Il n'use pas sa salive inutilement.')

Neither was Tadj exactly spendthrift with his saliva, she thought. But, in deference, she modified her attack. Perhaps some stealth was necessary after all.

'So, maybe because something happened at that time, or maybe at a later date, Monsieur Petit-frères loses his job as a minister. What does he do? Let me guess. He's always had an interest in anthropology, I believe? Maybe he decides to take it up more seriously. Then when Independence comes – in the sixties – unlike most of the French, he stays on here. Would that be the broad outline of the story?' Tadj shrugged, but she felt there was beginning

152

to be less resistance. 'But how did he keep alive? He can't have made much out of studying Saharan tribes.'

Something happened. Was it because they were moving from reported history to Tadj's own experience, or his father's experience reported to him? Anyway, he looked suddenly a lot nearer to communication and finally managed several sentences in a row. From him it was a speech.

'He ran a small import-export business. He was never good at it of course. He was too generous. He was absent-minded, and never finished things. He lives now on the small pension they gave him.'

'I see. But why did he choose to live here in Tifgad? Presumably he lived in Lagoued when he was in the Government?'

Tadj blew his cheeks. 'Ah, you may well ask that.'

'Well, why did he?' She made a wild guess. 'Was it a woman? Did he marry an Arab girl perhaps, and was that the reason . . .'

Tadj turned away, but not before she saw the look on his face. She knew she'd struck on something. 'No,' he said, 'he didn't marry an Arab woman.'

'But he wanted to?'

'You might say that.'

'And there was some tragedy or other? They wouldn't let him perhaps?'

She'd exhausted her luck. Apparently fatigued by such a frenetic run of consecutive speech, Tadj decided to remove his clerical operations from the counter to the table behind it where he could sit. He began laboriously to transfer the objects one by one – the ledger, the pen, then the inkpot. She waited, hoping for further revelations when this was finished. But he sat down finally and, after a lot of blowing and smoothing of the two open ledger pages, took up the pen again.

'Vous me permettez, Madame?' he said.

She tried a last sniper's shot. 'Who is Ben Abbis? Why does he meet Petit-frères here?'

Either Tadj's energy was spent or she'd strayed on to forbidden ground again. She couldn't get another syllable out of him. It was a repeat of the Petit-frères situation.

She went upstairs. Enthroned, she tried to do some creative thinking. She'd had problem-solving success before at this time.

She tried to think of Petit-frères in the light of the little she'd just learnt about him. If Petit-frères's fall from grace had happened in 1936 or some time soon after, and if it had something to do with a woman, could this be linked in some way to a dislike of Alan? Could Alan even, as with Janet Brisbane and Neil Beazley . . .

No. She realised she was clutching at straws. For a start, she had no reason to think Petit-frères's tragedy, if such it was, was contemporaneous with Alan's expedition. Tadj hadn't said so. She was on the wrong tack. What she needed to do was return to the idea of finding someone else in the town, someone who'd been alive in 1936 and who knew Petit-frères. In such a small place the events of that year must have been discussed. Petit-frères must know a lot of people. It surely shouldn't be so difficult. Maybe she could find an old mullah, she thought, in or near the mosque. But first she needed an interpreter. Ouboussad, but for his unaccountable behaviour on their trip to the cave yesterday, would have been the obvious choice. Hocen? It was worth a try.

When she went down, Hocen was alone in a corner of the empty dining-room having his own breakfast. Still embarrassed by their former exchange, he got clumsily to his feet as she approached. She sat down beside him at the table. She and Michael had already told Hocen what they were doing in Sahara, and they'd found he knew all about the expedition and what happened at the end of it. She explained she was interested in people who were alive at the time. Monsieur Petit-frères had been a little disappointing as far as information was concerned when they went to see him two days ago, she said. Did Hocen happen to know of anyone else who might be more forthcoming?

Her opinion of Hocen rose even higher. He stopped eating to reflect, but she had the idea it wasn't the first time he'd thought about this, even perhaps that he'd expected her question.

'I'll take you to someone now,' he said firmly, eyes lowered.

'Take me to someone who was alive in 1936?'

She thought Hocen looked a bit sheepish. She thought it was because he was doing something he shouldn't in working hours. 'That'd be marvellous,' she said, 'but haven't you got duties in the hotel? I wouldn't want you to get into any trouble with Monsieur Tadj . . .'

He interrupted her. 'I must go to the souk with the chef to buy food for the kitchen. We can also make the visit.'

She still wondered if she shouldn't square it with Tadj, but self-interest and a further look at their taciturn proprietor, still sitting behind the reception desk and looking even more incommunicado, convinced her. She had to go to the bank in the next street to cash a traveller's cheque. She agreed with Hocen to meet there in twenty minutes. It seemed justifiable.

There were only three clerks and a cashier visible in the tiny bank office, but it took more than twenty minutes for her simple operation to be completed. It was as if this was the first time they had been called upon to execute such a critical function of international finance. First, with numerous pauses in which he looked to see what his colleagues were doing and made remarks to them, a young man covered a whole side of paper with details from the cheque and from her passport. While the idle cashier smoked and pared his nails in his glass cage, the paper then began a leisurely circuit of the other two male employees. Claudia watched its snail-like progress from one in- or out-basket to the other, until it finally arrived with the cashier who, after completing a lengthy operation of rolling, licking and lighting a new cigarette, rose momentously for the critical act. She supposed they had to make the most of such a choice morsel of business.

But she needn't have bothered about wasting Hocen's time. It seemed he knew exactly how long her bank visit would take. Just as she hurried into the street, a car was approaching. It pulled up, with Hocen sitting in the passenger seat. It was one of those ancient black Citroens she associated with old Simenon films. Presumably, the driver was the chef, and the Citroen belonged to Monsieur Tadj. The chef and Hocen were allowed to use it for this morning chore.

She glanced at the chef's face for confirmation that all was in order. It was impassive. He didn't even look at her, let alone speak, even when Hocen courteously offered her the front seat and himself climbed into the back.

She'd thought they would be walking, so was relieved to have the lift. It was past nine o'clock and it was already stoking up. She'd no idea how far they had to go. It was in fact on the other side of the town in a suburb of small poor-looking dwellings, huddled together in a tight honeycomb, with only minute passageways between them. The chef dropped her and Hocen and went on, presumably to do the shopping. Perhaps this explained his moody silence. Without Hocen he'd have to do the humping himself this morning.

They dived into one of the alleys, Hocen leading at a furious pace. Half-naked children, playing in the dirt, stood up from their games to gape at her. Two women gossiping in a doorway drew their veils more tightly over their faces. Silently, with a kind of extra resolution, she thought, Hocen led the way.

After turning to left and right several times, they stopped by what seemed a rather better-built even quite a substantial house which had a heavy double door big enough to admit a vehicle, with a smaller one cut into it. Hocen beat on it robustly.

A voice called within and Hocen answered.

They stood there waiting. Hocen, with his head bent, stood close against the door, anxious for it to open, not speaking. They must have waited half a minute. They heard ponderous movements, and eventually a female voice muttering. At last the smaller door opened to reveal a large old woman in a thin saffron-coloured dress suitable for a teenager, which left her arms bare and revealed a fleshy cleavage of Grand Canyon proportions. She had an eccentric headdress which was bandaged on like a medieval nun's wimple, leaving only the oval of her tattooed and wrinkled old face visible – a curious paradox, Claudia thought, considering the arms and the cleavage, even for indoor wear.

The woman began questioning Hocen in Arabic. Hocen's answers were short. During this, the woman didn't look at her. She had only, initially, given her the most peripheral glance.

When the conversation finished there was a long pause. They were standing in a dark, unevenly-cobbled tunnel which led into a patio where a few scruffy hens were pecking without much enthusiasm in the dirt. The woman then looked at her suddenly – fully, almost insolently it seemed, ranging her from head to foot like a producer interviewing for the front row of the chorus. To her surprise she spoke in French. She'd imagined Hocen would have to interpret. 'Suivez-moi,' she said. She turned her back, and walked towards the patio. Claudia and Hocen followed.

It was quite a large house with two storeys. Round the patio was a wooden balcony where there were two other, younger, women leaning over the balustrade. They rapidly vanished as Claudia looked up. In the centre of the otherwise bare patio grew a huge fat palm which towered well above the roof of the house.

They went into one of the ground-floor rooms, which amazed her. It was chock-full of obviously quite valuable nineteenth century French furniture. There were half a dozen armchairs, a sofa, and a fleet of upright Empire-style chairs, all of which were upholstered in a gaudy red velvety material, the woodwork gilded. They looked as if they'd been designed for opera house boxes but had never been sat on. On the walls were large heavily-framed nondescript portraits. The room smelt musty and felt more like an antique shop than somewhere where people lived.

Their hostess lowered herself into one of the more substantial armchairs and Hocen helped her to raise her foot onto an embroidered stool. As she issued no invitation, Claudia sat in another chair. Hocen left the room without looking at her again, and was replaced by a young girl who came in with a round brass tray with two tiny cups and an Arabian Nights jug. Apparently this was standard procedure for visitors. No order seemed to have been given. The woman rapped a single syllable in Arabic and the girl poured, obediently handing Claudia a cup of the fragrant mint tea and placing the other beside her employer. The girl went out, and there was another long pause while they both sipped. The woman then put down her cup, and began speaking in strongly-patois-ed but correct and literate French. 'So you write books, eh?'

She explained. The woman's eyes misted over as soon as she mentioned Gérard Petit-frères's name and began to speak of their visit. The gaze, which had regarded her steadily, was removed to the ceiling. She was interrupted suddenly.

'Oh yes, I know Gérard Petit-frères. You've come to the right person if you want to know about him. For that matter, you've come to the right person if you want to know anything about what goes on in this town. I see everything, hear everything. Hocen says you want to know about that Englishman. I knew him, too. He was here several times. Men talk, you see. If they don't talk to me, they talk to the girls, and the girls always tell me. We're one family here.'

'You mean this place . . .'

'Didn't Hocen tell you? No, he wouldn't have. He doesn't approve of his Aunt Jezi doing what she does. But he's a good boy, Hocen. Got a head on

157

his shoulders. He knew where to bring you all right.'

Claudia recalled the girls on the balcony, Hocen's embarrassment – as she now understood his reticence to be – and plunged. She saw no point in being devious. Aunt Jezi was apparently willing to be frank with her. 'You run – an establishment?'

'I was brought up here. My mother had it before me, and her mother before that. I took it over in the early thirties when my mother died. I'm nearly ninety, you know.' She gave a humourless laugh. 'It's the most important building in Tifgad – a lot more important than the "mairie" certainly.'

Like the Oasis Hotel, it seemed, it was another once-thriving family business – maybe, unlike the hotel, still thriving to some degree. Claudia was given further enriching information about the enterprise, a great deal of which was about the colonial period when – as with Tadj's hotel no doubt – she was to understand times were so much better than under 'ces gens-là.' It wasn't until she began a long inventory of the celebrities who'd purchased her wares, that Claudia saw a chance to bring her to heel. Would she be equally revealing on more specific topics?

'And I suppose Gérard Petit-frères, Minister of Justice in the French Government, was a particularly interesting client?'

Jezi halted, and gave her another piercing look. 'Ah yes, I was forgetting. You want to know about poor Gérard. Well I don't see why not. Nobody in town knows as much about him as I do. I saw most of it happen under this roof. And the main lines of the story are well enough known. Gérard won't mind me telling you.' She paused, with an arch look. 'You'll be mentioning me in your book, I suppose?'

'Not if you don't want me to.'

She looked affronted. 'Oh, I've no objection. It's about time someone gave me a bit of credit for a change. I've lived all my life in this backwater, but I'm not a nobody, you know. You put my name in – that'll do something to put the record straight.' She smiled rather charmingly. 'Someone important might read it. Never too late, is it?' She again raised her eyes dreamily to the heavily-moulded ceiling from which hung a huge but apparently no longer functional fan.

'The girl – Sawsan – was beautiful, but a nobody. Her father was a clerk in the post-office here. In those days under the French, Arab women had more freedom than they do today. A few even had jobs, like Sawsan. She worked as a maid in the Oasis Hotel. Gérard used to come to the town at week-ends for his hobby. He was interested in old tribes, and went off on treks into the desert. It wasn't long before he spotted Sawsan, or rather – the way it was – it wasn't long before Sawsan spotted him. As soon as he realised she was interested in him, Gérard was helpless.

'Gérard had been to this house once. It wasn't a happy occasion. He wasn't the sort of man for what we were offering. But he liked me, because I understood his problem and was kind to him. It was only a month or two after this that he met Sawsan and came to ask me to help him.

'I didn't like what he asked, I can tell you. You don't get into what he wanted in my business unless you're a fool. For a start, what would the girl's father think of me if he knew, which he soon would in a place like this? In a few weeks I might have no business at all. And anyway – I thought of the girl. You can imagine what might happen. I give them a room to meet in, they make love, maybe he gets her pregnant, a type like him, minister or not, wouldn't know how to take precautions in those days, or wouldn't bother, and eventually she's dropped. Arab familes are strict, where would she be then? That isn't the way I like to recruit my family.

'But things were unusual. First, Sawsan wasn't just beautiful, she was bright and had a strong will. As soon as I met her, I could see she wasn't the little flower type I'd expected. That first time she came here she told me exactly what she wanted. She wanted to leave Tifgad, she said. She wanted to marry a rich Frenchman and live in a luxurious villa on the south coast of France.

'You can imagine how I reacted to that – she, an oasis town girl whose father was a clerk. But what I said made no difference. I might not have spoken.

'The other unusual thing was Gérard. Not just that he was a minister in the Government and therefore very much a feather in my cap as well as hers. What was clear from the start was that he didn't want to have sex with the girl, not at once anyway, and not on my property. What he wanted was just to meet her in a discreet place – in this room, he said – so they could get to know each other. He said he wanted to marry Sawsan and that eventually – when he'd given her an opportunity to know him better and decide if she wanted him – he'd be speaking to the family.

'I'll admit he was willing to pay for the service I was giving him, but I swear that wasn't the only thing. I didn't think Sawsan would succeed with her plan, and told her so, but I really did want to help her. Perhaps, I thought, because she was unusual, and Gérard was the man he was, she might just achieve the impossible. Stranger things have happened, and as long as she didn't get pregnant, what harm was there?

'I was surprised. I could see Gérard wasn't up to much as a man, but I didn't expect to see a high-ranking Frenchman like him used in the way Sawsan used him. She told him she wasn't going to marry him unless he provided her with that villa in France. I remember telling her she ought to drop her sights a bit. If she wasn't careful, I told her, she'd lose him. No Frenchman, let alone a Government minister, was going to be pushed around like that by a poor Arab girl. But she wouldn't give up. One day Gérard himself told me what she was asking. He said that he'd willingly give up his job here and find one in France but, though not exactly stint, he'd never saved – he'd spent most of his salary on his hobby – and knew he didn't have anything like the money he'd need to satisfy what Sawsan had in mind.

'I told him to keep on and Sawsan would see reason. I even suggested he went to see the family and got them on his side. But Sawsan was one move ahead.

'One week-end they didn't come here, and I learnt that Sawsan had left her home. She'd made Gérard rent her a flat in Lagoued. It's my view she'd already seen Gérard didn't have the kind of money she'd set her sights on. I think she thought it all out before she went to Lagoued. If Gérard couldn't give her what she wanted, she was going to use him to find someone else who could. It wasn't long before she met someone else, another Frenchman, who was rich and lived in France. He was only visiting Sahara. She married him – and still is married to him, I believe.

'Gérard was heartbroken. It wasn't long after this that he lost his job and came here to start a business and to live. He said he wanted to be near all his memories of Sawsan. For a time he continued to come and see me occasionally. He never wanted a girl. I don't believe he's ever looked at another woman. What he wanted was a friend and, though I was younger than he was, a mother. But then he stopped coming for some reason. I guess he didn't like me telling him he ought to forget Sawsan – who'd never have been any good for him – and find another girl. I haven't seen him for years now. It's sad, a good man like him going to waste when there are so many rotten men about treating women like dirt.'

Tantalisingly, the woman broke off from the story and looked aside wistfully. 'But I envy Sawsan. I could have got out of here, too, if I'd played my cards better. There were Frenchmen who came here for my girls, plenty of them, as rich as the one Sawsan got. I wasn't bad-looking. I could have had a place bought for me in Paris and be there now. Lagoued at least,' she amended more realistically.

She began to talk again about her own life and its missed opportunities. She embarked on what threatened to be a long list of the Frenchmen who could have been her saviour and the father of her children, had she not been thinking of her girls. Claudia understood now why she'd been so open with her. She had a lot to unload.

But Claudia remembered what her own purpose was. She had eventually to interrupt quite rudely, or the interview might have run away from her. 'You said you also knew Sir Alan Silverman,' she said, as gently as she could, 'the famous English archaeologist who was here in the thirties.'

It took Jezi a moment or two to detach herself from her memories. She was staring at the wall, as if her past was being visually displayed on it by some hidden projector. 'Eh,' she said – that Arabic vowel sound that comes from half-way down the throat.

'You knew Silverman, the archaeologist?'

Her expression changed rapidly. 'Oh yes, I knew him all right.'

'It doesn't sound as if you have very good memories of him.'

Her more pragmatic tone returned. 'The Englishman was all right – except he was about as mean as you can get, mean as a stone. He'll bargain with Allah if he ever gets the chance, which I doubt – he'll never find himself in those regions, I fear. Tried to beat me down when he came here first. He said the girls weren't pretty enough for him and didn't have big enough breasts. I knew how to deal with him all right. If he didn't pay money down in advance he didn't get a girl – that was simple. But others in the town he'd bought things from weren't so lucky – poor people who couldn't afford to be stood up. He left debts when he went.'

'He came here often?'

'When he first came to Tifgad, yes. Three or four times. Always wanted the best. Went through the girls as if it was a pair of shoes he was buying before he made up his mind. Then he took up with a girl on his expedition.

They used to meet in the Oasis Hotel, they told me. I didn't see him again until about the last day he was here.'

'Really? You mean he came for a girl?'

'No. As I told you, he was fixed up in that direction. He came here to meet Gérard Petit-frères.' Claudia's pulses skipped a beat or two. 'Petit-frères?'

'Gérard phoned me from Lagoued one afternoon. It was after Sawsan had gone to Lagoued with him and I still hoped they'd be married. I thought at first he was coming here to speak to the parents. But he made it plain on the phone it was someone else he was meeting, a man. He was coming that evening after dark and he wanted it to be kept quiet. It turned out to be the Englishman. They sat in this room an hour or more, talking.'

Aunt Jezi was showing signs of boredom, or perhaps she was tired. Her vigour easily made one forget how old she was. She began to collect herself together. She leaned forwards to ease her leg off the stool. Any moment Claudia thought she'd call for Hocen.

'But what did they talk about?'

'How should I know? Business, I suppose. They'd known each other some time, I think.'

'Gérard gave no hint afterwards why they'd met?'

'I know one thing – he was pleased about it, whatever it was.'

'But what could he have been pleased about, do you think?'

'I don't know. If you want to know you'd better ask him, hadn't you – if he'll see you? He lives like a mole these days.'

'And Silverman said nothing to you about the meeting, either?'

'The Englishman never said anything to anyone unless it was in his interest and, as I tell you, this was the last time I saw him. Hocen,' she shrieked suddenly. 'Well, I hope I've told you what you want. I'm sorry for Gérard. He's a fool, but he can't help being that, and he did love that girl. If she hadn't been one in ten thousand he might have had a happy life even though he lost his job with the French. Maybe you can put the record straight for him, too, when you write your book. And don't forget to say Jezi told you all about it.'

There were a host more questions Claudia wanted to ask, but she knew that even if Jezi had some of the answers she wasn't going to get them. For whatever reason, she'd had enough.

Hocen entered. Jezi spoke a few Arabic words to him. He turned back to the door, making a gesture to her to accompany him. She rose. Jezi had clasped her ring-laden hands in her lap and was staring at them. Claudia thanked her, and followed Hocen.

Hocen led the way to the front door, opened it to let her pass, and when they were both in the alley, banged it shut behind them so that the lock caught. They returned to the main street without speaking. The chef and the Citroen were waiting. They got in.

As they drove off, Hocen remained silent. He turned away from her, looking out of the window. She wanted him to know she was grateful and that he needn't be embarrassed about Jezi on her account.

'Your aunt is a kind, intelligent woman,' she said.

He didn't answer, and didn't change his position, but she thought the tension slackened a little. Then her attention was distracted. She noticed in the driving mirror a helmeted male figure on a motor scooter driving behind them. She remembered she'd noticed him on the way here. He must be tailing them. The vehicle was issuing a cloud of blue smoke. It accompanied them almost all the way back to the hotel, and only at the last moment shot off into a side street.

It chilled her at a moment when she was beginning to feel rather pleased with herself for her morning's work, but she didn't mention this to Hocen. He'd done quite enough for her for one day. She had the idea he wouldn't want any further conversation about his aunt.

She wrenched herself from worrying about the motor-cyclist by thinking about Hocen. She thought she should give him money. She decided not to. Maybe he wouldn't like it. She'd give him a very generous tip when they left. At the hotel she just thanked him warmly.

17.

The heat was rising inexorably again. When Claudia got inside the hotel and Hocen had disappeared with the chef, she felt exhausted and parched with thirst. Iced water was a necessity. She peered through the open door behind the reception desk. Tadj didn't seem to be there. With no energy or inclination to find Hocen again, she slumped into one of the tattered armchairs in the hall. She supposed Tadj would appear in a moment.

Sitting in the semi-darkess, she found herself unaccountably depressed. Surely her morning had to be accounted something of a success? Was it the motor-cyclist who was upsetting her? He'd certainly renewed all her apprehensions which Michael had so pooh-poohed. But that surely didn't account for the force of her feeling. She went back over her visit to Jezi and no immediate explanation offered. Petit-frères's story, sad as it was, had told her nothing especially about Alan. After all, she'd known Alan knew Petit-frères and guessed that he'd probably made use of him in some way. It wasn't also exactly startling news to hear Alan had been with a prostitute or two during his life.

She realised then what was at the back of her mind. It wasn't the way she was interpreting what she'd heard that was getting to her at all, it was what Michael would make of it. Michael of course was going to say it was obvious why the two men had met. He'd say Silverman had some kind of a hold over the minister – probably his knowledge of his affair with the girl – and he'd used it to force Petit-frères to help him out of his 'predicament.'

Why should she care whatever Michael's self-interested imagination came up with? The hypothesis he'd construct about Alan's meeting with Petit-frères, whatever it was, would be no more mind-boggling a piece of conclusion-jumping than any he'd indulged in so far. Her depressing discovery was that she did care. In plainer words, could she any longer feel so hundred per cent sanguine of her own point of view? If she was right about the skeleton in the cave, it would be fine. But supposing the skull sitting upstairs did prove to be Beazley's, and the perforations traceable in some way to

Alan's gun? How then would she interepret this clandestine and possibly hastily arranged meeting between the two men just at the time of Beazley's disappearance? Not, certainly, to cover up a murder committed by Alan and to frame Beri for it – she'd never easily bring herself to believe that. But for some less than honourable purpose? That had surely now at least to be entertained.

She faced it head on. Could it be then that in some fundamental way she'd been wrong from the start about a man she'd known and studied daily for several months, a man the nation had honoured, a man who with very few exceptions had charmed, amused and interested pretty well everyone he had come into contact with? Would it any longer be reasonable to reject the idea that, for whatever purpose, Alan might perhaps have blackmailed a lovesick Frenchman? If he had, she might have to revise her whole approach to the biography, possibly even abandon it. Far worse, she thought, would she have to admit – as Michael had so casually suggested – that hitherto her own viewpoint had been conditioned, conditioned by the mores of her social position, to believe what the nation did? Could she face that?

Hot, angry, finally confused, she again had an impulse of weakness. She'd go home and wash her hands of it, she thought. Tifgad, as she'd always realised, was only a small part of Silverman's long life and career, whatever circumstances might have made him do at a particular juncture. Let a triumphant Strode set about his grizzly self-remunerative research alone, while she got out of this disagreeable and quite possibly dangerous place to continue with the much larger picture of a man's whole life.

The thought did not diminish her depression. Tadj was still nowhere in the offing. Luke-warm bottled water would have to suffice to quench her thirst. She went upstairs. Her room being next to Michael's, she had to pass his door and noticed it was ajar. She hadn't seen a femme de chambre about, but there must be one, for her bed had been made after both nights. She unlocked her own door. Then something made her have second thoughts. She went back into the corridor and listened. There was no sound from Michael's room. She pushed the door fully open.

She was confronted by chaos. There wasn't much in these entirely functional rooms, but someone had done their best with the few items there were. The bed was turned on its side, the mattress ripped from end to end.

A chest of drawers had been searched, the drawers left pulled out, the wardrobe door hung open. Michael had taken his bag, but not all his things. These were scattered over the floor where they'd been flung.

She thought again of the sinister figure on the motor-scooter, the glint she had seen on the further mountainside opposite the cave, and for a moment was plain scared. Someone pretty ruthless had been after something. Of course – the skull, she thought. Presumably it had been found and taken. She couldn't see how an object that size could be concealed for long in this room.

She rushed downstairs, shouting. Hocen appeared, and she sent him scuttling for Tadj. In a few moments Tadj appeared in a dressing-gown. She thought he'd been shaving, he was bleeding in several places.

'Monsieur Tadj, my friend's room has been ransacked – I guess in the last hour or so. Presumably not by one of your staff.'

Tadj was not greatly perturbed. Puffing and wheezing, he seemed more concerned with getting his spectacles perched on his nose. Claudia thought he was about to disappear again to put his clothes on, which could take half an hour. She made him come upstairs with her as he was. Viewing the chaos, he blew his cheeks out.

Emotion overtook her. 'Who has done this?' she shouted. He heaved his massive shoulders. 'You mean you don't care? Your hotel is invaded in this brutal way, your client's property is attacked as well as yours. I ask you again, who is capable of an act like this?'

He raised a hand the size of a ping-pong bat and oscillated it. 'Such things, in Sahara, are not uncommon these days.'

'You mean you're going to do nothing about it? Not even inform the police?' He made a noise she had to assume was a laugh. 'You mean, it's the police who are responsible? But why . . .'

Why indeed? But another thought had taken precedence. How had she not had it before? This could surely only be an act of the state, and if this was an act of the state how was Michael faring in Lagoued? So much for his idea that the Government would be pleased to see him. For whatever reason, or none at all, he could be in danger. She controlled her anger, gave up on Tadj, and told him to give Michael another room or repair the damage to this one. She herself picked up his bestrewn belongings and put them on top of the chest of drawers.

She knew Michael's appointment had been for ten – three hours ago – but she had to try to reach and warn him. After more bullying from her, and a great deal of grampus-like blowing from Tadj as he pored over an out-of-date telephone directory, she got the number of the hotel in Lagoued, whose name she'd fortunately heard Michael say when phoning for a room.

Mr Strode was registered, yes – he had checked in last night – but he was not present in his room, nor anywhere else in the hotel. Yes, he must have gone out. She left a message for him to call her at once when he got in, and said it was urgent.

Claudia no longer thought of going home. The violence in Michael's room set her adrenalin moving. She went up to her room again to think. Until Michael phoned she could do nothing to help him. But couldn't she in some way pursue the information about Petit-frères she'd gleaned?

It came to her suddenly. Could he somehow be involved with this assault? She could see at once, once having had the thought, how this could be. If he had connived with Alan in some way, any new evidence of what had happened could be dangerous for him. He would surely want to remove it. Was it possible that Ouboussad was working for him, that Ouboussad had followed them to the cave after all and had seen the bulge in Michael's rucksack? They had said nothing of what they had found in the cave on the journey home, but could he have put two and two together and reported to Petit-frères? Ouboussad, or some other hireling of Petit-frères, might be responsible for this assault on Michael's room. Another thought occurred to her – the cigarette butt she'd seen near the entrance to the cave. Perhaps she'd been wrong to think the skeleton had been planted. Perhaps it was Beazley's, perhaps it had been there all the time, and the cigarette butt had been dropped by someone else Petit-frères had sent recently, after he'd received Michael's letter and before their arrival in Sahara, to try to find the body – as it turned out, unsuccessfully.

It was not an idea which appealed much to her, but shouldn't she try to see Petit-frères again after all? If he was acting in this hostile way, he would hardly be hand in glove with the authorities whom he would certainly not wish to know what he was up to. Could she somehow use the information she'd gained from Jezi to try to get some sort of cooperation from him? It was surely better than sitting here doing nothing. Maybe, by letting him suspect

167

she knew more than she did of his story, by showing him she sympathised and that she and Michael would protect whatever part he'd played in 1936, she could get him to help Michael if he needed it – and even, she thought secondarily, at the same time extract a more detailed statement from him about his relations with Alan?

She decided to phone him. The line buzzed, but didn't ring. She got Tadj to speak to the operator. Apparently, the number hadn't been disconnected. Either by mistake or on purpose it must be off the hook. She wasn't going to phone Ouboussad, and couldn't face the midday heat without a taxi – anyway, she was expecting Michael to phone at any minute. She had some lunch, asked Hocen if he'd listen for the phone in case Tadj proved non-functional, and went upstairs for the daily endurance of the afternoon inferno, determining if Michael hadn't phoned, to walk down to the oasis as soon as the heat was anything like bearable.

There was no call from Michael. Soon after five, she found the temperature had dropped a little. She got up. She phoned the Lagoued hotel again. Michael hadn't returned. She left a message with Tadj that if Michael phoned when she was out he was to tell him what had happened upstairs, and also to ask him to stay in his hotel without fail until she called him back. She tried Petit-frères's number again with the same result as before, and went out. There was enough shadow at this time to keep out of the direct sun for most of the way to the oasis. Nonetheless, in a couple of minutes she was streaming with sweat.

Petit-frères's gate was locked with a padlock and chain, which it hadn't had before. The windows of the house were shuttered and barred. She pressed the electric bell, and it peeled loudly – like one of those railway station bells. There was not a stir – no dog, no boy. Could he have died, she thought, or taken his own life? She dismissed this. If he had, the boy would have surely have reported it. There was every sign that, for whatever reason, Petit-frères had disconnected his phone and gone away.

Claudia thought vaguely she should tell someone about Petit-frères, just in case, but when it came to it she found she was too preoccupied with Michael. Whom would she tell anyway? She spent time sitting at the so-called bar in the hall, drinking a bottle of Algerian wine Hocen had conjured, talking to the oil men who had just come in. On the other side of the hall was the mouthpiece of that absurd telephone protruding from the wall. It remained doggedly silent.

At half past six she phoned the Lagoued hotel again. The reception man, having answered her call, kept her waiting five minutes while he seemed to be dealing with several people. At last, still talking to someone else, he picked up the phone again. He focused rapidly on her anxious question, however, and answered with disconcerting certainty. No, Mr Strode hadn't returned to the hotel and hadn't had her message. There was a slight pause. 'He's no longer registered,' he added nastily.

'You mean he checked out? Then why didn't he get my message?'

Another pause. 'He didn't get your message because he didn't check himself out.'

'You mean he sent someone else to do it?'

'The police came to search his room, Madame.' The 'madame' had an acid tone.

'The police?'

'We were told he wouldn't be returning.'

She began to remonstrate. It was scandalous, she railed. Mr Strode was an ordinary western journalist going about his business. She knew this was pointless and, indeed, in a moment or two realised she was talking to a dialing tone.

Claudia was used to thinking of herself as a reasonably resourceful person, even the sort others might turn to in a crisis. But Michael's sardonic view of her sheltered bourgeois existence never seemed as close to the truth as it did now. What was she to do? What could she do? Phone the British Consul if there was one, knowing how they might regard Michael's visit here? Phone The Times? What would they care about a freelance who, probably without their knowledge, let alone their blessing, had gone out on a limb?

It took her a moment or two to realise that of course she did have to try to contact the Consul. However un-grata Michael might be, it was a consul's duty to do his best to protect any British citizen, wasn't it? She'd gathered that in Sahara evening working hours were five until eight, but would the consulate still be open at this time? She began the nightmare of trying to get through on that phone. There was a consulate and the number was in the directory, but there must have been a caravan of camels on the line somewhere. At last she got a frosty English female, into whose ear she gave her name, and Michael's, and poured out her predicament.

'I see,' the woman said when she'd finished, her tone already admonishing such a display of emotion. 'Well I'm afraid the Consul has just gone home, but I'll certainly tell him what you've said in the morning.'

'In the morning?'

'There's nothing he could do this evening anyway, I'm afraid. All the Ministries will be closing just about now.'

'But the police?'

'I think you said it concerned the Ministry of Culture?'

She made up her mind in this moment. Michael had said there were two buses a day to Lagoued. It was too late for the evening one. She'd go in the morning. She told the woman this, and said she'd call the Consul in the morning on her arrival.

'Very well, Mrs Drake.' The tone was now of a headmistress dealing with a wayward child.

In view of Ouboussad's untrustworthiness, she had to walk to the square where the souk was held, as Michael had done the evening before last. As the bus left at six, she had to start a good hour before. She was afraid Tadj would oversleep again, but all went well. The chef was also up to give her breakfast. By just after five she was on her way through the dark deserted streets with her overnight grip, expecting to be stopped at any moment.

She wasn't stopped, there were only six other people on the bus, and the journey was uneventful apart from the most beautiful dawn. Entering Lagoued, the route went right past the five storey hotel where Michael had booked. She saw its name suddenly – 'Le Cosmopolite' – in Latin script as well as Arabic. The driver allowed her to get off.

She suspected the receptionist was the man she'd spoken to on the phone. He looked at her with a little-concealed sneer as she asked for a room. She knew it was useless to ask if Michael had returned. There was a stack of newspapers on the counter, in Arabic. She decided if she was already identified as an acquaintance of Michael's, she wasn't going to lose anything by being open. She asked the man if there was anything about Michael on the front page. She was handed her key wordlessly, as he turned away to deal with someone else.

The room was air-conditioned with a modern bathroom, and it had a telephone. She allowed herself a few minutes to wash after the journey and to cool down. Then she called the British Consul. The same woman answered. There was no improvement in her manner. The Consul was not in, she was told, but he had been informed of her friend's 'alleged' arrest and he would be making enquiries. Claudia told her where she was. The woman said she was sure the Consul would call her when he had some information. Claudia asked if she thought he'd want to see her. She was told he probably would, but first wished to find out what had happened, 'if anything.'

Claudia couldn't be sure how strenuous and prompt the Consul's efforts to help Michael would be, and she decided to do some research of her own. It might not endear her to the Consul if he found out, but she asked the hotel operator to get her the Ministry of Culture and – a forlorn hope – to try to get the minister himself for her. She told him to say her name, that she was a British writer, and that her call concerned the disappearance of a British journalist, Mr Michael Strode. She thought the operator might refuse, or at best put her through to the ministry and dump her there, but he told her quite courteously to hang up and that he'd call her back.

The bell shrilled in about ten minutes. She was connected with a male voice speaking almost perfect English. 'Is that Mrs Drake?' She said it was. 'Please wait in your hotel. A car will arrive for you.' She asked him who he was. 'Kindly wait in the hotel,' he repeated.

She felt a gust of anger. This wasn't just faulty English, it was the usual arrogance towards women. 'How can I just get in a car without knowing where I'm going?' she asked. There was a curious hesitation for a moment, but then whoever it was rang off.

She found her pulses were thumping away like the Muppet Show band. She was stark crazy, she thought, coming here and walking straight into the jaws. A cautionary voice told her she should certainly phone the Consulate again and at least tell them what she was doing in case she got arrested, too. But she ignored the warning. It was only too obvious what that woman would say, and she found she did want to speak to these people directly. There was no need to be diplomatic. Logic and the simple truth were surely all that were required. Neither she nor Michael were doing anything against Saharan interests.

She spent the next minutes dolling herself up. Not excessively – a clean

171

white shirt to go with her yellow cotton skirt was all she had to change into. But she did a spot of work on her face.

The phone buzzed again. It was reception saying the car had arrived. Was it her optimism or was there a humbler note? She went down in the lift. As the doors opened, a tall smart Arab in a very white sheet, rather jazzy sandals with gold buckles on his bare feet, and full headdress – which she'd always found attractive – was waiting for her. He wore dark glasses, through which he glanced at her. He inclined his head fractionally and began to walk towards the front door. She followed, trying not to feel like a pet dog.

Parked outside under the awning which stretched across the pavement, was a vast Mercedes, one of those King-size ones with darkened windows and three rows of seats which make one think of Godfathers and street massacres. A driver leapt from his seat and sprinted round to open the rearward of the three doors. Her escort motioned her to get in. He climbed in after her, having slipped money disdainfully into the palm of the hotel flunkey who'd been beaten to the door-opening by the agile driver.

The car was air-conditioned. They glided off in cool silence, blaring at sparse traffic which consisted mostly, apart from jay-walkers, of animals – mules, a skinny horse or two, and camels. Claudia glanced at her highly-scented companion who had seized a tassel hanging from the side of the car and was looking straight in front of him. She could see conversation wasn't going to flow, in English or French. She turned to look out of the window, remembering stories of European women being carried off by Arabs never to be seen again.

It was soon apparent they weren't bound for a ministry building. They were leaving the town. She felt a surge, not so much of fear, as of anger again. 'Look, I think it'd be at least courteous if you told me where we're going,' she said in French. There wasn't a flinch. She resigned herself. In truth there was nothing else she could do.

They were soon out of the town on a good metaled road heading west. They passed a line of camels loaded with sacks and their pedestrian tenders, journeying towards the town. The flat landscape was parched and utterly devoid of vegetation. Claudia suddenly had an idea where they might be going.

In the Tifgad hotel yesterday she'd idly glanced at the one newspaper in Sahara written in French. The lead story and colour picture of the front page

172

was of the President, Djebal, meeting some foreign dignitary, an African – she hadn't taken in from which state. The two men were standing at the top of some plushly carpeted steps in front of a large building. The Presidential Palace? She remember noting it was not in Lagoued but outside somewhere. They were approaching a fork in the road. They went right. The signpost said, 'Ain Mokhtar' in both scripts. That, she remembered, was the name of the place.

Trust a man like Djebal to pick himself a spot like Mokhtar, Claudia thought. It was about twenty miles out of the town, a private oasis in the middle of nowhere. She'd seen a curious feature ahead of them for some time, a little posse of unreal-looking pinkish hills rising from the shimmering rock plain. The oasis was inside these hills, which seemed to be of the same rock as the mountains where Alan had found the hoard. Some sort of hardy residual, she supposed, which erosion had separated from the main massif.

She saw the oasis as they breasted a shallow col between two of the hills, much larger than the one in Tifgad beside which Petit-frères had pitched his bungalow, and not as closely cultivated. It was thickly palmed, however, and in pockets were clustered some kind of a desert bush – a variety of cactus – which was covered with scarlet blooms. The palace was a huge concrete monstrosity, relieved only by a wide green canopy over the front door, built a little way up the hillside.

Her companion made a small movement, and she glanced at him out of the corner of her eye. Did she imagine a slight diminution in the arrogance of his mien? Was the bully about to enter a domain where he was bullied? It didn't encourage her.

They swept to the green canopy, and the front steps she recognised from the newspaper photo. They were still covered with a red carpet. A soldier with a machine-gun approached, one of three who were visible, and opened her escort's door. The Arab got out and waited for her to follow. They mounted the steps, passed through glass doors which parted for them, and entered a huge marble-floored hall.

It was an incredible thing to find in the middle of a desert. It was like stepping inside a huge refrigerator. The place was ice-cool. There were several fountains plashing, one cascading down an illuminated wall of simulated ice. There was foliage everywhere, and two or three tropical plants in massive bloom. On one side a flamboyant staircase, also marble, mounted to a huge mural of Tintoretto proportions. It was similar also to that artist's work in that it was densely populated with figures. There any similarity ended. The work seemed to depict the idealised socialist endeavour of mixed races. It was crudely painted in garish colours.

She was led to a sumptuously furnished room, which had a table entirely made of glass, a magnificent woolly wall-to-wall white carpet, luxurious damask curtains of a light blue colour and leather armchairs to match.

'Wait,' she was told again. Her escort departed.

There was again no option. Having admired the view of the oasis below, she sat in one of the chairs, thinking what an obscenity all this was in a country so desperately poor, and wondering if Socialist purity had yet even thought about eliminating the subjection of women. On the evidence of her escort's behaviour to her it certainly hadn't. Was she about to be added to the harem? Illogically, she caught herself glancing in her hand-mirror.

She was kept waiting about half an hour. What amazed her was the silence. Presumably the place was teeming with people, but she couldn't hear a sound. At last there were two or three footsteps beyond heavy double doors on the inner side of the room. The doors opened and another extremely handsome man appeared, this one bareheaded and rather European-looking, in a well-cut lightweight white suit, pink shirt and tie to match.

'The President is ready to receive you, Madame Drake,' he said. He spoke in Parisian French, but she knew at once it was the man who had spoken to her on the phone earlier.

She hadn't realised she'd been sitting next to what seemed to be Djebal's office. It must be Djebal, surely, who sat, also in a shiny suit – of lilac hue – at a gleaming semi-circular desk in the centre of the room, which was much larger than the one in which she'd waited but similarly furnished. She then recognised him from the photograph in the paper – just. Without his headgear he looked very much what he probably had once been, a small-time thug. There were smallpox marks in the centre of one cheek, two gold teeth showed, and it didn't look as if he'd shaved for a day or two. He didn't get up, but leaned back staring at her. One of his eyes had something wrong with it.

The man who had come to collect her took up position at his side. Folding his arms, he peered over them at his feet, his eyebrows raised.

174

Claudia had the distinct impression he wanted her to know he didn't approve of his master.

Neither invited her to sit down. There was a chair on her side of the desk. She sat on it in as composed a way as she could muster and waited, trying to make her face look as if it was expecting an explanation for her virtual abduction and that it had better be a good one. She doubted if she succeeded.

'Why have you come to Sahara?' Djebal rapped in abominable French.

She thought for starters she'd keep it as haughty as her own French allowed. 'As I told your consulate in London when I obtained my visa, I'm writing a biography of Sir Alan Silverman, the archaeologist who led an expedition here in 1936.'

'But you're here with a journalist.'

'Mr Strode's newspaper is also interested in the expedition. Mr Strode thinks there were irregularities in Sir Alan's account of his discovery which, you may know, he wants to investigate. Our interests are different but there was clearly good reason to travel together.'

'That's a cover. You're spies, both of you, sent by your Government. Strode's confessed.'

The bottom fell out of her stomach like the trap of a scaffold. 'Where is Mr Strode?' she managed to say. 'If you've arrested him you've no right to. He's an ordinary journalist . . .'

'You know what we do with spies in this country, Madame Drake?'

'We aren't spies.'

'We shoot them. Strode will be shot.'

'This is madness. Michael Strode's interests are Sahara's. He wants to prove Silverman lied, even that he may have taken part in a crime. If he finds what he hopes to find, Sahara's case for the return of the Carthaginian hoard will be greatly strengthened. The Times has already . . .'

Djebal's protuberant eyes seemed to protrude even more. He rose, and shouted. 'You're spies. We have information. Make her talk Salek – and fast. The matter must be cleared at once.'

He left the room.

Claudia was immediately sure that Mohammed Salek, the Minister of Culture, whom Michael had gone to Lagoued to see, was her only hope. She certainly didn't trust him an inch, and knew she had to keep her wits sharpened, but all her instincts told her he was at least, unlike Djebal, an educated, cultured man.

He continued to give every evidence of this. As Djebal closed the door behind him he seemed to relax. He smiled pleasantly, as if a disagreeable irrelevance had been removed. He eased the cuffs of his suit and switched to his immaculate English.

'Shall we sit more comfortably, Mrs Drake?' They adjourned to the leather upholstery. 'Would you care for something to drink?' he enquired, as if they had dropped in to Phyllis Court at Henley Regatta.

'What I want is Michael Strode's instant release.'

He smiled indulgently at such naivety. 'No drink? Are you sure? Very well, we'd better plunge straight in then, hadn't we? It's true, I'm afraid, that I do work for a man of – executive habits.' He paused, and sighed, as if again to rue the vulgarity of the man he was forced to serve. 'So, you think that what Mr Strode, or you, or both of you wish to find might be of interest to my country?'

'Of course it is. Mr Strode thinks Silverman killed Beazley, one of his British assistants. If that's true, it'll surely improve your chances of getting the Carthaginian collection back here.'

'Why would that be so?'

'You would surely know better than I would. The international scandal you'd be able to stir – are stirring? Isn't that what you want?'

Salek blinked affectedly. 'That could be so – if such a thing turned out to have happened – certainly.' He paused thoughtfully, looking at her with an intensity she found very uncomfortable. 'And this is what you think, too, is it? That Silverman was a murderer. You use qualifying words, I notice.'

She could see the man was clever. He'd already picked up her reservations about Alan's guilt. She made a quick calculation. There was no need to mention anything about Petit-frères and about what Jezi had told her, but what was to stop her relating what had happened in the cave? He might know already, but she surely had the best chance of winning his confidence by being open.

'My view of Silverman, as his biographer, has hitherto been mostly a sympathetic one. When I first came here, frankly I didn't agree with Michael Strode, whose view seemed to be sensationalist and not based on evidence.

But though I'm quite honestly still not sure Silverman could have done something so evil, what has happened in the last day or two has forced me to question my previous opinion.'

She was still sure he must know everything already. Could she really doubt now that it was he, not Petit-frères, who was behind the hidden sleuth who'd tailed them, that it was he who had ordered Michael's room to be raided? But if this was so, it was even more reason to be as accurate as possible. She told him about their visit to the cave and of their discovery. She mentioned the skull and the bullet holes in it, and said they'd taken the latter back to Tifgad. She didn't mention the cigarette butt, nor her suspicions they were being watched. She also told him about the raid on Michael's room and the disappearance of the skull. While she spoke, Salek gave nothing away. Throughout, he continued to look languid and maintained a faint smile of incredulity. She knew nonetheless he was listening to every syllable. Was he hoping to trip her up?

When she'd done she felt parched. 'I'd like that drink after all,' she said. He went to the door, called out something, and returned. Until the drink came – glorious iced orange-juice made from fresh fruit – it was Henley Regatta again. He did actually talk about England where he'd been to school, he told her, at Stowe. He was also fascinated by royalty, another distinctly unsocialist enthusiasm. Was he some sort of well-born Saharan Talleyrand, she thought, who had by guile survived the transition from colonialism to revolutionary independence? What was for sure was that, charming as he could make himself, he was almost certainly a twister of cobra-like proportions.

When the man who brought her drink had retired – Salek didn't have a drink himself – he crossed his legs with conscious elegance, easing his trousers at the knee, and clasped his hands like a priest. 'Well now, this is a most interesting statement you have made, interesting from several points of view. A special highlight of course is your discovery of these mortal remains. Forgive me, but a small matter comes to mind about that. You and your colleague come out here – with no prior consultation with my ministry, which one would have expected from a newspaper like The Times – and on the very first day of your enquiries you stumble upon the very thing you're looking for. Forgive my scepticism, but was it only your undoubted powers of deduction which led you so rapidly to the right place?'

'No – that is, partly it was, yes. As Silverman's biographer I had all his material, including a detailed diary he kept during the expedition. This enabled us to find the cave where the hoard was discovered – and also, it appears, where the murder took place. But having found the cave – and the breach in the rock fault behind which the hoard was hidden – it was entire luck that made us come upon this pit in a lower level of the cave, and what lay in it. It was just about the only place we saw where a body might have been thrown. Frankly . . .'

She checked herself. Was it mad to be giving everything away like this? Michael might have said nothing and would be furious if they ever saw each other again. Madder still was she to say anything that could be offensive. But she was committed now. She felt Salek was watching her with a kind of infra-red penetration which would enable him to know the moment she deviated from the truth.

'"Frankly?"' he prompted. 'Frankly what, Mrs Drake?'

It came out in a rush. 'Mr Strode doesn't agree with me, but I had a distinct feeling that what we'd stumbled on was not a coincidence. I had the feeling it had been set up.'

'You mean you think someone had put the bones there for you to find?'

'Yes. There were several odd things. While I was waiting for Strode just inside the entrance to the cave I thought I saw something move outside – on the further mountainside. I could have been mistaken. It was very hot. But I thought there was someone there, watching. I thought it might have been the driver of the car we hired who'd followed us up, though when we got back to the car he was there apparently asleep.'

'You're suggesting that someone was following you to see if you entered the right cave?'

'Yes, or to observe what we were doing. There was also the cairn. In Silverman's account there was a cairn of stones outside the cave. If you're familiar with the story, Beazley is alleged to have put it there to mark the cave for Beri, the Berber worker, to identify. It was still there after all these years. I found that extraordinary, and unlikely. Finally, in the entrance to the cave I found a cigarette butt, an Arab cigarette. I have it. It must have been thrown there very recently.'

Salek's face was still inscrutable. He remained silent when she'd finished. Then he rose suddenly and went to the window. He stood like there for some moments with his back to her, then he turned.

'Then there was this theft of the skull from Mr Strode's hotel room. Now I wonder who it could be who would want to possess such a thing?'

She went over the top. In this moment she was sure he was manipulating her. 'You?' she said.

He contrived a convincing look of amused surprise. 'Me? What would I want with an Englishman's skull?'

'You want evidence of Silverman's wrongdoing as much as Mr Strode does. It could have been you who's had us watched ever since we've been here. You could have planted a skeleton there for us to find – with two bullet holes conveniently made through the skull – and then you could have employed someone to steal it from the Oasis Hotel. If this is true, you've surely now achieved everything you want. Why don't you let us go, so that we can get on with our respective jobs?'

Salek looked aside with an actor's theatricality. 'You make it all sound very easy, Mrs Drake.'

'It is easy, if you'd stop thinking Strode and I are spies.'

'Ah yes – the paranoia of the third world. That is a problem, is it not – for us sophisticates?'

'Are you saying you didn't set it up?'

'That would not have been at all a hospitable thing to do to foreign guests, would it?'

'Are you saying what I've told you is news?'

Salek didn't answer her question. The smile left his face, and for a moment he looked a great deal closer to the kind of operator he must be. The levity left his voice. 'Very serious charges have been made against you and your companion – from a reliable source. These are charges any state would investigate. I must remind you of the seriousness of your position. As I see it, nobody should be declared guilty until the proof is clear. Meanwhile, I fear I must detain you until things become a little clearer. I do hope, however, at least until this time you will consider yourself a privileged guest of the President. Please do not hesitate to ask for whatever you want.'

With this, to her acute discomfort, he bowed and left. In a few minutes an unshrouded woman wearing European white overalls appeared. She had cropped henna-ed hair. She indicated to Claudia that she was to follow her. She did so. She was no longer a free agent.

18.

The woman led Claudia to an ultra modern lift at the far end of the hall. They mounted to the third floor and processed down a corridor lined on one side by doors. The woman opened one of these.

Claudia thought the rooms must be guest accommodation. But for the fact that the woman turned the key in the door as she left, she could just about imagine herself a state guest. The suite of rooms was ornately, gaudily furnished. In a few moments a gold-coloured mock-antique telephone tinkled discreetly. She was asked, in French, what she would like for lunch.

She contemplated a fast, but what was the point? She asked for an omelette. She sat in one of the three armchairs and tried to think rationally. Until this moment she hadn't allowed herself to think of Michael and what they were doing to him. Now she couldn't stop herself. Was he lying in a ghastly cell somewhere, tortured, bleeding, perhaps dead? Was he in this building? She pulled herself from such thoughts. She must think of Salek. What did she make of him?

It just didn't add up, nothing added up. If Salek, or whoever was running this charade, had set up Beazley's remains for them to find – if they were indeed his remains – why were they being treated in this way? Was it that some unknown party had accused them of spying? If so, who, and why? Who could have any motive to do so? Was it Petit-frères? If so, why had he disappeared from his home? Had he come here to Lagoued to do his dirty work?

She really decided it must be Petit-frères after all. Only he had a motive to stop Michael's investigation. Ouboussad must have been conscripted into working for him. No wonder they'd thought him shifty. It might well be Ouboussad who'd raided Michael's room and taken the skull, and it was Petit-frères who was 'the reliable source' who had denounced them as spies to Djebal. She imagined Salek consulting now with Djebal. Would she be tortured? What would they use? Cigarettes? Electric horrors? They thrash the soles of your feet, don't they? She began to feel weepy. What had she done to deserve all this?

The same woman brought the food. Claudia had to force herself not to talk to her – anything for a kind, reassuring word. When it came to it she couldn't eat. She abandoned the omelette after two mouthfuls.

She took off her skirt and blouse and lay on the brass four-poster bed. Eventually she must have dozed off. She woke with a start. The woman was back again, having let herself in without knocking. She pointed with ugly force to her clothing on the chair. Claudia asked her what was happening. She didn't answer. It was doubtful if she understood French.

They went into the lift again. Would it be some basement, below the hall? She tried to see which button the woman pressed, but her body blocked her view. Imperceptibly then, the lift was down. The doors rolled. It was the hall.

They marched across it towards the front door. The doors opened obediently. At the bottom of the red-carpeted steps stood the same limousine. The woman stopped, stood aside, and motioned her to continue to the car. On either side of the front door the armed soldiers were lolling, both chewing gum. They watched her vacantly, like cattle.

'Where am I being taken?' she asked the woman. She gave no answer and again jerked her head.

She had no escort this time. Apparently it was to be just the driver. She thought of remonstrating, of refusing to go, of demanding to see Salek. In the end she complied. She didn't want to be forced physically, which she was afraid she would have been.

She was sure she was being taken to a gaol somewhere and began to think desperately of the British Consul and what he might be doing on their behalf. She'd been mad not to tell them where she was going. Needless to say the driver proved no more communicative than the others. They were heading back to Lagoued.

She imagined some castellated construction on the outskirts of the town, but they seemed to be making for the centre. They entered the main street, where the Hotel Cosmopolite was. Her stomach bounded. They were drawing up alongside the faded awning. The driver half-turned his head to her, indicating they were at journey's end.

She needed no bidding. She was out of that hearse like Lazarus reborn. The heat cuffed her, and she loved it. She just stood there for several moments as the car pulled away, savouring the full force of the sun. She was free. She had to remind myself that Michael wasn't. The Consul, she thought – she must get on to him at once.

She went in. There was a different man on the desk. He handed her her key without expression or interest, but as she turned towards the lift, he spoke. 'Your friend is in number seventeen,' he said flatly.

She swung round, but he was disappearing into the room behind the desk. She looked at the keyboard. Seventeen was missing. She rushed up the stairs, not able to wait for the lift. The key of room seventeen was still in the lock, on the outside. It had not been turned.

Michael was lying on the bed, face down, naked. His clothes were in a heap on the floor. For an instant she thought he was dead. Then she saw his back and heard him groan.

His back and buttocks were streaked with appalling red welts amid blue-black flesh. Some of the welts were still bleeding. As she reached the bed, he turned his head and she saw the mess that was in, too. One eye was completely closed, both cheeks were puffy and his mouth seemed to be split. She thought he recognised her.

She forced herself not to give way to emotion by just thinking of practicalities. Isn't this what nurses and doctors have to do? If she allowed herself to acknowledge the swell of mixed horror, pity and anger she felt, she wouldn't be much use. He was alive, that was what mattered, and apparently, like herself, free. She put her hand on his, which was splayed on the pillow and free of injuries. She asked him if he had any bones broken.

'I'm filleted,' he managed to say through a horribly swollen mouth.

She was sure she had to persist with the unemotional practical tone. Sympathy could come later. She put her question about bones again.

'No,' he said. 'I don't think so.'

She told him to lie as still as he could. She was going to find a doctor.

She went out, locked the door, and took the key with her. Somehow the savage brutality and callousness was expressed by the key being left in the door like that. They'd taken him into that room and just dumped him like goods. The hotel had done nothing. She went downstairs to reception.

'I want a doctor urgently,' she said to the same man.

Of course he knew – he must have seen them bring Michael in, and the state he was in. Her fierceness at least confused him. She couldn't imagine much explanation had been given by Djebal's henchmen. The hotel staff probably didn't know what attitude to take.

'There isn't one,' he said, sullenly.

'What do you mean, there isn't one? Are you telling me there's no doctor attached to this hotel or that there are no doctors in Lagoued?'

'I don't know any doctor.' She asked to see the manager. 'He's not in,' he said, and turned away.

She couldn't imagine the manager would be any more helpful. She went out to find a chemist. Surely they'd know a doctor? There was a small shop down the street. They did know of a doctor, a Frenchman. They gave her the address and told her how to find it.

It was walkable. She half ran there. It was a private address in a block of flats. The name was on a black plastic plate beside the bell panel. She rang, and was invited through the intercom to come up. The door catch was released from above.

The man was dressed in trousers and a pyjama jacket. When he opened the door of the dingy-looking flat, she told him at once that her friend, a journalist, had been beaten up. He had bad cuts on his face and back. She didn't say who had beaten him up. He said he'd come with her. He went into another room, put a shirt on, and picked up his bag.

When they got to the hotel he went up to the reception clerk and exchanged a few words in Arabic. Claudia imagined this was a courtesy of some sort as he was seeing a patient in the hotel. But when he turned back to her his expression had changed.

'I'm sorry, I cannot attend your friend,' he said, and began to walk towards the front door.

'You mean the hotel won't allow you to?' She had to run after him. He didn't check until they were in the street and out of sight of the man. Then he stopped briefly.

'Go to the chemist further down this street, in about fifteen minutes. I'll prescribe something, on the phone – an antibiotic and an antiseptic ointment. Clean the wounds as best you can, dab them with the stuff, and don't cover them until they're healed over. You'll have to look after him yourself. I'm sorry.'

He was as good as his word. There was no problem at the chemist, the same one she'd been to before. He must have phoned at once when he got home. The man gave her a huge, exotically-shaped bottle that looked as if it had come from a medieval apothecary's. It was filled with a brown substance. There was cotton wool, a sedative, and a card of antibiotics. For the latter item Claudia was particularly grateful. She was sure the doctor was right, the main problem was to avoid infection. She just hoped to God Michael was right and he had no broken bones. The prescription was very expensive. It cost the equivalent of thirty pounds. As an afterthought she saw a stack of bedpans in the corner. She bought one. That cost another fifteen.

Michael could raise his head a few inches from the pillow and she managed to give him the antibiotic and two sedative pills with a glass of water she held to his lips. Then she set about the wounds. First she tried gently to clean up some of the blood with the cotton wool, then she set about the ointment. She was afraid the antiseptic was going to be a further torture for Michael, but she had to withdraw her uncharitable thought about medieval apothecaries. It didn't sting him at all, and when she'd coated the wounds with a generous helping of the odious-looking brown stuff it seemed to give him some immediate relief. She thought she could risk a little humour.

'You look like a baked jam roll,' she said.

She didn't know if he appreciated the remark or not. He was trying to concentrate on saying something. 'Don't do anything,' he said.

'What do you mean, Michael?'

'Embassy. Not a word. We've won . . . I think. Keep it to ourselves.'

She wanted badly to know what he meant, but there was a very nasty wound on his head and she feared he might be concussed. She knew she mustn't press him. She managed to get him to move over a bit, first to one side of the bed, then the other, so she could straighten the sheet. By this time the sedative seemed to be taking effect. She put the bedpan handy, told him it was there – though she couldn't see how he was going to move himself to use it. She hesitated whether to touch his hand again.

As she hesitated he held out his hand. 'Thanks Claudia,' he said as she took it. 'You turning up here's brilliant. Did they phone you . . .'

His voice faded and his grip was slackening as the powerful drug took effect. She laid his hand back on the bed.

She knew from the number of keys hanging behind the reception desk that the hotel had very few guests. Her room was on another floor from Michael's.

She went down and told the man she wanted to move nearer to him. She thought it might have been the expression on her face which did the trick. He went into the room at the back. There were low voices. When he came out he handed her another key. It was number eighteen. Maybe he was human after all. Who knew how anyone would behave if they lived in a state like Sahara? She thanked him.

She moved her few things into the new room and found there was a communicating door between it and Michael's, and that her key unlocked it. She was thankful for this, too. She had no idea how ill Michael was, and if he would need her. By leaving this communicating door ajar she could now rest, and if he stirred or cried out she'd hear him. He was asleep, she saw thankfully, though breathing painfully through his wounded mouth. She felt a swirl of protective affection for him, above all for that humorous certainty of his and for his open-eyed courage. She hadn't considered this before in the emergency, but she felt then a puritanical guilt because she was looking at his sleeping naked body. She wanted to draw the sheet over him, but knew she musn't until the wounds had dried and the ointment was no longer necessary.

She went back to her room and lay down. She realised how exhausted she was. She tried to think what Michael had meant when he said he'd 'won'. If they'd released him, and herself, it had to mean something, she supposed. But how could their present state be in any way thought of as a victory? Perhaps he was semi-delirious.

She decided she didn't want his words to mean anything. What she principally thought, until sleep overtook her, was that now they'd be going. Just as soon as Michael was up to it, they'd be flying back home, away from this torrid sink.

She was woken by the telephone. She reached for it in a panic. It was the British Consul's secretary. She realised that in the turmoil of finding Michael alive and of looking after him she'd completely forgotten she'd phoned the Consulate. The prissy voice informed her that the Consul gathered Mr Strode's short detention had been an administrative error and that he had now been released. She asked her to confirm this. When she did, there was a pause.

'If you had informed the Consul of this some hours ago, it would have saved us a considerable amount of work,' she said. ·

It was on the edge of her tongue to give her a short and acid resumé of what had happened. Remembering what Michael had said, and fearful the phone might be bugged, she didn't. Instead, she apologised, and thanked for the Consul's trouble.

She slept for three hours. When she woke, Michael was still sleeping. She began to think about food for him. It was important he got something into his stomach when he woke. It was quite possible, if he'd been arrested the day before, he'd had nothing since then. There was a small breakfast room downstairs, but she'd seen no dining-room. While she was thinking what to do, she heard Michael stir. The bedsprings creaked, and there was a heavy thump. Then he groaned, and cursed.

She rushed into his room. He was kneeling by the bed, bent forwards. It seemed he'd edged his legs off the bed and tried to stand up.

'My bloody legs gave way,' he said. 'I've got to get to the loo.'

'I got you a pan thing. Use that.'

'I'm not using a bloody pan. I want to see if I can walk. Give me a hand.'

She got behind him, put her arms under his armpits and, avoiding the wounds, joined her hands on his chest, which was free of injuries. He levered with his own arms on the bed and together they got him upright. Turning, he transferred his hands from the bed to her shoulders. With her walking backwards, they began a ludicrous shuffle towards the bathroom.

'Take your partners for the Lagoued Gallop,' he said grimly.

She feared his legs would give way and he'd fall, herself on top of him or the other way round, but as they made progress he seemed to get more control of his muscles. They reached their destination and, turning again, he lowered himself gingerly, with his hands clasped now behind her neck. He cursed again as the wounds on his behind made contact with the seat.

Then he looked at her and began to laugh – as well as he could, poor man. There was he, starkers, looking like Frankenstein, and her with the sticky brown ointment on her hands and front, standing in front of him in pants and bra. She'd completely forgotten she'd taken off her top clothes. In a moment, she laughed, too.

Michael had been flogged viciously with a cane, punched and kicked but, apart from lacerations and terrible bruises, there was nothing seriously wrong. The main danger was infection. But the ointment, the antibiotics, and Michael's rude health and strength and courage did the trick. The next day he could sit in his underpants on a chair, if with care and innumerable oaths. Claudia thought the hotel must have realised the same thing she had, that if they'd been released and reinstalled in their premises they were still tolerated on Saharan soil and that therefore, from their point of view, they were not totally untouchable. She was right in thinking the hotel did no food beyond breakfast, but she persuaded them to allow her to use the kitchen to warm packet soups she bought, and she was allowed to borrow crocks and cutlery.

As if realising they needed a period of convalescence, Michael and Claudia both avoided discussion until later the following day. There was also the thought, initially, that the room might be bugged. She did what she could to look for gadgets, even on Michael's sign-language instructions buying a small screwdriver to take the telephone to pieces. Michael had just finished spooning her soup into the operative side of his mouth and had managed to chew some bread soaked in it. He dabbed his chin with the paper napkin.

'Yes, it dawned into their thick heads at last I was telling the truth,' he said suddenly. 'Some bugger's been telling them we're spies. I just managed somehow to keep saying the same thing. I didn't really have an alternative. If I'd "admitted" anything I think they'd've shot me. They had the tape-recorder going throughout. Confession was all they wanted. They stripped me, and it went on most of the day, all night, and into the next day – yesterday was it? Then suddenly it stopped. For a whole hour or more I was left alone. I thought they must have knocked off for a meal or to watch a football match or something. Then two of them came back with a stretcher. I was heaved onto it, still without my clothes, taken out to an ambulance and driven back into town.'

'Back into town?'

'Yes, they'd taken me to Djebal's palace at Ain Mokhtar. It's about twenty miles out, in another oasis. I thought I was on my way to a grave in the desert somewhere. But we were driving in the direction of Lagoued. To my astonishment they pulled up outside this hotel. They carried me up here with a sheet over me as if I were a corpse, tipped me on the bed, and left. Boy, was I pleased when you turned up. Did they phone you? They must have known you were in Tifgad. I never mentioned you.'

Claudia thought it was time she told him her end of the story. She'd found nothing in the telephone, but not to take any risks on bugs, she turned on the radio built into the bedside table. She began with her reasons for staying in Tifgad and how these had led her, through Hocen and his remarks about Ben Abbis, to the brothel-keeper and her revelations about Petit-frères. She was tempted for a moment to suppress the crucial bit about Alan's meeting with Petit-frères, and so avoid the constructions Michael would put on it, but she found she no longer felt any pride about this, or any rivalry. Events had rendered pride superfluous. She told it all straight. She also related what seemed to lend credence to the idea that Alan had done some sort of a deal with Petit-frères – she told Michael about the raid on his room and then how she'd tried to see Petit-frères. She explained how he'd disappeared, maybe after framing them with Djebal.

Involved with these conjectures, she hadn't realised she'd left the story with herself still in Tifgad. She was about to continue, but Michael got there first. He was frowning.

'But they couldn't have phoned you in Tifgad, now I think about it,' he said. She didn't realise what he was getting at for a moment. 'If they had, it would have been yesterday morning, when they'd changed their minds about beating me up. You couldn't have got here by bus until the evening, and you were here in the morning. Did you get Ouboussad moving again?'

She told him how she'd tried to get him at this hotel after the raid on the room and finally learnt he'd been arrested. She'd taken the early morning bus.

Michael realised she hadn't been here when they'd slung him into this room, somewhere about midday. So what had she been doing all the morning, he asked? When she told him she'd also been a guest at the presidential palace he was horrified. 'Christ you mean they . . .'

She assured him nobody laid a finger on her. 'I saw Djebal,' I told him, 'who thought I was a spy, too, and ordered, I think, the kind of treatment you got. Then I saw Salek, who'd been in attendance throughout the interview.'

'That fucker.'

'You saw him?'

'No, I never got to him and spoke to an underling. Salek just gave the orders behind the scenes.'

'I'm sure you're right about him, but as it turned out he did seem to be an improvement on Djebal. He's rather suave and western. He went to an English public school, Stowe, and speaks perfect English. Djebal had told me you'd been "interrogated" and I was terrified what they'd done to you. I'm afraid I told him all about the morning we spent in the cave, including about the skull. It seemed the only way to get us out was to be frank. You'd made the point all along that what you're doing is in their interest, and there's clearly no love lost between Salek and Djebal. I thought if I was frank with Salek he might wonder about this spy story and intercede for us. Apparently, that's just what he did. What time was it they – left you alone?'

'I don't know exactly. I was in an underground room somewhere. They'd taken my watch – and kept it, the fuckers – and, down there, I couldn't tell from the temperature. My estimate would have been towards midday.'

'That would fit. It must have been about then I finished talking to Salek and was taken upstairs.'

Michael was staring at her. 'Christ,' he said.

'Where does Christ come into it?'

'You came steaming up here to save my neck, and I've been saying the things I have to you. The bastards could have hurt you.'

'They could have, but they didn't. They didn't because, as I say, Salek must have changed his mind. For some reason he decided to forget the spy accusation – if indeed there was one – and saw he was going against his own interest.'

Michael wasn't listening to her again. 'I really owe you, Claudia,' he went on. 'You almost certainly saved my life. And there was I thinking I'd done it single-handed.'

Compliments from Michael Strode. It was, she realised, one of the better moments of her life. Had she been trying all along to win his esteem? He went on to say what a good job she'd done, and more about how guilty he felt at having landed her in such an ugly situation. It was some time before she could return him to the subject of Jezi and what she'd told her.

As she'd expected he would, he pounced on Petit-frères's meeting with Alan. Alan, with Beazley's blood on his hands, had 'plainly' done some sort of a deal with Petit-frères, and that was why Petit-frères was trying to get rid of them. He grew excited. 'And if Petit-frères was involved, that explains a great deal of the mystery surrounding the murder. Silverman didn't need to cover his tracks. He left Beazley's body where he'd thrown it, even with two incriminating bullet holes through the skull, because he knew he had the law on his side. All he had to do was somehow rig up a case against Beri.'

She let him go on. Though she didn't see how certain aspects of the Beri story could have been rigged, it was obvious to her now that Alan had probably done something a bit shady. But at the back of her mind she knew there was something else – quite apart from her feelings about Alan. All right, perhaps it had been Petit-frères who'd tried to shop them. The man on the motor-bike who'd followed her to Jezi's house could have been his sleuth. But Ouboussad's behaviour, the cigarette butt, and what she thought she saw on the far mountainside outside the cave? How did all that fit in? She was still convinced that in some way their discovery of the human remains had been set up for them. If so, who had set it up? If not Petit-frères, who apparently had every reason to hope for their failure. Salek? It was possible . . .

But she was beginning to get subliminal feed-back from her interview with Salek. She'd thought at the time he must know everything she was telling him, but had he? She could recall exactly the look on his face as she spoke. Was it passively ironic in face of a rabbit squealing, as it would have been in that circumstance? She didn't think so. He'd surely been intrinsically interested. He'd hung on her every word. And a few minutes later he must have got to work on changing Djebal's mind, and succeeded.

19

They stayed in Lagoued three more days. Air-conditioning certainly hastened Michael's recovery. It reduced the risk of infection, not only because of the lower temperature but also because it reduced the flies. Claudia couldn't stop a few getting in – she thought they must enter through the cracks round the doors. But those which did she was able to slaughter, shamelessly using as her murder weapon a spare pillow she found (French style) in the wardrobe.

After that first brief conversation about Petit-frères, they didn't talk much about Alan, or the situation they'd got themselves into. Claudia felt there was no doubt their shared experience, and Michael's injuries, had created a new climate between them. Their conversations became personal. She learnt a great deal about Michael's life – which hadn't, as she'd guessed, been a very happy one. His father, a building-site navvy, had been sent to gaol for violence. His mother had had to survive on a very small income. Michael also showed an unexpected interest in her existence. He was especially interested in her marriage to Jack. Because he asked a lot of penetrating questions, including some on matters she hadn't considered herself, she told him quite a lot. She thought he really wanted to know about the source of their happiness together. This moved her. It didn't seem he'd had too much of that commodity in his life.

As he couldn't see through one eye and not too well through the other, she read to him. As a sort of reflex action when she was throwing things into her bag at Tifgad, she'd included a large paperback compendium of great short stories and a book of modern verse she'd brought with her from home. She chose some of her favourites. Michael seemed to agree about them, especially about one of Elizabeth Bowen's beautiful and sensitive stories, which he made her read twice. It merited repetition, it was as tightly written as poetry.

Because of this and because, like a painting in the process of being created – a little added each day – she felt a real relationship taking shape, she'd really pushed to the back of her mind the question of what they did when he was well enough to move. At the beginning she hadn't been able to think he'd abandon the mission but, because they didn't talk about it, she slowly began to think he would. The reason they weren't talking about it, she thought, was that he'd realised he couldn't now write a story that was going to be in any way beneficial to the abominable regime in this country. Any morning now he'd say, 'well, let's go.'

It was bright and early on the third morning since Ain Mokhtar. Michael had decided to shuffle downstairs to breakfast for the first time. Amid a pyrotechnic display of atmospherics, a radio was blaring Arab music. It was good enough cover for any bugging devices.

'We'll get the evening bus to Tifgad, shall we?' he said out of the blue.

Her good spirits at his recovery plummeted. Every day she'd dreaded a change of Government policy and their recall to that concrete palace. She strove to hide her chagrin. 'Are you sure you're well enough?' she said, turning her head away.

'Yes.'

He meant it all right. She tried her luck on another tack. 'Do we have to go back to Tifgad?' she said. 'Our air tickets are open. We could have them changed and fly from here, couldn't we? You didn't leave much stuff in Tifgad, did you, and the less you have to travel the better, surely?'

He looked at her in amazement. 'Claudia, we're not going home. At least I'm not.'

Uncontrollably, she felt the colour rising to her face. How could he be thinking of going on here when he'd been treated as he had been? 'Of course we must go home,' she said. 'They could change their minds at any moment.'

'Why? They obviously made a mistake and have admitted it. And I'm on to the best story of my life. Do you think I'm going to abandon it now when I've proved to them they've behaved like idiots and I've almost got the thing tied up?'

'You've got all you want already for a story.'

He looked at her fixedly. 'Isn't what you mean that you don't want the truth about Silverman?'

Was it now so easy for him to remove the detonator from her anger? She wasn't angry, she found. The question he'd put to her was no longer sardonic and superior as it would have been before. It was simply a question of fact, and the fact was, he was right. She didn't really care about Alan Silverman at this moment. What she cared about was their safety. She tried a last card. 'But you no longer have the skull,' she said. 'You won't be able to prove anything.'

'You think not?'

'Whoever did your room over – Petit-frères – must have found it.'

'It wasn't in the room.'

'You mean . . .'

'I mean it's safe, and Salek doesn't know it. What you said to him suits our purposes admirably. He thinks someone else has got it. What we want now is the other piece of the jigsaw-puzzle – the bullet. It's got to be somewhere in that cave. We're not going to find Silverman's gun, I'm sure he got rid of it if he had any sense, but we know its make. There are those mentions of it in the diary, and we have photos of him wearing it. If the calibre of the bullet is right for the gun, it'll be good enough for me and, I guess, for Bellerby – not to mention our readers.'

'Supposing Djebal does change his mind again?'

'Why should he do that now?'

'He may think you'll describe what they did to you when you get back to Britain.'

'I can't think that'll worry him. He'll just deny it and make up some story to explain the scars on my back, if he even bothers.'

'You don't think they'll let you fish around in that cave unmolested, do you?'

'I don't give a damn what they do. What I'm going to do to Silverman is in their interest. They now realise it is.'

It would have been easier for her to go home alone before all these events. It would have been easier to convince herself Michael was crazy. Now she knew he wasn't crazy. She also knew she could never write her book unless her own curiosity was satisfied – with her own eyes. She still didn't believe Alan Silverman was a cold murderer. Something else, most peculiar, must have happened. They agreed to return to Tifgad that day.

Persuaded by her, Michael changed his mind about the bus. They decided to hire an air-conditioned car for the journey. In the later afternoon they'd paid their bills and were waiting for the car to arrive, sitting in the hotel lobby. Claudia was worried about Michael travelling so soon, but also aware, under her concern, that there was some kind of a shemozzle going on behind the reception counter. The surly man she'd originally encountered was on duty. With him was the manager, a smaller man. She thought they must be expecting someone. They kept whispering remarks to each other and looking towards the front door like two girls at an old-fashioned hop, hoping to be asked to dance. It also occurred to her that she and Michael were involved in some way. Were they deliberately not looking in their direction? Michael's attention was also caught. They heard a vehicle draw up outside. The two men seemed to give themselves a final preen. In walked Salek.

Salek saw them sitting there at once and, ignoring the two men behind the desk, walked straight up. With his back to Michael, he addressed her, in English. 'All ready to go, are you?'

Michael of course didn't know Salek. 'Who the hell are you?' he said.

'Mrs Drake, you have no doubt told your friend of our pleasant and – I would have thought from both our points of view – our rather fruitful conversation. Please introduce us, will you?'

Michael didn't need introducing. He'd guessed. 'You're Salek,' he said, with no attempt at courtesy.

'At your service.' Salek made a small ironic bow and again turned to her. 'I thought my car would be rather more comfortable than anything Lagoued can provide. Our friends here have excelled themselves in keeping me informed of your plans, and I've taken the liberty of cancelling the limousine you ordered. I imagine, alas, your companion may still be a little tender from his unfortunate experience.'

Claudia thought the humour grotesque. She could see Michael was fuming at the cancellation of the car he'd ordered. The hotel operator must have been listening in to his call. But for once, on a strong instinct for self-preservation, she took the decision for both of them. Michael, she was sure, was on the point of turning the toad down, whatever the consquences. She preempted his fury.

'All right, we accept your lift, Monsieur Salek – thank you,' she said quickly, in the nick of time.

For once, Michael, if combustibly, concurred with her realism.

It was the same mafioso Mercedes. There were two men in the front seat, the driver – and another, who Claudia later learnt was the impassive chef-du-cabinet at Salek's Ministry whom Michael had met. When the driver opened the boot to put in their small bags, they saw that it was filled with expensive leather luggage.

She exchanged a glance with Michael. 'You're coming to Tifgad?' Michael said to Salek.

'But of course, Mr Strode. You'd hardly expect me to miss the investigation at this exciting stage, would you?'

Claudia thought it was still in Michael's mind that they should refuse the lift and remake their arrangements. But maybe his curiosity at this turn of events overtook his dislike. After all, his purpose in coming to Lagoued had been to obtain Salek's cooperation, and he'd already said the Government must have changed its mind about their mission. He said nothing.

Nonetheless he kept only just within the bounds of courtesy. Salek sat in the middle row of seats. She and Michael were behind. 'Why the U-turn?' Michael said offensively as soon as they'd got going.

'I've made no U-turn, Mr Strode.'

'What do you mean? One minute your thugs are flogging the hell out of me, and now this.'

Salek clearly didn't care at all for the lack of deference, but he kept his cool. He turned his head away from them. 'For a journalist, you have a naive appreciation of third world politics.'

'It's naive, is it, to wonder at a hundred and eighty degree swing between criminal violence and apparent cooperation in the space of hours?'

Michael's insolence took her breath away. Salek leaned forward and closed the glass panel that divided the front seat from the rest of the car. 'You were denounced as a spy,' he said.

'Which – if I really was denounced – you must have known was a fabrication. I bet you know exactly what I've been up to since being in Sahara. If I was a spy, why would I go rushing off in the heat to look at a cave? What was I supposed to be spying on, anyway – your latest Saharan uranium extraction plant?'

She thought Michael was being an ass. Salek, who must after all have saved their skins, was bridling like a maiden aunt. 'For your information,' he said, 'the first I knew of your arrest was on the morning you were released.'

'I was arrested in your goddam Ministry for God's sake. You must have given the order. I had an appointment with you, made the evening before, and that jackass sitting in the front seat came to tell you I'd arrived.'

'He did nothing of the sort. I was not in Lagoued that day. I was unexpectedly delayed abroad. My subordinate was, I admit, a little hasty, but understandably. It was he who received that morning, anonymously, the accusation that you were a spy. He naturally passed this on to a higher authority and was ordered to send you to Mokhtar.'

'You expect me to believe that?'

'It's rather in your interest that you should, I'd've thought. Perhaps it would also be a courtesy, as I possibly saved your life. You will recall, Mrs Drake, that when you came to see the President he was not in a very amiable frame of mind.'

She felt this was her cue to enter the lists. 'You knew nothing of what I told you then?' she asked.

'Did you doubt it?'

'I had no means of knowing. You mean you didn't know we were here in Sahara, in spite of the fuss in London?'

'I knew naturally of the "fuss" in London, as you describe it, but not that a journalist was coming. A number of people do obtain visas to come here, you know, despite our backwardness.'

'And you didn't know we'd been to the cave and found the skeleton? You didn't have us followed?'

'Of course not.'

She looked at Michael. He was staring out of the window, thinking. He made his mind up with characteristic decisiveness. 'OK, Monsieur Salek,' he said. 'As an act of faith I'm going to believe you, and I'll consider whether or not I report my barbaric treatment to Amnesty International. It's certainly in both our interests that I believe you. We'll do a deal. You help me find that bullet, I'll write the story you want. Let's hope it makes you the next President. I guess that would have to be an improvement. I'll need transport, lighting, proper climbing equipment.'

Salek grinned at her, and winked in a way she did not find at all agreeable. 'Arrangements are in hand,' he said. 'Perhaps next time you come here you will inform us in advance. It would have saved a lot of fuss had you done so this time.'

When they got to the Oasis Hotel Claudia couldn't believe her eyes. The missing 'O' of the hotel sign had been replaced and the tilting 'I' assisted to a vertical position. All the letters had been sloshed with fresh green paint, and the walls, including the brickwork from which bits of rendering had fallen, had been newly whitewashed (but only the front wall Claudia observed, the others hadn't been touched). Finally, from the end of a previously naked flagpole projecting from the first floor balcony, flew a rather crumpled version of the yellow and purple national flag.

Further marvels were apparent. Three men they'd never seen before came springing from the door. Behind them emerged a transfigured Tadj. Over his paunchy body hung a splendid kaftan, a rose-tinted garment which had elaborate coloured embroidery round the neck. On his head was a round Moslem cap of the same material. He bowed unctiously as the Minister got out of the car, and said something, Claudia was sure, of extreme obsequiousness.

Inside, also, modifications had taken place. To begin with, you could see in the lobby. Where there'd been two light bulbs, there were now a couple of dozen. The place blazed with light, and it had clearly been thoroughly cleaned.

Salek made a movement of his head towards Tadj but didn't look at him. 'My rooms are prepared, I presume?' he enquired in French. 'My friends here will join me in them for an aperitif about eight perhaps? We shall also, I trust, dine together in my apartment. You are seeing to that, as ordered?' Tadj was seeing to it.

Salek explained to them, still within earshot of Tadj, that he'd sent his own chef to the hotel, his own dinner service, provisions, and two waiters – you couldn't rely on a small oasis hotel to provide the necessary. He hoped the food and the service would therefore be 'in a category marginally acceptable.'

In the background Claudia saw Hocen lurking, his eyes bulging. She felt more warmly than ever towards him. Even Tadj now came within her sympathy. Poor man, to have this thrust on him. Queen Elizabeth the First couldn't have caused more consternation on her progresses. She wished they were back here alone, with Tadj in shirt-sleeves, with garlic soup and lamb for dinner, and without their poncey accompaniment.

Michael came into her room when they were upstairs. They searched again for a bug in the phone. She wanted to say something which had occurred to her. Though they again found no gadget, she took the precaution of going into the bathroom and turning on all the taps.

'I don't like it,' she said. 'I think he was probably telling the truth in the car. I'd had the same feeling already about my interview with him at the Palace – he didn't know anything about us and was listening to every word I said. But it could be only sunshine until the bullet's found. How are we to know what he'll do next? He may not accept my story about your room being raided and the skull being stolen. He probably doesn't know about Petit-frères. We could easily be re-arrested.'

Michael nodded as she spoke. 'It's possible. But he hasn't got the skull, and isn't going to get it. That's the trump card. He won't touch us without it. It's the main evidence.'

'Where is it?'

'I told you – safe.'

'If you've got it, he could force us to give it to him.'

'That would be difficult. By now it's safe in England. Before leaving Lagoued, I posted it to a friend and asked him to get cracking on forensic tests. Whatever tricks Salek may be up to, our use to him will extend beyond our return home.'

'Michael, you're brilliant,' she said, greatly relieved.

20.

Claudia began to feel familiar symptoms during Salek's dinner party, a sudden sore throat and a headache in a particular part of her head. She knew it was a fluey cold and that it would last for its statutory three days minimum. Out here it could be worse. But, also ritually, she pretended it wasn't what she knew it was. It was just a sore throat brought on by the dust and dry air, she told herself, which an aspirin would cure before the morning.

She endured the evening and kept her end up. If Salek was playing a double game, he was certainly putting on a good show of being on their side. In his complicity with them, she thought he steered pretty close to indiscretion, his servants being within earshot. There was also another man present, who had come in another car – a tall Sudanese called Kaftu, who was to conduct the search in the cave. Salek made it very clear indeed what he thought of Djebal and his thuggish entourage. He as much as said that she and Michael were his civilised allies in the unfortunate predicament in which post-revolutionary Saharan politics had pitched him. Claudia played up to him within reason. What was the point of making things worse than they might be? Michael, needless to say, was less sycophantic than she was, though not totally uncivil.

After they'd gone to bed, the storm swept down on her with unusual speed and force. The washers in her nose seemed to collapse, and a cataract started with such volume she thought she wouldn't have any juice left in her body. Then after three hours it stopped as suddenly as it had begun, and she had a bad fever. They were due to get up at five. Salek had a helicopter waiting at the airport to take them to Silverman's camp. When Michael came in to wake her she was in the thick of it. She had decided hours ago she couldn't go.

She had no doubt she looked like a spectre. Michael was gentle and sweet – really concerned. He damped her flannel and bathed her face. Unbidden, he got her spare nightdress out of the drawer for her to change into.

'I'll get Hocen to bring you a bucket of orange juice,' he said. 'I imagine we'll be back by midday, then I can look after you.' She told him not to worry, and again asked him if he felt up to what would surely be a rough day even with the helicopter. He gave her the predictable answer.

She could tell from the sudden silence which followed the bumps and general commotion which raged for about an hour in the badly-built building that the party had left. Soon after this Hocen knocked timidly on the door and staggered in with, not a bucket, but a whole crate of little red bottles which turned out to be fizzy orangeade. This was the only item on the hotel's regular drink repertoire – except for its sister, lemonade, which came in yellow bottles. Hocen had taken Michael's instructions literally. Professionally, he produced an opener from his pocket, and with one hand held both the bottle and the opener and lifted the metal cap. He levelled the neck of the bottle inside the glass and poured.

Hocen deployed to effect his few words of English. 'This very good for desert grippe,' he said. 'I leave you opener. You drink five, six, seven. By twelve o'clock you better. You see.'

She was inclined to disagree with Hocen's optimistic forecast, which among other considerations seemed to downgrade the severity of her affliction. She looked at the label on one of the bottles. She couldn't think that J.Lebrun, Marseilles, had prepared his brew with any curative intentions. But – perhaps it was Hocen's and Michael's concern, maybe it was the effect of the soda – by mid-morning the fever did seem less. She began to feel drowsy and eventually fell asleep.

When she woke, the full heat of the afternoon seemed to be past. She felt the remnants of her sweat dried on her skin like a membrane. Hocen had obviously been in. The heavy slatted shutters were drawn and on the bedside table was a tray of food. There was a spread of – surprise of the month – a glorious trinity of cold garlic soup, bread, and lamb – but also a tempting-looking, quarter-moon slice of red water-melon. Propped against the soup bowl was a note in Hocen's essential English.

'I see you drink four bottles only, but you better yes?' It was signed with Hocen's intentionally illegible signature, which took up half the paper and looked like the reading of a seismograph during an earthquake.

She examined herself for an answer to Hocen's question and – yes, quite definitely – she was a lot better. She looked at her watch. Half-past four. They must be back. Probably the continuing silence was that of exhaustion. They were all asleep.

She swung her feet to the floor and tested. All systems perfectly-in order. She put on her just opaque dressing-gown and reached for slippers. Out of one fell a siesta-ing cockroach which ran for the wainscotting. She opened the door. She was sure as soon as she got into the corridor that they weren't back. She glanced down the stairs. The hall was deserted and all the lights were out. Tadj was economising again. She didn't believe he'd have dared turn them off if Salek was in residence. Just then she heard a sound behind her and a loud whisper.

'Madame Drake?'

She made out Hocen in the gloom. He was advancing towards her while putting his white burnous over vest and underpants She thought he'd been sleeping on the floor in the corridor. He seemed very excited about something. She asked him if the party had returned. 'Not yet,' he said, as if this were of secondary importance. He also went to the stairs and bent to peer down. Apparently pleased no one was about, he returned to her. He spoke French now. 'Madame is better? I told you. Our juice is very good medicine.' He indicated he wanted to come into her room. He opened the door and turned his back against it to let her pass. 'I must speak to you, Madame,' he said, still in the urgent whisper. 'I was waiting in the corridor until you woke.'

Her pulses began to thump. 'Why, what's wrong?' she said. 'Is Mr Strode . . .'

Hocen closed the door behind them and drew himself up like a guardsman. 'Monsieur Ben Abbis is here,' he announced.

For a moment she couldn't think who Monsieur Ben Abbis was. Then she remembered. Ben Abbis was the date merchant who made occasional visits to Tifgad, stayed in the hotel, and invited Petit-frères for illicit whisky sessions. Because of their misgivings about Petit-frères's intentions towards them, his presence wasn't welcome news. Hocen saw the look on her face.

'Monsieur Ben Abbis is a very nice man. He wants to see you, alone – if possible now. He has asked me to speak to you immediately you are better. You are better?'

Her thoughts were ranging in all directions like a spaniel after a scent. What could this man possibly want? If Petit-frères had tried to frame them as spies, and failed, he surely wanted them out of the way.

201

She sat on the bed. 'I'm a bit better, Hocen, but I'm not sure I feel like talking to a complete stranger in the middle of the afternoon.'

'Oh but it's very important. He says it's important. It's important he speaks to you before Monsieur Salek returns. I must tell him you agree.'

She did a quick calculation. If Ben Abbis had evil intentions he'd hardly have gone to these lengths and involved Hocen. Hocen then clinched matters. 'Monsieur Salek is a very dangerous man,' he added.

This was no news to her. Hocen had proved his acumen to her, she couldn't entertain the idea that he was in any way duplicit. 'All right,' she said. 'Give me a few moments to put some clothes on. I'll be downstairs in ten minutes.'

Hocen wasn't sold on this idea. 'Oh no, Madame Drake. You stay here in the very pretty dress you are wearing. I will bring Monsieur Ben Abbis here and stay in the passage outside. If the party comes back I will knock and Monsieur will return at once to his room.'

Was she about to be raped? She couldn't believe it. Ben Abbis, as far as she knew, had never seen her, and how would Hocen connive at such a thing?

'Very well,' she said.

She nonetheless felt very uneasy, and for a moment began to feel weak and trembly again. She poured herself another glass of J.Lebrun's elixir and swallowed most of it. Her weakness was probably only dehydration. She kept feeling parched.

Hocen had left the door ajar. There were quick footsteps, it was pushed open, and a hardly Adonis-like, seventy-plus Ben Abbis appeared in summer sportswear – perforated white kid shoes, light-weight trousers, a dark blue shirt, and dark glasses which he peeled off as he entered to reveal deep-set eyes overhung by bushy eyebrows. Hocen closed the door discreetly behind him.

Ben Abbis looked very un-Arab. He faintly resembled that actor who always plays highly-respectable, exaggeratedly Scottish parts. Not at first sight anyway your prototype rapist. He looked very distracted, and apparently nervous at seeing her in her slippers and nightwear. By this time she was perched on one of the two hard-back chairs in the room.

'Madame Drake,' he began in excellent French, 'I apologise for asking you to see me like this when you are not well. But you must realise my coming here to speak to you involves some risk, and the opportunity may not so easily present itself again. May I?'

She had placed the other chair about a yard from hers. He sat on it, and with a very French gesture briefly held his hands together at the level of his chest as if he were making a rapid selection from a great number of things he might say. He then plunged. 'First, you may be relieved to hear, Gérard Petit-frères is safe. You could not know of course when you came here how your enquiries endangered his life. But he knew how likely it was that you would come across that body, which the French police made such little effort to look for in 1936, and he'd always suspected it might contain evidence which would be dangerous to himself as well as Silverman.

'However, he wasn't on reflection too worried about this. He calculated that if you proved Silverman had been up to something and dragged Silverman's reputation in the dirt, it was unlikely he'd be implicated, with Silverman dead. He'd after all been Minister of Justice in the French Administration at the time, in no way responsible for the day to day affairs of the colonial police. But then he heard you'd been to see Jezi, the brothel keeper. This was another matter. He had at once to get in touch with her to find out what she'd said.

'Gérard doesn't blame her for telling you about the disastrous love affair in his youth which ruined his life, but of course when he found out she'd told you he'd had a secret meeting with Silverman at the end of his expedition – just when all the unpleasantness was occurring – he grew alarmed. He knew it was possible you'd draw unfortunate conclusions. He couldn't take the risk that you would. You did, no doubt, draw conclusions?'

'Well, we did wonder . . .'

'Naturally – you are looking for evidence of Silverman's guilt. I won't tell you the ins and outs of the conversation Gérard had with Jezi and how he knew you'd been to see her. Sufficient to say that when he'd finished talking to her he began to think he'd have to leave the town. In the past he's always got on reasonably well with the authorities here, but the present regime is quite unpredictable. If they had any inkling of what had happened between himself and Silverman in 1936, after which a Saharan citizen died, in the present highly-charged circumstances no one could guarantee what attitude they'd take. When he realised your companion had gone to Lagoued, almost certainly to gain the cooperation of the authorities for further searches, he phoned me and asked my opinion about what he should do.

'I advised him to shut up his house and leave the country at once, at least until things clarified. This is what he has done. I shall not reveal where he is. Sufficient to say that, where he is, he is safe.

'I can guess what you have been thinking of Gérard, and I want to tell you quickly – I haven't much time – what Jezi didn't tell you, what she has never known in fact. Gérard made a great mistake, not only in the infatuation he had for Sawsan – who, right from the start, saw him only as a means to an end – but above all in falling in with Silverman's suggestion. The agreement he made to pervert the course of justice – in return for a large sum of money – was a criminal act. Though he never knew precisely what Silverman had done, he certainly suspected that the Berber was being wrongly accused for the Englishman's death. He got the police to accept at face value the evidence Silverman presented, and a minimum of effort was made to look for the body. It was intended that proceedings could be delayed until Silverman was safely out of the country, and then that the trial would be held in camera. After the trial, when the young Berber had been convicted, Gérard was going to make sure the death sentence was commuted to life imprisonment, and then that, after a month or two when everything had calmed down, a pardon would be arranged for the man on some technical grounds. Of course he couldn't foresee that the man would kill himself in prison. Then, not long after this, Gérard lost Sawsan. I think Jezi told you she married another Frenchman and went to live in France. This had been her intention all along.

'The double tragedy struck Gérard down. An additional blow was that Silverman never paid all he'd promised. He argued that the Berber's death reduced the value of the service he was receiving. He knew Gérard could never do anything about it if he refused to pay up. If he did, he would be incriminating himself. Within a year Gérard had lost his job. I think you have some idea of the rest of the story from Jezi.

'Many times I've tried to make Gérard forget it all. I've told him Sawsan would never have married him anyway, even if Silverman had paid up. She was only using him to find the sort of man she very quickly found. But he wouldn't forget. His experience became a bitter obsession with him that conditioned his whole behaviour. In time he came to believe – against all the facts – that but for Silverman Sawsan would have become his wife and they would have lived happily.'

Poor Petit-frères. Claudia almost repeated Alan's phrase. But she forced herself to think. Here she was beginning to feel sorry for the man who could have caused Michael's death and perhaps hers. 'And this is why Petit-frères made such strenuous efforts to get rid of us?' she said.

Ben Abbis stared at her. '"Get rid of you"? I do not understand.'

'It must be Petit-frères who followed our every move and who denounced us as spies to the Government. You do not know that my companion was arrested and severely beaten?'

'No, there is a misunderstanding. Of course Gérard would never do such a thing.' Ben Abbis could not surely be faking the frown that had leapt to his brow. 'Your companion was beaten? I had no idea. Neither, I am sure, did Gérard. He'd have told me this. I saw him only yesterday.'

She felt her weakness attacking her again. Perhaps it was to try to control it that she raised her voice. 'And Petit-frères had Michael's room next door ransacked the morning after he went to Lagoued. He knew we had Beazley's skull and he wanted to get possession of it, to destroy the evidence. Who are you? Why are you telling me this?'

She thought she was practically shouting. Ben Abbis rose from his chair and went to stand by the window. 'I am very sorry, Madame Drake. If these things have happened, I can understand your alarm. But what you are saying makes no sense to me. I've told you exactly what my friend's part in the affair has been. I'm absolutely sure he hasn't concealed anything from me. We are the closest of friends. Clearly there have been things happening of which he has no knowledge. You will forgive me, but whatever explains these matters you mention, I must pass now to the chief reason I've come here to speak to you. Your last question I can and will answer, however, as it is relevant. Who am I, you ask? Why am I here? In a phrase because I am Sawsan's brother.'

He left a pause for her to look blank in, and she had no doubt she obliged.

'Yes. I am younger than Sawsan. At the time she was having her affair with Gérard, I was only a young boy. But I understood exactly what she was doing. I was ashamed of her, as were our mother and father when they found out. She was selfish and ruthless. She knew what she was doing to the man who loved her, but she used him cynically.

205

'I felt at the time the same way as our parents. But I have to admit that I, too, gained from her marriage, and this, there is no doubt, in time muted my criticism. We were a poor provincial family. I also wanted to leave Tifgad and arrange a better life for myself. Sawsan sent money to the family from France after she'd gone there with her husband. My education benefited. And later it was Sawsan's husband who set me up in this profitable business I now run. It was only when I started coming to Tifgad on behalf of my company that I began to see Gérard again and realised fully what Sawsan had done to him. I determined to do what I could to atone in some way for Sawsan's acts. I knew that in an indirect way he'd been responsible for the change in my fortunes. Unknown to Sawsan I became Gérard's friend and always visited him, or met him at this hotel, when I came here. He always wanted to know how Sawsan was, and no detail about her life was too trivial to relate.

'You have, I see, made the acquaintance of the remarkable Hocen. Last night when I got here it was he who told me that Salek is here and why. Because of what he told me I rang a friend in Lagoued. Never mind the name of my contact. Sufficient to say he's a very highly-placed official and that I've never known his information to be wrong. In speaking to him I was of course principally concerned about Gérard. I wanted to know if anything was known in the Palace about Jezi's revelations.. Apparently not – your friend must have been discreet if he was interrogated. But what I did learn was that your friend is cooperating with Salek in searching for evidence of the Silverman affair.

'Madame, you are undoubtedly in great danger. As soon as he has what he wants, Salek will arrest you both. He was suspected of having been behind the unsuccessful coup against Djebal a few months ago, and he's under pressure from Djebal. If you are arrested, no one could guarantee your safety.'

'But surely, Salek – and Djebal – want the English press to print Michael's story?'

'Not if they have the proof themselves of Silverman's guilt. They will not care about an English newspaper and what it prints. They would probably prefer to have the British press raging against them. You and your friend could just disappear. An accident in one of those caves perhaps? It will not be difficult for them to rig a story. What I am saying is not to alarm you, but

206

to convince you that you must both get out of Sahara now – tonight if possible, while it is still possible.'

There was a loud crash downstairs. Ben Abbis turned, startled, towards the door. Hocen opened the door a fraction but did not come in. 'It's all right, it's only Monsieur Tadj,' he said. The door closed.

Ben Abbis put his hand in his trouser pocket and drew out a car key on a ring. 'I usually come from Lagoued to Tifgad by air,' he said. 'This time, fortunately, I was late for the Tifgad plane and had to use the company car, which is kept in Lagoued. If you are wise, you and your friend will take the car tonight and make for the Moroccan frontier. The car papers are in the pocket. If you start before midnight you should make it soon after dawn. I need not discover the "theft" of the car, which I shall declare it to be, until much later, but it's likely, when they find you are not in the hotel they will also find the car missing. The manager knows I came in one. I understand Salek has a helicopter here. Maybe he has others he can summon. He will know you have taken one of three routes north. Two are to Algeria, and one to Morocco. Algeria being a bit further, he will guess you will be making for Morocco and almost certainly attempt to pursue you. But with any luck you will be over the frontier in time. The car has a full tank of petrol, and there are two full twenty-litre cans in the back. That will get you to the frontier town. I will leave the car in the street, not in the hotel park.' He handed her his card, which had a Marseilles address. 'Let me know, if you can, when you are outside this country, where you finally leave the car. The company's insurance will deal with it. It will be reported as a theft.'

Ben Abbis looked briefly at his watch. 'A last thing. I am doing this for you because I want to. I know this man Djebal. He is a ruthless criminal, and Salek, I suspect, would not be much better if he got the chance. There has been quite enough bloodshed in this country. But I do also have another motive, a personal one. I cannot, I know, prevent your friend from making full use of this story. I do not think Gérard will object to most of the Silverman story being told – whatever that turns out to be. But in return for my service to you, will you try to find a way to keep Gérard's name out of it – at least for as long as he lives? It should not be difficult. The two stories are separable. It is perhaps a small request to make for an old man who has suffered enough.'

Ben Abbis did not wait for a reply. He was crossing the room to the door. He seized the handle and held it an instant. 'Good luck. I know Gérard would also wish it to you. He is a good man, you know.'

He had gone before she could begin to offer any kind of thanks.

21.

Claudia lay on the bed thinking, first in one direction then the other. Was Salek really as devious as Ben Abbis made out? Even if he was, and assuming that Silverman had been involved in some way in Beazley's murder, how could he lay hands on them when the principal evidence, Beazley's skull, lay beyond his beyond his grasp in England? Then she thought one of them could be held to ransom for the skull's return to Sahara. They could be arrested this evening. Michael might already have been.

She tried to stop thinking and conserve her energy, all of which might be needed in the near future. It was probably only anxiety, but she felt the fever threatening again. She drank more orange juice.

She must have been dozing. She came to about six, aware that the hotel was full of noise. Salek and his men had taken over the whole of the top floor – she heard heavy boots clamping in the room above. Michael came in looking exhausted but, she could see, a great deal more concerned about her than himself. 'How are you?' were his first words, and despite everything she knew for sure in this moment that his feeling for her went beyond just liking.

'Much better.'

'Hocen brought the juice?' He looked at the crate.

She climbed out of bed, and with a bit of eyebrow-raising and head nodding got the bathroom routine going. With everyone in the building drawing on the no doubt limited supply of oasis water, there wasn't much of a splash, but enough to conceal their conversation from electronic ears. She told Michael what had happened and the amazing offer made to them.

He was sitting on the edge of the bath. His fatigue seemed to fall from him like a discarded skin. From his pocket he drew out a small object and held it up trimphantly. It was clearly a spent bullet.

'There's now nothing to stop us going,' he said, and in his confident way began to tell her what had happened in the cave. 'I showed them the pit where Beazley was slung. They got so busy getting the rest of the bones up, with Salek giving orders left right and centre, they forgot about me. I slipped away, went up to the upper cave, and started looking. I first found what seemed like a ricochet mark on the rock, then another. The bullet was just lying there on the floor where it's been all these years. The police certainly never tried to look for Beazley, or they must have found it.'

'Salek doesn't know?'

'No. I was afraid he'd realise I was missing from the party and guess why. But I just put the thing in my pocket and rejoined them. He was so pleased with himself for having raised the rest of the skeleton with all his fancy gear, I don't think he'd noticed I'd been absent. I had to hang about all day while they searched for the bullet. They're going again tomorrow.'

She told him of her fears about being held to ransom.

'Right,' he said. 'I think it's very possible Salek could be up to something. He's been curiously silent about the skull, when you'd think, today, it would have been very much in his mind. We go tonight then, yes? You think we can trust Ben Abbis? You don't think he's setting us up?'

'No. What he said rang all too true. Anyway, what other option do we have?'

She was worried of course whether Michael or herself would be OK physically – and there was still at the back of her mind a major unresolved problem about the whole business – but she said nothing. Thanks to Ben Abbis, they were going at last. That was the thing to concentrate on. They fell to discussing in a lot more detail the surely hazardous journey they'd have to make.

It was the longest evening of Claudia's life. She decided with Michael that she should stay in her room, feigning to be iller than she was. It might help to allay any thoughts Salek might have that they were about to do a flit.

It was an error. After dinner, which again took place upstairs in Salek's room and which Michael had to attend, Salek came down to see her. Though she protested it was quite unnecessary, he insisted she saw a doctor. As there was no one half-competent in Tifgad, he said, he would send the helicopter to Lagoued to fetch his own man. It would only take a couple of hours. Nothing she said would dissuade him, and she did not like to over-protest, which might have aroused his suspicion.

The doctor didn't arrive until nearly midnight. Salek came in with him. The doctor, Claudia knew, understood he had been called unnecessarily, but he had to go through the motions of a lengthy diagnosis for the sake of his standing with his powerful patient, who remained a fussy witness to the consultation. He had brought with him a chemist's shopful of remedies in an old-fashioned black bàg. He repeated each instruction several times. Every minute he stayed was bringing the dawn that much closer.

When they'd gone, she dressed and packed her bag, but it was an hour later and nearly one o'clock before the hotel stilled. She had left her door unlocked. Michael slipped in, carrying his own bag.

A frightful thought struck her – the front door. It would be bolted and barred as it had been on the first morning. As she whispered, Michael raised his finger to his lips. He'd thought of it. The bigger danger, he said, was from two guards on the upper floor outside Salek's rooms.

Their saviour was Hocen once again. Primed by Michael, he was down in the hall, waiting in the darkness to perform this last service to them, and risking his neck. He gently eased the bolts and turned the heavy locks. When he had the door open,Claudia pulled him to her and held him tightly for a moment. 'Send me an address where I can write safely,' she said, and slipped the envelope she'd rapidly prepared into his hand. She would have liked to give him more, but she had only travellers' cheques which might be dangerous for him to cash. The envelope contained nearly all her remaining Saharan currency, about a hundred pounds. She only hoped that, for Hocen, that would be a small fortune. What else could repay him for what he had done?

They couldn't delay, not least for Hocen's sake. They slid into the deserted street, which was lit much too brightly by star and moonlight. Ben Abbis had thoughtfully parked the car as far from the hotel as he reasonably could. Michael had already identified where it was – he pointed to it. It was on the opposite side of the road in an alley between two houses and on a slight slope. It was, Claudia saw gratefully, a largish car, which looked like a Peugeot.

As she made towards it she was aware Michael wasn't following. She looked round, and he'd moved into the shadow on the right side of the front door where there was an old cannon and a pyramid of large cannon balls, a strange relic of Sahara's colonial past which had somehow survived the revolution. Michael had remarked about it earlier. He seemed to be lifting one of the balls.

This *was* what he was doing. He carried it across the road and put it in the back seat of the car. 'Souvenir,' he said. Not for the first time she thought him totally daft.

Michael wanted her to drive. The slope was useful. She'd be able to avoid using the starter. Seated, for a moment they regarded the hotel. There was only one light on the front side of the building. Salek's rooms were at the back, she remembered. Hopefully, the guards were dozing. They rolled forward. The engine took, stumbled, and recovered. In the silence of the sleeping town it sounded ear-splitting. Michael looked back as they went away down the street. He said there didn't seem to be anything stirring in the hotel.

Neither was there, it seemed. The slumber of the oasis town stayed undisturbed. They'd been a little unsure of the road they had to take, but Hocen had given Michael instructions. They passed Petit-frères's house, where no light showed, and circled the oasis. There was a crossroads, and a home-made looking signpost cheered them on their way. Nobody was following.

For a few kilometres the road was metaled. Could it really be like this all the way? No such luck. As if it had started out bravely but lost heart as soon as it contemplated the vast prospect of the desert ahead, they plunged abruptly on to the usual, not very compacted, dirt. They were accompanied, as ever, by the dense cloud of choking dust their tyres raised, which soon penetrated the car, sucked back through the boot, and coated everything including their skins. She felt it even inside her clothes.

They had calculated it was about seven hundred kilometres to the frontier. If they managed a steady hundred and twenty kilometres an hour – the maximum one could undertake on this road -and if they didn't have to stop, it would take something under six hours. That would make their arrival at half past seven, about half an hour after dawn. But an even more relevant fact than daylight was when Salek would discover they'd gone. If the frontier post had been alerted, they would have had it. It was doubtful if there was any way of circumventing it.

Claudia had been so caught up in the events and the driving, she hadn't given much attention to Michael's physical state, except to marvel at the way he seemed to have recovered from his ordeal. The idea was that they should take it in turns to drive, in one hour stints. When they'd been going for half an hour, she realised he was in some kind of discomfort. She switched on the inside light. To her horror she saw that the back of his shirt was badly stained with blood.

'I think I opened up one or two of the wounds in the cave today,' he said, as if he'd just acquired a couple of mosquito bites.

She stopped at once. She still had some of the brown liquid from the Lagoued chemist. They both got out. She got his shirt off, doing more damage to the wounds which had stuck to the cotton, and plastered the stuff on while he lay over the bonnet of the car. His back was again not a pretty sight, even in the moonlight. He agreed the best thing was to keep the shirt off and kneel on the front passenger seat, facing backwards. When she'd finished anointing him, he kissed her on the mouth. They held each other for several moments.

By mutual agreement, it seemed, they broke away from each other. They would sort out that side of things when they were safe, it would be dangerous to do otherwise. Claudia guessed that was what Michael was thinking, too.

They travelled nonetheless in an enchanted silence. For many miles Claudia could think of nothing else. Had she foreseen that this would happen? Was it happening, was Michael in love with her and was she falling in love with him? Or was it some purely reflex action to the joint strain they had been under? She couldn't decide, she couldn't decide anything except that a new delicious hope and peace had descended on her despite the danger they were still in. She had to make a conscious effort to sever herself from this feeling. Time enough, she had to keep saying to herself, time enough when they were free of this benighted country, free to contemplate again the things life was really about.

The road remained deserted. Early on, they passed a lorry making for Tifgad, that was all. For the next hours, Claudia forced herself to think that avoiding a broken axle was the major concern, and watching to the east for the first unwelcome signs of the rising sun. Not that daylight would make them much more conspicuous than they were already. A helicopter following the road would have no difficulty in spotting them miles ahead from the cloud of dust they were raising.

Michael wanted to do his share of the driving. He said if he leaned forward and didn't let his back touch the seat he could do so perfectly well. Claudia wouldn't hear of it. He'd been working through the heat of the day in that cave, she reminded him, while she'd been lying on a bed drinking orange-juice. But she was still ill, he insisted. She happily denied it. 'I'm cured,' she said.

And actually, though she was feeling pretty peculiar, driving helped. Wasn't pain or sickness or faintness supposed to be a signal to the brain that something was amiss and that action was needed? If the brain ignored the signals, didn't the signals give up? It seemed like it. Instead they had another giggling session. Michael had taken several soft garments out of his bag and hers and made himself a sort of cushion to lie over. It was certainly an eccentric position to travel in.

Apart from a pee stop, they kept going – an Aix to Ghent situation. But long sections of the road were bad and she had to reduce speed. They passed along the edge of what she believed was called an erg – an area of sand rather nearer to most people's idea of what the Sahara was like perhaps than the reality of rock-waste. In patches the wind had blown sand across the road. She was afraid they'd get bogged down in one of these drifts, some of which were quite deep. She'd noticed a spade strapped to the lid of the boot – no doubt it was often necessary equipment. They nearly came to a standstill once or twice, but with Formula-One-like revs and a little skewing to the right and left they survived. When dawn first showed, according to the kilometre-meter they were still a hundred and fifty short of the frontier. They stopped to put in the two reserve tins of petrol.

Daylight broadened with horrifying speed. In his back-to-front position, Michael was constantly scanning the sky behind them. She was doing the same forwards. The most likely thing, they agreed, was that the frontier would be alerted and the frontier police would be looking for them from there. Would the frontier have a helicopter handy, or would they just send a car down the road towards them with a couple of armed men? There was indeed no alternative route they could take if they were on this road. To go cross-country was out of the question. The barren landscape abounded with impassable dry wadis.

A half hour passed, then nearly an hour. Still they travelled an empty road, and the sun was beginning to make itself felt. Then on the horizon a vehicle appeared ahead.

'Here it comes,' Claudia said.

Michael had found he could alternate his kneeling posture with sitting forwards on the seat without undue discomfort. He switched to the latter posture. They wondered if they should pull off the track. But what use would that be? They would have been seen by now. They decided they had to chance it and keep going. They clung to the possibility of bribery, though they both knew this was not really worth trying. If they wanted the money Michael had, they'd take it, and make them both countersign their remaining travellers' cheques.

'Stop, could you?' Michael said, a short way on. 'Pull right into the side.'

Mystified, Claudia did so. Michael got out, opened the back door and took out the cannon ball. He told her to stay where she was. In the driving mirror she saw him burying the cannon ball in some loose stones just behind the car. She asked him what on earth he was doing.

'Simple precaution.' He recovered his seat and changed the subject. 'I think as we've stopped we might remain stopped. Less provocative, don't you think?'

The imminent danger displaced Claudia's puzzlement about the cannon ball. They waited like a couple of dazed rabbits – one dazed rabbit anyway, Claudia thought. It was at least a private car approaching, she saw, not a police or an army vehicle.

It was a huge car, almost of the dimensions of Salek's vehicle. It was black, and had curtains in the back windows. It stopped just in front of them, and from the back seat emerged a large character out of the Arabian Nights. Bare-headed, he wore a newly-laundered white burnous and enormous yellow slippers with turned-up toes. There was a suspense-laden pause.

'Vous êtes en panne?' he enquired genially, and looking at the car as if the fault might be apparent.

The car wasn't en panne, Claudia nearly said, they were. She resisted the temptation. Michael, bare to the waist, was making sure he kept his back out of view, but there were still bruises on his chest and face as well. How would the man react to this? He grew curious all of a sudden. He walked forward, peered at Michael's side, then, moving round, at his back.

'Had a bit of a fall,' Michael said, in French. 'We're speleologists.' ('Des spéléologues', was the word he used – Claudia wasn't sure if it was the right one).

Right word or not, it did the trick. The man nodded his head gravely, then clicked his tongue with sympathy.

'Mais ce n'est pas bon, ça. Vous aurez dû consulter un médecin.'

A bright notion in the middle of the desert, Claudia thought. There was more humming and haa-ing, warnings about the danger of having such wounds in the heat, doubts about the efficacy of the ointment they had applied.

'These Saharans know nothing about medicine,' he added in good English. Apparently their nationality was apparent.

Claudia doubted his judgement there, but other thoughts were uppermost. Who was he – not, thankfully, a Saharan obviously – and what would he do? His line of thought had come ominously to an end, and he seemed to be thinking.

'Attendez,' he said then, and marched purposefully back to his car. He got into the back seat leaving the door open and, not entirely to their comfort, they saw him reach for a telephone. Michael made a move to try to stop him. She held his arm. In their apprehension, neither of them had noticed until this moment the number plate of the car. It was Moroccan. With any luck . .

The man re-emerged. 'C'est tout organisé,' he said. 'I have just spoken to my secretary in Rabat. He will arrange something for you at the frontier – on our side of course.'

As they stumbled into abject thanks, he brushed them aside and took out a wallet. From it he produced a card which with a flourish he held forward to Michael between two manicured fingers. She looked over his shoulder.

The name was an essay. It took up two lines. Underneath it said: 'Ministre de Commerce.'

They allowed him time to drive off. When he'd gone a fair distance, Michael told her to get into the Peugeot and back it a few yards. She did so. The stones in which the cannon ball were concealed were thus hidden from the rapidly retreating Minister if he happened to be watching.

As he uncovered the object, Claudia guessed. She'd fleetingly thought Michael must have buried the cannon ball because it might have been a difficult thing to explain at the frontier, either side – and after all he had stolen it. But of course it wasn't a cannon ball at all. Looking at it, she realised it wasn't even stone.

'I'd've left it here, buried, if it had been the Saharan fuzz,' Michael said.

'It's the skull?' He nodded. 'But you said you'd sent the skull home by post?'

'I know. I did think of it, but it wasn't really on. Couldn't rely on the mail here. It's a neat job, don't you think? I used clay and water. It didn't look so different from the other cannon balls. Only the weight is different of course.'

She didn't ask why he'd deceived her, because she knew. He hadn't told her the truth because he thought she would have been anxious. He was dead right about that. She didn't pressure him to say this, it was better left as it was. Anyway, they were still confronted with the immediate problem ahead.

'I think we keep up the speleologist line, don't you?' Michael said as they got under way again. 'The giant fossil sitting there on the back seat is just what a speleologist might have in his knapsack. The main problem may be persuading them what a fossil is.'

They did not discuss that they might simply be arrested and have no opportunity or need to explain the skull.

22.

When Claudia woke she panicked for a moment. The air was different – softer, damper – the light less stark. She realised there were curtains, dainty curtains of a pinkish lacy material which were stirring in a gentle breeze coming through two open windows. She sat up in the huge double bed and found herself surrounded by a foam of frilly bed linen. Of course. She was in Marrakech in a five star hotel and, surely, safe.

They'd survived the Saharan frontier post without trouble. No message had come from Tifgad, and two dazed soldiers peered into the back seats but didn't seem to notice the round object on the floor. On the Moroccan side, ministerial instructions had arrived, a telex was handed to them. They were to wait for an hour or two in the one-horse hotel the small town offered. A vehicle would arrive – they gathered from the phraseology it would be an ambulance – which would 'transport' them, it did not say where. Presumably to a hospital for the treatment of Michael's wounds.

They imagined at first that Claudia would follow in Ben Abbis's car. They decided, however, if an ambulance did arrive, to leave the Peugeot in the care of the hotel – which the manager was happy to allow. If it was to be returned to Lagoued, this was surely the most convenient arrangement for whoever was to recover it.

They had to wait over three hours. Claudia couldn't help thinking they'd have been well on the way to Casablanca and an aeroplane in this time. But they could hardly turn down so generous a bounty from such a high level, and Michael was able to rest in the room the hotel gave them. He lay on the bed on his stomach and soon went to sleep. Though dropping, Claudia couldn't sleep – she was too scared a message would come through to the Saharan frontier post and an armed posse would come over to seize them.

They were unmolested. It did prove to be an ambulance which arrived – huge, air-conditioned, and sprung like a mattress. The driver, who also seemed to be a para-medic, cleaned up a couple of Michael's wounds which had opened up. He anointed them anew with the last of the Lagoued apothecary's brew, and Michael was able to stretch out full-length on the bed, lying on his stomach. Claudia travelled with him. Not to be driving, and not having all that anxiety hanging round their necks was bliss.

The very amiable driver only spoke Arabic, but before they left the hotel the manager had translated for them. They were destined, it seemed, for Marrakech, where they'd been booked into the famous Mamounia Hotel. Again, Claudia would have preferred it if Casblanca airport had been their objective, but Michael was delighted. 'It'll cost us, but I suggest we have a couple of nights' swan,' he said. 'We deserve it.' She didn't feel she could demur.

Dazed from the miles they had travelled (and Claudia feeling like a scruffy tramp in filthy clothes she'd had no chance to wash) they staggered up to the huge reception desk to be told they were booked in for as long as they wished to stay 'as guests of the Morrocan Government.' They were not even required to sign in. Their two bags had been seized outside and their key was handed to a page boy with a fez at a rakish angle. It seemed to Claudia like fate. She succumbed to it willingly enough. Who looked a gift-horse?

They followed the page and the luggage porter – Michael, like a referee who had confiscated a football from an unruly children's match, bearing the skull, alias cannon ball, alias fossil, under one arm. Would their benefactor have assumed they slept together, Claudia remembered wondering drowsily as they mounted smoothly in the lift?

He, or his secretary, had taken care of every detail. Every combination was catered for in this palatial suite. There was this huge double bed she'd woken in and, in the adjoining room, twin beds. Michael had collapsed into one of these.

She looked at her watch. It was nearly eleven. She'd slept for ten hours. She felt entirely well, she noted with joy, except for a bit of stiffness from the driving. Her bout of flu had been cast off like an unwanted skin. She flung back the bedclothes and went in to Michael's room. He wasn't there, neither were his shoes and clothes. She felt a sharp disappointment. Waiting for him to return, she rang for someone to collect her meagre selection of laundry. She discovered thankfully that the hotel had an efficient three-hour service.

Michael appeared in about three-quarters of an hour when she was still in her now very grubby housecoat, having had a luxurious bath into which she'd tipped a soapy unguent from the battery of exotic packets which were lined up on a glass shelf, and having given her nails – hands and toes – the full treatment.

'I've despatched the skull,' he said. 'I'm fed up with carrying it, and it'll be safer this way. It cost a fortune but I've sent it by special courier to the friend I mentioned before, with instructions to get cracking on the forensic – the teeth, and the bullet perforations.'

She knew from the way he said this what was happening. It was a give-away tone, almost as if it were said by someone else, in another room, about something quite irrelevant to them. They looked at each other, and she flung herself into his arms, only at the last moment remembering she had to be careful of his back. He held her, and kissed her – not so much passionately as tenderly. At the back of her mind she was conscious of a mild surprise at this. Had she anticipated he'd be a tempestuous, perhaps rather a ruthless sort of lover?

In the event he was grave and deliberate. He took off her two items of clothing, slowly, deliberately, and laid them on the chair. He took off his own, then, naked and aroused, in an almost leisurely way picked her up and carried her to the bed. He made her feel like a citadel from which initially he was barred. It seemed he circled the fortification, not with apology certainly, but gently, almost politely. Michael had surely had many women before her, but she sensed in these moments a certain deference. Was this to womenkind in general, or just to her? Was he in some way uncertain of her, nervous of offending her? At all events this withholding ignited her own passion in a sudden overwhelming surge. She felt a rush of impatience. She did not want to be wooed. Perhaps it was the accumulated tensions of the last days, perhaps it was more than that. She wanted him to possess her, to overcome her, to bear no regard to anything but his own desire, which would automatically gratify her own.

He knew at once what she wanted of him. Perhaps because he responded with such immediate and intuitive understanding, he gave her what she had never experienced before. Successive waves of sensation heaved and burst, like rollers breaking on a shore. She felt her whole being was exploding, exploding – the big bang.

The moment when at last they came to a breathless halt, was perhaps the best of all. While they lay, still interlocked, they looked into each others' eyes. 'File that to The Times,' she said, and they both started laughing. The shaking of his shrinking object gave her a last flutter of physical delight. She didn't think Michael Strode had any idea what he was taking on when he asked her to go to Sahara with him. She certainly hadn't. Would it last? She refused to think.

They didn't know if food was included in the generosity of their absent benefactor, and didn't feel like asking. But, ravenous, they decided not to think about it. If they got an astronomic bill they'd shut their eyes and pay with a credit card. 'Don't forget I should have more than something coming to me for my story,' Michael said.

Though by now it was past midday, they began by ordering a vast breakfast to be sent up, which included Parma ham and melon – for which Claudia said she would sell her soul.

They inevitably began talking about the story Michael was going to write. He was going to be hamstrung of course by their moral obligation to Ben Abbis and Gérard Petit-frères. But with the skull, and the bullet, Michael thought, there was plenty for a pretty strong hypothesis story. Re-interviewing Archie, primed as they now were with the new information, was also going to be interesting. Under cross-examination Archie might be forced to reveal a lot more which he'd hitherto concealed.

Claudia kept, still, her tacit reservations, but she was now resigned to the fact that, however innocent he might still prove to have been on larger counts, Alan had in practice connived at the circumstances which had caused Beri's death, and must surely deserve some retribution. In her happiness, she kept away from the central issue.

'How will you handle Djebal and Salek?' she asked instead. 'Your own story, I mean. You know I don't want to be in it.'

'I'll tell it straight. That is, Salek's version. I go to get the cooperation of the Ministry of Culture. I'm arrested, accused of espionage, and beaten up. I'll include your story about Salek intervening on my behalf, without mentioning your name – unless I can persuade you to let me – and speculate, not entirely in his favour, about his motive. Salek and I go to the cave and I find the bullet, just as it happened. Then I say I decide to scarper because I don't trust Salek. I nick Ben Abbis's keys, his car – and away. I won't be able to mention any of this stuff here in Morocco of course. Don't want to embarrass the minister when he's being so incredibly decent.'

221

'Salek must be gnashing his teeth.'

'Let him gnash.'

Claudia began to have a nasty thought. Salek wouldn't surely know where they were, but he must know by now they were in Morocco. They'd had to sign a currency declaration form at the Saharan frontier post and everyone in the adjacent Moroccan border village knew that two British people, one with a badly lacerated back, had left a Peugeot car at the hotel and had been taken northwards in an ambulance. The hotel manager knew they were bound for Marrakech.

Michael wasn't in the mood for such a pessimistic supposition, neither really was she. She kept it to herself, along with her thoughts about Alan.

She gave herself to their idyll. When her clothes arrived, beautifully restored, they dressed – Michael in a tropical suit and a new sports shirt he'd bought when he went out that morning – and walked in the enchanted garden full of dizzy scents, which put Falla's Gardens of Spain into the shade. They soon found this too hot in the mid-afternoon sun and went back into one of the bars where they gulped ice beers, first at the bar counter, than in a smoochy little corner seat to which Michael led her with his arm round her waist. She felt like a teenager.

He told her he was in love with her. With the total frankness she'd come to expect from him, he told her it was the second time in his life. The first time had been when he was sixteen – his first affair – and the girl had jilted him.

She knew Michael's declaration was no kind of a gambit, but she did make again the unspoken reservation – perhaps, now, it was of the touch-wood variety. Michael's feelings might well have arisen, as might her own, out of the ordeal they'd been through together. It was surely much too early to quantify them? But her answer was to squeeze his arm and to hope her face expressed the happiness she felt. She knew he wouldn't be in a hurry to press her with further questions. She knew he was the kind of man who would put his tender on the table as it were, and wait. She knew that, despite his modern approach to most things, that was how Michael saw the male-female relationship – in rather an old-fashioned way, the man proposing, the female disposing. She supposed it was something of a paradox. It might have been expected that he'd've wanted to carry her off like a Roman with

222

one of those Sabine women.

After a long session in the bar, they were seriously hungry again. They ate a huge and delicious lunch in the ornate dining-room. After it, they went upstairs for a siesta, and slept for the first time in each other's arms. They woke, and went for a delicious swim in the pool. Then it was the bar again, another meal – fortunately dress wasn't too formal and a blouse and skirt just about passed muster – then dancing to a live band providing music for what was called 'A Bygones Evening', presumably to please the ageing foreign visitors, mostly American, who made up the majority of guests. The band played waltzes and quick-steps, into which, stumblingly at first, they found their way. They congratulated themselves for performing so creditably at them. Claudia didn't still know how serious her feelings were. All she was certain about when they went to bed in the small hours was that the past day had been among the happiest and most memorable of her life.

They both woke early the next morning, full of energy. Michael said he was going to start thinking about his story. While he sat in the other room immersed in that journalistic concentration which was as impervious as deafness, Claudia began to think of thank-you letters.

She most wanted to write to Hocen, but of course couldn't think of doing this until all the fuss had died down. Not having his home address, she would have to write to him care of the Oasis Hotel. Michael had already posted money to Tadj a generous guess at the sum they owed, in travellers' cheques, half of which she would refund to Michael on their return home. She thought a brief note to Tadj was in order. It might cheer him up a bit when he recovered from the wrath Salek would quite likely have expended on him when he discovered their departure. Ben Abbis was easy. His business address in Marseilles was on the card he'd handed her. She thanked Ben Abbis with all the words she could summon for probably having saved their lives, and assured him that Michael would steadfastly respect his wishes concerning Petit-frères. She told him where they'd left his car and said she'd be refunding him for the petrol and the cost of the recovery when she returned home. She sent a message of goodwill via him to Petit-frères, and gave him her home address. Lastly she wrote to their Moroccan benefactor who had treated two total strangers with such truly wonderful Arab hospitality and kindness. She determined also to buy something expensive and English to send him when they got back. She didn't say anything about the real reasons for their being where they were and for the physical state Michael was in, though he'd no doubt hear about this if and when Michael's story broke at home.

When Michael had finished what he was doing, he clearly felt a little restless. To her relief, he'd volunteered the idea before that an attempt could be made to kidnap them and return them to Sahara. He'd said it was probably a good safety precaution to stay inside the hotel. But the thought of being in Marrakech and not seeing it proved too much for his curiosity. Neither of them had been here before. Why didn't they risk it, he said? Claudia thought it would have been silly as well as chicken to resist when she, too, was anxious to see the place.

They strayed out into the famous market place and watched, with the mass of other tourists, the various entertainments – the juggler, the fire-blower, the snake-charmer, the several story-tellers and their little knots of wrapt listeners, of all ages. They wandered into the crowded lanes of the souk. Claudia looked inconclusively at jewellery and materials, none of which she had the money or the inclination to buy, and Michael wanted a pair of shoes, which could be made in a couple of hours and delivered to the hotel.

Michael was negotiating with the shoemaker and she was looking into a shop window opposite. For some reason she had an uneasy feeling someone was observing her. As unobtrusively as she could, she turned her head. Sure enough, about twenty yards away down the covered twisting way between the crowded stalls and shops a man was standing looking in her direction. For a moment before he turned away, she saw his face. She was sure it was Ouboussad. When he saw her looking towards him, he quickly disappeared into the mêlée.

She rushed into Michael who was in the back of the shop. The bargaining was taking an age to resolve. She hissed the news into his ear. He took no notice.

She lost her nerve and forced him to attend to her. Michael said she couldn't be sure it was Ouboussad in this crowd. It was probably delayed action shock on her part, he said, resulting from what had been happening in the last days. To the shopkeeper's annoyance, she forced him to abandon the shoes and go back to the hotel immediately. On the way she said they must fly home at once and not tomorrow, which they had tentatively thought should be the limit of their indulgence.

Michael was reluctant to go. She still felt quite adamant, but agreed to discuss it in the bar with him before they spoke to the travel agent who had a booth in the hotel. As he carried the beer to their corner seat she realised that, other honeymoons as there might be later, this first unscheduled one was over. They were back on the job, and the job, she was now certain, was by no means finished. A number of thoughts she'd had from that first day in the cave came together in a concerted rush.

'There's a third party,' she began. Michael looked at her blankly. 'There's been a third party all along. Whoever it is, I think Ouboussad's working for him, or "it." Right from that first day in Sahara I've been aware of something which doesn't fit. The cigarette butt at the cave entrance has never been explained, neither has the figure I thought I saw on that further mountainside. Until my conversation with Ben Abbis, we both thought it could have been someone working for Petit-frères, but Ben Abbis made it clear Petit-frères didn't consider himself in any kind of danger until I went to see Jezi. Then there's the ransacking of your room in Tifgad and the attempt to find the skull. That could have been Petit-frères trying to destroy evidence, whatever Ben Abbis said, but it happened while I'd gone to see Jezi. I can't think he could have acted so quickly. I can't think it was Salek, either, without destroying the whole of his story. Finally, there's the question of who shopped us to Salek's office. Again, Petit-frères had the motive, but could he have so misled Ben Abbis, who was clearly astounded at the idea he'd done such a thing? What makes sense is that someone else – someone who pretty desperately wants to stop us getting to the truth – has been working against us all the time. And it's highly likely Ouboussad, whose attitude to us throughout was strange, is that person's accomplice. I'd swear it wasn't just your being angry with him which made him so shifty that day we went to the cave. Someone had got to him about us. Ouboussad may well have followed us up to the cave – and then feigned sleep when we got back to the car.'

Michael interrupted. 'If it was Ouboussad you saw in the souk just now. You're basing an awful lot on that.'

'I'm as sure as I can be it was him.'

She was expecting to have to argue, but Michael put his hand on hers. 'OK, if you're worried, Claudia, we'll get a flight tonight, if we can. Even if this proves to be a hare, we won't enjoy it here now.'

Michael phoned British Airways right away, got two tickets which they could pick up at Casablanca airport, and cancelled their flight the next morning. They'd get a car to Casa, Michael said.

Claudia supposed she could be getting paranoid, but she didn't trust the hall porter whom Michael asked to book them a car. Immediately it was done, she slunk up to the reception desk and quietly asked for their bill. There wasn't one. They'd paid cash for their drinks, but apparently meals, including wine, were on the Minister of Commerce as well as the suite. As soon as they got upstairs, she told Michael what she wanted to do.

Her idea was that Ouboussad, or whoever, might well have been in and done a deal with the hall porter to keep him informed of their movements. The man could at this moment be tipping off Ouboussad that they were going. Ouboussad could arrange for a limousine to pick them up, but it would be to Sahara that they'd be driven, at gunpoint, not Casablanca. It was quite against Michael's style to accept this cloak and dagger stuff, and he resisted. But she knew he wasn't so dismissive as he would have been a few days ago.

'It's too fantastic,' he said, 'a Tifgad taxi driver going in for all this. Even if it was him you saw in the souk, which I can't believe.'

She began to think so, too, for a moment, but she yielded no ground, and she supposed it was a sign of Michael's feelings for her that he finally agreed to what she suggested, even half joining in the cloak and dagger atmosphere. They packed their bags and on his suggestion, to avoid going through the main hall, slipped into the service lift, which took them down to the ground floor and released them into a delivery bay at the side of the hotel. They walked through the grounds and reached the road through a garden gate. As they went, they were watched by an Arab, probably an off-duty hotel employee, leaning against a wall. Claudia was afraid he'd dart back into the hotel, assuming they were trying to slink off without paying their bill. But if he did have this thought, he didn't appear to be about to act on it. He continued to stare until they were out of his sight. Claudia hailed the first cruising taxi. The man agreed to take them to Casablanca, and Michael haggled a price.

She sat back in the seat and began to feel her muscles relaxing. She was back to the feeling she'd had earlier that morning. She took Michael's arm and put her head on his shoulder.

He laughed. 'Perhaps we should have bought false wigs and moustaches.'

In her haste to depart they hadn't had any food. They had time to kill before their flight left. When they'd been going about an hour they began to look out for a place to stop. It was a parched landscape, towns and villages were few and far between, and those there were didn't offer anything that would be acceptable. But in the middle of nowhere a place hove into view ahead of them, surrounded by a posse of eucalyptus trees. Their driver said it was a hotel, which had a restaurant.

It was off the road, a blindingly white building with a roof of crinkly red tiles, which was shaped in the style of a Spanish ranch. There were no animals in sight, but it had wooden fences enclosing the several acres of barren land which surrounded it. A similarly functionless white fence avenued the track that led to the front entrance. They were approaching the Hotel Hacienda, they were informed on a section of a tree-trunk onto which the letters had been archly burnt. Clearly, the place was designed for tourists.

There was a pleasant inner patio overgrown with a vine – just the place they wanted to spend a couple of lazy hours. There was every reason, Claudia thought, not to get to the airport early.

Their driver didn't seem to mind stopping and extending the hire time, and didn't try to up the fixed price they'd agreed. They saw him parking the car in the shade of the trees and making preparations for a siesta on the back seat.

There had been three other cars parked outside. Their occupants were already eating. At one table there were two men in earnest conversation. The other party, which must have owned two cars, was a family – three generations by the look of them, grandparents, parents, and three children. Claudia relaxed further and, as the wine began to percolate, began to feel ashamed of herself.

They must have sat there talking for getting on for two hours. They'd eaten a delicious set lunch of another melon and Spanish-style ham (not up to Parma but delicious), a scrumptious chicken cooked with almonds and served with ratatouille, then cheese and a huge bowl of fruit. The white wine was local, they were told. It was certainly good. The other two tables had been vacated and they'd heard the cars drive off.

The sound of another car approaching didn't worry her. She'd been rather surprised more people hadn't stopped on this main road. No new customers appeared. She half thought it was a delivery maybe or someone visiting the proprietor.

They still had an hour to kill in addition to the time it would take to reach Casablanca. They thought they would go, get to Casablanca, and drive around the town a bit before going out to the airport. They paid the bill, thanked the proprietor for such a good meal, and left.

The taxi driver had moved his car to a position right beside the front door. As soon as he saw them emerging, he leapt out of the driving seat to open the rear door for them. At some level Claudia registered the oddness of this. He'd struck her before as a particularly lethargic man. They'd kept him too long, she thought, and he was anxious to go.

She noticed another car, which must the one that had arrived a few minutes ago. It was parked some way from the house on the far side of the parking area. It looked like an American sports car – red, low, and unnecessarily bulky. As they drove off at a greater speed than she expected, she just managed to see there were two people in the front seats. They seemed to be looking for something on the floor, their faces hidden.

It was then she noticed the state their driver was in. His head was shaking, so were his hands as they clutched the wheel. Michael was sorting out credit cards in his wallet. She caught the driver's eyes in the driving mirror. He was looking back, terrified, towards the house. She turned and saw the red car starting out behind them.

'Ne regardez pas,' the man said in a grotesque whisper. 'Ils sont des bandits.'

They dragged it out of him in bits. He'd been dozing in the car. One of them had got into the seat beside him and put a gun to his head. He was to drive right up to the front door, as he had, and when his clients came out move off quickly in the direction of Casa. They would follow. At a certain point on the road to Casa they would indicate with a flash of their headlights that they were to turn off to the right on to a track. Any attempt to stop, or contact another car, any failure to carry out the instructions exactly, and all three of them would die.

Claudia's stomach was water. She looked at Michael. He'd also looked back at their pursuers. 'What did the man look like?' he asked the shaking driver.

The shoulders hunched. 'Short. Dark hair. Spanish maybe.'

'Was he Morrocan, do you think?'

'Didn't look like it. Talked French. European, I'd say.' The man was cracking up. 'For God's sake give them what they ask,' he burbled. 'They're killers. Someone was shot on the road last month by bandits. I've got nothing to do with this. I've a wife and four children . . .'

Michael sat back in his seat. Claudia envied him his apparent calm. 'Don't worry,' he said. 'We'll just do everything they say. It'll be all right.'

She wanted to talk, to discuss who it might be. It might just be bandits, who would take Michael's remaining money and let them be. But they all three sat in tense silence while they drove on across the flat featureless landscape. They saw no tracks leading off the road. In the driving mirror Claudia could see the red car keeping a steady distance behind them of about five hundred yards. Two cars and a bus passed them going the other way. It wasn't exactly Bank Holiday traffic.

They began to go downhill slightly and the road curved. Claudia saw they were entering and crossing a shallow wadi. At the foot of the incline a small bridge came into view. The red car's lights began to flash. On the far side of the bridge was a track leading off to the right. Their driver made a noise that sounded like a whimper. He slowed, turned off the road on to the unmade surface, and began to negotiate the stones and pot-holes.

The track followed the old wadi. In half a minute they rounded a bend and the road was no longer visible. Claudia had the thought this might be the last sight she'd have of this planet.

They came to a large hole in the road where there'd been some sort of erosion or subsidence. They were obliged to stop. In a few seconds the red car came into view. It parked a hundred yards from them and the two men got out, both wearing stockings over their heads. Claudia had a spark of hope. If they were going to kill them, surely they wouldn't bother to hide their faces. All three of them got out of the taxi, and faced the music.

The smaller man, who certainly didn't look like a North African – he wore rather grubby white trousers, a black T-shirt, and pinkish-coloured trainers – carried a hand gun, and looked muscular. The other clearly was an Arab – he wore a brown habit and sandals. Claudia thought he could be Ouboussad, he was the same build and height. The clothes certainly looked like those worn by the man she'd seen in Marrakech souk.

The smaller man approached them. He thrust the gun at Michael's stomach. 'Put your hands behind your head,' he said roughly in a French which had a strong Midi accent. He nodded at the other man, who searched Michael for a weapon.

Finding none, Michael was allowed to lower his hands. The European nodded again at the Arab.

It seemed they had a prearranged plan. The Arab went to the taxi, opened the front and back doors and began to take it apart. The European continued to cover them with the pistol.

'You're wasting your time,' Michael said.

'Keep your mouth shut.'

'Your sleuth obviously didn't see me post what you want in Marrakech.'

The Arab's search went on. He'd begun by taking out the upholstery of the seats and flinging them onto the ground outside the car, then he'd raised the bonnet. Now he was opening the boot. He took out the two suitcases. Opening them, he emptied their contents onto the ground, then stood back, blankly facing the other man.

Again, the pistol was thrust into Michael's stomach. 'Where did you send it?' the other man said.

'You'd like to know that, wouldn't you?' Michael said.

'Don't argue with me, or you're dead.'

'You're not going to shoot me. If I'm dead you certainly aren't going to get it, are you?'

'I could take you back to Sahara and hand you over.'

'But you won't do that, either, will you, because Salek's interests are as opposed to yours as mine are? You're nothing to do with the Saharans.'

There was a long pause. Claudia expected the shot, Michael falling. Should she try to intervene, distract the man's attention somehow so that Michael could knock the weapon from his hand? She knew she wasn't considering this seriously. What hope would Michael have against this brute and his accomplice, even if he temporarily removed his weapon. The taxi driver, she knew, would be useless. He was a shivering wreck.

There was no shot. With an irritable movement, the man suddenly withdrew the gun from Michael's ribs, reengaged the safety catch, and put it in his pocket. 'I'm warning you. Your every movement will be watched in England. You'll get your instructions for the delivery of the skull. Fail to

230

deliver, and you're a dead man.'

Michael's cool amazed Claudia. 'Who's paying you for this?' he said.

The question was ignored. There was another final jerk of his head towards the Arab, and the two of them retreated to their car. They watched as it backed out of sight. They concluded from the noise that they must have turned right on the main road, towards Casablanca.

They waited until silence reclosed. For a moment they continued to stand, as if enjoying the silence, which Claudia thought was the most benign she'd ever experienced.

Michael then broke the spell. 'It seems you're right again. He's certainly not working for Salek. Petit-fréres, we know, is eliminated from our enquiries. A third force – there must certainly be one, and it would seem it exudes as obnoxious a smell as Djebal and Salek. If I'm not wrong that fellow was hand-picked from the murkiest elements of Marseilles.'

In a state of shock, the only thing Claudia could think about was how they'd been traced to that restaurant. She said this. Michael was barely interested. 'Someone must have been watching the hotel. They found we'd gone, and guessed which road we'd take to the airport. Having done that, the Hacienda was a good bet, I suppose. Not a great deal to choose from, was there?' He returned to the major consideration. 'But who the heck can be behind this? It can't have been that type himself, he was obviously hired. When he saw we didn't have Beazley's skull, he didn't know what to do. He had no orders.'

She still wasn't in a mood for such deduction. 'That was Oubousssad with him, I'm sure,' she said.

This time Michael wasn't listening. Meeting a wall of mystery which they were not going to surmount in the immediate future, he did the most obviously Strode-like thing. He turned and went in the other direction. He gave a shrug.

'Well, whatever, let's get to Casa,' he said. 'Maybe we won't be troubled again.'

She could not accept his optimism, but she also accepted this formula. She needed space to realise they still had their lives intact.

23.

They had difficulty persuading their driver to continue to Casablanca. Only an offer of more money and the assurance that there would be no more unpleasantness persuaded him to finish the journey. As it was, he wouldn't go to the airport and dumped them on the outskirts of the town where they had to take another taxi for the last miles. Michael was right, however. Even if their movements at the airport were being monitored, their assailants didn't show.

They named the man with the Midi accent Alphonse. Airborne, they gave themselves anew to the riddle of who was giving him his orders. Michael made another half-hearted attempt to make Salek responsible, but this made no more sense than it had before. If Salek was involved, they would almost certainly be on their way back to Sahara. He had a new idea. Could it possibly be the Foreign Office or MI5 or both, indulging in cloak and dagger? They certainly had every motive to hinder their efforts. The Consulate in Lagoued hadn't exactly jumped to Claudia's help. But could one really imagine, Claudia said, a British authority acting with the sang-froid of the CIA at the height of the cold war? Eventually, Michael also thought one couldn't. They were brought back to the idea of individuals. Who, in England, if it wasn't the State, was interested enough in trying to suppress an awkward bit of history? They agreed that, within their knowledge, there could be only two candidates.

Janet Brisbane? Surely not? She'd refused to attend Alan's memorial service in the Abbey. Everything she'd told Claudia that day she visited her in her South Devon house had been redolent of her dislike of the man. Surely she would relish his disgrace, even if it were posthumous? How also would she have known they'd gone to Sahara? This left Archie Fieldhouse. Archie did know of their trip to Sahara – Michael had told him he was going at their last interview – and Archie had as strong a motive for wishing to protect Alan's reputation as anyone. He worshipped the man. Was it possible to believe an old soldier, even one of Archie's unusual qualities, could have got someone to follow their movements so closely and behave in such an apparently ruthless fashion?

For a good half an hour Michael went to town on this possibility, with Claudia in the role of Archie's defence counsel. Money, she asked? Even given his wish to carry out such an enterprise, where on earth would Archie have got the funds? Michael had an answer to that. Silverman had left him a chunk in his will, hadn't he? Claudia had mentioned this to Michael some time back. What better cause could a man like Archie spend it on, Michael argued, than the defence of his benefactor's honour? Fieldhouse obviously knew the whole story, he said. He'd known all along exactly what Silverman did. He might even have done the murder himself on Silverman's behalf. It would be typical of Silverman to get someone else to do his dirty work for him.

Then why, Claudia countered, if Archie was involved, had he begun the whole fuss by adding details in the lecture she'd heard, which were likely to arouse suspicion? He'd surely have wanted to let sleeping dogs lie.

Michael had to think about this. He came up with an ingenious theory. 'Look, Archie clearly has two motivations,' he said. 'One is to extol his hero, the other to exploit his recently found ability to give graphic lectures. The latter is given an impetus on Silverman's death for, apart from Janet, he alone now is alive to tell the tale. He can't resist giving the story an extra twist, dangerous as this is. Then, realising too late that he's let the cat out of the bag, he has to do something about it. When he hears I'm going to Sahara, he knows very well what I may find. So he somehow hires Alphonse to put a spoke in the wheel.'

Through his network of contacts in the international underworld, Claudia asked? By this time she didn't think Michael was believing his own story. As they crossed the English coast, it lost impetus and he changed his tack. He began to wonder if they needed to bother about Alphonse anyway, now they were home. What he'd said was almost certainly bluff to cover his failure to get his hands on the skull, which had certainly been his brief. Once the Silverman story was published as a fait accompli, the chances were they'd hear no more.

Claudia was a great deal less sanguine. She suggested the first thing they should do at Heathrow was inform the police. Michael wouldn't hear of it. 'The first thing I'm doing is to check on that skull,' he said, 'which my friend, David Suter, should by now have had examined. I'll then have them check the bullet to make sure it fits the Webley calibre, and if all goes well I'm there.'

Claudia had a brief attack of weariness. Why should she involve herself further with this? She had the grotesque thought of going to ground with her dismal sister-in-law until it was over. The idea was rejected almost before she'd thought it.

'All right,' she said. 'While you're talking to David, why don't I go to Donnerton to check Alan's collection of armoury for the revolver? It's unlikely he'd've kept a murder weapon, if that's what it was, but it's worth a look. If it's there, I shall begin to suspect it wasn't a murder weapon.'

She'd meant her phrase 'if that's what it was' half in jest, but Michael took it at face value. He gave her a look. 'It's the murder weapon all right,' he said, grimly. But then, only a second later, he seemed to listen to himself, and smirked. 'All right, Claudia, touché. You can still be right about Silverman, of course you can. It could still all amount to something we haven't thought of. Yes, do go to Donnerton. We do need to know about that gun and – OK, if it's there and my bullet turns out to be of another calibre my story's in pieces.'

Michael conceiving that he might in the bowels of Christ be wrong? She really began to believe they'd travelled more than spatial distance in the last days.

As they entered the terminal building at Heathrow, Claudia began to be scared again. In the safety of the flight, the fright of the incident on the road to Casablanca had temporarily faded. Why should they think, she thought now, that people who were prepared to pull a gun on them and who had quite likely shopped them to the Saharan Government, were going to give up? Whoever it was pursuing them was no amateur. Alphonse must almost certainly have been somewhere at Casablanca airport observing their departure. If he wasn't already on another flight to London she'd be surprised, and he would have immediately alerted his superiors. There was every chance a reception committee would be waiting for them the other side of customs.

Despite what he'd said, Michael was also thinking they might be followed. When they were through customs – and there was no apparent reception committee – with no prompting from her he made her sit down while he made a couple of manoeuvres, one to the gents, then another towards the exit carrying his bag. She was to watch to see if anyone was obviously tailing him.

There didn't appear to be, but she could feel he hadn't relaxed. They took the tube into London. 'Look, there doesn't seem to be anyone on to us yet,' he said when they'd been going a few minutes, 'but on second thoughts I wonder if it is such a good idea for you to go home. If they haven't got on to us at Heathrow, the places they'll watch have to be my place and your's.'

The thought had occurred to her, and she'd already been considering an alternative. 'Right,' she said, 'but I don't need to go home. At Waterloo, I'll phone my friend Ann who's the housekeeper at Donnerton. I'll ask her if she can put me up. If she can, I'll go straight to her from Salisbury station. I can lie low at Donnerton. They won't expect me to go there. And I'll check on the pistol at the same time.'

Michael wasn't happy about this arrangement. But he finally agreed, and went to Waterloo with her to see her on to the train. They did another sleuth-checking operation in the sparsely populated concourse, and again thankfully drew a blank.

Ann was of course surprised, then alarmed, when Claudia got through to her. Why on earth wasn't she going to her own home, she asked? But she agreed to put her up, and finally accepted that Claudia would tell her all on arrival. She then offered to meet Claudia at Salisbury station.

Michael fussed to find a carriage for her which had several respectable-looking people already sitting in it. They kissed, and he retreated to the platform. They talked through the small aperture in the window. A whistle blew, and the train jolted them apart. She had a sudden desire not to leave him. It was too late. For days maybe, they would be apart.

It was nearly midnight when Claudia got to Salisbury but there, waiting anxiously at the barrier, was Ann. She was thankful – particularly when, outside, she saw the one taxi on the rank being grabbed by someone else.

'What is all this, Claudia?' Ann asked anxiously, as they scuttled towards her car on the other side of the road, Claudia setting a marathon pace. She still couldn't be sure there hadn't been someone on the train.

Claudia hadn't even told Ann she was going to Sahara, let alone that she was going in the company of a man she'd only known a few days. She'd debated in the train what she'd tell Ann and decided it couldn't be much less than all – apart from her affair with Michael, that was. Ann was totally discreet, and she was being decent to hide her like this. By the time they got to Donnerton, she'd related the main outline of the story, including the last episode with Alphonse. Ann was flabbergasted, not only at the danger she and Michael had been in, but also that any suspicion should have been thrown on Alan's integrity. Then Claudia came clean about the gun. She was afraid Ann might feel she was being implicated with this, but it was quite the reverse. She threw off her astonishment and became as excited as a schoolgirl.

'Do you really think Alan could have been a murderer?' she said. 'I can't believe it.'

When they got in, they flew up the stairs together, two at a time. They burst into the library and put all the lights on. The armoury was arranged on the walls between the bookcases. There were half a dozen groups of larger musket-like guns, and one of pikes. The pistols were arranged above the stone fireplace in two fans. Claudia had never really noticed during all the hours she'd spent brooding in that place, but one of these was of antiques, the other was of modern weapons. She then saw there was an empty space in the latter group. The wallpaper where a weapon had hung was less faded, and there was a black line on the top edge of the area, where dust had collected. Someone had surely removed the weapon very recently.

Ann whistled. Then she remembered that only a month ago she'd made an exhaustive inventory of all the objects in the house for the trust. She had a copy of it in a file sitting on one of the bookshelves. Sure enough, the pistol had been there at this time. Tired as Claudia was, they began a search of the house. They found evidence of the break-in in the basement. Someone had broken the glass of one of the small windows and forced the lock. So much then, finally, for her thought that Alan's pistol wasn't the murder weapon. How could she now think this when, as with Beazley's skull, someone needed it so desperately?

Michael had said he was going to stay with his friend David Suter if he was home. Though it was now one o'clock, Claudia tried the number he'd given her, but there was no answer. She left a message on the answer machine, telling him to call Donnerton no matter what the hour.

Her sleep was undisturbed. First thing, she tried Suter's number again.

To her relief David answered. Yes, Michael was there, still asleep. They'd been out talking until the small hours, he said. She asked him to wake Michael as she had some interesting news. Michael must have woken as she'd been speaking to David. He came on the line almost at once. She told him about her discovery and its implication.

He seemed less than interested. 'Good, well done,' he said, as if she'd won fourth place in the under-fourteens sack race. 'Proves someone's on the warpath in this country all right, doesn't it?'

They discussed this desultorily, but she knew he was bursting with something. She asked him what he'd been doing last night. There was a pregnant pause. 'Claudia, I think I'm there,' he said. 'Nigel Bellerby, editor of the Sunday Times News Review, wants my story – as it is if necessary, and of course with the rest, and conclusive proof, if I can get it. It'll be in next week, displacing the story he'd pencilled in. We also discussed price. Claudia, it's serious money, plus any expenses from now on, possibly some retroactively, Nigel says, if he can swing it.' He paused. 'I've also got a headline – "Skullduggery." Like it?'

She enthused. She was really glad for him. He'd worked hard for his story, and as things had turned out risked his life for it. But suddenly the void in her stomach was back. 'Conclusive proof if I can get it,' he'd said. They weren't finished yet.

'So, what's next?' she said with false levity, knowing he'd see through it.

'Next? Archie of course – news on the skull front being good. It arrived safely by the way, and David's expecting the forensic report this morning. Archie may well be my last port of call.'

Her spirits sank. 'Have you been followed?' she asked anxiously.

'No.'

'But – going to Archie? If you phone him in advance, and if by any chance he is criminally involved, he'll have time to tip someone off, won't he?'

'Right. That's why I'm not phoning him. I'll arrive, and hope to find him in.'

'But is that wise without back-up? It's true we haven't eliminated Archie. He could be dangerous.'

'An old man? What do you think he's got, an oubliette under his front hall?'

237

'I'm coming with you.'

She couldn't bear suddenly to be cooped up in this house doing nothing. A protracted argument followed. Claudia supposed it was a sign of her enhanced status in the Strode view of her capabilities that she won it. He agreed to meet her at Waterloo in the early afternoon.

At Waterloo they embraced as if they'd been parted for weeks – for Claudia's part it felt like weeks – but Michael had now recovered all his bounce. He was again bursting with something. 'It's Beazley's skull all right,' he said as soon as it was decent. 'David's come up trumps. He traced Beazley through his Oxford college. He got his home address from their records. It turned out his younger brother still lives in the family house in Stafford. The dental practice they'd both attended as children is still going and they had the records right back. Beazley had three fillings before 1936 – one up and two down, in the same teeth I identified. Also, and this is the conclusive thing – David took me this morning to see his forensic friend in Hackney. The bullet's the right size for a .445 Webley model. It doesn't matter that we haven't got the gun. Its theft merely compounds the case against Silverman. I tell you, the man's nailed. There's no doubt Beazley was shot through the head with Silverman's gun. We can now say, at the very least, that the story he told about Beri, however he rigged it, has to be a lie and that he, inadvertently or not, sent the poor man to his death. But I suspect Archie's going to give us a lot more than that, now I've got him cornered. Silverman's had it.'

She supposed she should have been decimated by this. She found in the event she wasn't. She was merely excited.

It looked as if Archie might be out. In the fine weather, a number of the occupants of the houses in his street were outside. Young children played. Archie's house was immaculate but motionless, the orange-striped curtain drawn across the front door, all the windows closed except in an upstairs room.

'Perhaps he's away doing a lecture,' Claudia said.

'All to the good if he is,' Michael said. 'We'll move into the lane behind the houses, wait till the coast's clear, then hop over the garden wall and break in. He could have Silverman's gun stowed. If he has, we've got him.' It had occurred to her Archie might be the Donnerton intruder, it seemed now an even bigger possibility.

Michael rang the front door bell. In a moment they heard someone coming down the stairs. Archie appeared, wearing white overalls.

Claudia was ready, mentally, to photograph Archie's face when he saw them. Would it show surprise, fear, menace, puzzlement? It showed none of these. 'Oh hallo Mrs Drake,' was what he said, as if she called every day. He didn't look at Michael.

'We'd like to talk to you if that's convenient,' Michael said.

Archie grinned at her. 'Oh yes, it's convenient,' he said. It was as if he and she were in cahoots in some way and were playing a joke from which Michael was excluded.

'Can we come in?'

Archie turned his back to the open door to let them pass. They entered the polished parquet hall decorated with strategically-placed mats and well-polished Indian brass objects on the hall dresser. In the small sitting-room Bounder was as laid-back as his master. When he saw them, he rose dutifully from his basket, yawned, stretched and gave his back legs a couple of brisk backward movements. The tail then managed a couple of wags.

'I'm sorry to descend on you like this,' Michael said, 'but there've been some dramatic developments since I last saw you, and time is short.'

Archie still looked at her, not Michael. 'Oh, I've been expecting you, Mr Strode.'

'Expecting? Why?'

'When I last saw you, you said you were going off to Sahara, didn't you?'

'And?'

'And you've now been no doubt.'

'Yes, but why should you think my visit to Sahara would make me want to see you again?'

'You journalists are all the same.'

'Meaning?'

Archie began to take his overalls off. 'You must excuse me, Mrs Drake. I quite forgot I had these on. It's my make-and-mend day. I was doing a little repair work upstairs when you rang. Please sit down.'

While they did so, he took his time picking up a metal hanger that was lying on a chair. He hung the overalls on it and carried them to the hall-dresser which had a hanging cupboard built into one side. He then returned and sat very straight on one of the hard-back chairs he pulled from the table.

Michael was getting impatient. He did one of his straight-to-the-point acts 'We've got evidence that Alan Silverman murdered Neil Beazley,' he snapped. 'It was not Mustapha Beri, as Silverman alleged, and as you have been informing your audiences for some time.'

'Oh no, you're quite wrong about that.'

'I don't think so. We found Beazley's remains in the same cave where he was murdered, and recovered the skull. It had been pierced by a bullet. I also found the splayed bullet, which turns out to be of the same calibre as Silverman's pistol.'

'You say, "We?"' Archie said, still looking at her.

'Claudia came with me to Sahara.'

Archie nodded at her reflectively. 'I see.'

'This morning I have forensic confirmation that the skull is Beazley's.'

Archie gave a little chuckle. 'You have been busy, haven't you?'

'I'm surprised you find this a laughing matter. I'd've thought this news might put you in a more reflective frame of mind.'

'I'll reflect if you like, Mr Strode, but I dare say what I might reflect wouldn't be exactly what you and your newspaper are looking for.'

'What's that supposed to mean?'

'I mean of course that, being a newsman, your job's to tell stories that will entertain people. This skeleton, you say, is Beazley's. No doubt, if you say so, it is – but it hasn't occurred to you apparently that it could've been put there for you to find by the Saharans, after they'd put a bullet hole through it to prove your case for you?'

'It has occurred to us, yes. But it wasn't the Saharans, even if they could have found a British-made bullet of the right calibre to shoot the skull with. We have other evidence – from the Saharans themselves and – via other people – for example from Gérard Petit-frères, the ex French Minister of Justice, who is still alive. Though I'm still not exactly sure how it was done, I know also that Silverman framed Beri and caused his death. There's only one thing about the murder I'm not sure about – whether Silverman did it, or whether you did, for him.'

'You've got a good imagination, Mr Strode.'

'Good enough to bring about an almost certain enquiry at which it is most probable you will be required to give evidence.'

'I'm not afraid of giving anyone evidence. What I tell is the truth. I leave the twisting of facts to others.'

'Are you really telling me you're not prepared to admit any of your story is a lie?'

'Mrs Drake here knows the two or three footnotes I was able to make to the story – after Sir Alan's death. There's nothing to add to those.'

'I think there is, and I think, in your own interest, you're going to tell me.'

Archie turned his full attention to Claudia. 'Mrs Drake, Mr Strode here is saying Sir Alan shot Neil Beazley – I expect he thinks because of the difficulty Beazley was making. You will know as well as I do that he was incapable of such a deed. You don't acept this story, I'm sure, do you?'

'Like you, I'm trying to find the truth,' she said.

'Which you think includes Sir Alan being a criminal?'

'On the evidence it seems certain the story as it has been told is wrong.'

'And the evidence against Beri? Above all Beazley's note to him which Sir Alan found among Beri's gear? Are you suggesting that Sir Alan made Beazley write that note at gunpoint before shooting him?'

'The note has certainly to be explained.'

'And someone's been trying to stop our researches,' Michael interrupted. 'How do you explain that? How do you explain that someone tried to shop us to the Saharans as spies, that someone's been making desperate efforts to recover Beazley's skull, that a hired gunman with a stocking over his head held us up at gunpoint on the road to Casablanca, and that Silverman's murder weapon has been stolen from Donnerton Hall.'

For the first time since we'd arrived, Archie seemed to lose some of his cool. 'I don't know what you're talking about, Mr Strode,' he said.

'Don't you? You've got Silverman's pistol upstairs, haven't you?'

'I have no such thing.'

'You've been spending Silverman's legacy to you to defend his name, and probably your own neck.'

Archie went silent. After a few seconds the perplexity left his face. He stood up, and suddenly there was an immense tension. At any moment Claudia expected him to draw a weapon from his pocket or from the nearby chest of drawers. She thought Michael must have had the same idea. He also got up and moved a step towards Archie.

But Archie's arms continued to hang harmlessly at his sides. Then he seemed to draw himself together, like an accused soldier commanded to give an account of himself. 'I do not follow what you are saying, Mr Strode – the money Sir Alan left me is invested as it was when I first received it, as are my other savings – but I do know this. Sir Alan Silverman was a very great man, the greatest man I've ever known or read about. He was incapable of a mean act, let alone a criminal one. If there's meanness and criminality, it's others who are guilty, not him. The story I tell is the essential truth, and I shall go on telling it.'

'"Essential" is the operative word there, isn't it?' Michael said.

'What I'm saying is that if there ever was an occasion when Sir Alan did not say the exact truth it'd've been to cover someone else.'

'Ah, covering, was he? At last we have it. Covering who? You?'

Archie paused again, and looked at the ceiling. He spoke even more slowly and deliberately. 'There's one small detail I have left out of my account. I've always left it out because in a general way it isn't relevant. But I'll tell it to you now. On that evening of Beazley's disappearance and as we now know his murder, after his late return from Tifgad Sir Alan stayed up talking outside to Miss Brisbane. I retired. A bit later Sir Alan came into our tent. I thought he was going to retire, and made no movement. But after a few seconds I realised Sir Alan hadn't turned in, and had gone out again. My immediate thought was that he'd changed into his sports gear and gone for a jog. One of the reasons Sir Alan was the man he was, was because he kept himself fit. Every night, however arduous the day had been, he usually went for a long jog. But something, I cannot exactly say what, made me curious. There was no moon, but it was as usual a bright night. Through the flap of the tent I could see that all seemed to be quiet – I could see Miss Brisbane's tent and presumed she must have turned in. But then – I don't know why – I began to think there was something funny about the silence. Curious, I got up. There was no sign by now of Sir Alan. I went towards Miss Brisbane's tent and called her name. There was no answer. I went in. She wasn't there.'

'You mean you think Janet Brisbane went for a jog with Silverman?'

'Miss Brisbane did not take jogs.'

'So?'

'Just that, Mr Strode. It's an interesting detail, don't you think?'

'Interesting from what point of view?'

'What I'm saying is there's others who know things and Sir Alan's name must be cleared.'

'I see. And when did Silverman and Miss Brisbane return?'

'I do not know.'

'How can you not know? You were there.'

'I was there but I turned in again. It was none of my business. I went to sleep. Sir Alan was of course there in the morning. That's all I know.'

Michael was showing signs of exasperation. 'Look, what the hell are you saying – that Miss Brisbane and Silverman were lovers and the two of them went off to have it away somewhere? Or are you suggesting something else a great deal more relevant to what we're talking about?'

'What I'm saying is what I've said. When there's falsehoods about it's the duty of those responsible to put matters straight.'

This, effectively, was all they got out of Archie. Michael tried every angle. Was Archie suggesting Janet Brisbane was involved in some way, that she'd conspired with Silverman to implicate Beri? But Archie would add nothing to what he'd said.

'Facts is what matters, Mr Strode, not theories,' was, as usual, his punch line.

24.

Claudia and Michael were virtually silent as they walked back towards North Harrow's main street. They found a cafe that smelt pleasantly of coffee and doughnuts – the latter on display like mounds of cannonballs on the bar. They sat at a yellow plastic-topped table and began to grapple with the interview.

'Archie gave a very convincing display of not knowing I was with you in Sahara,' Claudia said. 'If that was an act, he's a consummate liar and we can't believe anything he says.'

'Right,' Michael said.

'But I can't believe he was making that up, can you?'

'No.'

'He was equally convincing about his ignorance of Alphonse, etcetera.'

'Right again.'

'So where does it leave us? If he's ignorant of Alphonse, surely he finishes up again as – what he's always been – quite a shrewd but rather a peripheral observer.'

'He's more than that.'

'He obviously thinks Silverman was innocent.'

'He would, wouldn't he?'

'It's possible he believes it.'

Michael was silent a moment. 'Archie's covering on Silverman of course, as he has from the start. But it's for sure, whatever his mumbo-jumbo about Silverman and Janet going off together like that, he's trying to pass the buck to Janet in some way. I think we've got to see her.'

'Maybe, but I cannot see how Janet can possibly be Alphonse's employer. We've been over this. She's going to rejoice at your headline.'

'Ah, but does she hate Silverman? Let's think – what do we know really about her? We know that during the expedition she was his lover. It was the 1930's, she was young and, though relatively liberated, upper middle-class with romantic ideas about love and marriage. Then Silverman lets her down with a bump. Maybe, subconsciously, she still loves him, even though he dumped her. Maybe she does so a lot more consciously since Silverman's death – that could make psychological sense. Defending his reputation could be her last act of homage to him and a release for her own long-suppressed feelings.'

As with Michael's theory about Archie, Claudia thought this a lot too subtle and shrinky. She reminded him how vehement against Alan Janet had been when she went to see her. An argument developed, rather half-hearted on both their parts. She broke off from this, realising its futility.

'All right then,' she said, 'we go and see Janet. She's our one remaining loose end. But if she knows nothing, I think you've just got to publish your story as it is, implicating Silverman as he clearly must have been in some way, and leave some question marks, including a large one about Alphonse and his superiors. Isn't that about it?'

Not to her surprise, Michael disagreed. 'I'm going to get to the bottom of it,' he said. 'If you ask me, they were all involved somehow.'

'Janet?'

'Janet at that time was still sleeping with Silverman. Are you telling me she knows nothing?'

He talked about going down to Devon alone, but this time he knew it wasn't worth the breath.

Claudia thought a visit to Janet was not only a waste of time, it was an unnecessary exposure of themselves to further danger from their unknown assailants, but she kept it to herself. Unlikely as it had seemed, she was returning to the idea it could be the Foreign Office through MI5 who were trying to quash Michael's evidence. The Foreign Office's problem was Sahara, and the use Sahara would make of any story, particularly one which had solid evidence of criminality. God knew what high politics were involved. Vincent Galleon had told her the Foreign Office had hinted at Middle East implications. Did they still, after all, live in days when British agents as well as American could hold people up at gunpoint and burgle private property? She just wished Michael would write up the story he had and hand over to the police.

She thought Michael would want to go down to the West country right away. Certainly, from her point of view, the sooner it was done the better. She suggested going to Paddington and getting a train. 'No, we can't,' he said. 'I've phoned a security place in Exeter to make sure Brisbane's at home – and to check if she's alone. I've got to wait for their report.'

He declared a day at leisure. They went on a river cruise to Greenwich, which neither of them had ever done. The only thing that marred the day for Claudia was the pocket telephone Michael had. He phoned the West country agency at least half a dozen times.

It was getting on for eight when after a meal they returned to Central London. Michael wanted to drop into the Strand Palace Hotel, whose secretarial facilities he often used for his journalism. 'Better and cheaper than one of those cretinous clubs,' he'd said. He wanted to see if there were any messages left for him while he'd been away. He had a private deal with the hall porters.

In the lobby, while he began using his mobile again, she went off to tidy up. When she returned he looked pleased. He'd at last got the news he wanted from Exeter. The 'quarry', as they described Janet, was at home, and apparently unaccompanied except for a cleaner who came and went. During the afternoon, Janet had been 'sighted' in her garden, reading in a large sun-hat. 'We'll go down overnight,' he said, 'and beard her in the morning.'

They ordered two beers. Just then Claudia saw a page boy circulating among the tables carrying a board. He turned the board in her direction. 'Mr Michael Strode' was chalked on it. She jogged Michael's arm and nodded in the boy's direction. The page told Michael there was a message for him at the porter's desk.

She watched Michael cross and speak to the man, who handed him an envelope. She saw him open it, standing there where he was, frown, then continue towards her at a slower pace. He held out the note to her ironically, between his finger tips. It was typed in capitals.

'DELIVER SKULL DONNERTON TONIGHT AND LEAVE BY SUNDIAL, OR EXPECT CONSEQUENCE. NO ATTEMPT POLICE. NO ATTEMPT NEWSPAPER ARTICLES. NO ATTEMPT CONTACT FIELDHOUSE. NO MESSING. YOU ARE BEING WATCHED.'

She noticed it was hotel notepaper, and pointed to the name and address at the top. Instinctively they both looked about them. Not one of the couple of dozen respectable people visible seemed to qualify. The note was concrete evidence, Claudia thought, on which the police would have to act. Surely they must give up now. But Michael was thinking.

'That phrase about Fieldhouse is interesting,' he said, lowering his voice. 'If they don't want us to contact Fieldhouse, it's because he knows something. And what Fieldhouse knows, he's told us. He's told us that Janet's our objective.' He looked about him again, less intently. 'There's another point. It looks as if they don't know we've been to Archie. Either someone's just picked us up, a few minutes ago, or . . . wait.' He jumped up and went to the porter's desk again. He returned triumphant. 'It's as I thought. The porter says the note was handed in yesterday afternoon by an Englishman he'd never seen before who asked him if he knew me. They're not immediately on our tail at all. Whoever it is knows, or has got to know, my movements very well. They know I use this place a lot and left the note here hoping sooner or later I'd come in. I bet there are notes all over the place – my place, yours. It looks as if we have a short head advantage.'

Claudia wanted to know who among his acquaintances might wish him ill, but she knew in this mood nothing was going to draw Michael off the scent. 'We're going to have to be a bit careful,' he went on. 'I'd already thought we should take some precautions in Devon if there was anyone with Janet. Now I think they're essential anyway. Look, Claudia, if you don't mind I've got things to do for a few minutes. Among other things I'm going to hire a car. I don't want to go home to get mine, they could well have someone lurking there. Could you stay here, maybe in the television lounge over there? Shan't be long.'

Though there were only half a dozen young children in the telly room, Claudia wasn't so sure as Michael that they weren't being observed by someone in the hotel. She was relieved when he appeared nearly an hour later, and a waiter spirited them through the kitchen regions and out of a delivery door into a side street where another hotel employee had a taxi waiting. She felt even more relaxed when they'd driven off from the hire garage in a brand new Escort and again confirmed that there was no one following them.

She drove. For a while they didn't speak. The traffic was quite heavy, and Michael had said he had something to write up and was busy with it on a pad he'd bought in the hotel. As they reached the M.3., he finished what appeared to be a long letter, folded it, and put it into an envelope – which was already stamped, she noticed.

'Your last will and testament?' she said.

'Something like that.'

She saw he'd addressed it to David Suter. 'So, am I to be privy to these elaborate "precautions?"'

'Yes, of course. I'm sorry about all this cloak and dagger, but I didn't think it was a good idea to linger in the Palace any longer than necessary.'

'Right. Well?'

'For starters I got on to the Exeter agency again. They're lending us a man.'

'You mean a bodyguard?'

'You could call it that. But what I have in mind requires the three of us. It's struck me that if Janet is somehow behind all this it's not advisable just to knock on her door. The Exeter people say there was no one with her this afternoon, but that doesn't mean to say there won't be by the morning. It's essential we see her alone.'

'That sounds sense, but how are you going to be sure of that?'

'I've got an idea. It's a long shot, but it might just work. Somehow we've got to lure her out of her house. It occurred to me there's only one person who might be able to do that, someone whom she must be aware knows as much as I hope she does – Archie.'

He fished into his pocket and brought out another typed letter. He handed it to her. 'I did this in the hotel,' he said. She drew into the safety lane and stopped the car. Intrigued, she read.

'Dear Miss Brisbane, I must see you, alone. You've no doubt read what's been in the press about Sir Alan lately. Well they've been visiting me again – a young journalist called Strode. You may have seen his earlier reports. Well, now he's been out to Sahara, and seems to have a lot of new stuff, which it looks as if they'll be publishing any day. I need urgently to discuss with you what is to be done. We cannot allow things to go on like this.

'You will understand that a meeting between us in present circumstances could be misunderstood. Conclusions will be drawn! I shall therefore deliver this letter to your house under cover of darkness and will be waiting for you at the spot marked with a cross on the enclosed Ordnance Survey map at 11.00 hours this morning. I ask you to approach the tor as indicated, leaving your car at the other spot I have marked on the map. This will enable me to be sure it is you approaching. You will realise that, in my position, I cannot be too careful. May I repeat that our meeting must be alone.'

The signature was typed under a 'Yours truly.'

Claudia drew breath. 'But this is an incredibly long shot, isn't it? It assumes for a start that the two of them have had no contact.'

'Do you think they have from the way Archie spoke?'

'No, probably not, but . . . she could phone him to check, couldn't she?'

'She could, but we'll have to risk that.'

'You're also assuming of course that Janet's got something to hide.'

'That has to be our assumption, doesn't it, until we're proved wrong?'

She thought. It was bold, it could just come off. And Michael was right about one thing, a knock on Janet's front door was surely to be avoided. 'Right,' she said, 'so we somehow deliver this letter to Janet. We then sit on top of a tor and wait for her. Where's the ordnance survey map you mention?'

'Our sleuth says he has one of the Dartmoor area. He's also working out the geography and marking in the two crosses. I spoke to him on the phone just now and told him to choose if possible a feature which has a road on either side of it, so we have a line of retreat if necessary. He'll be meeting us at Newton Abbot at six.'

'And if Janet comes, what do you say to her?'

'I'll keep that as a surprise. If it proves she knows anything about it, I'm going to offer her a deal.'

They'd thought to stop at a motel for a few hours' sleep. As they turned off the M.3. on to the A.303 Claudia had a strong wish to go home, ill-advised as this was. As Michael had thought before, if someone was trying to pick up their scent, their two addresses were the most obvious places to keep watch. But she was imagining all the things that could have happened to her property while she'd been away. Most of all she wanted to change her clothes. A five star laundry and the largesse of a Moroccan minister had restored the few she had with her, but they'd been packed with desert temperatures in mind. Anyway, she'd left them at Donnington. The English summer weather was fine and sunny, but after a hundred and ten degrees plus it did seem almost chilly. Michael didn't like it, but he agreed. As far as they knew nobody had actually been on their trail since they'd arrived in England, and they could take a few precautions in the village.

About five hundred yards from the first houses she parked the car in an old chalk pit beside the road. She felt absurd making a detour down a lane to avoid the main street, then into her home through the garden gate. In her changed mood she nearly forgot and put the light on as they went in. Michael hissed at her from behind just in time.

Apart from a musty smell, there was nothing amiss. She collected a fistful of letters from the mat and put them on the table. Michael pounced on them and took them to the window through which a street light shone. Sure enough, there was a hand-delivered envelope. She found him her pocket torch. The note was identical to the one Michael had had in London.

'It almost proves they haven't found us, anyway,' he said.

Leaving him with a beer from the fridge, she went upstairs to wash and change. Undressing, she felt suddenly languid and sexy. Quietly, she opened the window on the garden side and stood naked for a moment, allowing the faint night breeze to course coolly over her body. She went out on to the minuscule landing.

'Come up,' she said.

'I've been thinking again,' he whispered.

She didn't answer. He came up. She purposely stood in the shaft of light that came from the street light. She was not only full of physical desire. She also wanted to prove to Michael, and to herself, that everything was normal, gloriously normal, that they were in love, and that perhaps they would live here together now in this house. For however short a time, she wanted to shut out the rest.

She heard the escape of air from his mouth. They made love again. It was made the more delicious this time because of the secrecy, almost the illicitness. It was different from their Moroccan love-making. That had been questing, miraculous. This was no miracle. They both knew it was there, and took it greedily, joyfully.

They lay in the pin-dropping silence of the village, the only noise the playful rustle the wind made in her silver birch. Michael held her tightly, and gently nibbled her ear. She felt triumphantly light-hearted.

They must have slept two or three hours. Michael stirred, and sat up with a lurch, waking her. He grabbed for his watch. 'Christ, it's three-thirty. Come on, we'll only just make it.'

He threw on his clothes, and while she dressed went downstairs to phone. She listened, with her nerves – a moment ago so deliciously relaxed – reined up like a coach and four. As she guessed, it was this man David Suter he was calling.

'David? Sorry to dig you out of bed. Look, it does seem they're at it again – the same games, yes. You had anything?' There was a short pause. 'Good. But look, as a precaution, hide the thing. It should only be for today.' He lowered his voice. 'And if . . . you know what to do. I've written down the new developments since I saw you. I'm posting them now. You have the rest.' He hadn't intended her to hear these last words. 'Call you tonight then,' he finished.

All the tensions of Sahara were back. She knew exactly what he was saying. If anything happened to them, David was to carry on. But she was aware of a difference. She was scared, yes, but wasn't she also excited, as excited as she knew Michael was? Was she getting a taste for danger?

It was still dark. They crept out of the cottage the same way they'd come in. There were the couple of lights in the street on the other side of the houses, and a light glimmered in one of the windows of the pub, otherwise the place still slept. They kept to the grass growing on the sides of the path. Even so the noise of their feet seemed earsplitting.

Michael drove, and stepped on it. Apart from stopping at a post-office in a small town to post the letter, they kept going. They were ten minutes early at Newton Abbot.

The man, who said he 'answered' to the name of Jim, was waiting as planned outside the railway station. Claudia was sure Jim wasn't his real name. Like everything else she began to learn about him, it was probably a compulsive evasion. 'Shall we say?' was a phrase he used in every other sentence. 'Shall we say my name is Jim?' 'Shall we say here-abouts,' he replied when she asked him where he lived. Michael had gone off in search of a loo. She was glad when he returned and discussion began about their plan of action. The man gave her the creeps.

Jim didn't have a car. In the broadening early morning light the three of them drove north to Bovey Tracey in their hired vehicle. There was a surprising amount of traffic on the road – people going to work. The sight of two empty tourist buses setting out from a garage made Michael reflect.

'The trouble is, the Moor's going to be swarming with holiday-makers today, isn't it? We do not, repeat not, want company for our rendezvous.'

He regarded Jim in the driving mirror. Jim was reclining with studied ease on the back seat. 'Not to worry about that, sir. All under control. You'll find the place I've selected will meet your requirements.' Jim looked out of the window, sideways. They were on his territory, they were to understand, such anxiety on their part was superfluous.

'And supposing she spots you delivering the letter? What are you going to say?'

'I've just been thinking about that, sir. I was about to suggest a small amendment – an open approach. Be sure she gets it then. Nothing to hide really, is there? Special courier service being employed – all above board and accounted for?'

'Supposing she questions you, asks for the name and address of your firm and of the sender of the letter?'

'Oh, confidential, sir, confidential – in the politest way of course. That's what I'd put to the party, and it'd be understood, I'm sure.'

Michael was getting snappy again. 'Well I'm sure it wouldn't,' he said. 'She was alone yesterday, you say. But by now it's quite possible she's got someone with her. If she has, he'll stick a gun in your back, or she'll do it herself. Get it in the letter-box, unseen, please.'

Claudia tried to pour a little oil. Jim, for all his irritating characteristics, was after all their lifeline and she was beginning to feel more every minute that they might well be needing him in the very near future for a lot more than his duty as guide. She wondered fleetingly if he carried a gun. Was that legal? She turned to him. 'If I remember from a visit I made to Miss Brisbane's house, on one side you can get within twenty yards of the front door without breaking cover. It's woods and bracken all round.'

'I was there yesterday afternoon, madam,' Jim said stiffly.

He had to take it out on her, OK. She nodded acknowledgement of her naivety and failure to recognise his professionalism. The atmosphere eased a little.

As it turned out, they did owe Jim an apology. They went first to the proposed venue, and the place he'd picked seemed ideal. A barren tor, it was crowned with the typical Dartmoor feature of a heap of large granite slabs, which would provide good cover for their vigil. It was west of Haytor, not too far from Janet's house, but far enough for Jim to have time to alert them on his mobile phone if she didn't concur with Michael's instruction to come in her car, alone. Also, being on the southern rim of the Moor, though barren and open on the north side, to the south there were woods reaching up to within five hundred yards of the peak. If for any reason they had to abandon the operation in a hurry, they could reach the wood in a few minutes, running downhill.

There were roads on both sides of the tor, as Michael had wanted. They observed the tor first from this, the Moor side, from the point where Janet would, hopefully, leave her car. Having to make a four mile detour, they then drove round to the southern aspect and chose a pick-up point which was well-concealed from the summit of the tor, should this prove necessary. The final advantage of this tor was that the tourist buses seldom came here, Jim explained. The only danger was from the one-off hiker. Michael was satisfied.

It was now after seven. Jim and Michael did a last check on their telephone numbers, and Jim left them – taking the car and the letter. A thought occurred to her.

'God, what time is the post in these parts? If it's early, and Janet has already had her mail, she might not look again in her box and the letter could lie there all day.'

'The post arrives between nine and half past,' said Michael. 'I had the agency check.'

Full marks again, she thought.

Michael admitted, however, as they began to climb the tor, that there were a number of things which could go wrong in addition to those they'd considered. The most important thing was the letter itself. They knew nothing of the relations, if any existed, between Archie and Janet. Claudia went back as carefully as she could over everything Archie had said to her in her meetings with him – so did Michael, who had interviewed him twice over the original story. Neither of them could remember any mention of a meeting after the expedition. But of course they might be wrong, in which case the tone and content of the unsigned letter could be out of key and Janet would spot it. They didn't know if she had a henchman at hand, and if she had – to what lengths he, and she, were prepared to go. Despite the wood, an armed thug sitting in a vantage point with a rifle and intent to murder could make things very unpleasant for them if they had to run for it. Even if Janet took the bait and thought it was Archie's letter, and their conjectures about her knowing something were right, would she come? Wouldn't she be much more likely to send someone like Alphonse, with a gun?

The permutations were endless. Half-way up, they decided to stop thinking. There was a good chance that, whatever she thought, Janet's plain curiosity would get the better of her and she would come even if she were not involved. They had to cling to that.

Just then the phone started bleeping. Michael drew it from his pocket and pulled out the aerial. Claudia tilted her ear as near as she could get.

'So far a hundred per cent success,' they heard. 'The letter's delivered safely and it's all quiet. No sign of the party being up yet. I've found a vantage point above the house and have it under surveillance. I'll keep reporting further developments.'

'He's having fun,' she remarked. Michael didn't answer. She thought he was rather less cool than he'd been in Sahara – or was she transferring her own feelings? They continued their ascent doggedly.

When they broke clear of the trees on to the open moorland, Claudia had an unpleasant feeling of exposure. They were certainly invisible to a pair of binoculars trained from Janet's house, which was hidden by the several wooded reentrants between them. But that didn't eliminate imagined perils. She kept listening for a shot from a sniper's rifle – or would the bullet arrive before the noise caught up? The fantasy was not scotched by a further communication from Jim. The lady was now 'abroad' – he had seen her visit the dustbin – and he'd just spotted the red mail van coming up the hill from Bovey, stopping at houses as it went.

They reached the granite slabs and found there was a kind of ravine between them in which they could conveniently conceal themselves. From their position they had a good view down the north slope of the tor to the road which ran along the bottom. Added to the stiffness in her legs from the climb, she felt a wave of mental fatigue and remembered that, but for those three or four delicious hours, they'd lost a night's sleep.

The bleeper went again. This time it was bad news. Apparently 'the party' had no mail this morning. The van had visited another house, then driven on past Janet's drive. Would Janet go to her letter-box if she didn't hear the van? The body heat generated by their climb was evaporating. Claudia felt a chill. They had two more hours to wait in this narrow granite corridor. During this time nothing could be happening – or worse, Brisbane could be deploying her snipers.

A further development lent credence to the latter idea. At nearly ten o'clock Jim reported that a private car had turned into the drive and was approaching the house. He kept on the air and gave them a blow by blow report. It was a vintage M.G. – green. A man was getting out – sixtyish – tall, grey hair, casually-dressed. He was going to the door, ringing. The door was being opened. Yes, it was Brisbane all right. She was holding the door open for the man to enter. He was going in. The door was closing.

Claudia felt her blood had stopped flowing. The same thought had occurred to Michael. 'The man is tall and grey-haired, you say?'

'Yes.'

'And ageing?'

'Spry, I'd say, but the age I said.'

'You're sure of that?'

Michael clipped the radio off and rammed home the aerial. 'Well, thanks be for that. It's not Alphonse.'

Ominous as the visitor was, there was another consolation. It looked very much as if Janet had read the letter, and summoned this person in consequence. Didn't this indicate in some degree her involvement?

25.

The next hour was tense. Jim reported the man reemerging. He was letting himself out. No sign of Brisbane. He was getting into the car and driving off. There was a pause, then they heard he'd turned left at the end of the drive in the direction of the Moor – their direction. Jim asked if Michael would like him to follow.

'No,' Michael said at once. 'Stick to the plan.'

It was an unwelcome addition to the enigma. Jim had said nothing about any firearm, but one could be stowed in the car. Was the man substituting for Janet as their visitor? It seemed more than likely. If he was, would he come the way Michael had directed? Would they stay put if he appeared? They began to watch anxiously the road to the north of them.

They waited ten minutes, a quarter of an hour. The M.G. did not appear. What did this mean? Michael kept ranging the skyline to the east of them with the binoculars. Had the man parked out of sight of them somewhere, and was he now taking up a position from which he could shoot at them with a rifle if they broke cover?

The sun rose higher and brought with it a little warmth. Above them larks trilled. The light breeze was audible in the heather. Grazing sheep were dotted about the slopes. The odd car sped along the road below. At a quarter to eleven Jim called them once more. His voice was lowered and animated.

'She's coming out. Looks as if she means business. Strong-looking shoes, denim trouser-suit, handkerchief thing round her head, a shoulder-bag with a long strap. She's making for the garage. Yes, no doubt now, she's opening the doors. She's going out somewhere. It's a blue BMW. Registration number . . .'

They were kept on tenterhooks until she reached the end of the drive. Would she turn right down to the town or left towards the Moor?

Then they heard it was all right. The car had turned left towards the Moor. Jim was going to follow it, as planned. As he drove up the hill he called again. He confirmed he'd seen the BMW ahead of him, and there was no sign of the M.G..

In a few minutes they saw the BMW come into view below them and draw up precisely at the place Michael had indicated on the map. Michael observed Janet through the glasses but Claudia could see her as well with the naked eye. Janet locked the car and after a brief glance upwards began to move towards them. She didn't look round as she walked.

'She strides like a woman in her twenties,' Michael said. He'd been afraid earlier that the slope might be too much for her. Claudia reminded him she still went on massive treks in the Andes and probably outwalked younger companions.

They let her advance to within twenty yards before they broke cover. There was a chance if she saw it wasn't Archie she would turn round and go back. They both climbed forward into the open.

Claudia was sure they astonished her. She stopped in her tracks as she saw them. 'It's Mrs Drake, isn't it? What's all this?'

'We were going to ask you much the same question,' Michael said. 'I'm Strode. I write for The Times.'

'It was you who delivered that letter?'

'Yes.'

'And Archie Fieldhouse . . .'

'Let's say, he couldn't make it.'

She was recovering her cool fast. She turned away from them and sat in the heather. They had to approach her.

'I'm sorry,' Michael said, 'but I'm going to search you before we begin.'

She swung her head away. 'Don't be ridiculous.'

'Could you stand up please?'

'I certainly will not.'

Michael seized the handbag from her shoulder and opened it. It held nothing untoward. He tried to return it. She made no move and he was forced to put it on the ground beside her. Michael continued.

'You hired an assassin to stop us finding the truth, but we found it. Fieldhouse now knows we know what happened, we've been to see him, and the game's up.'

Janet snatched up the handbag and drew out a carton of cigarettes. She put a cigarette in her mouth and rummaged again for the lighter. The cigarette alight, she drew in a long breath of smoke then snapped the cap of the lighter shut and threw it back into the bag. Dislike her anew as Claudia did, she could not help admiring her cool. 'You typed that letter,' she said to Michael.

'What gives you that idea?'

'Fieldhouse wouldn't have the nous to do a thing like this.'

'Apparently you thought he had, though. Your coming up here is proof of it.'

She appeared to take no notice. 'Fieldhouse is a bloody ass. He started all this foolery. I knew as soon as Silverman died that sooner or later he'd blab something. Things were perfectly all right as they were.'

'What things were perfectly all right?'

'The official story. We didn't need all this muck-raking.'

'Muck's the word, isn't it?'

'I hold no brief for Silverman. As I told you when you came here before, Mrs Drake, Silverman was a vain, single-minded, womanising bastard who didn't give a damn for anything except his precious reputation. But we didn't need all this.' Janet continued to address Claudia. 'You at least, I'd've thought, could've seen that. I formed the impression, obviously wrongly, that you had some judgement.'

Michael persisted. 'So you're confirming that Silverman shot Neil Beazley and framed a Berber for his murder?'

'I'm not "confirming" anything. I don't have to say a word to you.'

'You'd be wise to. If you don't say it to us, you're going to have to say it to the police.'

'Why should I have to say anything to the police?'

'Because, for a start, I can prove to them you've been using criminal methods to interfere with my enquiries, that at this moment I strongly suspect you have a gunman concealed somewhere here within gunshot – and because Archie knows what happened and knows he's cornered. If you don't spill the beans, we know enough to force him to.'

Janet sniffed but I could see Michael had scored something of a hit. 'You're entirely on the wrong track,' she said sulkily, 'as you newspaper people usually are.'

'Has Archie got it wrong, too? If so, why did you come up here to talk to him? I'll tell you why. You came because you know Archie knows the truth, and you hoped to head him off somehow. What would you have offered him, I wonder? Money? I doubt if that would have worked. Fieldhouse has proved bribery-proof so far. Tried to scare him, as you tried to scare us? I doubt if that would've worked, either. Archie's the Bunkers Hill type. So what cards do you hold? Quite frankly none.'

The cigarette looked as if it was going to explode when Janet dragged on it. Each time she sucked, the curve of ash seemed to grow half an inch. Claudia felt the determination and neurotic will-power which drove her energetic personality and were responsible for her remarkable achievements.

Her voice dropped a little. 'What have you come here for?'

'I've come because, in certain circumstances, I might be able to offer you a deal.'

Again, the sniff. 'What kind of a deal can you offer me, and why should I want one?'

'Let's recapitulate. You've been doing your best to stop us discovering what happened on the Silverman expedition. You were unable to head us off what we were doing in Sahara, and you now want to get possession of the evidence of the crime. You have the gun – you, or one of your minions, nicked it from Donnerton. But you don't have the skull and the bullet. Without these you aren't going to avoid an enquiry and, quite possibly, a prosecution. At the very least you are guilty of withholding evidence. It's obvious you were in it somehow, up to your neck. You were Silverman's lover. It's perfectly obvious to me, despite what you pretend to think about him, you're protecting his good name. If there's a trial, it'll be your word against a considerable body of evidence – which incidentally could include a statement from Petit-frères, who can be found if necessary. You may not know he's alive, and no longer in Sahara. He's now quite accessible. With all this, are there any guesses whom the jury will believe?'

'So?'

'So I want the whole truth. I publish the story, and I'll do my best to get Beazley's skull and the bullet sent to you, to add to the gun. I'll say it was stolen. If you want to, we'll allow you a short time to go abroad and avoid the fuss there's bound to be, certainly an enquiry.'

'I thought you said you had the story already from Fieldhouse?'

'Only part of it so far. He speaks in instalments and hints. I guess he'll only tell the rest when he has to, under oath in a witness box.'

'So you did write the letter?'

'Yes. But it doesn't change anything, does it?'

She turned her head away sharply. 'I doubt if Fieldhouse does know the story. Not all of it. It's certainly clear to me you don't know the story.' She paused, stubbing the cigarette, unfinished. She sighed deeply. 'But that little runt probably does know enough, and the rest he guesses. He never liked me. He doesn't like women. Women threaten to strip him of the little suit of khaki armour he's worn all his life. And of course he doted on Silverman like a dog. As you've got the wrong end of the stick and are trying to frame Silverman, he'll be even more inclined to blab. On balance, if it has to come out, I'd rather do the blabbing myself. Come back tomorrow – to my house – when I've had time to think about it, and I'll tell you.'

'Oh no, you tell us right away or the deal's off. We don't want any further attentions from your criminal friend.'

'You won't have them. I've just sent him home. And he's not a criminal. He's a local friend of mine.'

'Not criminal, you say?'

'No. Ludo's a romantic ass with far too much money, and time. He doesn't know what to do with himself now he's given up his gun-running and the other semi-shady ventures which filled his life.'

'One's heart melts for him. He may not have done the dirty work himself but he certainly employs some colourful friends, including a very choice specimen from the Marseilles mafia who wasn't above sticking a gun in my ribs.'

'I'm sure he wouldn't have hurt you. I doubt if the gun was even loaded.'

'Really? And shopping us to the Saharans as spies? I suppose that was part of the big joke, too. You know we could both have been killed? As it was, I was flayed alive.'

Janet made a movement with her shoulders as if to shrug off a minor irritation. She frowned. 'Ludo said nothing about violence. He thought they must have let you go on condition you cooperated.'

'He didn't observe the condition of my face and back afterwards?'

'Of course he didn't.' She turned away distastefully. 'I'm sorry if anything happened to you. Though Ludo went much too far in hiring whoever he did, he's never left England. Ludo never shopped you.'

'How very comforting. And now, here in England, death threats and ultimatums – and Silverman's gun stolen from Donnerton? Are you saying that's the work of the mafia, too?'

'No, that was Ludo. He's an incorrigible ass. All of this was his absurd idea. I never really wanted him to do it. He heard about your daft expedition to Sahara. He also tries to write for The Times now and then – more then than now – and someone on the staff told him what you intended. He persuaded me one evening to let him have you followed, to keep an eye – at his own expense. I agreed because I thought you might be headed off. I always thought it better that sleeping dogs lay. He went far beyond my wishes, and now, as I say, I've packed him off home. When I read that letter I summoned him. He's just been with me to report his infantile goings-on.'

She did not elaborate and went very quiet. Claudia was aware of the Moor – the huge expanse stretching away, those scattered sheep still grazing, unchanged by their drama, the clouds dragging bulky shadows across the slopes of short grass and heather. Out of sight, towards Haytor, a bus's hooter brayed, the noise absorbed at once into the heavy silence.

Janet drew in a sharp breath and sat very straight. 'All right, I'm going to tell you. But not – let me make it plain – because you're forcing me to. I don't give a damn what you do about poor Neil's remains, except to give at least the part of them you've got a decent burial in England, I suppose. You're as good an audience as anyone and there's no point in hanging about. I should probably have told the story years ago, I've nothing much to be ashamed about. You're quite wrong about my feelings for Silverman. They are as they ever were – ones of total contempt. It's myself I've been protecting, not him. I didn't see why the end of my life should be beset again by Silverman. I killed Neil Beazley, in self-defence. But it was Silverman's fault. If he'd behaved differently, it wouldn't have happened.

'I've told you, Mrs Drake, about the affair I had with Neil and how it started when we were undergraduates at Oxford. It was doomed to end and of course, out there in the Sahara, it did. We had a sexual relationship of sorts, but Neil was realising he was a suppressed homosexual before we left England. Before anything started between me and Silverman, he more or less admitted it to me. I think I'd known, or subconsciously guessed.

'I don't think, after an initial period of pique, Neil really minded when I started going in to Tifgad with Silverman. We remained civil to each other and went on sharing a tent. But that was when Silverman began to behave despicably. I think in a curious way he was jealous of Neil's intelligence and sensitivity, which were much greater than his. He also hated homosexuals.

261

Neil started something with Mustapha Beri. They always worked together. Silverman began mocking him in front of me, and – worse – in front of Fieldhouse who, as you might expect, joined in any sycophantic refrains of amusement and applause required of him. It was unnecessary, vindictive, and cruel – and Silverman was meant to be our leader, holding us all together.

'The heat and the strain were getting to us, but with this additional burden to bear it got most of all to Neil. He and Silverman began to quarrel in an uglier way. More than once, Neil said that if we found the hoard it should be given to the Saharan state, to which he maintained it belonged. He knew that was the most riling thing he could say to a man like Silverman. The day before the tragedy Silverman stopped Beri working with Neil, took Beri in his own group and gave Neil one of his men. Out of pique, unknown to Silverman, Neil spent that morning working in a cave on another mountainside, and not the one Silverman had designated for him.

'This was the background to what happened the next morning. When we arrived at the site for the day, Neil was even more trucculent than he had been and demanded to work with Beri again. Silverman flew into a rage, threatened to send him home, and ordered him back to camp. Neil lost no time in going. When he'd gone, Silverman then had another thought. Neil had gone off by himself yesterday, the chances were that was what he was planning to do again. He told me I had to follow him and observe what he did. Actually I didn't have to go very far. There was a vantage point just above where we were from which I could observe Neil's route. I saw him make his way down to what we called the 'Red facet' of 'Gold Mountain', which was to be our next area of search. I saw him stop outside a particular cave and build a cairn of stones outside. I reported back to Silverman.

'Silverman was due to go into Tifgad that day to contact the firm which was paying for the expedition. Because of this, he asked me to go down to Neil and see what he was up to. He also thought, I guess, that in view of my relationship with Neil I might somehow head him off his rebellious attitude and persuade him to return to the camp. When I'd done this I was to return to where we were to supervise the Berbers. "As a precaution" – that's how he put it – he then made me strap on to myself the heavy webbing holster and the loaded gun he always carried. The gun was "in case the Berbers ever get out of hand," he'd once told me. I remonstrated. "What on earth would I want a gun for?" I asked. He burbled something about his pending absence

262

and said I ought to have it until he returned. More to avoid an argument than anything else, I did as he said. This had never happened before when he left the camp.

'It wasn't difficult for me to re-identify the cave where Neil had gone because of the mysterious cairn he'd built. I went in and immediately found him in the entrance chamber. He was in a semi-hysterical state. At first I thought he was ill and having delirious hallucinations. "I've found it, I've found it," he kept shouting. "I'll make him look an idiot now" – by which, of course, he meant Silverman. When I saw from the excavation he'd made that it looked indeed as if he'd found something, I realised what it was he intended to do. We'd always known that in the strict terms of the very complex Saharan law of treasure-trove prevailing at that time, the actual finder had certain legal rights. That's why we always split the Berbers up so that one of us was always with them. What Neil was saying was that he was going to exert the rights he thought he had and give the hoard to Sahara.

'I was excited about what he might have found. I didn't know for sure at this moment whether he was telling the truth – he might well have been hallucinating. But the immediate priority was Neil's state of mind. I didn't relish the task Silverman had given me. I thought he'd treated Neil abominably. But I tried to calm him down and reason with him. It'd always been understood between us, I said, that any one of us could be the lucky one, but that we'd always expected, whoever it was, that Silverman, as the instigator, organiser and leader of the expedition, would naturally carry all the honours. I said I understood how he felt about Silverman, and to a large extent sympathised with him. Silverman had not behaved well. But I said that on this – the matter of the hoard – I thought he, Neil, was wrong. This was not just because I was then still loyal to Silverman and was sleeping with him. It was because I believed it. I did think Neil was wrong.

'Suddenly he flew into a rage. I'm sure at this moment he was over the edge, and my siding with Silverman over the hoard was the last straw. He launched at me with the axe he must have been using to hack out that fault line behind which the hoard was concealed. I think, in falling on me, the axe must have slipped out of his hand. The next thing I was aware of was that he'd crashed me down on to the floor of the cave on my back and that his hands were encircling my neck. I was certain he intended to strangle me.

'In the state he was in, I don't think he'd noticed I had Silverman's pistol. Somehow as we struggled I got it out of the holster and undid the safety catch. I shot him through the head. The force of the bullet drove his body away from mine as if it had been lifted up. I think he died at once.

'I don't know how long I lay spluttering – a matter of minutes, I suppose. It could have been longer. The next thing I knew, Silverman was there. Perhaps he'd feared for my safety with Neil in this strange mood – that's what he told me later. Maybe he heard the shot. Though I doubt the latter – the cave would have muffled the sound and anyway he couldn't have got down to this place in the time. I can't say, at the time or afterwards, I much cared. What I cared about, apart from the horror of Neil's death, was that from this moment on I began to realise what kind of man Silverman was.

'I was expecting he'd attend to me. I was just sitting there, shaking. Neil's body was motionless and bleeding a few feet away. But I and the body might not have been there. I'd said nothing about Neil's find. I was hardly in a state to think rationally. But Silverman had spotted something in the cave entrance some yards from us, which must have shown up in the light from outside. What he saw turned out to be the two alabaster pots which Neil must have found loose in the cave – we afterwards supposed they must have been dropped in haste by the original band of brigands – and which almost certainly had led Neil to the main find. "It's here, somewhere close. The bastard's found it," I remember hearing Silverman shout.

'It seemed he said the phrase over and over again, though probably this was the ghostly echo the cave had. Leaving me sitting there, he began searching frantically, and of course came across the partly excavated fault line I'd already seen, and then what lay behind it.

'It must have been a considerable time later before he returned to me – in almost as hysterical state, it seemed to me, as Neil had been in. "We've done it, we've done it," he kept saying. "It's the hoard all right. A mountain of stuff from what I can see – glass, copper, probably silver, and a number of earthenware figures. It's incredible."

'He calmed down at last, began to take in fully what had happened to Neil and to realise that I'd been within seconds of death, and spoke the first words which might be construed to imply any comfort for me.

'"Don't worry about this. He had it coming to him. Attack you, did he?" He'd spotted the axe by this time – I don't think he realised, still, I'd shot Neil with his pistol. "You had to do it. I'll get you out of it somehow."

264

'His mind then worked at lightning speed, just how fast I didn't for the moment realise. He told me to go back to the main party and continue as if nothing had happened. They shouldn't of course be left without supervision. If Beri was curious – he was the only one who spoke any English – I was to say I hadn't been able to find Neil. He was going to hide the body temporarily somewhere, then continue into Tifgad as planned. I did what he said. I was in a pretty numbed state.

'That evening, when he returned to the camp from Tifgad, he told me what he'd done and what he planned to do. On the way through the camp that morning, he'd placed the alabaster pots at the bottom of Beri's kitbag, and had taken his knife. In Tifgad he'd seen someone he said was "pretty high up in the Government" – yes, it was a man called Gérard Petit-frères, the Minister of Justice – who had agreed, for money, I presumed, to help on the legal side. That night, when everyone had retired, we talked. He told me what he planned. He said he was going to go up to the cave, plant the knife near the bloodstains, and dispose of Neil's body. To my horror, he made me accompany him. He said at the time he'd need my help. I was pretty sure afterwards he was making sure to involve me as fully as possible in case things went wrong with the police and he had to leave me to my fate. The next morning he and Fieldhouse would go up to the cave again in search of Neil and "find" the knife and the blood, but not of course the body, which he threw down a deep pit he found on a lower level of the same cave. He would also simulate a second finding of the hoard with Fieldhouse as his witness. This would neatly eliminate any difficulties about treasure trove, as well as ensure that his own glory was undimmed by anyone else's effort.

'It was typical of his cunning that he allowed Fieldhouse to make the actual find of the hoard the next morning, and then make him shut up about his part in the action, even the bit about him following Beri the previous afternoon. You know the rest of the story – the midday search of the Berbers' belongings and the discovery of the pots – and Neil's real letter, which of course with Fieldhouse's activities the previous afternoon, was an amazing extra piece of luck, which doubly sealed the cover-story Silverman had invented. Neil had obviously found those pots the day before, suspected the hoard was near, and wanted Beri with him the next afternoon. He quite possibly engineered the renewed row with Silverman on the morning of his death in order to ensure his being alone for the day. The cairn had been built to enable Beri to identify the cave. Beri had not had the sense to destroy the note Neil had slipped to him.'

Michael had been listening, as Claudia had, to every syllable. As Janet momentarily paused, he put in a rapid thrust. 'And Beazley's note also sealed Beri's fate, didn't it? How did they do him in? The old French garrotte, was it? Then the body set swinging on the man's belt in the cell to persuade a few people it was suicide?'

Janet sat, unflinching. 'Beri was the worst part of it, the part which makes it impossible to forget. Maybe he was killed. I don't know. Personally I think it was suicide. The Berbers were fatalistic. Beri thought he was for it, he probably preferred to die by his own hand than by that of French justice.'

'And you and Silverman hardly cared one way or the other.'

Janet again ignored Michael. 'Silverman told me Petit-frères had promised he'd have the death sentence commuted to life-imprisonment and that, after a month or two when the fuss was over, he'd arrange for the man's release on some legal technicality. Silverman said Beri would be out of work when the expedition was over. The only difference for him, therefore, would be that he'd be well-fed and have a roof over his head for a period. I was young, and scared. I thought it was a reasonable thing to do. And Silverman was insistent. He was powerful, you know, when he wanted something. I also knew that by this time that if I went against his wishes in any way, at the drop of a hat he'd leave me to a murder charge which, in view of my previous relationship with Neil, couldn't have had a pleasant outcome. There was only one motive in his mind, to get the hoard out of the country. That, I knew, would have taken precedence.

'As for Silverman's attitude to Beri – I can only tell you this. We didn't hear of Beri's death until after we'd left. I was with Silverman at the time. He just shrugged his shoulders. One Berber less meant no more to him than had Neil's death.'

Janet, they realised, had finished. She was staring away over the Moor. Claudia didn't feel she'd had any consciousness of their presence in the last moments. She'd been speaking as if within the anonymity of the Catholic confession-box.

At that moment Claudia saw a cyclist on the road below. It was a young boy, peddling uphill. It was a strange relief somehow, to fasten on his movements weaving from side to side until finally the gradient became to much for him and he got off and walked. Perhaps it was a piece of normality one clung to.

She realised then she totally believed Janet. So, she thought, did Michael. He'd dropped the cynical look he'd worn for most of the time she'd been speaking. 'OK,' he said at last. 'So we got things a little wrong, but not too much.' His tone wasn't exactly conciliatory but it was going in that direction.

Janet hardly noticed. 'I'll be going abroad in a few weeks anyway, and I'll be away for several months,' she said, 'it'd be easier for me if you held up your story till then.'

The journalist surfaced in Michael. 'I'm sorry, I can't wait that long.'

'Very well. Publish away then. It's neither here nor there to me.'

'You don't want the evidence?'

'No.'

'What about Silverman's gun?'

'I've got it. Ludo brought it this morning. You can have it back.'

'You mean you're going to face the music?'

'I very much doubt there'll be much music, except some not very pleasant and drawn-out publicity I could do without. It was self-defence, a long time ago, in another country. Silverman's the one who'll be exposed. That will be the justice.'

'You could be charged with manslaughter.'

'If I am, I won't care. My conscience is clear.'

Janet's words had dignity and poignancy. Her mind then seemed to drift from them, and from the story she'd told. After a few moments of silence she rose. 'Come and get the gun if you want it,' she said. 'After that, it'll be a good idea if we leave each other alone.' With no further word, she began to walk downhill.

26

Claudia felt almost sorry for Janet Brisbane as they watched her set off back to her car. She was glad Michael had his story. From her own biographer's point of view, too, she was beginning to feel the challenge of a new and stimulating viewpoint on her subject. But perhaps it would have been better, as Janet had maintained, if none of this had come out. All right, the perhaps unjustified reputation of a 'great' man was going to be justly modified, but an old woman was going to be unnecessarily exposed for an act of violence she had committed in self-defence, and an even older Frenchman – admittedly as a result of his own misdeeds – had been obliged to end his days in an unwanted exile from the land of his choice. A brutal left-wing dictatorship had the ammunition with which to bully Britain.

She awoke from her thoughts to find Michael was on the telephone to Jim again. Presumably he'd told him all was well and had asked him to come over to collect them at the agreed point on the south road. Then she heard him add that they'd be calling in to Janet Brisbane's house to collect a weapon. She had one of her worst and least rational outbreaks of panic.

'Surely we can leave it,' she said, 'how do we know Ludo isn't still lurking? Janet could have been lying.'

Michael chuckled. 'I hardly think so,' he said, 'and Silverman's gun's the last bit of evidence.' Gently, he enfolded her in his arms. 'It's over, darling. We can start breathing again.' It was the first time he'd used that word, but she was in no mood to appreciate it. While Michael walked at a leisurely pace yards behind her, she half ran until they reached the trees.

They drove to Janet's house. Michael sent Jim in to collect the gun. He came out with the thing wrapped in a Sainsbury bag. But Claudia didn't feel happy until they had dumped Jim in Newton Abbot and were back on the road up-country. Even then she kept a weather-eye on the driving mirror. At any moment she expected to see a green M.G. on their tail.

Meanwhile Michael talked of practicalities. He talked of cameramen, skulls, guns, and bullets. He'd been weeks collecting his story but, journalist as he was, he'd already phoned Nigel Bellerby and promised him copy and pictures for the day after tomorrow.

Claudia's fears were groundless. No M.G. pursued them. Ludo had apparently faded into the Dartmoor landscape. Michael wanted her to go to London with him and stay at his place in Finsbury. She would have liked this, but she had a deeper desire. She wanted him to finish his business with the paper then come to her as her lover, without the trammels of Alan Silverman. There was another reason. She could well imagine what it would be like without him tonight. Perhaps it was cussed, but it was because of this she wanted to be alone. She wanted to regain her independence and belief in her own life before she saw him again.

But when he'd left her at home and driven off and the silence of the village reclosed, she thought she'd been mad. What on earth would she do with herself for the two days Michael thought it would take him to put his story in the can? She just stood there in her kitchen staring at the pots on the shelves. Plan meals? Go over to Donnerton and begin the immense task of reorientating her view of Silverman, which she knew was going to go far beyond the Tifgad chapter? As she stood there, her neighbour knocked and put her head round the back door.

'Hi, saw signs of habitation. Had a nice break?'

She decided to make her sister-in-law her accomplice. Jen knew all about Beatrice. 'Oh, it was the usual thing,' she said airily, 'but I managed to do some research.' The latter at least was not a lie.

When Jen had gone she realised she was ravenous. Michael had been in such a hurry to get to London they'd only had a cup of tea in Newton Abbot. She made herself two mounds of baked beans on toast. Then two more people dropped in expecting tea and an exhaustive explanation of her absence. She realised a lot later, when they'd gone, that there was something she desperately wanted to do and that was go to bed. She pinned a notice on both doors to head off other visitors. 'Late night debauch. Sleeping it off. See you soon.'

She slept for twelve hours and woke refreshed at six the next morning. She ate a huge breakfast, then set about cleaning the house from top to bottom. It was in the middle of this she realised there was something she ought to be doing. She'd gathered the political storm raised by the Saharan embassy had died down whilst they'd been away, but when Michael's story broke it would all flare up agan. Alan had previously only been accused of giving a false account of the last days of the expedition. Now, on the best interpretation of Michael's story, he was going to be held guilty of gross malpractice. It wasn't difficult to guess what the Saharans would make of this. The collection would be under siege again. She felt she owed it to Vincent Galleon at least, and probably Walter Claridge, to give them advance warning. There was also the question of her biography. Should she continue – would she be allowed to by the trust – with things as they had turned out? Promptly at nine she called Vincent's office.

Elizabeth told her Vincent had just gone on holiday. Disappointment must have been apparent in her voice. After a pause, Elizabeth added that though he was off to France with Mrs Galleon later today she thought he might still be at home. Claudia thanked her and said by way of apology that she did have something rather important to tell him.

She phoned and knew at once Vincent wasn't pleased. He covered up quickly, but not before his distaste showed at being bearded on the first day of his holiday. She said she'd got something important to tell him about the Silverman business which she thought he ought to know about before he read about it in the newspapers.

His voice altered quickly to its usual friendly tone. 'Well, in that case, Claudia my dear, it's a very good excuse for you to come round for some coffee, isn't it? Will you come straight away? We're not off to the ferry until eleven – and Min, as you'd expect, has everything packed up ready to go.'

She was used to Vincent in a suit, not in shorts which revealed white rather unhealthy-looking legs with visible bluish-coloured veins etched on his shins. But he was relaxed-looking and obviously in a holiday mood.

'I gather you've been with your tiresome relation. Was she less intolerable this time?' he said as courtesies with Min were completed and she withdrew. Min had supplied them with a tray with two coffees at a white iron table set in the garden. Standing, Vincent was pouring.

She thought she'd better get on with it. 'I didn't visit my relation,' she said, 'I've been to Sahara with Michael Strode, the freelance journalist who did the original Fieldhouse stories.' It wasn't often she surprised the Vice-Chancellor of Sarum University. His thin sandy eyebrows raised to the high

270

position and his hand was arrested as it travelled to the tray to lift her coffee cup. 'I bumped into him in London and he asked me to go – as Alan's biographer. It was rather an expense but I thought it'd give me some colour for the Tifgad chapter. It was certainly a colourful experience. In fact it's been the most extraordinary time in my life.'

Vincent was recovering. Still standing, he continued with the coffee routine, and grinned. 'And what did you do – search for the murdered man's remains?'

'Yes, we did.'

'Don't tell me you found them?'

'Yes. On our first day – in the cave where the discovery was made. At first I couldn't believe they hadn't been planted for us.'

'Well, well. And no doubt from them your indefatigable companion was able to deduce Alan's dastardly involvement in some way. I recall the innuendoes in his original article came as near to libelling the dead as makes no odds.'

It was her turn to be surprised, though she realised at once it was just an intelligent guess. 'That's more or less what happened, yes,' she said. 'The skull we found, if it was Neil Beazley's, had been shattered by a bullet. At first it did appear Alan could have shot him. As it turns out, he didn't, someone else did, but he doesn't come out of it at all well. I fear when the story's published, as it seems it will be in a day or two, the row over the collection is going to break out with renewed fury.'

Vincent was unfazed. He sat in the other seat, boyishly ladled two heaped spoonfuls of sugar into his cup, and began to stir. Though overlain with the usual concession of fairness and willingness to listen, the look on his face remained humorously sceptical.

She took him through the story inch by inch, chronologically, and he listened intently. He showed concern at the parts where they'd been in physical danger – particularly when she told him what they'd done to Michael – but behind this she was aware of his cool mind calmly hauling in each item as she presented it, labelling it, card-indexing it, so that when the time came he'd be able to make his overall objective judgement. She relaxed a bit. She wanted to hear his judgement, which would surely confirm her own.

She had dealt with the story up to their escape from Sahara and their

271

arrival in Marrakech. It was now time to talk about her sighting of Ouboussad in the souk, Alphonse's hold-up on the road to Casablanca, and the 'third party.' Up to this point it still seemed Alan was guilty of murder, and Vincent's manner was grave, even at times apprehensive. But as Janet Brisbane's involvement became increasingly clear, she was aware of a change in his manner. She described their interview with Janet and made plain how she'd shot Beazley to save her own life. Though she was at pains to explain how badly Alan had behaved during and after this episode, she had an odd sensation that the atmosphere was lightening.

'Well, that's about it,' she finished. 'Alan, as I say, doesn't come out of it at all well. I'm afraid it's going to be bad for the University from whichever angle you look at it. It seems Michael's Strode's original instinct about Alan, though exaggerated, has been regretably vindicated.'

She was expecting Vincent to agree, but he bunched his mouth in a dismissive way. 'Oh, I don't think all this is too bad, Claudia,' he said after a moment, making an adjustment to the coffee-pot. 'In fact I'd say it's all rather splendid.'

'What's splendid?'

'Alan had to deal with a very unpleasant situation, and simply did the proper thing to cover his employee. The Saharans will argue otherwise no doubt, but Beazley's state of mind, and his attempt to kill this woman, puts an entirely different complexion on things. Most people will see it that way.'

She couldn't believe her ears. The most honest man she knew taking a purely pragmatic line? 'In my view Alan's part in the affair was despicable,' she said.

Vincent gave a little laugh. 'A little Star Chamberish perhaps, but not criminal surely?'

'Not criminal to be responsible for an innocent Berber's death?'

'How could Alan know the man would take his own life?'

'How could he know at all what would befall Beri if he framed him? It's true he didn't know the man would commit suicide, but he didn't know for sure, either, that Petit-frères would be able to fulfil his pledge to save him from execution and get him out of prison – this quite apart from the almost certainty that he blackmailed or bribed a minister of justice to get his way. Anyway, it was a frightful thing to do to anybody to put them through such mental agony. The fact was, in my view, Alan didn't care. He didn't care about Beri, and he didn't care about Janet Brisbane, either, according to her. His behaviour to her in that cave just after the murder shows how little he felt for her in her appalling situation. All that mattered to him when she was spluttering there on the floor of the cave was the hoard and the reputation he was going to establish by finding it.'

'You say you believe Janet Brisbane. She's a rather interested party, isn't she? As it turns out, a jilted party, or one who considers herself so. She has a motive to blacken Alan, hasn't she?'

'She certainly has after the treatment she got from him. And there's Alan's earlier treatment of Beazley, after he'd seduced Janet – what do you make of that?'

'Again, it's tainted evidence from an interested party.'

'Fieldhouse also indicated his hostility to Beazley – as a homosexual. He was almost certainly replicating Alan's attitude.'

'Beazley, gay or not, may have been obnoxious. And in those days people had a different view of homosexuality.'

Claudia checked herself. It was, she felt, a crucial moment for her. Around them was the orderly garden. A couple of chaffinches were drinking at the bird-bath. In the street an ice-cream vendor was dispensing an electronic version of 'Greensleeves.' All in all it was a normal, soporific, easy-going English summer morning with middle-class children playing on their bicycles next door, everything in place. Vincent's grin was now boyish again. In an hour he'd be off on holiday. Somehow the very ordinariness of the scene helped her to make up her mind.

'If I go on with the book I'm going to show Alan as I see him,' she said, no doubt more fiercely than she intended.

'How will that be?'

'I am sure one major aspect will be that he was a single-minded man who cared only about his reputation and who was capable of gross and callous insensitivity if anyone tried to get in his way.'

'Surely that's an exaggeration?'

'No, it isn't. He fooled me, as he fooled a great number of people. Now I see him differently.'

'I'm sure you'll see it more in perspective when you've reflected – and digested it all.'

'I don't think I will. Vincent, I'm not sure I should go on being paid by the Silverman Trust. I think I should resign my commission and work independently.'

A shrewder look shuttered across Vincent's face. It was still smiling, but behind was the steel which had won him his eminence. 'This Michael Strode – he must be quite a character,' he said amiably, and as if changing the subject.

She knew he wasn't. He knew just where to dangle the bait. Before she could check herself she'd risen to it – in a top huff. 'He is,' she said.

The way she was shown to the door further nauseated her. What she had thought was warm courtesy to women became at this moment blatant male patronage. What he meant to imply was that her female judgement was warped because he sensed she'd been attracted to the man whose views he wished to denigrate. At the door he took her hand in both of his and patted it.

'Well, thank you for telling me in advance, Claudia dear. I'll be able to think of possible repercussions while I'm away. And meanwhile you must have a good think about it, too. Shall we talk again when I come back from France? By then the new political row will have subsided – if indeed there is one, there may not be. We must have dinner together again.'

She recovered her manners but not her temper. 'I hope you have a nice fortnight, Vincent,' she said. She was pretty sure they wouldn't be having that dinner.

Michael had not phoned her the previous night. She was tempted to go home in case he did today some time. She quickly talked herself out of it. Waiting for a call you wanted from Michael Strode, even when he'd declared he was in love with you, was a recipe for frustration. Instead, she thought about Walter Claridge. If he'd been through the ordeal she (and now Michael in his reformed state) suspected, even though he'd saved his skin by withdrawing his remarks about Archie Fieldhouse, surely she owed him a visit as much as the one she'd paid Vincent? She got into a call box up the road from Vincent's house and phoned him.

Marjorie answered. She was surprised to hear her voice, especially when Claudia asked if she could come round to see Walter, if he was in and wasn't too busy. But Marjorie didn't hesitate before inviting her to lunch. 'I think Walter will be very pleased to see you,' she added. This was mariginally odd.

Marjorie was renowned for her hospitality, but she didn't know the Claridges that well, and the Walter-being-pleased bit wasn't what she would have expected.

As she was in Salisbury she did the shopping she'd been going to do tomorrow and got to the Claridges' house about twelve. Through the iron gate which bordered the Close she saw Walter in the garden with Ursula and Gideon. Dressed in light-weight mauve trousers with an open-neck shirt, Walter was mowing the lawn. The children were helping him, efficiently taking the bin to a compost pen at the end of each swath. She was engaged by the tableau she briefly witnessed. Whatever else he was, Walter was probably an affectionate and considerate father. She continued to the front door.

Marjorie opened it. 'I'm so glad you've come, Claudia,' she repeated warmly. Again, her manner was noticeable. It went beyond even her ubiquitous hospitality.

Marjorie led the way onto the terrace where the family lunch was laid, simply but attractively, on a chequered cloth. Claudia was already revising uncharitable thoughts she'd had only too recently about Marjorie. What was wrong, she thought, with being a thoroughly nice gregarious woman, naturally and spontaneously hospitable? Marjorie called to Walter, but he couldn't hear because of the mower. She waved her arms about humorously until Ursula saw, ran to tug her father's sleeve, and pointed. Walter immediately halted the machine and switched it off where it was in the middle of the lawn. He approached in a cumbersome sort of run, mopping his flushed face with his handkerchief, the children jumping at his side.

'You're very welcome, Claudia,' he said. 'I was really hoping to speak to you, you know. Marjorie, I say, do you think we could have some drinks? We all deserve them on a day like this.'

The children, without prompting, stepped forward to greet Claudia. Ursula shook her hand gravely and Gideon grinned infectiously at her side.

Walter's greeting, added to Majorie's, had again made Claudia wonder if something was up, but during the delicious home-made apple wine and a lovely summer lunch of Marjorie's cold chicken pie with a sumptuous salad, nothing was said which wasn't commonplace. She thought she must have been wrong. She began to think the occasion might conclude with nothing said about Sahara, unless she broached it. Could it pass off then as a routine drop-in requiring no explanation, though she had said to Marjorie she wanted to speak to Walter? She almost began to want it to be that way. If it was true Walter had been threatened, he might not have told Marjorie, and she certainly couldn't bring up the matter with her there. Did she really have to tell him? He'd be hearing soon enough.

The children had been excused and ran off inside the house. Claudia wondered if Marjorie would stack up the dishes and go, too, which would have cleared the decks for action as it were. She didn't. Instead, there was a sense of imminence. Both Claridges went silent. Walter cleared his throat.

'Naturally, I didn't want to say this in front of the children, Claudia,' he said, 'but the Vice-Chancellor phoned me an hour or two ago, just before he went on holiday. In confidence, he told me in rough outline what you told him earlier this morning. He told me you, and Michael Strode – whom I have no doubt you know I know – have been to Sahara and have been in great danger.'

Marjorie stretched out her hand and laid it on Claudia's sleeve. 'We're so terribly sorry to hear what you've been through,' she said. 'It must have been a frightful ordeal.'

Claudia said that from her point of view she was not sorry it had happened, as what she and Michael had discovered was certainly going to give her a more realistic view on Silverman for her book, but that she wasn't sure how it was going to affect the University. She said she hadn't known Vincent was going to phone Walter, but that she had felt she should let him know, as well as Vincent, before they read it in the newspaper.'

The Claridges exchanged a glance. It seemed Marjorie was expecting Walter would say something, but at the last minute he funked it and raised his napkin to his lips. She had to do it for him.

'Do you know that Walter has also been involved with these dreadful people?' she began. Claudia gave her an encouraging look. 'You remember the garden party we gave earlier in the summer when Walter seemed to have been taken ill . . .'

Claudia was sure Marjorie was a great deal more explicit than Walter would have been. Walter had had a threatening call about his family all right – undoubtedly from a foreigner, who from his accent was probably an Arabic speaker, Walter had thought – and had been forced to make that statement to the press about Archie Fieldhouse. For weeks he had kept it to himself to shield Marjorie and the children from anxiety. It was only a week ago that he'd changed his mind and told her about it.

Claudia was assuming that was all, and was privately questioning whether it amounted to very much. Having retracted his statement about Archie's lecture to Michael, Walter couldn't actually have been in much danger. He'd done what the Saharans wanted. But she was conscious there was more. Marjorie was looking at Walter again.

'And now,' she said, 'we've decided together we're going to face the music.'

Claudia sat up, and looked at Walter. Certainly a look of rugged determination had replaced his usually rather uncertain expression. 'Yes,' he said simply. 'If a little late in the day. From the start I've been ashamed of caving in to these people, good reasons as I had for doing so. I've discussed it with Marjorie and together we've decided to make public our small part in what happened. I'm going to declare the blackmail I was put under, and take steps to protect ourselves. We decided this a few days ago, but what we've learnt from Galleon this morning about your courageous operation makes us even more determined. These appalling gangsters must be exposed.'

'You mean Galleon agrees?'

'I'm afraid he does not. We don't see eye to eye at all on the matter. I went to see him a few days ago, after we'd taken our decision. Galleon was against any kind of a public statement which might embarrass the Foreign Office again. His advice was to leave things as they are. This morning he made another attempt to persuade me on the phone. In the light of your friend's imminent revelations, he told me he thought a statement from me would be pointless.'

Walter's voice faded. Marjorie filled the gap. 'The Vice-Chancellor made Walter feel he was morally splitting hairs and trying to create a storm in a tea-cup,' she said definitively. 'Walter feels his act of courage in standing up to this despicable state is being thrown back in his face.'

Walter stirred himself for a more explicit statement. 'I'm afraid you're right, my dear, I do feel somewhat aggrieved – support from Galleon would have been gratifying. As the matter seems to be turning out, a statement from me will maybe seem somewhat academic but I shall do what we've decided for my own reasons. My family and I were criminally threatened, almost certainly with the knowledge and possibly at the instigation of the

277

Saharan embassy here. Naturally I shall avoid libel, but I shall do my bit to expose them by implication.' His face broke into an attractive, craggy grin. 'I'd like for a start to relieve myself of the reputation of being subject to mental breakdowns.' He paused. 'And it's an ironic footnote, isn't it,' he added, 'that, though against my wishes at the time, my enforced recantation turns out to be rather nearer the truth than I imagined? Silverman did lie, it seems. If the press interview me again, I shall say that, too.'

It was Claudia's chance to express a thought she'd had about Walter since returning to England. 'And you're saying that, for whatever reason, this is quite consistent with the view you always had of Alan, aren't you, Walter? I think you never did like him, did you? I think you only ever protected him out of loyalty. You thought he was rather a superficial showman. Am I right?'

'Claudia's entirely right, that's exactly how you saw him, Walter,' said Marjorie.

The smile broadened. 'It would be nice to bask in that view, Marjorie. It's true I didn't care for the man. It's also true I tried not to let a personal view influence my behaviour in public. But I regret to say there was another factor in the equation. It was not just loyalty to my superior and to the profession which accounted for my performance. It was also what I now realise is far too great a respect for elitist traditions for their own sake – a form of elitist back-scratching if you like. If these events we have been through have taught me anything, it is that conformity of this sort is wrong, that it leads to self-esteem of quite the wrong sort, it leads to establishment tyrannies, and to gross inner falsehoods.'

Walter was ponderous, Claudia thought – his morality was ponderous. This wouldn't cease to be so. But she realised from this moment her view of him would be different, as her view of Galleon would be different. Walter might be a bore, but he had integrity. Also, wasn't what he had said a rather oratorically-expressed version of her own experience – an escape from lip-service to established assumptions and certainties?

The occasion died a bit after this exchange. It wasn't long before Claudia took her leave. She thought that, paradoxically, this was also somewhat to the Claridges' relief. Apart from what they had just said to each other, and apart from the lasting impression events would leave, perhaps the three of them hadn't the ingredients for more than an amiable acquaintance, once outward topics were exhausted.

Her departure was emotional nonetheless. Walter's handshake was firm, and Claudia responded warmly to its pressure. She and Marjorie embraced as they had never done before. They had shared an ordeal, and in the end had finished with attitudes a great deal closer than any of them might have imagined possible a few weeks ago.

27.

To her surprise Michael was waiting for her when she got home about four. He'd climbed on to the garage roof and got in through the loo window she'd carelessly left open. He was sitting with his feet on her footstool and a pint of beer in his hand. As she entered, he struggled to his feet. He looked hot and tired, but triumphant.

'I needn't have rushed. It'll be in The Sunday Times "News Review" next week, displacing what they had – front-page story, with a page and a half, probably six pictures. Five grand and all expenses – retroactively. I tried to swing expenses for you, too, but they wouldn't buy that. We'll go shares on yours.'

She began to apologise for not being there when he arrived, but he lifted her up in his arms and bore her to the sofa. He took her shoes off – she raising her feet in turn like a horse being shoed – then his own. They lay clutched together in peace, both of them now feeling Sahara was over. It was perhaps a kind of convalescence.

In a little while she wondered if he'd eaten. She discovered he'd been up writing most of the night and had had almost nothing. Full of Claridge food herself, she felt ashamed not to have thought of it before. She was only thankful she'd done some shopping in Salisbury, the fruits of which lay where she'd dumped them on the hall table, including half a salmon and a bottle of Pouilly Fumé. They agreed on an earlyish nosh. While Michael had a bath she set about poaching the fish, doing Delia Smith's instant mayonnaise and throwing together a salad. She had home-made ice-cream in the freezer to go with the fresh peaches.

Michael came down looking pink and fresh. He'd put on a clean white shirt. After huge gins, they tucked in. Michael raved about her hastily concocted meal. 'An improvement on the Oasis Hotel, anyway,' she said. They went to bed before it was dark and made the sort of love that pays no attention to time schedules.

The next day they went for a long walk across Cranborne Chase. Naturally – because they both felt like talking about it, not because it was necessary for any practical reason – they began to discuss aspects of 'les événements'. She told Michael about Vincent Galleon and how his attitude to Silverman had surprised her. 'He really thinks Janet's story restores everything to base,' she said.

'A bit predictable, isn't it?' Michael said.

'I wouldn't have said so only a week or two ago.'

'You're either an "inner" or an "outer". He's a liberal on the surface, but when the chips are down you see the nickel under the gilt. That's how you build a public career. He's a Vice-Chancellor.'

'Is it really as cut and dried as that?'

'No. But pretty cut and dried nonetheless. Ever heard of politicians beginning to tell the truth when they get elevated to a peerage – Socialists veering to Toryism and vice-versa? It's not only politics. Institutional back-scratching – what is politely called party-loyalty, enforced by party whips – gets into every branch of life. Doctors, lawyers, trades-unionists, you name it. And it's what an increasingly educated and sophisticated nation is sick of.'

She also told Michael about Walter Claridge and how she thought he'd come out of it rather well. Michael was glad Walter's U-turn hadn't been the result of Christian soul-searching but straight fear – it made it a lot cleaner. Then she told Michael about herself. 'Is it possible,' she asked him, 'to become a different person in a few days?' 'No,' he said. She told him she thought she had. 'No, you haven't,' he insisted. 'What's happened is that you've shed a skin someone, or something, wrapped you in.'

'If that's so,' she said, 'I could've been wrapped in it all my life if I hadn't met you.'

They walked on another hundred yards. It was warm without being oppressive. Around them the post-harvest countryside glowed gold. Though it was much too early to think of autumn, peewits were already beginning to gather. A party of them were wheeling untidily overhead with their odd squeaky cries.

'I feel unwrapped, too,' Michael said then. 'You were a good deal right about Silverman and Sahara, and I was a prat. You rumbled me. Perhaps we've both given up the party whips. I was subject to one, too. By the way, I am in love with you, you know. I want to marry you. I'd like us to have children.'

She reminded him she was several years older than he was, that they'd

281

been in very unusual circumstances, and that she wasn't sure if she could bear children. She and Jack had never bothered to find out which of them was deficient. He said piffle on all three counts. She felt gloriously happy.

Michael and Claudia have not married, not yet anyway. Michael's Sunday Times story was, as he'd hoped, a breakthrough for his career. He now has all the work he wants and keeps at it very hard. He comes down to Claudia's village whenever he can and they have idyllic week-ends and holidays, seldom less intense than that first one. Michael continues to want marriage. Claudia is not sure. She thinks she likes it the way it is. She doesn't want children now. If she'd had them with Jack it would've been OK. Michael says, though he'd wouldn't mind having kids, he's not avid about it. She supposes she knows that one day he might prove to be more avid than he'd realised and find a younger girl who'd give him a family. He might go off – she has faced this. But her life is alight again, so much more so now she has formally resigned her membership of the respectability club.

She has done the biography and shown Silverman as she now sees him – in spite of Vincent's further efforts to head her off. Vincent did even hint more once that she owed a sanitised version to the money she was getting, and had received, from the trust. It was this rather sordid pressure which determined her not to resign. It wasn't her fault Silverman had turned out as he had. She waited for them to sack her. Perhaps because Michael's story had already tarnished Silverman's reputation, they didn't. The book has had some predictable stick from certain quarters but on the whole it has been well-received as a fair assessment of a man admirable only in parts.

There was a great bashing international row about the Beazley business and the hoard. Sahara made the most of it. But the brutal despotism of this state is wreaked upon its Moslem and African neighbours as well as on the western world, and Claudia suspected that underneath the anti-British third-world rhetoric was a silent recognition that Britain's exercise of its right to refuse to go to the International Court was justified. After all, what did the majority of them care about a few ancient artefacts? (Incidentally, Michael, too, these days, under what he calls Claudia's subversive influence, no longer talks about Sahara's glorious cultural heritage).

Claudia's book has been able to add to Michael's journalistic account of the Tifgad expedition for two reasons. She and Michael have heard via Ben

Abbis, with whom they keep in touch, that Petit-frères is dead. Also, Ben Abbis himself, for reasons explained below, no longer visits Sahara and is unlikely to until the unforeseeable event of a successful liberal revolution. He has given willing permission for his part in the story, as well as Petit-frères's, to be told. Claudia has also been able to be freer in her account of Janet Brisbane's role in the drama. Since they met her on a Dartmoor tor, nothing has been heard of her. Michael found out that her Devon house was sold, and there has been no public mention of her since she left England. It is possible she is also dead or, more likely, that she has decided to end her days in some Andean fastness. Archie Fieldhouse is not dead, but Claudia feels he's quite capable of looking after himself in face of any embarrassment her book may cause him. She has heard he has ceased to 'give talks', however, which does cause her regret. He clearly derived such pleasure from them, and was such a good lecturer. What she and Michael do not know, and have confessed they almost certainly never will, is just how much he knew or guessed. Probably most of it, in view of the final cryptic remark he made to them about Janet. In which case does his view of Silverman persist untarnished? She hopes it does. Although such admiration might now be thought rather less than justified, people, especially old people less able perhaps to make painful mental adjustments, should be allowed their heroes.

As the world knows, Djebal has been overthrown by a coup d'état organised by Mohammed Salek. Astonishingly, soon after the event, Michael and Claudia received – disturbingly at Claudia's home address – two huge gilded cards inviting them to Salek's installation as President. On the back of Claudia's, someone – surely not Salek himself? – had scribbled, 'All expenses paid.'

Not on either of their nellies. The controversy over the hoard has ceased. Salek is soliciting western capital. But Ben Abbis has told them of the silent executions that have accompanied Salek's elevation to power, and the seizure of selected assets in Sahara, among them his own.

Michael and Claudia have invited Ben Abbis to come and stay with them and he has promised to do so. They realise with even greater certainty that he probably saved their lives.